I0685076

A Good Man's Life

Book 2 of The Real World
Series

Barbara Cutrera

Published by On My Way Up, LLC

Cover art by Lisa Anderson of Barefoot in the Glass
www.barefootintheglass.com

ISBN- 978-0-9858255-8-4
Second edition

To my mother, Connie. You're such a loving, talented, intelligent, resilient, good woman.

Part One

An Unexpectedly Brief Introduction in the Search for the Truth

Prelude

My dear son, since you're reading this, it means that I've passed on. Death always brings about shock and grief, no matter how much we tell ourselves we're prepared for it. I hope that you and your mother and the others are holding up well. I'm sure you and Sarah will do an excellent job of explaining things to Kristopher. Perhaps by the time you read this, my grandson will be old enough not to need much explanation. But he is so young now, and I feel that my time on Earth is extremely limited.

There's so much I want to tell you, so much I want to explain. I would like to believe that you and I are close, but the dynamics of all relationships are complicated. Fathers and sons, mothers and sons, sons and their wives, sons and their sons – every nuance of a man's life has some bearing on his relationships with others.

Lillian and I have tried to be good parents despite our unusual family circumstances. As if your own traumatic childhood would not have been enough, it was certainly unusual for you to have a white adoptive father and a black adoptive mother in 1970s Baton Rouge, Louisiana. I believe, however that we all managed remarkably well.

Maybe my journals will be unnecessary, and I'll have told you everything before my death. If that is the case, then do what you like with these "manuscripts." Throw them away or save them for Kristopher when he gets older if you deem them appropriate. However, if I haven't told you, then please read them carefully.

I would ask that you not rush through this process or skip ahead. It has taken me many years to document the story of my life. I've tried to do so in a way that will reveal the reasons for my actions and the truth.

As for the truth, it is my wish that you should know it. I've attempted to be a good man in life, and I hope I've succeeded. Nevertheless, I am human and have made mistakes, mistakes that have affected not only my life but others' lives as well. Telling you about those mistakes has been the one thing I haven't been able to do, yet. It is the one area in which I find myself afraid.

Afraid of what? Afraid that I will lose your love, your trust, your respect. It's this fear that's haunted me for almost two and a half decades. It haunts me as I write these words.

So, why exactly did I not sit down with you years ago and disclose these revelations, including the knowledge that I am not only your adoptive parent but am also your biological father? When Lillian and I first took you in, you were a twelve-year-old, motherless boy who had almost been beaten to death by the man he knew as his father. As a psychiatrist, I was very concerned as to whether or not you would ever recover emotionally from repeated abuse and from the episode that almost killed you. And, frankly, I was unaware of the truth at that time.

When I did accidentally uncover the information that confirmed you are my biological child, you were still in an extremely precarious state, both in mind and body. Your recovery was slow and steady if you recall. I didn't want to do anything to jeopardize it.

As time progressed, you adjusted well. Regardless, there were obviously still problems – and not only with your recovery. Sarah and her father went through such a terrible period for a second time, and then she manifested the condition that slowly destroyed her central vision. All of this greatly affected you as well. Of course it did. You loved her long before she became your wife.

Each time Lillian and I thought about revealing the truth, something made us hesitate. We didn't want to set you back. Your well-being was our top priority.

And so it has gone for many years. Perhaps explaining things this way is cowardly. The psychiatrist in me is railing against my avoidance of discussing these issues with you. The man in me could not bow to what he knew was the rational path.

I've pursued directness in my written musings, although I've not breached any professional confidences. What I've written of my birth and early life was told to me by my father and mother and those around us. Perhaps I've been too brutally honest or descriptive about everything I've documented. I hope I've told the complete truth.

Forgive me, Daniel, if I've ever hurt you in the past. Forgive me if I hurt you now. Take care of your mother and your wife and your son. No father could ever be more proud of his child than I am of you. I love you more than life itself.

Max
November, 1993

Refolding the letter, Daniel laid it on the nightstand next to the bed in his hotel room and then raked his fingers through his graying black hair. According to the date the attorney's office had stamped on the front of the envelope, Max had written it almost exactly one year before his death.

Daniel rose from the bed and went over to the dresser. He stared at his reflection for a long moment. He was almost six feet tall and had some gray weaving its way into his black hair. He had very dark brown eyes and was slim, thanks to the self-imposed regimen of daily exercise that he employed in order to keep his previously abused body functional. His jeans and sweater hid the terrible scars that covered his torso. He looked several years older than thirty-six.

He opened one of the cardboard boxes that he'd brought with him to the hotel room. Inside was a stack of hardcover notebooks. Each had a number written neatly in the upper right-hand corner.

Sighing deeply, Daniel picked up *#1* and sank onto the beige couch cushions. It was 7:00 p.m. on a Friday, and he had reserved this room until 11:00 a.m. Sunday morning. There was no way that he could rush through these journals, the books that hopefully held the key to the biggest mystery of his life. Would forty hours be enough time?

It would have to do. His wife, Sarah, and their son, Kris, were spending the weekend with his mother. He had cleared his calendar of all other obligations for these two days. It was the ideal opportunity. Daniel wanted to make the most of it.

Stretching out his long legs, he reached up behind his head and switched on the lamp. He kicked off his Nikes, which bounced on the carpet and landed next to the coffee table. Daniel rubbed his sweaty palms down the front of his sweater and then ran his fingers through his hair once more. He touched the cover of #*1* with his fingertips. His heart was racing.

Get on with it, he thought. *If you're too scared to do it for yourself, then do it for your son. You know you can't leave here without uncovering the truth – or at least Max's version of the truth. If you don't read his account, it will shadow you for the rest of your life. Now, open that book!*

Daniel opened the book. He had no way of knowing that what he was going to read in the course of the next twenty-four hours would only be a precursor to his true search for answers and the beginning of an even more difficult journey. Believing that all would be revealed in the journals, he started at the top of page one.

Chapter One: A Good Man's Life Begins

On the evening of April 12, 1912, Warren Nash was presented with his newborn son. He gazed down at the tiny baby, who'd been tightly wrapped in a clean infant blanket. Stroking the soft hair on the baby's head, the father smiled and exclaimed, "Hello, Maxwell! Welcome to Cornwall, England. You've given your mother some thirty-two hours of trouble, don't you know? I don't suppose you could help that, though." When the baby cooed at him, he laughed and proclaimed, "You'll be a truly good man, Max. Just you wait and see."

"Warnie, the baby's less than an hour old," Edith said then smiled up at her husband. "Don't you think he's done enough for one day without starting him fretting about living up to our expectations?"

"Oh, my! I hadn't thought of it like that," Warren replied frowning. "I didn't mean –"

"Of course you didn't. And of course, he'll be a truly good man. You're his father."

"He's a long one but a might scrawny," the midwife remarked pleasantly, as she arranged the bedding in the cradle. "He'll be a tall one like his Da, I reckon."

"I do hope he's taller than I am," Edith said seriously. "It would be nice if he could mount a horse without assistance." She looked studiously at her husband and speculated, "I wonder if he'll have your hair or mine?"

"At the moment it appears he'll have yours," Warren commented. "See how black it is?"

"That'll all most likely fall out," the midwife put in.

"Well, I wouldn't mind a bit if he had all of your features," said Warren. "Edith, you are the most beautiful woman I know."

"As is every new mother to her husband," muttered the midwife under her breath. Then, more loudly, "If you're wanting to have more, you'd better not wait too long. You're, what, nearing forty, Sir? And the missus here is twenty-nine. Not much time for more healthy births. Specially seein' as how it took you five years to get with this one."

Edith smiled; Warren stiffened.

"Course, you won't be tryin' at all for at least three months. You understand that, Mr. Nash? She's got to have time to heal inside and out."

"At this moment, nothing could be further from my mind."

"Warnie, may I hold the baby again? I know I've had him for nine months, but it's a bit different being able to see him and not simply feel him."

Warren lowered their son into Edith's outstretched arms. The baby began to root around for his mother's breast.

"Well, he's certainly got an appetite, hain't he?" crowed the midwife. "You'd best be gettin' back to your accounts, now hain't you, Sir? Let the mistress have a long rest."

"Yes, Dear. I am tired. Don't be cross. Mrs. O'Rourke will take care of us nicely." She stared at him appraisingly and added, "You look rather tired yourself. Why don't you lie down and have a rest as well?"

"All right, my love. You will send for me if you need me?"

"I will. Now, go."

Warren left his wife and crossed to the water closet. He stooped down and took a long, hard look at himself in the mirror. His golden hair, cropped just below his ears, stuck out in all directions. His moustache needed a trim. The shining blue eyes were dimmed by hours of worry and lack of sleep.

"I do look rather a sight," he muttered. "At least it's finally done."

It had been torture for him to listen to Edith's cries as the labor had dragged on and intensified for a day and a half. He would never do that to her again. He wouldn't be able to stand it.

Nonsense, his father had written in response to Warren's mention of this in his letter announcing Max's birth. *She'll be expecting again next year.*

And he was right. A few months after Max's first birthday, Edith had come to her husband while he was restocking the shelves in their dry goods shop and had told him that she was expecting another child. She seemed happy enough, but Warren was beside himself.

"Be calm, my dear," she said reassuringly. "Max deserves a brother or a sister. He's such a ducky boy," she continued, as she admired her son, who was banging pot lids together on the floor. "I do think he's a good combination of both of us. He will be taller like you, but his hair and features are mine." She placed a hand on her belly and predicted, "This child may be short like I am with your hair and your features."

Warren stared silently at his son.

"Aren't you excited about the child?" his wife asked.

"I'm merely anxious about knowing what it will take to bring it into the world."

"First births are usually longer and more difficult. I'm sure this one will go more smoothly. You'll see." She took his hand and slipped it under hers before saying gently, "It's another baby, Warnie. It will bring us as much joy as Maxwell has."

Warren remained unconvinced. For the next several months, his anxiety mounted. A worried "Are you all right, my dear?" was asked with such frequency that Edith grew tired of hearing it and became restless, both with her condition and with her husband's concern.

In the early hours of the morning of February 4, 1914, Warren was awakened by Edith's frantic grip on his arm.

"Wh-what?" he stammered, reaching blindly for the lamp. "Edith?"

"The baby! It's coming!" She covered her mouth with her forearm, trying to stifle the cry that might wake Max. Then she begged, "Warnie, please! You must help me!"

"I'll get the midwife," he said, surprised at how steady his voice sounded.

"No!"

Startled, Warren turned from the lamp, which was now lit and glowing brightly.

"Edith, I must get the midwife." He sat gingerly on the bed and took his wife's hand before reassuring her, "It will be all right, my dear."

She shook her head and bit her lip in order to silence another cry then declared, "The baby is coming! There's no time! I can…I can feel it coming at this very moment!"

Warren froze. He had lived in terror of this birth and of hearing Edith suffer through it. Now, he was going to be forced to *see* her suffer through it and to deliver the child himself? What if he did the wrong thing?

"Warnie, I'm frightened. The baby's arriving so fast and early, too."

That was it. Warren Spencer Nash called himself to attention. How dare he be afraid? His poor Edith was the one in pain. She was the one who would be forced to bear the brunt of the child's birth. What a coward he'd been!

"You'll both be fine." When she appeared doubtful, he added, "Max is such a serious child. Maybe this little one will be more impetuous. That's why he's coming so quickly."

Edith smiled gratefully at her husband. For a moment, she seemed certain that everything would, indeed, be fine. Then, the pain jolted through her, and the fear resurfaced with tremendous force.

She grabbed wildly at the sheet underneath her and groaned, "I can't do this!"

"You *are* doing it, my dear," he assured her. "It's almost done."

As he watched in awe, the empty space between Edith's legs began to fill with the wet head of their child. From some faraway place, he could hear his wife's pleas and his son's cries from the nursery, but his entire attention was fixed on the inexorable emergence of the infant he had helped to create.

When Edith went limp, her husband leaned down to touch the baby. It was cold. With infinite care, he turned the infant over.

"Warnie?" Edith said meekly. "Is it…all right?"

"It was a girl," he said softly.

"Was? Oh – oh, no. Please." She started to weep and insisted, "No, she's fine. She has to be fine. I want to see her."

He lifted the baby up so that his wife could see the perfect, lifeless body of their daughter.

"It's my fault," Edith sobbed.

Laying the body of the baby back onto the bed, Warren went to his wife and took her in his arms.

"You did a sterling job, my dear. It's not your fault. If only I had been able to get the midwife, perhaps she would have known better what to do."

"It would have taken you two hours to fetch her with the weather the way it is. It's not your failing either." Still crying, she confided, "I was so looking forward to her arrival. I felt her kick just before we went to sleep. Sh-she was alive only then. And now…."

As Edith lay sobbing, Warren wrapped the stillborn baby in a blanket and placed her in the cradle. He kissed his wife, then he left the room to attend to their son.

Once Max had been rocked back to sleep, Warren laid him in the crib and started back towards the master bedroom. Three steps from the door, he heard Edith cry out.

He rushed into the room, an irrational thought entering into his mind. Perhaps he'd been incorrect. Perhaps their daughter had not been stillborn after all.

But the first thing he saw when he threw open the door was not his daughter alive and kicking. It was the head of another baby.

"It can't die!" Edith cried. "I won't let it! Don't let it die!"

Before Warren had time to cross the room, a small son lay wriggling and wailing on the mattress between Edith's knees.

"Thank God!" Edith breathed. "I want to hold our baby!"

He brought the boy to her as soon as possible. She kissed the bloody hair and cradled the baby tightly against her chest. Warren stood over them, alternately kissing his wife and son. Edith nursed the baby, who drifted off to sleep. When Warren reached down to take the boy from his wife, she shook her head.

"Not in the cradle. Not where the dead baby has been. Put him in the big drawer of the bureau until we can get another cradle. Then bring me our daughter."

"Edith, no," he said hoarsely.

"I want to hold my daughter. We'll have another daughter someday, I swear it. But I won't let them take this one to bury until I've held her in my arms. Alyce, she'll be."

A week after the birth when Edith was feeling stronger, Warren brought Max in to see her and his brother. Max took one look at his sibling and cried, "Piglet!"

Edith smiled for the first time since the birth. Warren found himself laughing uncontrollably.

"That's just cheeky, Max. Meet Milo. Milo would you mind squealing a tad for your older brother?"

Over the next six months, both Max and his younger brother thrived. Max continued to be an inquisitive child but could be content to sit for hours and look through children's books or play with blocks. Milo was more impetuous than his brother and, once crawling, never ceased trying to go out through the back door into the yard.

Their parents delighted in Milo's antics and Max's questions and observations, but Edith continued to feel an empty place in her heart and at her table when she thought of Alyce. When Milo had been three months old, she'd begun an ardent campaign to conceive again.

In October, Warren's father, Colonel Edward Nash, came to Cornwall from Manchester for a month-long visit. It was the first time he'd seen his new grandson. Edith hoped it would be the last.

The Colonel, as he was called by everyone, was a stern, imposing man who had no qualms about telling others how they'd made all of the wrong choices in life. If one didn't enter into the military as early as possible, he was not considered to be a true man in the Colonel's opinion. How someone who was so unfeeling could have fathered such a sensitive soul as Warren Nash, Edith had never been able to fathom.

At dinner on the first evening of his visit, the Colonel was speaking about the propriety of having heirs to carry on the family lineage.

"Such as ours is," he said scathingly to Warren. "Our proud family name should have continued to be associated with serving our King through military service, yet here you are, a shopkeeper. You could have been a man of honor."

"I *am* a man of honor," Warren said tersely. "I chose not to be an emotionless cad like certain others who share our proud family name." He took a bite of bread and remarked, "That celebrated family name has been no more than a title for more years than I can count."

"If you will recall, I gave you several thousand pounds when you reached the age of majority. I believe you used all of that money to open your business."

"Then you are misinformed. I would hope that I'm a better businessman than that. Would you honestly believe that I could squander all of my inheritance on one investment?" He refilled his glass from the pitcher of honey wine on the table and continued by saying, "As for the inheritance itself, your father earned all of that and more. I would have received quite a substantial sum if you hadn't mismanaged your own inheritance."

Ignoring his son, the Colonel devoted his entire attention to refolding the napkin in his lap.

"You've done your duty," the Colonel informed Edith. "You've given birth to two Nash children."

Edith stared at her kidney pie.

"Father, that's enough," Warren said testily. "I believe you've forgotten that my dear wife has given birth to three Nash children."

"That one doesn't count," the Colonel said gruffly. "Stillbirths are of no consequence. Besides, it was only a girl. Better to lose a girl than to lose a healthy male heir."

"If you say anything like that ever again, then I will put you out of this house in an instant," hissed Warren.

"You wouldn't dare!"

"Wouldn't I?"

The morning of the Colonel's departure, Edith stood next to her husband on the steps of the railway platform and whispered, "I never want him in our house again."

"I couldn't agree more," he nodded, still waving at the departing train. "I know it's bloody awful to say, but I do so detest my father." He kissed her and murmured, "I do so love you."

For the next several years, Max and Milo enjoyed a happy existence as shopkeeper's sons. They were not wealthy, but neither were they poor. Their parents doted on them, and they romped and played in the stunning stark beauty of Cornwall.

Then the Colonel became ill with rheumatism. One October day, he arrived at the Nash home with all of his worldly belongings.

"It's only right that I come to your household, Warren. Your mother, God rest her soul, would have wanted to know that you fulfilled your familial obligation and took care of your ailing father."

Edith bit her lip and waited for her husband's reaction to this statement. Warren's face turned to stone, but he remained calm and silent.

"You don't look much different, either of you. Those boys of yours are bigger. That younger one is much too small, though. You have to make him eat more. The older one seems stout enough. Have you managed to have any more children?"

"Edith has conceived twice, but…no. We've had no more children, yet."

"Well, you'd best stop having relations with her, Warren. You're getting too old to father any more sons, and your wife is getting too old to birth them. You have two. Should one die, you'll still have a male heir.

"You don't need a female child. Girls are nothing but trouble. I believe that it was for the best that your sister was taken by the influenza. Better to be taken at nine than to die in childbirth at nineteen."

His face purple with rage, Warren balled up his fingers and shook his fist at his father exclaiming, "I said that we'd had no more children, *yet*." He stalked over towards the hearth. "I'll be damned if I stop lying with my wife from now until the day I die, and I'll be damned if either of us is too old for a child. God simply hasn't seen fit to send us another one."

"*Yet*," Edith muttered. "Bully for you, Warnie."

"As for my sister, maybe it was better that she die young. She didn't have to grow up to listen to you pontificating about how right you are about everything or for you to try and arrange her life the way you tried to arrange mine. As a man, at least I was able to break away from you. As a woman, she would have been at your mercy."

"I'm ashamed to call you my son!" the Colonel roared.

"Right-o. And I'm ashamed to call you my father!"

"Enough!" Edith whirled off towards the kitchen calling, "Warnie, I would speak with you, please?"

As they stood in the doorway to the yard, Edith said, "I will not have him here. He is cruel and horrible, and I want him gone!"

"And he will be, my dear. I'll tell him that he must find another place by the end of the week, that's all."

"That's all."

Two days later, Edith and Warren were closing up the shop for the evening when they heard the Colonel's voice booming from the kitchen.

"And you, Maxwell, will never be a truly honorable man if you continue to misbehave. Didn't you run through Mrs. Crabb's garden this morning?"

"My – my ball –" the child stammered.

"No excuses!" his grandfather declared. "And you, Milo, you didn't eat all of your peas last night!"

"I don't like peas," the small boy insisted defiantly. "They look funny."

"You must learn to be flexible! You can't be such an ungrateful little monster."

"GET OUT OF MY HOUSE!"

Everybody turned to stare at the normally soft-spoken Warren Nash.

"You stride in here, descend upon my home, upset my wife, and domineer over my children! I won't have it!"

"My, my," the Colonel said smoothly. "Finally showing some real spirit? I never could understand why you were so timid as a child."

"Maybe because you took every opportunity to smash me right down," Warren spat bitterly. "I had to get away from you in order to find out what kind of a man I really was. Even then, I don't think I was truly certain, not until the night Milo was born.

"I can tell you that I'm a much better man than you'll ever be! You dare tell my son to be flexible? You are the most inflexible person I have ever known! And the most appalling!"

"How dare you!" growled his father. "Your mother spoiled you and made you weak. That's why we could never be close as a father and son. It was all her doing!"

"Mother tried her hardest to shield me and my sister from your behavior! You're an extremely pathetic man, Father. I pity you." Warren walked over, picked up both boys, and headed for the parlor doorway where his wife stood waiting. "I'll expect you out by sundown."

"I won't leave! I won't stand for this!"

Warren paused and lowered the boys to the floor.

"No, you won't, will you? You will hound us in a twisted attempt to make our lives as miserable as yours."

He suddenly found himself growing very calm.

"Edith, the boys, and I will leave. You will vacate these premises by 9:00 tonight. I won't tell you when we'll be leaving or where we'll be going, but I will tell you that you'll never find us."

"You will not do this, Warren!"

"You're sixty-nine, Father. You don't have many years left. You'll simply enter Hell a trifle early and spend your last days alone. You've done it to yourself, so there's no use blaming anyone else, although I daresay you'll try. Now, go gather your things and get yourself to the inn."

At 9:30, Warren returned home from accompanying his father to the inn. His wife and sons were seated around the kitchen table. Upon their father's entrance, the children leapt from their places and ran to greet him.

"Bravo, Father!" cheered Milo. "You showed him but good!"

"You were so brave," Max said earnestly. "Maybe someday I will be as brave as you."

Hugging the boys, Warren smiled across at his wife, who was beaming at the three of them.

"So, my brave lord, where are we going? What sort of an adventure are you taking us on?"

"And can we take the cat?" Milo piped in.

"*May* we take the cat?" Max corrected.

Rising, Warren walked over to his wife and leaned down to brush her forehead with his lips.

"It's a surprise, a wonderful, daring surprise. Are you up for it, my Guinevere?"

"We have nothing to hold us here, not really. We've no other living relations. I'm quite ready for something daring. Lead on, my Arthur."

"I want to be Sir Lancelot!" cried Milo, jumping up and down.

"And I will be Sir Gawain," added Max stoically.

"What's all this, then?" Warren stretched out his arms. "We're even at a round table!"

Within six months, the shop had been sold. The furnishings for the rooms had been included in the selling price.

"We'll start a new life," proclaimed Warren. "It will be a glorious new life."

And so it was that in May of 1919, King Arthur, Lady Guinevere, Sir Lancelot, and Sir Gawain set off for America, armed with only five steamer trunks filled with their clothing, the family china and linens, and a photograph they had taken the previous December.

"We're lucky to have our own room," Warren commented as they stared at their cramped accommodations on board the ship. "Some must sleep downstairs all together in one large hold."

"We're lucky because of your forethought," Edith remarked. Addressing her sons, she said, "Father is a shrewd businessman. You'll do well to let him teach you how to handle your finances as you get older."

"Yes, Mum," the children answered in unison.

"At least we have a window," Max pointed out.

"Maybe we'll see giant whales!" Milo exclaimed.

"Maybe," agreed Warren. "Tomorrow. We've all had a busy day. It's bedtime. We've got a long journey ahead of us, and I don't mean only on the water. We must get our rest."

"But where will we go when we get to America?" asked Milo. "Will we see cowboys in the West? Or maybe Indians?"

"I don't know about cowboys and Indians," Warren answered. "We may go out West someday. However, when we get to America, we will go to a place called Ellis Island then to New York City. From there, we will take the train to Louisiana."

"Louisiana? Why Louisiana?" inquired Max.

"Tommy Fleming, that's why."

"You mean Mr. Fleming, the banker?" Milo closed his eyes, as if he was trying to picture the man's face and asked, "What about him?"

"Milo, use your head!" Max cried in exasperation. "He left last year for America. He must have gone to Louisiana."

"Very good, Max, although don't be so contrary with your brother. He is only five."

"And I'm only seven. At least I have more than half a brain."

"Mum!" Milo cried.

"Maxwell! Say you're sorry to your brother."

"It's only normal for siblings to tease one another, Edith."

"That was ungentlemanly. What is it, Max? Why are you being so cross?"

"I'm sorry, Milo," her son said grudgingly.

Max walked the few steps to his brother and punched him affectionately on the arm. Milo swung back not so affectionately.

"But isn't it right, Father? Is Mr. Fleming in Louisiana?"

"Baton Rouge, Louisiana. He and his wife, Mary, are expecting us. We'll stay with them until we can get things going on our own."

"How exciting!" Milo offered.

Warren rubbed at the space between his upper lip and his nose and muttered, "I do so feel disconcerted every time I reach up to touch my moustache."

"It was your decision to remove it before we left," Edith reminded him. "I rather like you without the thing. You can always grow it back if you like."

"I can, but I don't think I will, not for a while." He smiled at his wife and announced, "It's bedtime, boys."

Milo wailed, "I'm not the least bit tired!"

"Me neither, Father," added Max.

"It's bedtime, children," Edith said firmly. "Put on your nightclothes, please."

An hour later, both boys were sound asleep. Edith and Warren lay wide-awake in their not-quite-wide-enough bed.

"Are you pleased?" Edith murmured, poking her husband in the ribs.

"Exceedingly. We're heading for a foreign country where we have no relations and will attempt to earn a good living and raise our children. I can't remember when I've had more excitement."

"Me neither. I am rather sad to leave England. Maybe we shall go back and see it again someday."

"Perhaps."

Sliding his hand underneath the covers, Warren fingered the top button of Edith's nightdress. In a matter of seconds, he had the first four buttons undone.

"Warnie! Whatever are you doing?"

"I am cupping your breast in my hand, my dear. After twelve years of marriage, I would hope that you were familiar with that – or even this." Moving his hand, he pushed it under her nightdress.

"Stop that!" she giggled. "We're in the same room with the children. And an exceedingly small room it is at that. What if they wake?"

"Ah, that's what makes it so thrilling, don't you know?"

"Seriously –"

"Seriously," he sobered. "I am forty-seven years old, Edith. I have thrown all reason to the wind in regards to the future. I would now like to throw all reason to the wind in regards to our present. I want to be with my wife all night. And I want to do it without waking the children. Do you have a grievance with that, my lady?"

"Not at all, my lord. I will enjoy it as long as we don't rouse our sons."

"Excellent."

"Warnie?"

"Yes, my dear?"

"Am I still…a handsome woman?"

Warren leaned on one elbow and grinned down at his wife.

"I've told you that I want to be with you so much that I'm not capable of rational thought. Do you think I would tell you that if I didn't find you overwhelmingly appealing?"

Edith blushed and admitted, "I'm thirty-six and have given birth to three babies and been with child five times in all. I'm not as slender as I was when we first married. I've nursed the boys, and my chest is larger."

"And I like it that way," he chuckled. "And I like you this way. You become more lovely to me every year. It's my old body that's sagging, not yours."

"It's not sagging in the least. You've only got a bit of gray in your hair to tell the truth."

"And quite a few lines around my eyes."

"Not so many."

"Oh, but you will turn my head, Edith." He lowered his mouth to her shoulder and murmured, "What do you want, my love?"

"You and your children. The boys are getting older. I want as many children as we are able to have before I cannot have more. I'm afraid we're running out of time. It's been two years since I was last with child."

"And if we have no more? What if I get you with child again and the same thing happens? It upsets us both so. Is it worth going through it again?"

"If we don't try, then we'll never know if there's another child waiting to be born to us. I think God will give us another chance, another child. I want to keep trying."

"We can certainly enjoy ourselves trying," Warren agreed. "Two daughters would round things out nicely. We'll all have a splendid life together in America."

Edith shifted awkwardly in the bed and told her husband, "If that's what you want, then you'd better get to work and help me to start a new life right here."

By the time Ellis Island was in sight, Max had developed a cold, Milo was exhausted from repeated bouts of seasickness, Warren was suffering from continual lack of sleep, and Edith was expecting another child.

Interlude

Daniel shut the notebook, rotated his head back and forth, and rubbed his stiff neck muscles. He glanced at his watch: 8:20. His stomach growled.

I should have brought food in an ice chest. I don't have time to go out.

He went to the phone, dialed Room Service, ordered a pizza, then fished in his pocket for some change and set out to find a soft drink machine. Five minutes and three wrong turns later, he found it. He punched the Coke Classic button and listened as the can bounced its way down to the opening. Daniel took two large gulps before starting back towards his room.

He made it to his door in time to collide with the girl from Room Service.

"I am soooo sorry!" the girl cried. "It's, like, only my first day!"

"It's okay. Really," Daniel assured her, as he stooped down to pick up the fallen pizza box and said, "Look, it landed right-side-up." He tentatively opened the top of the cardboard container and said. "Don't worry about it. It's still intact, and there are only a few drops of Coke on the floor."

"You won't report this?" she asked nervously. Fighting back tears, she added, "I really need this job."

Daniel frowned down at the girl. She could be no older than seventeen. Blonde hair. Blue eyes. Nice chest. The All-American Cheerleader. He estimated that she was at least five months pregnant.

"No, of course, I won't tell anyone. There's nothing to tell." He reached into the front pocket of his jeans for the room key and asked, "Are you hurt? I mean, we crashed pretty hard."

"I'm okay. I have to be getting back. They, like, might think I'm taking too long."

"Oh. Sure. Let me get the tip."

Unlocking the door, he put the pizza box on the coffee table and located his wallet.

"Here you go. Thank you…"

"Celeste." Accepting the tip, she said, "Thanks, Mister…"

"Dan Nash."

"Maybe I'll see you again tonight."

"I wouldn't doubt it."

"I guess I'm supposed to go now," she said reluctantly.

"This is your first job?"

"You can tell?"

He shrugged and said, "Everybody has a first job. Once you get used to working, it gets easier. It helps when your boss gives you a break."

"Then I guess I'm, like, not so lucky."

"Not good, huh?"

Celeste reached for the doorknob and said, "I'd better get back."

"Good luck."

Once he'd closed the door behind her, Daniel went back to the coffee table. He thought about eating and reading at the same time but dismissed the idea. He'd only get pizza grease on the notebooks. So, he ate three pieces, finished off his Coke, then went to wash his hands.

Returning from the bathroom, Daniel decided it might be more comfortable to read while sitting in the chair across from the couch. He flipped the pages to the place where he'd left off and discovered what life in America had been like for his father's family.

Chapter Two: A Good Man's Life Begins Again

"Up you go there, Milo. It's time to board the train."

"Noooo!" the child wailed, struggling to free himself from his father's grasp.

Warren looked to his wife for guidance.

"Milo, we must get aboard. There are other people who are waiting to get on the train."

"Noooo!"

"Hey!" yelled a burly man behind them. "You get on, yes?"

Edith looked imploringly at Warren and asked, "Could we take a later train?"

"No. It must be this one."

Max stepped forward and said cheerfully, "Come, Brother. What's wrong, then?"

"I don't want to be sick again! It makes my sides hurt! What if I do it all the way to Louisiana?"

"You won't get sick," Max said with authority. "You won't throw up your dinner once. Now, take my hand, and let's climb aboard."

Milo took hold of his older brother's outstretched hand and stepped up obediently. Their parents exchanged relieved looks and followed.

Once they were crammed into yet another small compartment, Milo immediately fell asleep to the soothing rhythm of the chugging train.

"How on earth did you know that he wouldn't be sick?" Edith asked her oldest son.

"I didn't, but I couldn't see any other way to get him on. I was only hoping that he wouldn't be sick. He'd never forgive me if I told him a story."

"That's my good man. I know you're not feeling well yourself with that congestion, but you've still been so helpful,

Maxwell," she said, smoothing his hair. "Warnie, I may take a short rest myself."

"Aren't you feeling well?"

"I'm ready to be home, although I daresay that won't happen for some time. Days on the ship with such terrible weather, hours on Ellis Island, days in the boarding house...." She sighed and admitted, "It's been wearing, and we have been squashed into each place like lemmings. I keep dreaming that we're stuck in a tiny tin and that we're waiting for someone to unroll the top so we can breathe easier." She leaned back against the seat cushions and laid a hand on her stomach. "And I do feel dreadful, I must admit. I can't keep anything down in the mornings."

"Maybe the baby's ready to stop moving, too," Max suggested.

"It won't be long now," Warren assured them. "By the end of the week, we'll be able to roost for a while. I know it won't be a permanent home, but we can at least plant our feet for a time and plan for a place of our own. Tommy and Mary have two extra rooms, so we'll have a bit of space."

"I'd settle for the lemming tin if I could take out my things," grumbled Max.

"Why don't you come for a walk with me, while Mum and Milo have a nap?"

"No, Father. I'll stay and read if it's all the same to you."

"That's fine, Max. I'd actually like to read a bit myself. Perhaps we can take a walk later."

As it was, they didn't leave the compartment for the remainder of the afternoon. After supper that evening, they returned to it and collectively agreed that they were ready for bed. They were asleep before dark.

Cough! Cough!

Edith was instantly awake.

Cough! Cough!

"Max, what is it?"

Edith turned on the lamp and hurried over to her child. Laying her hand on his chest, she bent forward and kissed him on the temple.

Cough! Cough!

"Warnie!" she whispered urgently. "Warnie, wake up!"

"Hm? Edith?"

"It's Maxwell."

Warren climbed quickly out of bed and knelt beside his wife.

"He's running a high temperature." She took her husband's hand and placed it across their son's chest before urging, "And feel this."

"What?"

Cough! Cough! Cough! Cough!

Warren looked anxiously at his wife in the dim light of the compartment. She nodded.

"What do you need to help the fever and the congestion?"

"Water and a washcloth to start. Ice, if you can find it."

Cough!

"Edith, I don't think you should be taking care of the boy in your condition."

"And what should we do then? Should I sleep on the steps of the train or should he?"

"I only meant –"

"I know what you meant. I agree with you, but there is no place for me to go. Even if there was, Max needs me. I want this child, but I'd much rather lose the one that's hardly begun instead of the one I've had for seven years."

"Quite. I must confess that I am worried, Edith. He's had that blasted runny nose and congestion for a fortnight. That it could worsen so quickly and completely is not a good sign."

"I've just had a horrible thought. What if he dies? What if that's why I'm expecting again?"

"He won't die. You're with child again because…because it was time for us to have another one, not because anything will happen to our first. You stay here with the boys, and I'll go find the things you need."

By the time he returned, Edith had stripped off all of Max's clothes, except for his underwear. The boy lay coughing and tossing on top of the bedclothes.

"Mum." Max tried unsuccessfully to sit up and said, "Father."

"It's all right, my darling," Edith cooed. "Father and I are both here." She dipped the washrag into the water and began to drag it across her child's fevered skin murmuring, "There, doesn't that help?" Without waiting for his answer, his mother continued her ministrations and said reassuringly, "You'll be better soon."

An hour later, the cot was soaking wet. Max's fever had escalated, despite his mother's best efforts. Warren took the basin and wiped at his son's face, arms, and legs in the same manner as his wife. Edith sat heavily on the floor and laid her head on the edge of the cot.

"Lie down," Warren quietly commanded. "I'll watch over him."

"No," she insisted. "Why won't his fever come down?"

"Mum!" Max shrieked, jerking on the cot. "Mum, where are you?"

Scrambling up from the floor, Edith took her son in her arms. She could feel the intense heat from his body where their bare skin made contact.

"I'm here, Darling. It's all right. Mum's here." She flashed a terrified look at her husband. "You have to see if there's a doctor on the train!"

Warren reached out and touched his son's sweat-soaked hair.

"Leave my brother alone!" Max stared up at his father with glazed eyes and mumbled, "He's too young to know about the wire! His cat is too big!"

"He's out of his head," Warren muttered. "I'll bring help presently. Be brave, my dear."

Help returned with Warren Nash in the form of Dr. Aloysius Portsmith. Tall, robust, and kindly, Portsmith had been awakened by the porter and was, therefore, clad only in his pajamas and dressing gown.

"Excuse my attire," he said immediately to Edith, as he followed her husband into the compartment. "I didn't want to take the time to dress. Dr. Aloysius Portsmith at your service."

As the man began a cursory examination of her sick child, Edith almost cried with relief.

"Your husband tells me that your son's been ill for two weeks but that this intensification of illness came on quite suddenly and that you found him congested and with great fever earlier in the night."

"Yes, exactly."

"Has he had similar illnesses in the past?"

"Not like this, no. He tends to be a rather healthy child." She tilted her head towards the sleeping form of Milo and continued, "My younger one has more respiratory illnesses."

"Has he been sick?"

"No, not at all, unless you count the seasickness he had on the boat."

Portsmith reached forward and effortlessly took Max from his mother. The boy moaned and twisted weakly in the large man's arms.

Cough! Cough! Cough! Cough!

"Hm."

He placed the child on the soggy cot and started a more thorough examination. Removing a bulky stethoscope from the black bag he'd brought with him, Portsmith lowered the end onto various locations on the boy's torso.

"Why are you doing that?" asked Warren. "The problem's in his chest, isn't it?"

"A good physician leaves nothing to chance. His bronchial passages are most definitely under siege from bacteria, but I must listen to his bowel sounds and other abdominal functioning to determine if there are further problems or obstructions."

"And are there?" Edith asked in hushed tones.

"I'll let you know when I've finished."

He pressed his fingertips on Max's abdomen, then his groin, then felt under each side of the child's jaw. After looking carefully at the boy's ears, nose, eyes, and throat, Portsmith took Max's pulse then turned to the porter, who was waiting near the door.

"I'll write a list of the supplies you can round up for me."

"Yes, sir."

The doctor withdrew a pencil and piece of paper from his bag and jotted down several items. The porter took the list and left, pulling the door shut behind him.

"Can you tell what it is?" asked Warren nervously.

"He has an acute infection in his lungs. At first I was concerned that it was pertussis or diphtheria."

Edith covered her mouth in horror, and he hastened to reassure her.

"Upon examination, I find that's not the case. In pertussis one sees the wretched coughing spells where the child cannot even take a breath then the deep intake of air afterwards." He rooted around in his bag and continued, "In diphtheria the mucous membranes are so affected that there is a threat of asphyxiation."

"But that's not what he has? You're certain?" Warren asked hopefully.

"No pertussis or diphtheria." He went on by saying, "However, your son is seriously ill. Whatever the source of the bacteria, it's leading to double pneumonia. His temperature must come down and the congestion must be broken up if he's to recover without any permanent damage to his brain or other organs. I'll mix a plaster for his chest that will be hot, while attempting to cool his extremities to bring down the fever." He pulled a bottle from his bag and said, "I'm also going to give him some aspirin and an injection of a sedative. He's in no shape to fight us, but I'm certain he'll try."

"How can you know?"

"My daughter had a similar illness ten years ago. In her delirium, she fought the attending physician so hard that he had to retire from the room for a brief time. I won't make the same mistake."

Portsmith unscrewed the top of a bottle and motioned for Warren to hand him a glass filled with water. He poured a powdery substance that Warren and Edith assumed was aspirin into the glass and stirred it with a spoon.

"My daughter recovered completely, although it took some time. Gave me my first grandson last month. I'm on my way home from visiting them." Glass in hand, he rose and went back to the cot and then announced, "We'll lift him and get him to drink this."

Supporting his son under the shoulders and the back of the head, Warren lifted him slightly. Portsmith put the glass to the child's lips and tilted it. At first, Max swallowed automatically. Then, as the bitter taste of the aspirin went down his throat, he choked and tried to turn away.

"There, there," the doctor prodded encouragingly. "Drink it down."

With some effort by the adults, Max was forced to drain the contents of the glass.

"Good. Now that we've got that in his system, I can give him the injection."

The door to the compartment slid open, and the porter entered and placed the requested materials on the empty bed.

"Mum, why are all these people here?"

Edith hurried over to her youngest son, trying to shield him from seeing his ailing brother.

"Max isn't feeling well, Darling. This nice man is a doctor come to make him get better."

"It would be advisable, Mrs. Nash, for your other son to leave the room for a time," Portsmith said as he nodded to the needle he was concealing at his side. "No use predisposing anyone to anxiety, you understand."

"Father," Max groaned. "Mum."

Cough! Cough! Cough!

"How would you like to see the engine of the train, young man?"

Everyone stared at the porter.

"In my pajamas?" Milo asked incredulously. "Could I meet the engineer?"

"I think I can see to that. He and I are like this," the man said as he crossed his fingers. "Maybe you can help him up front for a while."

"Hooray! Can I, Father?"

"If you let your mother dress you in something more appropriate. Quickly, my dear."

As his wife hastily pulled out Milo's pants and shirt, Warren mouthed the words *thank you* to the porter.

"I've got four children at home. It's pitiful to see them sick. Makes your heart bleed. I'd hope that someone'd do the same for mine." He held out his hand to Milo and said, "C'mon, young fella. We can start with the conductor."

When their footsteps could no longer be heard down the corridor, Portsmith spoke frankly to Warren and Edith.

"He'll have to be held tightly. All children detest injections, but intravenous injections are particularly nasty for them. I'm glad he's feverish. Perhaps he won't remember when he comes to."

"I'll do it," volunteered Edith.

"No, my dear," protested Warren. "You'll never be able to hold him securely enough. If he flails about, he may injure you or the child."

"You're with child?" Portsmith asked, as he removed a length of cord from his black bag.

"Only just, offered Warren helpfully. "I'm concerned that she could contract this infection."

"It's too late to worry about it now. You've all been exposed. If you're going to catch this, then you're going to catch this. The next week or so will tell. If the symptoms begin to manifest themselves, seek treatment immediately." He nodded to Warren and commanded, "You hold him against you. Leave his left arm free." Turning to Edith, he said, "You can help me by holding the arm itself. Keep it as steady as possible."

They took their positions. Portsmith secured the cord around the upper part of Max's arm and worked on locating a suitable vein.

"Ready yourselves."

Having said that, he slid the needle into the vein. Max howled, his cry muffled by his father's chest. He fought and kicked and twisted, but his parents held him fast. It was all Edith could do to keep the arm steady and to contain the tears she was blinking back.

Portsmith withdrew the needle and undid the cord. He relaxed his own hold on Max's elbow, as the exhausted child went limp against Warren.

"Now, we can get to work."

When Dr. Aloysius Portsmith stepped off the train ten hours later, Max's fever had broken. Although the congestion would take longer to dissipate, the physician assured the parents that their son would live.

The remainder of the Nashes' train trip was spent coaxing Max to drink liquids and to take the aspirin mixture and cough medicine his mother had been instructed to prepare every four hours for her son. Milo, although worried about his older brother's condition, enjoyed his time spent with the train crew and became the engineer's pet. He stepped out onto the platform in Baton Rouge wearing the conductor's hat.

Tommy and Mary Fleming stood scanning the faces of the descending passengers. Milo pointed them out to the ever-friendly porter, who led the boy across the platform to greet them.

"Mister and Missus Fleming?"

Tommy's brow furrowed, as Mary bent to give Milo a brief hug and asked, "Is something the matter?"

"I'm afraid so."

Mary straightened quickly as her husband asked, "Where are the boy's parents and his brother?"

"Well, they're still on the train. They'll need some help. The older boy, he's been mighty sick. Didn't know if he'd pull through. Seems to be doin' well, but it'll be a while before he's feelin' up to snuff."

"Follow us!" Milo cried, tugging at Mary's hand.

"Oh, my!" Mary exclaimed upon seeing her friends and their child. "You poor dears! Tommy, do be a love and help Warren. I'll stay with Edith until the last minute so we don't have to move poor Max until then. Milo, will you keep us company? It has been a while." She leaned down and patted the boy's head before prompting, "Do tell me about your journey."

By dinnertime that evening, Mary and Tommy had heard various accounts of the long trip from Milo, Edith, and Warren. Max, who was weak and drawn, slept almost continually, only waking to drink, eat, or go to the water closet.

"Bathroom!" Milo chirped. "That's what the men on the train called it."

"Bathroom," Max repeated before dozing off once more.

For the next two months, Max learned about life in Baton Rouge from his brother. As his congestion lessened, Max's strength gradually returned, yet he was still confined to bed. His parents brought him books and toys to occupy his time, and Milo regaled him with tales of the city and the small shop their father had purchased.

"It's on Main Street," Milo explained, brimming with pride at being the brother with all of the answers. "It has things like we had in the shop at home, but it has other things, too. There are baskets for catching fish and odd spices and things. Some people come to the shop on foot, some by motor car, and some come by horse. Lots of people come by boat!"

"Boat?" Max echoed, intrigued. "How do they get the boats down the street?"

"They don't. They leave their boats in the river and walk up and down and up and down and buy everything. Then, they go back to their boats and row home."

"Is it as hot outside as it is inside?"

"Sticky," Milo nodded. "Uncle Tommy says there's not usually snow in the winter, but it can get quite cold."

"No snow? It certainly rains enough. I wonder how cold it does get."

In early September, the local doctor released Max from his imprisonment in Tommy and Mary's upstairs room. Max came bounding down the stairs, ready to see and do everything. By the end of breakfast, he was exhausted and asked if he could go back to bed.

Each day, he was able to push himself a little further. By the end of the month he took his first trip to the new store, which his father had named Nash & Co.

"When you're stronger, you can help me here," Warren told him. "I've already put Milo to work."

"I sweep!"

"But what about school?" asked Max. "We need to go to school, don't we?"

"Of course. However, with our lives in this new country just beginning, I need the whole family here. You'll go to school in the mornings and work here in the afternoons. Think you're up to the task?"

Max nodded enthusiastically, his inner strength surging and bolstering his tired body.

"Good. The first thing we must do is to get some weight back on you. You look as though you've lost a stone since you got sick."

"I have?" Max lowered his head and said apologetically, "I'm sorry, Father."

Warren crouched next to his son and took his hand.

"It's not your fault. Things happen in life that we can't control. We make the best of them and forge ahead."

And forge ahead Max did. By the time the Nashes celebrated their first Thanksgiving with the Flemings, his weight had increased, and he no longer tired easily. He and Milo had made friends and were kept busy by school and by the store. Except for his loathing of mosquitoes and his longing for snow, Max found that he was very happy in his new country.

On Christmas Eve, they all gathered around the Fleming table for supper. The culinary fare was a curious blend of English and Cajun. Max loaded his plate with roast goose, shrimp and cornbread dressing, blood pudding, clotted cream, and boudin balls.

"Max'll get a bellyache!" Milo taunted.

"I don't care. I mean to eat it all!"

"But there's pecan pie and shortbread!"

"And I'll have some of that, too!"

"Ahem." Warren tapped his wineglass with a fork and said officiously, "I've a very important announcement to make."

The others laid down their utensils in anticipation.

"Edith and I have purchased a house."

Exclamations of surprise echoed around the table.

"We'll still be right close," Edith put in quickly. "It's only two blocks away from here."

"Is it the little peachy one with the gray trim?" asked Mary. "That one's been needing someone to buy it for a while."

"It's the yellow one on the other end of that block," Edith answered. She smiled at her sons, who were grinning madly at her and remarked, "I see the boys remember it."

"We'll be out from underfoot in the week after New Year's," Warren told Tommy.

"You haven't been 'underfoot,' old boy. I'm pleased for you, but we've rather enjoyed the company. Mary and I adore these boys, and I, for one, was quite excited by the prospect of having an infant in the house."

Mary excused herself and hurriedly left the room.

"By God, that was a damned foolish thing to do!" Tommy admitted angrily. "How thoughtless of me!"

"I'll see to her," Edith said and went through the door that led to the kitchen. She called back over her shoulder, "You men get started with dinner. We'll be back shortly."

Confused, Max and Milo shrugged and attacked their full plates with gusto. The men also began to eat, but there was a tension in the air between them. Twenty minutes later, the boys sat back, full and content.

"Father, may I be excused? I have to go to the bathroom."

"Max, I know that some people call it a bathroom in this country, but I would prefer it if you used the word 'restroom' when you are at the dining table. It sounds much more polite."

"Yes, sir. May I be excused to go to the restroom?"

"You may."

"And may I have some pie when I get back?"

"Not until your mother and Aunt Mary have finished their supper."

"Yes, Father."

After relieving himself, Max started to walk back to the dining room. He heard voices coming from the kitchen and crept closer, curious to know what the trouble was with the grown-ups.

"…and it's not as though we haven't tried, because we really have," Mary was saying. "But every time my monthly comes, I feel so…so useless. It rather dampens my enthusiasm for trying. I'm worth nothing to Tommy if I can't have a child!"

"Don't talk like that. It may not have anything to do with you in the least. It may be Tommy."

"Oh, but it doesn't matter if it's one of us or both of us!" Mary cried. "Is it so much to ask that we have a child? Just one? Mrs. Fairwood, she's got eight and that's seven more than she needs. And we can't even have one!" She sniffled and daintily blew her nose before continuing, "It's not as though we couldn't provide for a child. I know we'd be good parents like you and Warren. Your children give you so much joy, even the one that hasn't been born, yet."

"That's true, but it hasn't all been joy, Mary. You remember the daughter who died at birth when Milo was born? And then there were the two that I lost almost as soon as I'd found out I was expecting. Even when they're here, one never knows what may happen. Why, look at what happened with Milo when the bronchitis overtook him two years ago." She sighed deeply and confided, "And what of Max? We actually thought he might die last summer. It was dreadful."

"Isn't it worth it, though?"

"I wouldn't give up a moment with Max or Milo. I'll say some extra prayers for you and Tommy."

"I daresay it might help. I'm thirty-five. Tommy and I have been married for fifteen years. Sometimes, I think it's hopeless."

"Oh, come now. It's Christmas Eve. Nothing should be hopeless on Christmas Eve. Let's return to the table and try to make merry."

Max scurried down the corridor and jumped into his chair.

"Told you you'd get a bellyache!" Milo said smugly. "You were gone for ages!"

Max chose not to enlighten his brother on the real reason he'd been away from the table for so long. There were too many questions running rampant in his head.

Why had his parents never told him that he and Milo had a sister who died at birth or that two other babies had been lost as well? Could this new baby die, too? Could his mother die? What was a monthly? Had he really almost died on the train?

Feeling bewildered and betrayed, Max refused dessert.

During the night, he lay awake, pondering unasked but important questions. He decided to go make inquiries of his mother and father and then changed his mind. Finally, in the hour before dawn, he rose and went to his parents' room.

He stood in the doorway and studied his sleeping mother and father. Warren snored softly on his back. Edith's even breathing could not be heard, but her stomach moved slightly with each breath.

Max turned to go. He couldn't ask them. He'd been eavesdropping, and that had been wrong. There must be a reason why they'd never told him. They were his parents, and they would do what was best for him. Wouldn't they?

"Maxwell?"

"Yes, Mum?"

"What is it?"

"I – I don't want you to die, Mum." Tears ran down his cheeks as he added, "Or the baby either."

Edith rose awkwardly from the bed and slipped on her dressing gown.

"Let's go to the kitchen where we won't wake Father or anyone else."

They sat at the table in the coolness of the December morning. Edith patted his hand and asked, "Why do you think I will die, my darling?"

"Because I…well, I heard you talking with Aunt Mary. I didn't mean to. Is it true, what you told her about my sister?"

"It is," she admitted sadly. "Your sister, Alyce, did die at birth."

"But why didn't you tell us?"

"Because you were too young to understand. I'd ask you not to say anything to your brother, yet. Someday, we'll tell him. I'm sorry that you found out. I don't want you worrying about me or this baby."

"Could it die? And you?"

"It is possible but not likely, Darling. Giving birth is a challenge for any woman and for the baby as well."

"But how does it happen?"

"You should ask your father to explain that. I believe he's been wanting to talk with you about it." She tousled his black hair and inquired, "Is there anything else you'd like to ask?"

"What's a monthly?"

Edith smiled into her hand.

"I believe that will go along with what your father wants to talk with you about."

"Oh. I'll ask him this morning." He sat lost in thought for a few seconds then went on, "Mum, may I ask you something that Father wouldn't know?"

"You may."

"What did it feel like when I was in your stomach?"

"It felt wonderful, just as it does with this baby. To know that the baby is growing inside of you is a joy. You love it so much, even when you can't see it! And when it kicks –"

"Babies kick before they're born? Does it hurt you?"

"No. It's delightful. It lets you know that your little one is getting stronger. Would you like to feel this one kick? When it gets closer to…when the baby is due to be born, you can feel the kicking on the outside a bit. Next time, I'll call for you." She glanced out of the window and said, "It's almost dawn. Why don't we go wake the others and see what Saint Nicholas brought?"

That evening as he played dominoes with his brother, Max reflected on the excitement of the presents and the Christmas Mass. He also ruminated on the wondrous and shocking explanation that his father had given him regarding men, women, and babies. He now carried with him a special secret that many other children didn't know. It would be hard not to tease his younger brother about this superior status, but he'd sworn that he wouldn't say anything to him.

"Max?"

"Yes, Mum?"

"Come here, please. You, too, Milo."

They clamored over the toys strewn on the floor and went to their mother, who was knitting in a chair by the fireplace.

"The baby is kicking. Would you like to feel it?"

"Me first!" insisted Milo.

"No, Milo. Max will be first." She took his hand and placed his palm on one side of her stomach then instructed, "Wait a moment."

For a time, nothing happened. Then a sharp kick lifted his hand slightly. He was astonished.

"Milo, you must feel it!" He grabbed his brother's hand and announced, "It's amazing!"

When Milo felt the kick, he cheered, "It's a boy! I know it is! He'll be a great ball kicker!"

As Edith chuckled and shook her head, Max happened to glance up towards the hall doorway. Mary stood morosely watching the happy family scene. She met Max's gaze and then hurriedly pivoted, darting out the front door.

The following day, Warren and Edith took Max, Milo, Tommy, and Mary to see the new house. A one-story structure, it had a parlor, a kitchen, a dining room, three bedrooms, and a bathroom. A picket fence edged the front yard. The back had no fence, several scrawny trees, and a multitude of weeds.

"It needs a bit of work in that yard," Warren remarked. "The house itself is fairly new, though."

"I'll fix the yard, Father!" Milo declared resolutely. "I'll get Max to help me. You don't have to worry. You take care of Mum and the store, and we'll make it look pretty. You'll see."

"Well, I do say that's a nice lad you've got there, Warren," said Tommy. "Will you work on my yard, if my man ever retires?"

"Yes, Uncle Tommy! I will!"

"I do believe he will," smiled Mary.

Despite their six-month stay in Baton Rouge, the Nash family had not acquired many material possessions. With the help of Tommy's yardman and a negro itinerant laborer, Moses, all of their belongings were moved to the new house in one evening.

"But Father, what about the furniture? Milo and I can sleep on the floor, but Mum can't."

"No one will sleep on the floor. The beds will be arriving tomorrow as will the rest of the furnishings. It won't be cluttered, but we'll have everything we need to live here. If we see that some other piece is required, then we shall have to acquire it." He turned to Moses and said, "You're a hard worker. Would you return in the morning to help with the furniture?"

"Yessa."

"Excellent. My wife will be here with my son at 8:00 a.m. to wait for the delivery. She can instruct you as to where she wants everything. It makes no matter to me."

"Yessa."

"Max, you will stay with your mother and assist."

"But it's Saturday! That's one of our busiest days at the store!"

"When I'm not about, you're the man of the house. The baby is due next month, and I don't feel comfortable leaving your mother alone, especially since there is no telephone in the house at present. In case of emergency, Milo is too young to be responsible and act in an acceptable manner. Do you understand?"

"I'll take care of her and the house, Father."

"Good lad."

The next morning, Max and Edith set out on foot at 7:30. When they arrived at the new house, Edith unlocked the door and busied herself by getting Max to help her open all of the windows. The air was cool. It was one of those Louisiana winter mornings that reminded Max of a spring afternoon in Cornwall.

At 8:00, there was a knock on the back door.

"Hello, Moses." Edith smiled and stepped back so that he could enter saying, "Please come in."

"Don' know if I should."

"I beg your pardon?"

"You ain' from aroun' here, so's I guess you don' know how things is. A black man don' enter a house wit' only a white woman inside."

Flustered, Edith sputtered, "But – you see – I – I'm not alone. My son…Max, come here, please."

The boy left the kitchen and came to the door.

"I'm not alone. I don't see how you can help arrange the furniture if you don't come in."

Moses nodded at the boy.

"S'all right, now dat I know he be here."

"Thank you. While we're waiting for the delivery truck, would you go with Max and begin to remove some of the silverware and dishes from the steamer trunks? You can put them on the counter."

Moses grinned and shook his head.

"Shore mus' be different where you from." He nodded to Max. "Bes' do as you Mum say."

As they unpacked the silverware and laid it out on the kitchen counter, Max blithely asked, "Why can't you be alone with a white woman?"

The large black man stared down at the child. He grinned and asked, "You really don' know?"

"Know what?"

"Most white folks, dey fear black men. Dey say we gon' steal dere tings and rape dere women."

"What's rape?"

Moses reached up a burly hand and scratched his bald head. Max watched the huge muscles in his arm ripple with the movement.

"You know 'bout men and women, yet? 'Bout what dey do wit' each other?"

"You mean about babies?"

"Yessa. Rape is when a man force hisself on a woman, when he do dat to her witout her sayin' s'all right."

"Why would anyone want to do…that with someone who didn't want to do it back?"

Moses shrugged.

"Some, dey crazy. Some, dey cain't get it no other way. Some, dey like to bring white folk down." He hoisted a large roll of felt from a trunk and continued, "Now, I ain't jus' sayin' it's black folk who rape. Dere's white ones, too. Lots of white folks raped black women when dere was slaves. Slaves didn't have no rights." He unrolled the felt and added, "And it don' happen all de time now, neither. But it do happen. Somethin' men been doin' from de beginnin', I imagine. Don' know what makes a man do it, though. Don' see how forcin' a woman could make a man feel good."

Max silently removed the knives from the felt and laid them near the sink. Eventually, he said, "Even if you wanted to rape someone, I wouldn't think that you would choose Mum. You're too nice, and her belly would get in the way."

Moses laughed uproariously at this in a deep baritone so thunderous that Edith came in from the front porch where she'd been surveying the yard.

"What on Earth is so amusing?" she asked.

"Oh, Missus Nash, you got yerself one smart boy dere. Thinks things through, yeah." He wiped at his eyes and declared, "He's one good boy."

"Thank you, Moses." She cocked her head and said, "I think I hear the furniture man."

As she headed excitedly towards the front door, Moses nodded down at Max and said, "We gon' finish dis for yer Mum later."

"Yes, sir."

Still shaking his head, Moses went to help the deliveryman with the sofa.

By 1:00, all of the furnishings ordered had been unloaded, arranged, and rearranged in the Nash home. Once the man from the shop departed, Edith went to the kitchen and retrieved a hamper from its protected spot near the back door.

"I have a basket with sandwiches, and there's lemonade. Would you like some, Moses?"

"Yessam."

"I'll set everything out at the table so that we can all sit and eat."

"No, ma'am."

"Excuse me?"

"No, ma'am. I cain't eat in dere wit' you. I'm beholdin' to you fer not bein' agin black folk, but dem other white folk, dey won' take a good look on you if you seats me at yer table. I 'preciates it, though."

"But where will you eat?" Edith asked.

"Back porch'd do."

Biting her lip, Edith nodded and proceeded to prepare a plate and glass for Moses.

"Mum –" Max began, as he picked up one half of his ham sandwich.

"Hush," Edith interrupted quietly. "He may hear you. He's right, my darling. There are things we're not familiar with, things I do not wish to be familiar with. Unfortunately, we may have to acknowledge and accept certain facts of life. Working with the store for so many years in Cornwall and now here, your father and I have dealt with many different types of people. There are good and bad of all kinds. Some may feel that we are…too accepting."

"But –"

"But it's unfair. Yes, it is. However, your father has always run a successful business and would like to continue to do so. We do not have to be unkind, but we may have to…conform somewhat."

"But –"

"Somewhat."

"But how will we know what people expect and what they don't?"

"Trial and error, I suppose."

After lunch, the unpacking and rearranging continued. By 3:00, Edith was tired and called a halt to the household activities.

"Would you return Monday, Moses? I think I'll leave the rest until then."

"Yessam."

"Has my husband paid you for today?"

"Yessam."

"Well, then. We'll see you Monday. Is 1:00 all right?"

"Yessam."

That night, as they sat around Tommy and Mary's dinner table, Edith turned to her husband and said, "Warnie, I had an idea today while we were at the house."

"I do hope you didn't overdo things, my dear."

"I feel fine. Now, listen. Moses seems to be a very good worker, don't you think?"

"He does."

"He's polite, quick, and good with people, isn't that so?"

"I must admit he is a great deal smarter than my yardman, God bless him," Tommy said grudgingly.

"I was thinking that perhaps you could use Moses at the store after we've finished at the house," Edith persisted. "That way, the boys could attend school all day and not have to spend the majority of their time studying when they get back from the shop. I know you'd have to pay the man a daily wage, and we've just bought the house and with the baby on the way…." Her voice trailed off, then Edith said, "It may not be feasible."

"I think it's a first-rate suggestion," Warren said, sitting back and wiping at the corners of his mouth with his napkin. "And don't worry about the money. I'm afraid I cannot afford diamonds or furs, but we're doing quite nicely here in America, even better than we were in England, actually."

"Oh, good show!" Mary beamed. "How excellent!"

"As is your idea, Edith," Tommy concurred. "Moses simply hasn't found his niche, yet. This may well be it."

"It's settled then. You mention it to him Monday when he arrives at the house. If he's interested, he can come 'round to the store that afternoon and work out the details."

"I don't want to go to school all day," Milo protested. "I don't like to stay still and stare at that old teacher. She must be a hundred and twenty!"

"At least we get to go to school. Imagine if we couldn't," Max said thoughtfully. "How would we ever go to university if we didn't learn at school?"

"I don't want to go to university! I want to work in the garden!"

"You will do both," Warren said sternly. "Uncle Tommy and I read mathematics together at Oxford. I don't expect either of us would be doing so well in life if we'd simply sat at home and grown vegetables." He smiled at his pouting son and said more gently, "And speaking of vegetables, enough talk. Concentrate on eating your peas. I know how fond you are of peas."

Moses did, indeed, warm to the offer of steady work at Nash & Co. Edith instructed him to be at the store, ready for work, on Tuesday morning. Then, she sent him, Milo, and Max to stock the pantry with the food that sat out on the counter.

Some time later, as Edith bent down to pick up a tin of beans that had fallen to the floor, she experienced what was unmistakably a labor pain. Leaning against the doorframe, she closed her eyes and breathed deeply, as the pain washed over her.

"Missus?"

Opening her eyes, Edith viewed Moses and Max anxiously hovering nearby.

"Mum?"

"I – I'm all right." She straightened, then said, "Moses, I'm afraid that I may need you to do a bit more than unpacking things today. Would you go to Mrs. Fleming's house and tell her to ring for the doctor? Then would you run to the store and let my husband know that the baby's coming?"

"Max and I can go, Mum!"

It was Milo, jumping up and down excitedly by the back door. He was covered from head to toe in mud.

Edith smiled at her younger son, her concern over what was to come momentarily forgotten.

"Milo! What in Heaven's name have you been up to?"

"Making the backyard prettier!"

"You look a sight!" she laughed and asked, "How did you manage to get so filthy? Moses, perhaps you and Milo could go together. Milo you will stay at Aunt Mary's, do you understand?"

"But Mum!"

"Not good to argue wit' yer Mum. Missus?"

Max saw him look at Edith. They exchanged some nonverbal message, and Moses nodded.

"Yessam. Mister Milo and I, we be goin' to Missus Fleming's. Seein' as he's already real dirty, maybe when I gets back from Mister Nash's, he and I can be helpin' Cleatus in the yard."

"Thank you, Moses. Perhaps you had better make haste."

The black man took the mud-covered child in his arms and hurried out through the back door.

"Max, you wait in the parlor while I put on my nightdress and get things ready in the bedroom."

"Yes, Mum."

She saw the fearful look in her son's expression and came over to him.

"What would you like, a brother or a sister?"

"Another sister."

"What would we call her? Or him, if it's a boy?"

"I – I'm not certain."

"Well, you think about it while I make ready. Then, you can let me know."

Max went to stand watch at the parlor window. Between contractions, Edith undressed, slipped on her nightdress, and spread some padding on top of the new mattress.

His heart racing, Max tried to distract himself by thinking of names for his soon-to-be-born brother or sister. His mind was blank. The only thought he seemed capable of having was: *They can't die.*

Just as he was wondering when the doctor would arrive, a low moan emanated from his parents' bedroom. In a panic, Max rushed through the house and flung open the door.

"Mum!"

Riding the crest of a pain, Edith was temporarily unable to respond. Max ran forward and took her hand. She squeezed it tightly then relaxed her grip as the pain diminished.

"Thank you, Max. It appears as though this one will come quickly, too."

"Did I take a long time coming?"

"A bit."

"Did I hurt you as badly?"

Edith weighed her words carefully before she answered.

"Having a child does bring pain to the mother, but one knows that, in the end, you will have a beautiful baby as a result of that. It makes it –"

Another contraction began.

"Maxwell, please leave the room. You shouldn't be here."

Panicked, he took her hand again and insisted, "I won't leave you!"

As the contraction passed, they heard a knock at the front door.

"Go!" Edith ordered.

Max went, praying fervently for the doctor to be waiting at the door. Instead, it was Mary.

"You wait on the porch!" Mary commanded. "The doctor should be here any second."

Sure enough, within five minutes, the doctor arrived. Max led him to the bedroom and was immediately told not to enter. He waited anxiously outside the door, trying not to cover his ears each time his mother cried out.

His father hurried in a half hour later. He opened his mouth to speak, just as Mary opened the door to the bedroom. She was extraordinarily pale.

"How is she?" Warren demanded. "Has the baby come?"

"No. It's…oh, Warren, I never imagined what birth was actually like. The doctor told me to leave so that I wouldn't faint."

"Damn it all, Mary! How is she?"

"She's…she's…"

Warren lurched into the bedroom and slammed the door behind him.

Beside Mary, Max started to cry.

Mary said suddenly, "I've returned to my senses. Everything will be fine. Come with me for a walk."

They walked to one end of the block then turned and walked to the other end. They had repeated this act twenty-two times when Warren came out onto the front porch and hailed them back. Mary tried to keep up with Max, who was running as fast as he could.

"Would you like to see your new sister?"

Max was radiant with relief and excitement. His father didn't appear so enthusiastic.

"Aren't you glad it's a girl, Father?"

"I am. It's only that the baby had a difficult time being born and a man doesn't like to see his wife suffer is all. I'm relieved they're both well. You and Aunt Mary need to come and see the new baby."

Edith lay cradling her newborn daughter at her side on the bed.

"She's so small!" whispered Max. "Look at her fingers how tiny."

"She's early," remarked the doctor.

"Well, Max?" Edith murmured tiredly. "Have you thought of a name for your sister? You got your wish after all." She angled her head towards her husband and said, "I do hope it's all right with you. I think that he deserves the honor, since he's been such a good little man with me here."

"As you say, my dear. Max?"

Max stared at the baby. He reached out and experimentally touched her cheek.

"How about the name Nora Mary Nash? Does that sound right proper?"

"Lovely," Edith proclaimed.

"Oh, Maxwell, you are such a cheeky boy!" Mary burst into tears and exclaimed, "How sweet!"

Warren concurred.

"Good," the doctor said. "Now that everyone's in agreement, I want you all to let Mrs. Nash and Nora Mary sleep."

In the months that followed, Max could see why the doctor had recommended that Edith get some rest in those early hours after Nora's birth. The baby never seemed to sleep. Even Milo, who normally slept through anything, was kept awake. Already irritated by the fact that he didn't get the little brother he'd hoped for, Milo openly showed his resentment towards the baby and the attention she received.

Nora grew healthy and strong. It was evident that she was as mild-tempered as Milo was hot-headed. Everyone adored her and praised her sweet disposition and her beautiful golden ringlets and blue eyes.

But it was evident that something was not quite right with the baby. Try as she might, she was unable to crawl until well after her first birthday. Walking seemed an insurmountable task for yet another year. She also seemed incapable of understanding and interpreting much of what was said to her. Constant repetition was the most effective method of keeping Nora on task. Local doctors speculated that there had been some injury during the difficult delivery that had resulted in her delays.

The summer after her fifth birthday, Warren and Edith took Nora to a New Orleans doctor who specialized in childhood disorders. Max, at age eleven, was put in charge of the store and his brother for two days – provided that Moses was present at all times.

"I do hope they find out what's wrong," Max told Moses, as they closed the shop on the evening of the second day. "Here, you put up those tables, and I'll put the other items over on this side."

"Nora is trouble," Milo said sourly. "She doesn't do what she's told. Sometimes, I think she's plain stupid."

"You stop talkin' 'bout Miss Nora dat way," said Moses, calm as ever. "Some folk born to be tall, and some folk born to be short. Miss Nora, maybe she born to be pretty an' sweet but not so quick to catch on. Don' mean she ain't as good as the next one. Maybe she even better. Folk who don' catch on tends to be nicer, least in my 'sperience."

"She's just contrary, that's all!"

"Don' you sass me, Boy," Moses said smoothly. "'Cept for all de night cryin' she done as a baby, Miss Nora ain't never been contrary in her whole life. You best mind yer elders. I work fer yer daddy, but dat don' mean I gots to take no sass from you."

Milo stomped out of the back door in order to stack the crates behind the store. Max and Moses began to stock the shelves with the merchandise that had arrived the previous day.

"He be strong-willed, dat one."

"You never seem to let it get to you. I think Mum gets rather outdone with him sometimes. Father, too."

"An' you?"

"Yes." Max straightened some notebooks that rested on a low shelf and asked, "Moses, why is it that you never got married and had children? Everybody likes you, and you're good with Milo, Nora, and me. You're good with all of the people who come in, adults and children alike."

"Right woman never came 'long."

"You're very kind about Nora."

"I gots me a sista who ain't too quick herself."

"You mean she's…like Nora?"

"Yessa."

"What…is she like?"

"Always gots a smile for you. Talks real soft. De man who married her, he takes good care of her. If I didn' think he would, I wouldn't a given my permission. Folk who's like my sista, dey need folk who's kind to dem. Dey don' know how to defen' demselves agin some who might hurt dem. Now, let's quit talkin' and close up dis here place."

Once the store had been straightened, the money counted, and the doors securely locked, Max, Milo, and Moses set out on the long walk back to the Nash residence. They arrived dusty and sweating to find Warren, Edith, and Nora sitting on the porch swing. Their suitcases were on the steps.

"Brothers!" Nora cried, scooting off of the swing and nearly tumbling down the steps as she added, "Moses!"

"I seem to have lost my house key," Warren said by way of explanation, as he came down towards the little group.

"And I left mine in the bureau," Edith added, as she rose from the swing.

"How did it go?" asked Max, as he picked up Nora and gave her a hug.

"In a bit," Warren answered a little too sharply.

Milo gave his sister a cursory hug, took the key from Max's hand, and ran up the steps to unlock the front door.

"Brother's mad?" Nora asked seriously.

"He's grumpy because he's had to take all kinds of orders from me and Moses for two days. It's good that you and Mum and Father are back."

"I'll go and cheer him up!"

They watched the little girl struggle up the steps and go into the house after her brother. As the door shut behind her, Max shrugged emphatically at his father.

"Well?"

"The doctors stated that she's mentally deficient," Edith said softly. "They wanted to institutionalize her."

"Because she's slow?!?" Max cried. "But you can't!"

"We never intended to," Warren said mildly. "She's perfectly healthy and not deranged in any way."

"Moses's sister is like her. She's all right. She's even married."

"Is that so?" Edith asked, brightening.

"Yessam. My sista's a good one, she is. Ain't nothin' wrong wit' her, 'cept fer some folks notions of what's good and what's not."

Warren rested his backside on a porch step and prompted, "Please, tell us about her."

As the three grown-ups and Max spoke in the front, Milo sulked in the bedroom. Nora, unable to get in, had left her place at the locked door and had wandered into the kitchen. She stood in front of the stove, looking up at the high shelf above it that held Milo's favorite cookies in a large green jar.

Milo heard the slow creak of the stove door. Curious, he left his room, went down the hall, and peered into the kitchen. Nora was kneeling on the edge of the stove. One foot dangled down towards the open door. One hand reached up towards the shelf. The hem of her dress was caught on one of the knobs that released the gas jets.

He had never run as fast in his entire life. Just as he reached his sister, the stove began to tip. He scooped her up, deposited her on the floor, and righted it. Then, he fixed the knob and shut the open stove door. Finally, Milo knelt on the floor and picked up his little sister, holding her close against him.

"What were you thinking?" he sobbed. "The stove could have fallen on you and killed you! The gas –"

Confused, she pointed to the shelf and said, "The Magic Cookies." She patted his wet cheeks and cooed, "Don't cry. We can get them."

"You…you were trying to get them…for me?"

"Don't cry, Brother." She touched his cheeks again and said sweetly, "I'm here."

Hearing footsteps on the porch, Milo picked up his small sister and carried her to her room. He sat in the white wicker rocker with her until his mother called them for supper.

"Come along, Nora," he said. "After dinner, we can share some Magic Cookies and milk."

"Max, too?"

"All of us."

"Tell me a story?"

"Any one you like."

And so began a new Nash family ritual. Every evening after supper, Warren, Edith, and Max would join Milo, who would sit with his sister, eat Magic Cookies, and tell her the story of the sleeping princess and the handsome prince who woke her with a kiss. Then, he'd wipe her face clean of the powdered sugar, and they'd go to wash their hands.

And life was good.

Interlude

After finishing a piece of leftover pizza, Daniel stood, slipped his sweater over his head, and pulled out his shirttails. He wandered about the room, considering everything and nothing. He ended up on the balcony and stood in the chill of the nighttime air, watching the cars go by.

Where are these people going? What are they like? Do they have normal, loving families? Daniel wondered. *That's what Max had and something I never knew as a child.*

Warren and Edith had been good parents. Milo and Max had been close, despite their very different personalities. Nora had loved both of her brothers and they her. The family had been well-off thanks to Warren's business savvy, and they were surrounded by good friends.

Of course, things weren't perfect. Max had that nasty grandfather, the dead sister, and the routine hardships of living in a world without modern pharmaceuticals and air-conditioning. It was evident that Nora was developmentally delayed. But none of that seemed to matter. Max and his family had been content.

Daniel reflected on his own childhood. Had there ever been a time before the summer of 1970 when he hadn't felt intimidated or afraid at home? Had there ever been a time when money was not an issue between his mother, Assumpta, and his supposed father, Zachary Samuels? Had there ever been a time when Samuels had not abused his wife?

The thought jarred Daniel. Had his mother been beaten from the day she met her husband? If so, then why had she married him? Certainly she wanted to keep her baby, but wouldn't it be better to go back to her family and raise her bastard son than to suffer constant beatings from a man she didn't love?

From what his adoptive mother, Lillian, had revealed to him after Max's death, Max had been a devastated widower with a full-time psychiatric practice when he'd begun teaching some classes at Louisiana State University. Daniel's mother, then called Tessa

Downey, had been a twenty-two-year-old graduate assistant. They had become sexually involved, and Tessa had become pregnant. According to Lillian, she'd run off, not wanting to ruin the reputation of her lover. Max had searched for both her and their baby for years but had eventually given up. He had unwittingly discovered that Daniel was his child after he and Lillian had taken the boy in during the summer of 1970. He had never told Daniel the truth.

What would Daniel's life have been like if his mother had stayed with Max and married him? The horror that had been her existence and Daniel's for twelve years would never have happened. How could she have chosen such a tragic path to follow?

Daniel wondered if the answer to that question would be in one of the later journals. How could it be when Max himself wouldn't be privy to Assumpta's motivations? Still, maybe there would be some clue. If there was, then Daniel could investigate further.

He threw away the cardboard pizza box and retrieved a plastic cup from the bathroom. After draining three cups of water, he returned to the chair and picked up the next journal. He'd wasted enough time. Max's future and his past were waiting.

Chapter Three: A Twist of Fate

In September of 1929, Warren Nash purchased a new home for his family. It was a white, two-storied dwelling directly off Highland Road. Nash & Co. had been good to him, and his investments were giving him excellent returns. He paid cash for the house.

"It's quite large," Edith said worriedly. "We have nice things, but I can't imagine that they will fill every room."

"They won't, my dear. We can have a jolly time cramming it with this and that."

"How many rooms, Father?" asked Nora.

"Let me see. There's a sitting room, a dining room, a kitchen, a parlor, three bedrooms, and two and a half bathrooms. Oh, and there's a garden choked with weeds off to one side. It's near the woods set back from the street. Quite nice, actually."

"Father, I've only just started at the university," Max put in. "I want to help with the moving, but I don't know if I'll have time."

"Rub it in," Milo teased. "My brother the bookworm who gets to go to college early."

"I still don't understand what college is," said Nora for the hundredth time. "I thought you and Milo went to that big brown school. Why do you go to another school now? Did you do something wrong?"

"Not at all," Max answered patiently. "When you get out of high school, you go to college. That's the only way I can become a doctor."

"Why don't I go to college? I want to be a doctor, too. I like to take care of animals. I could be an animal doctor. So, I should go to animal doctor school."

"Mum needs you here," Milo offered. "I think you already do a better job than most animal doctors, and you haven't gone to college at all."

Beaming, Nora skipped out of the back door.

"Hard to believe she'll be eleven this year," Edith remarked, as she removed a pie from the oven. "She's beginning to fill out some."

"Yes, quite," Warren agreed absently. "To get back to your question, Max, I've hired some men who'll assist Moses in moving the furniture and our belongings. Keep your mind on your studies."

"His mind is always on his studies. We could probably move, and he wouldn't notice until it was time for dinner."

"Milo, for shame!" Edith laughed. "But it is true, Darling. You are so serious. You'll be skin and bones soon if you don't pay attention to yourself."

Max stared down at his physique. He was tall and trim but muscular. He certainly wasn't wasting away.

Within the week, the Nashes had taken up residence in the house on Highland Road. Seven days later, the foundations of their happy world began to crumble.

On the morning of the 26th, Edith awoke with a terrible headache.

"Go back to bed, my dear," Warren suggested, as he entered the kitchen. "We can fend for ourselves. Remember when you had the influenza two years ago? We managed quite well."

"Nonsense, Warnie. Nora and I are baking pies today for the church meeting. I'll take some aspirin, and my headache will be gone in a flash." She cracked several eggs into the skillet and added, "We'll make a pie for us to have after dinner tonight. Does anyone have a preference?"

"I'd like apple," said Max.

"Me, too," agreed Milo.

"Me three!" cried Nora.

"I suppose my blueberry will have to wait," Warren moaned dramatically. "It seems I've been outvoted."

"Next time, Father." Nora patted him on the sleeve and repeated, "Next time."

Max took a sip of his milk then said, "By the way, I don't need a ride home from school today. I met a fellow freshman who has a vehicle of his own. He lives past here, and our schedules are much the same. He said he'll be pleased to drop me off, barring any unforeseen circumstances."

"Good show." Warren glanced at his watch and muttered, "We'd best be off soon, or we'll both be late."

"Not until you've eaten your breakfast." Edith laid down their plates and said, "Nora, get Milo, please. Tell him it's time to eat."

"That's all he likes to do is eat, sleep, and dig in the dirt," Nora said, as she trotted off to find her brother. "Is there college for that?"

That afternoon, Max rode home with his classmate as planned. He checked his watch as he inserted his key in the lock of the front door. It read 4:20.

Not bad, he thought. *We made excellent time.*

Carrying his satchel with him through the house, Max headed for the kitchen. The smell of baked pies wafted through the air and drew him forward. He stepped into the room. There were the pies, but his mother and sister were nowhere in sight. He noticed that the back door was slightly ajar. He pushed it open and froze.

Edith lay on the ground near the clothesline. Her eyes were closed, and her head rested in her daughter's lap. Nora was stroking her mother's hair.

For a few seconds, Max stood still and stared at them. His brain couldn't seem to process the images that his eyes were sending it. Then, he allowed for the possibility that what he was seeing was real. He dropped his satchel, walked forward, and knelt next to his mother and sister.

"Nora."

Trying to keep his voice steady, he repeated his sister's name. He took a long look at her. Her nose and eyes were red, and her cheeks were flushed and damp.

"Nora, what happened while Father, Milo, and I were gone to work and school?"

"We baked pies. Mum said she wanted to get some towels off the line. Then, she fell down. She was talking, and she fell down. I've tried to wake her up, but she won't. She sleeps and sleeps. She wet herself, Max. Why did she do that? Only babies do that."

Max knew that his mother was dead before he laid his warm fingers on her cool skin. A tingling feeling was seeping into his arms and legs.

Determined to stay calm, Max cleared his throat and said, "She's gone to be with Jesus."

The child looked first at Edith and then back to Max.

"But she hasn't gone. She's right here. Is Jesus expecting her?"

"Yes, I guess he is."

"Then I should get her hat."

Nora carefully laid her mother's head on the grass, slowly rose, and walked towards the house. Max followed her inside and telephoned his father while his sister searched for their mother's Sunday hat.

"I believe she had a cerebral hemorrhage," the doctor proclaimed after being summoned to examine Edith's body. "There's nothing anyone could have done. These things happen."

"I'm certain that they happen all the time," Warren conceded soberly. "It's only that they don't usually happen to us, you see."

"Death doesn't discriminate," the doctor replied. "It comes for us all one day."

The wake was a torturous affair. Nora was incapable of understanding that her mother was dead. As people came in to view the body, she would touch Edith's stiff hand and say, "Look who's here to see you! Wake up, Mum!"

The mood in the house was somber that evening, and the brothers and sister went to bed early. Max woke with a start shortly after midnight. Unable to return to sleep, he got up, put on his robe, and padded down the stairs in the darkened house. When he reached the bottom step, he stopped. The front door was wide open.

Pulse quickening, he tiptoed to the doorway and peered out. His father sat on the porch with his back against the wall.

"Father?"

"I should have gone first. I'm fifty-seven years old."

Max lowered himself down next to his father and said, "A hemorrhage doesn't have anything to do with age. It can strike at any time."

"Don't you think I bloody well know that!" Warren exploded.

Mortified by his outburst, the man reached out and put his right hand behind his son's neck and drew him close.

"Oh, Maxwell. I'm so sorry. Your mother and I have been together for so many years. I never imagined I'd outlive her. Here we finally moved into the kind of house she'd always dreamed of, and she's gone."

"She had it before she died."

"Yes, she did." Warren pulled away and leaned back against the house then groaned, "Whatever shall I do about Nora? She can't stay here alone."

"Take her to work with you," Max suggested. "At least until you find someone to stay here during the daytime to watch out for her. Put her to cleaning. You know how she loves to sweep and dust."

Warren nodded and agreed, "I suppose that would work for a time. It will have to do."

"Hello, Dearies!"

Startled, Max and Warren hurriedly got to their feet. In the moonlight, they could make out two approaching figures, one tall and one small.

"It's me, Louise Robichaux! I'm your next-door neighbor." The woman sauntered forward and gestured to the form behind her before announcing, "This is my daughter, Samantha. Samantha, say 'hello' to our friends."

The child shook her head and hung back uncertainly.

Warren glanced at his watch and asked, "Were you aware that it's 12:40?"

The woman said indignantly, "*I* have no need for clocks. Samantha and I live as we like. Right, Samantha?" Without waiting for a reply, she asked, "Doesn't she look like me? See her brown hair and her bone structure? Nothing like my husband. Right, Samantha?"

The silent child stepped closer to her mother.

"Mr. Nash, I heard about your wife. She didn't kill herself, did she? That's what my good-for-nothing husband did. Poisoned himself." She leaned closer and said in a stage whisper, "Some people say it was me who did it, but it wasn't. Not that I didn't think about it a time or two, but why waste good rat poison when a nice frying pan over the head will do?"

"Now, see here, Mrs. Robichaux! You – you shouldn't –" sputtered Warren.

"Louise," she emphasized, nonplussed.

"I'd think you should refrain from saying such things in front of the child. It's not seemly for one so young to hear such things about her father."

"Oh, he wasn't her father. That's why he took the poison." She glanced up at the moon and announced, "Time to go, Samantha! Goodbye, Mr. Nash and Mr. Nash! My condolences!"

And with that she took the child by the hand and led her back in the direction of their house. It was only then that Max realized that both the woman and the girl were in their nightgowns.

"I believe I'll take Nora with me to work indefinitely."

"The poor little girl," Max mumbled sympathetically. "She'll be warped by the time she grows to adulthood living with a woman like that."

"Unfortunately, she most likely already is. We have a lot to be thankful for, even now."

The next morning, Nora went to work with her father, while the boys returned to their respective schools.

"How was it, Nora?" asked Milo at the dinner table. "Did you have fun?"

"Tell them what you did," Warren prompted with a smile. "She was a very good girl."

"I cleaned everything in the store! Father says tomorrow I can do it again!"

Max took a bite of the tasteless meal that one of Edith's friends from the church had delivered after the funeral.

"You look tired, Father," he commented before forcing himself to take another bite.

"I'm exhausted. I must have pulled a muscle in my left shoulder today. My arm hurts like the dickens. Perhaps tonight I'll get some rest. You look tired yourself. You and Milo." Warren looked down at his empty plate. "I've been thinking that maybe this is all too much for us. You've started university so young, Max. With your mother's death, maybe you should–"

"I'm fine," Max said curtly. "I don't want to talk about Mum's death. I told her that I was going to be a doctor, and I don't intend to break my word."

"But your grades –"

"My grades won't suffer."

"You should take a break until the spring semester," Milo advised.

"I said I was fine! What about you, Brother? Will you take off the next three months of high school?"

"You know it's not the same. I don't have that option, unless I want to repeat the whole school year, which I don't."

"Milo's right," Warren agreed. "He may not be able to stop attending high school, but you can miss a term and –"

Max jumped up, his chair clattering to the floor.

"Why can't you all leave me alone? Why is everybody so worried about me? What about the rest of you? You can't give yourselves a chance to grieve, but you're going to afford me the opportunity? What a load of horse shit!"

He dashed up to his room and slammed the door. Throwing himself across the bed, he pressed his face into the bedspread and cried as he had never cried before.

It was Nora who eventually came to him. She sat on the edge of the bed and lightly stroked her older brother's hair.

"Max, do you want to get married someday?"

"Nora, it's not really the time to talk about this."

"I do. I want to get married and have lots of children." Placing her hands in her lap, she sighed and said, "I don't think I can go to college like you and Milo." She rubbed at her ring finger and asked, "Will you let me get married when I'm older? I promise I'd be a good wife and a good mama."

Rolling over onto his back, Max rubbed at his eyes and said, "I don't think it's up to me, Nora. That's Father's choice."

"If it were up to you, would you let me?"

He thought about this for a minute. Nora was sweet, pretty, and mentally slow. She loved to do repetitive household chores and was good at taking care of small animals. Max reflected on what Moses had told him about his sister and said, "If the right man came along and it was my choice, then I'd say 'Yes'. He would have to be a very nice man to marry my sister."

Leaning over to kiss him, she whispered, "I love you, Brother."

He fell asleep and dreamed of Nora in a wedding gown, then with a baby carriage, and finally with a cluster of children at her feet.

All the next day, Max felt better. The shock of his mother's death was beginning to fade, and he was once again able to concentrate on his studies. When his classmate dropped him off in the afternoon, Max hopped out of the car and swung his satchel as he walked towards the front steps. Ten feet from them, he stumbled on a stray stone. He thrust out his arms to try and break his fall, and the bag went flying.

There was a rustling sound in the bushes. As Max watched, Samantha Robichaux cautiously peeked out from behind some brush.

"It's all right," Max assured her. "I'm not hurt, and I won't hurt you."

The child took a few tentative steps towards him, picked up his satchel, and dragged it over to where he lay. Max rose slowly so as not to frighten her. He dusted himself off and said, "Thank you. Samantha, is it?"

A nod.

"Where's your mother, Samantha?"

"Sleeping. She sleeps a lot. She cries, too. Then, she doesn't sleep at all. Then, she laughs all the time."

"I see. Do you have a grandmother or aunt around?"

"My aunt, she lives in a silo."

"A silo?"

The girl nodded.

"A silo?" he repeated.

"They wanted to put Mommy there, too. But she didn't want the 'lectricity."

"Electricity?"

Another nod.

"Lectricity is for when you're bad. Mommy says that she's not bad and that she'd rather be here than have the 'lectricity."

Max was confused, but he could tell that the child wasn't making up nonsense. Whatever she was trying to explain, he was simply too bewildered to comprehend it.

"Let me walk you home."

He struggled to follow her through the deep overgrowth that edged her property. When the gray house was in sight, Samantha took off running towards the front door. Max hung back, uncertain as to whether he should accompany her inside or return home.

Samantha solved his problem by standing on the porch and calling out, "Come in!"

The Robichaux home was surprisingly neat. After witnessing the mother's eccentric behavior, Max had expected it to be in a shambles.

"The woman comes once a week," Samantha volunteered, as if reading his thoughts. "She's a colored lady."

"Samantha?"

Louise Robichaux stood in the doorway that led to the kitchen. It was evident that she had recently emerged from the bathtub. Her hair was damp, and she wore a white robe.

"I thought I heard someone. I hurried to get out of the bath." She smiled at her daughter and urged, "Go find Figgins, will you?"

The child skipped off down the hall and went out onto the back porch.

"Figgins?"

"The cat, Mr. Nash. She'll be gone for quite a while."

Louise swayed over to where Max stood in the living room. As she came closer, he studied her.

She was very young, perhaps only twenty or twenty-one. Her face was a delicate combination of high cheekbones, full lips, and pale skin. For the first time in his life, Max was truly uncomfortable in the presence of a woman.

His discomfort only increased as she moved nearer to him. Apparently, she hadn't dried herself well before slipping on the robe. He could clearly see her nipples through the thin fabric. A triangle of dark hair was visible lower still.

"I, ah, I should be going."

Trying hard not to break and run, Max edged towards the door.

"What's your rush, Mr. Nash? Stay a while."

"Samantha said you weren't feeling well." He took two steps and added, "Something about electricity."

Louise laughed, but it was not the crazed cackle that Max had expected. It was a bitter, reproachful laugh.

"I go up; I go down. I've had my share of hard knocks. My sister is the same way. They put her in an asylum. She gets electrical treatments to 'help' her. There's nothing of my sister left. I'd rather stay here, be crazy, and be myself than end up like a lump of clay with no will and no life." She bridged the distance between them and purred, "Won't you stay with me a while?"

"I need, um, to be getting back home. My, ah, father will be expecting me to help with the supper."

"You're welcome inside anytime," she informed him. "Just tell Samantha to go look for Figgins."

She leaned forward and gave him a kiss, making sure to brush up against him with her chest and her hips.

"Come again," she breathed. "Goodbye, Mr. Nash."

Max showed himself out. As he walked slowly home, he wasn't sure what had astonished him more – Louise's openness about being mentally disturbed, the decidedly off-beat way in which she and the child lived, the fact that such a thing as electrical treatment existed, or the woman's blatant sexual advances. He decided that what bothered him most was the fact that Louise Robichaux had aroused him so quickly and so completely.

He couldn't believe his reaction. Louise was crazy. Her husband had died mysteriously. She was possibly a murderess and certainly a questionable parent. So, why was he so smitten with the woman?

Because she's extremely available, he reasoned.

Max had been sweet on girls before and had even kissed a few of them rather passionately. However, the idea of being intimate with them, although tempting, had been undoubtedly out of the question. They were *good* girls from *good* families. He was the son of a prominent businessman. Young people of their class simply didn't consider being intimate before marriage, and he wasn't about to find some lady of the evening in order to satisfy his sexual urges.

"You're a prude," Milo said quietly, as they lay in their beds that night. He turned on his side and squinted at his brother in the moonlight before gloating, "You don't know what you're missing."

"And you do?" quipped Max.

Silence.

"Milo, you don't!"

Silence.

"Do you?"

Silence.

"Milo, do you know how dangerous it is? There could be a child and –"

"You wouldn't be lecturing me if you'd only do it yourself. You've never felt anything like it in the world."

"So, who have you done it with?"

"Sally."

"Sally Leger?" Max gasped. "But she's so…so proper."

Milo laughed devilishly and confided, "Not when we're together. God, but it feels good."

"I'll find out for myself someday."

"I certainly hope so," Milo concurred. "I'd hate for my older brother to die a virgin."

The next afternoon, Samantha was once again hovering nearby in the bushes. Pretending not to see her, Max unlocked the front door and went inside. He found it interesting that the mere sight of the child could immediately bring back his lingering desire for the woman.

He was engrossed in a chemistry assignment when there was a knock on the back door. Max laid down his pencil and went to answer it.

"Moses? What are you doing here?"

In a split second, Max realized that his father was dead.

"Where is Nora?" he croaked. "How did it happen? When did he –?"

Moses placed his hands on Max's shoulders and gave them a brief squeeze.

"I be tellin' you all 'bout it." He led Max back to the table and ordered, "You sit, and I be bringin' you a glass a water."

Once Max had drained the glass, Moses took a seat and folded his hands on the table.

"It was 'bout three hours 'go. We was puttin' some man's order in a box. Yer daddy, he says he was havin' indigestion. That arm was still botherin' him, he say, but now he got de indigestion, too. I axed him if he wanted to be takin' somethin' for it. The next thin' I know, he's staggerin' 'round, clutchin' up dere." Moses pointed to his chest then went on, "I catched 'im and laid 'im down. Miss Nora, she got real upset. I still don' think she knowed what happened to her mama, but she knows dat she ain't comin' back. And she smart enough to figger that de same thin' was happenin' to her daddy. I tol' her to go call Mista Fleming, to tell 'im to call de doctor. Didn' take de man long to get dere, but it be too late. He went real quick-like. Missus Fleming came and took Miss Nora to her house. I tol' dem I would come an' tell you and Mista Milo. Den I'd bring you back dere."

"You can take Milo with you, but I'm staying here."

"Mista Max, now why you wan' be doin' dat?"

"We've just lost our mother. Now, we've lost our father, too. I have to decide what to do."

"You ain't even eighteen. You think dey gon' let you stay here wit' yer brotha and sista?"

"I *will* stay here. I *will* sort it all out. Our parents may be gone, but we still have the house, the store, and each other. I'm close enough to the age of majority. I won't give up what we have."

"How you gon' handle it all? You in college; Mista Milo's in high school; and Miss Nora, she cain't stay by herself here all de time. And who gon' run de store?"

"You could run it."

"Dat jus' goes ta show how young you is. You think folks gon' shop at a place run by black folk even if white folk done own it?"

"I'll hire somebody to run it with you and somebody to stay with Nora, too. Or she can continue to go to the store if she's a help there."

Rising to his feet, Moses nodded.

"You think 'bout it. Talk to Mista Fleming. He be givin' you some good advice."

"You've always given me good advice. What would you do?"

"Close de store. Bury yer daddy. Cry over 'im and yer mama. Hire a woman to come keep house fer you and yer brother and ta watch out fer yer sista. Yer daddy was a good one wit' de money. Use it to live, while you and yer brother go ta school. Then, you get you a job and make yer own way."

Max stared at the wall, mulling over all of these suggestions and trying not to think about his father's cold body lying somewhere, awaiting embalming.

"I'll tell Milo when he gets home, and then you take him with you back to Uncle Tommy's. I'll call them, but I won't go there tonight."

"Yessa."

Later in the evening after a tearful Milo had driven off with Moses, Max had phoned the Fleming residence and spoken to Nora, Mary, and Tommy.

"Will you handle the arrangements, Uncle Tommy?" Max heard himself ask. "I simply need some time alone. I'll call first thing in the morning."

Max hung up without waiting for a response. Then he went outside and began to wander the yard in the moonlight.

He was standing on the Robichaux porch before he was even conscious of his decision to go there. He rapped lightly on the door but got no answer. Experimentally, he turned the knob. It gave.

There were no lights on in the house. He fumbled around looking for a lamp.

"Don't bother," came Louise's soft voice. "Samantha's asleep. As long as you leave the light off, she won't wake until dawn."

He turned slowly in the direction of her voice. She was standing naked in the hallway.

"You shouldn't go around like that with a child in the house."

Louise smiled and assured him, "Once she goes to sleep, she sleeps. I don't parade around like this when she's awake. I knew you were coming. I could feel it." She held out her hand and urged, "Come with me."

He allowed himself to be led to her bedroom. Within moments, he was naked and ferocious. Louise made love to him with an equally savage passion. Soon, they lay spent and raw in a cluster of bedclothes.

"What you lack for in experience you certainly made up for in enthusiasm."

His head against her chest, Max began to cry.

"Was it that horrible? I must be losing my touch."

"My – my father died this afternoon."

Lifting her shoulders slightly, she looked down at him in disbelief.

"You poor boy. Your mother last week and your father this week?" Wrapping her arms and legs around him, she cooed, "You just go ahead and cry it all out. You're the strong type, the I-can't-let-those-depending-on-me-see-me-cry type, right? Well, I'm not depending on you, so you cry your heart out. I've seen it all. It won't bother me."

Sometime before dawn, he woke and found Louise sitting next to him in the bed.

"What is it?" He pushed himself up on his elbows and asked, "Is it nearly morning?"

"No. Shhhh. I was thinking about things. Go back to sleep unless you want to make love to me again. I bet you don't even remember the last time."

"Not remember being with you? I'm lying here in bed with you, aren't I? How could I forget?"

"I don't think you could ever forget making love to me," she said haughtily. "But I bet you don't recall how it even felt in your heart."

She was right. In his shroud of pain, he couldn't seem to recall anything except the lust and intensity of their passion.

"I – I'm sorry."

"What, for being with me? For crying?"

"For not remembering how it felt in my heart."

She smiled.

"It's better that you don't, I imagine. You should do it with some nice, normal college girl, not some lunatic siren."

"I don't think you're a lunatic."

"Then you're mad as well."

"What…what happened to you to make you like this?"

"It runs in my family."

"No, really. I want to know."

"Now that you've fucked me, you care?"

"Fucked?"

He had never heard the verb before in his life, but it sounded extremely obscene.

"I wanted to know before I…before we were together like this."

Suddenly, she looked very sad.

"Mental instability really does run in the family. Men and women both. My parents didn't care about me or my sister or brother. All they cared about was their pleasures, and to hell with the results of their union. Do you know how old I was when my father married me off to the old man who owned this place? Fourteen. My husband was fifty-two. He was a lecherous son-of-a-bitch. He liked to hurt me when we were together. I thought that was the way it went with men and women. My sister, she'd been married at fourteen, too. That was before she was put in the institution. She'd told me that being with her husband was the worst thing in her life. So, I endured my own torment and tried to think of a way to escape. And then Sam came along."

"Sam?"

"My husband hired him as a gardener about six months after we'd been married." With a dreamy look in her eyes, Louise placed a hand on Max's stomach and said excitedly, "Oh, but he was the most handsome man you'd ever seen. Big and strong and with good features. He was a sweet boy."

"How did you end up with him?"

"He came to tend the yard while my husband was away to Chicago on business. I liked Sam a lot. I knew that he wanted to be with me, but he knew that I was married. I didn't care. I didn't even care that it would hurt. I wanted to make him happy." Her eyes widened, as if she were fourteen again and in bed with the gentle giant Sam for the first time. "And it didn't hurt at all! It felt wonderful. Every day for a month, he came to tend the yard. By the time my husband returned home, I was expecting Sam's child."

"Did he know it was Sam's?"

"No. He thought he'd done it before he'd left, but I knew different." She let out a pleasant sigh and explained, "Sam and I continued our affair as the months passed. We talked of running away. A month before Samantha was born, he fell off the roof and broke his neck."

"How awful for you," Max said emphatically.

"Yes, it was. My dreams of life with Sam and our child vanished. When my time came and the pain was all-consuming, I told my husband in front of the doctor that the baby wasn't his, that it was Sam's, and that I would never let him touch me again. I reminded him of it every day after she was born. I told him how

Sam had pleasured me in a way that he never could. He died when Samantha was three weeks old. I've enjoyed my life a lot more since then. I do as I please. I take men to bed when I feel they'll be good lovers."

"Don't you worry about having another child?"

"My, but you are the practical one, aren't you?"

"Was I a good lover? I'm afraid that maybe I hurt you."

"It's one thing to be bold and another to be masochistic."

"I don't understand."

"You will someday. No, you didn't hurt me, not in the way that you mean. Yes, you were a good lover. Someday, with a few more encounters, you could be a great lover." Louise went to the window and stared at the sky before declaring, "It will be dawn soon. Go home, Max."

He stepped out of bed and asked, "And how do you know it's almost dawn?"

"Years of practice."

"May I come here again?"

"To talk? Of course. For physical intimacy? No. You deserve better."

"Louise? Don't you worry that someone will come here someday and try to put you away or take Samantha from you?"

"I have the best lawyer in town. The best banker, too. My husband was a wealthy man."

"But wealth alone, especially for a woman, doesn't usually guarantee anything."

Coming away from the window, Louise pushed a lock of Max's black hair out from in front of his right eye.

"You really do care, don't you? And it's not just because we made love. You're like this with everyone, aren't you?" She lowered herself down next to him and agreed, "You're right. A man, especially a shrewd businessman, can turn on a woman and she has no recourse. But I'm an educated woman, Max. I completed nine years of school with honors before my parents took me out. I've read every book in my husband's library, which contains over three thousand volumes. Samantha and I go to the public library every week."

"But education alone –"

"I've also come to know quite a bit about men over the last few years. I know what keeps them happy and loyal. My lawyer is extremely loyal." Handing Max his pants, she added, "And extremely happy."

Tommy Fleming was waiting for Max at the front door of the Nash home.

"Where the devil have you been, Max? I've been worried, damn it!"

"Sorry, Uncle Tommy. I've been trying to clear my head." Unlocking the front door, he gestured to the older man and urged, "Please."

"Mary and I want you and your brother and sister to come live with us," Tommy declared before they'd taken five steps into the house.

"I've already considered that. Thank you, but no."

"Maxwell, this is preposterous! You're seventeen! Milo is fifteen! Nora is only ten and –"

"And she wants to grow up and get married."

"Ridiculous!"

"It's not," Max said calmly. "I'll see to it that she gets her wish, if the proper man comes along."

"You're distraught. That's understandable. I should have come myself to tell you instead of sending Moses. I was in the midst of taking care of things regarding your father. Your father and I, we've been chums for forty years," he said quietly. "I should be the one to take you in, all three of you."

"I'd like your help, but we're not your children. We've just lost Mum and Father in one week." His eyes filled with tears, but Max quickly blinked them back and insisted, "You can't replace them. I don't want you to try. Milo, Nora, the store, the house, the accounts – it's all my responsibility now."

"And if I say you're too young? I can take legal action, you know. I'll at least be granted custody of Nora and Milo."

It took Max a few moments to recover from the shock. Louise had told him she had the best lawyer in town. She seemed the sort of woman who liked to flaunt her power over men and over society's conventions. He could get her to help him and –

"The best banker, too," Louise had added.

It was a well-known fact that Tommy Fleming was considered to be the foremost banker in the community. He and Mary had long ago moved from their original house downtown to a large estate on the outskirts of the city.

Max shook his head and walked into the parlor. It couldn't be. Louise must mean someone else.

But what if she didn't? A wicked idea began to take shape in Max's mind.

"How long have you and Aunt Mary been married?" he asked blithely.

"Quite some time," Tommy said gruffly. "What does that have to do with the situation at hand?"

"And you've never been able to have any children," Max continued.

"No, Mary has not. We gave up on having a child of our own years ago."

"Did Aunt Mary stop sleeping with you then? Or was it your idea?"

"Maxwell! I cannot believe…I don't…How did you know that?"

Relieved and disheartened, Max sank into a chair.

"Do you think Aunt Mary would still love you if she knew you were in someone else's bed instead of working late all those nights? Do you think a judge would give guardianship of a mentally deficient very attractive girl to a man who has been unfaithful to his wife because she couldn't conceive a child? Do you think your prominent friends would associate with you if the scandal appeared in the papers tomorrow?"

"Mary is frigid. She has been for ten years."

Frigid? Max thought. *It does seem to be the day for new words.*

"Do you think people would care whether she was frigid or not?" Max asked. "Does that give you the right to break your marriage vows?"

"You can't possibly imagine what it's like!" Tommy growled menacingly. "It drives you to do things you can't explain."

"Do you think people would care?" Max asked again. "It would be a scandal, wouldn't it? Are you willing to take the risk?"

"I'm disappointed in you, Maxwell."

Max was surprised by how much it hurt to hear those words from Tommy after the exchange they'd just had.

"Get out of my house, please. I have business to attend to."

Max strode back to Louise Robichaux's and explained everything to her. She telephoned her lawyer, who telephoned Mr. Fleming. Max returned home to bathe and dress for his father's wake. An hour later, Mary drove up with Milo and Nora.

"I don't understand," she sobbed, as she helped Nora unlace her shoes. "Why don't you want to come live with us? Are we that horrible?"

Max stopped adjusting Milo's tie and crouched next to Mary.

"You could never be horrible, Aunt Mary. It's only that Father would want it this way. He'd want us to stay in our house, the house he worked so hard for, the house that he and Mum –" He broke off and set to unlacing Nora's other shoe before pressing forward, "We'll manage. I'll hire help. It doesn't mean that I don't want you around. I…I need you around. Please."

"I'll do whatever I can. I'll find a good negro to stay here and keep house and keep Nora."

"Thank you. Thank you so much."

The next week, Max made the decision to sell the store. There was no way that he could run it properly, attend school, and raise his brother and sister. A nice Italian family of grocers bought it. He was glad to see how excited they were, but it didn't take the sting out of seeing the removal of the Nash & Co. sign.

Then, there were all of the legal documents to be signed. He was designated Milo and Nora's guardian and was put in charge of all of the finances with the understanding that he would turn to Louise's lawyer, who was now also his lawyer, for advice before making any major investments.

Finally, there was Teal, the heavyset black woman whom Mary had sent over to the Nash house. Teal was a wonderful housekeeper and proved to be ever-patient with Nora. This had been Max's chief concern. To his relief, Teal was a welcome addition to their little family. Things were gradually improving.

Then Black Tuesday descended on October 29.

That night, after Nora had been put to bed, Max and Milo sat together on the staircase and worried about their future.

"What should we do now that the stock market has crashed?" whispered Milo. "How will we survive?"

"The house is paid for. We don't have to worry about a place to live. It's true that most of Father's investments are gone, but the money from the sale of the store hadn't been invested in anything yet. I hadn't had time. Some is hidden here in the house, and the rest is in the bank, along with the other cash that Father and Mum had there. We should take all of it out of the bank in the morning. I think we can stretch things and be all right, at least until I graduate from school. If not, I'll quit and work for a while."

"No, you can't!" Milo hissed. "If it comes down to that, *I'll* drop out for a while and –"

"No," Max interrupted. "You have to finish high school. You'd better finish college, too. I'm the man of the family now. It's my duty to take care of you and Nora and this house. Father worked hard to provide for us. I'll see to it that we stay here and do well."

"I don't see how you can be so calm about things."

As if there's a margin for panic, Max thought. *I must be strong. Father would be strong.*

By Friday, Max had deduced that there was enough money available to support them indefinitely, provided that no major catastrophe struck the house itself. That thought comforted him. As he closed his eyes that night, Max was confident that he could handle whatever lay ahead.

Nora's screams woke him in the middle of the night.

"Milo! Wake up!"

"Wh-what? Wha – Nora?"

They raced down the hall to their sister's room. No Nora. The Nash brothers stared blankly at each other in the near darkness.

Max scanned the bedroom. The window was shut and locked from the inside.

"Come on!" he cried, whirling and heading for the stairs. "You check up here! I'll check downstairs!"

As Milo ran from room to room, Max pounded down the steps. When he reached the bottom, he prepared to check the sitting room first. Then, he noticed that the front door was ajar.

"Milo!" he yelled. "Outside!"

He stumbled as he flew down the front steps. Quickly regaining his footing, Max ran into the driveway and called, "Nora! Nora!"

"I'll go around back!" cried Milo, as he took off in that direction. Max scoured the front. There was no sign of his sister. Hearing movement behind him, he spun around, heart pounding.

"It's only me!" Milo stood drenched with sweat in the shadow of a tree and added desperately, "I can't find her!"

"Go call the police! I'll keep looking!"

Max deliberated for a few seconds, then he darted towards the back of the house and plunged headlong into the thick woods. The branches of the trees above and the dense tangle of vines and bushes did not allow much moonlight to penetrate in the woods, and Max found himself tripping over roots and crashing into bushes. He didn't stop. He continued to careen about, calling "Nora! Nora! Nora!"

Suddenly, he found himself tumbling head over heels in the brush. He landed hard on his stomach. Trembling, he pushed himself up on his hands and knees and crawled slowly towards an embankment. He had never been this deep into the woods before. Perhaps that was why he'd fallen.

Max heard a strangled cry coming from somewhere. It took him thirty seconds to realize that it was coming from his own throat. He numbly finished his climb up the embankment and collapsed on the ground next to where his sister lay.

"Nora," he moaned. "Nora."

Never taking his eyes off of her face, he reached out and put his hand gently under her head. Instantly, his fingers were coated with blood.

"Nora, no."

"She's not yours anymore, is she?"

Max lifted his eyes and gazed up at Tommy Fleming.

"You couldn't share her with anyone, could you?" asked his father's closest friend. "All Mary and I wanted was a child."

The anger rose in Max so quickly that it seemed his vision went from normal to red in the blink of an eye.

"YOU MONSTER!"

Max slipped his hand from under Nora's head and lunged towards Tommy. They collided, and Max tumbled once again down the embankment, this time taking Tommy Fleming with him. Crashing with a thud at the bottom, Max swung his fists blindly in an attempt to gain the advantage before Tommy could recover himself. His fist made contact with the older man's gut, just as Tommy brought a rock down on Max's head. Then everything went black.

When Max regained consciousness, he was uncertain as to how long he'd been knocked out. The only thing he was capable of feeling was that he needed to vomit more than he ever had in his entire life. Once he started, he couldn't seem to stop.

"I've got you, Son," came a distant voice and a supportive arm. Max let himself sag against the stranger. He was unable to focus his eyes or clear his head.

"Concussion, yeah?" another voice asked rhetorically.

"*Mais*, yeah" answered the first. "Better get the doc down here as soon as he's done."

The blackness beckoned again, and Max succumbed to its sweet lure. The next time he awakened, he was in his own bed. He wore clean pajamas. His skull hurt so badly that it took all of his resolve not to throw his hands over his head and cry out in pain.

"Mista Max?"

"Moses?" he said hoarsely. "How –?"

"Mista Milo had dem call me. Teal and I goin' stay wit' you and him fer now. Don' you worry none."

Someone came into the room, but Max refused to look towards the door as he said, "Tommy killed Nora. What happened to Tommy?"

There was a long pause. The person who'd entered finally said, "It was your next-door neighbor, Mr. Nash. She heard all the commotion. Got the shotgun she keeps for protecting herself and her daughter. Says that when she came to the scene, Mr. Fleming was standing with a large rock poised over your head. She shot him."

With great effort, Max rolled onto his back and turned his head in the direction of the voice. The fuzzy image of a man in a suit faded in and out, but he recognized the voice. It was the man who'd held him when he'd awakened the first time in the woods.

"Detective Hargrove." The man touched the brim of his hat in greeting, then asked, "Mind if I sit down?"

"N-no. I – Thank you. You…you helped me before."

"Don't mention it. Even if it weren't my job, you think I could leave a kid in your condition alone when he's hurt?" He checked the time on his watch before remarking, "Your man here told me a little about you. You've been through some bad times in the last month or so. Lotta bad times, yeah?"

Max lay still and tried not to vomit again.

"I'm sorry to have to talk with you about this right now, but I need to make sure it's all official by noon today. It's already 9:30, so I've got to move things right along. Understand?" Without waiting for a reply, Hargrove pulled a notebook and a pencil from his jacket pocket and went on, "Let me see if I got this straight. You moved into this house in September with your mother, your father, your brother, and your sister. Right? Shortly thereafter, your mother died of a hemorrhage. Then your father had a heart seizure. Now, you're only seventeen, but a judge granted you custody of your brother and sister and gave you control of the family assets, despite the fact that Mr. Fleming, an older businessman and a family friend, offered to take control. Correct?"

Max agreed dully.

"And you're in college, too. How come you didn't take Mr. Fleming up on his offer? He and his wife don't have any children of their own. I'd think a young man like yourself would be grateful for the help."

"Then you'd be thinking incorrectly."

Hargrove smiled.

"You do have spunk; I'll give you that. So, you turn Fleming down. And how did he react to that?"

"He was…hostile."

"I'll bet he was. Why didn't he fight you? Seems like he could have won if it went to court."

Max wanted to think of something impressive to say, some believable lie. However, his head hurt too much, and he couldn't find his soul for anything.

"I blackmailed him. I knew he'd been having…relations with a woman who was much younger than his wife. He was acting cruel about assuming that he'd automatically take us in after Father died. I couldn't figure it out at first. He was acting so different. Then it all started to make sense. He had designs on having Nora when she got older. I threatened to tell Aunt Mary about the woman Uncle Tommy was sleeping with. Does she know about tonight?"

"Yeah. She does. She's taken to her bed. So anyway you and your brother and sister are here. Last Tuesday the whole world turns upside-down for all of us. Now, it's Sunday. Tell me about last night."

Max told him everything, everything except how guilty he felt for not being able to protect his little sister from the surprisingly inhuman Tommy Fleming.

"...and then it went black," he finished. "I don't remember much after that." As Hargrove tucked his notebook and pencil away, Max asked, "Will Louise Robichaux be charged with murder?"

"No. I'll see to that. She was defending you from a kidnapper and a murderer. I spent a considerable amount of time with Mrs. Robichaux last night, and I believe what she says. She doesn't appear to be a rampaging killer." He smiled and added, "Not at all."

Max shut his eyes and held his tongue.

"Your sister died from a blow to the head and –"

"Mista Hargrove, I don' think Mista Max need be hearin' 'bout dat jus' now. Maybe not never."

Hargrove nodded to Moses.

"I suppose you're on the mark there." He laid a hand on Max's shoulder and told him, "If you should ever want to know more about anything you can reach me at the station."

Max was unconscious again before Hargrove had left the room. He came to, disoriented and sweating, in the cold sunshine of Nora's room.

"Max? What are you doing in here?"

"Milo? I – I – What day is it?"

"It's Sunday." Milo walked over to his brother and touched his sleeve before urging, "Come back to bed, Brother."

"I can't. My paper on Milton is due tomorrow."

"Won' be doin' no papers for a while, Mista Max. Doc says you mighty lucky to be livin', but you cain't be doin' much fer a good while."

Max brought his hands up to his temples and cried, "I have to! I have to go to school! I can't stay here!" He cast about for something coherent, something to explain the attack of panic that had instantaneously descended upon him but found he could only say, "I can't breathe in here!" He pitched clumsily in the direction of his younger brother and whispered, "Her hair was soaked with blood. God, Milo, she was staring at me like, like…."

He fell into his brother's arms. Milo helped him out of the room and down the hall to their bedroom.

"Milo?" Teal said softly. "He needs to be lyin' down. You both do."

Max leapt to his feet and staggered a few steps to his right.

"No. I have schoolwork to do."

He edged forward towards his desk, oblivious to the entrance of Louise Robichaux.

"On the contrary, you have nothing to do but lie down." As Max stared at her, Louise nodded to Milo, Teal, and Moses before ordering, "Leave him to me. I'll get him to rest."

"I'm sure you will," Teal muttered. "Just don't wear him out no more than he already is."

Louise folded her arms in front of her chest and said seriously, "That's not what I came for."

Once the others had left the room, Max asked, "Where's Samantha? Is she…? Did she see…?"

"She was sleeping when it happened." Louise studied her hands, turning them over twice as she muttered, "I never thought I'd actually have to use that gun. I'm glad I had it, though. That son of a bitch would have killed you for sure."

"I wish he had."

She strode over to him and pushed him towards the bed.

"You don't mean that."

"I do."

As she covered him with the blanket, Louise said, "Don't bother with that now. You lie here and think about nothing. Nothing in particular."

"I'm glad you won't be charged with murder. You don't need that. Samantha doesn't need that. Was Detective Hargrove hard to convince?"

The slap was light, but in his present state it was enough to send him reeling.

"You'd better be thankful that you're hurt or I would have broken your jaw," she said coolly. "For your information, Detective Hargrove didn't really need convincing. It was evident what happened out there. Oh, a little reinforcement doesn't hurt, but he's no idiot. He's been on the force a long time."

"So, why did you…?"

Bending low, Louise whispered, "I wanted to help you; I wanted to help myself; and I wanted to have the good detective in my bed more than anything else. He reminds me of Sam. Physically, that is. And in his demeanor. He's a lot brighter, which makes him even more appealing. I think I'll be seeing him again."

"Louise –"

"No moral lectures, please. One day, you'll know. You'll know what it's like to want someone so horribly that nothing else matters. It's a terrifying and liberating feeling."

"But if you don't give in to it –"

"You will. It's human nature. We're animals, Max. Maybe we're smarter than the other animals on this planet, although sometimes I wonder. It doesn't make any difference. Our base desires are always tugging at the hems of our clothes. You can't fight them forever. Everyone succumbs at some point in their lives to lust or greed or hatred. You can either hone the tool or be destroyed by it." Gently massaging his thigh, she murmured, "Now, here is what will happen. You do *not* have to go to school. The lawyer will explain things to the Dean tomorrow. You can go back next term if you're ready. If not, you can wait."

"But –"

"But nothing. You've lost everyone in your family, except for your brother. Do you want to lose him, too? Do you want him to drop out of school and end up in the streets? Do you want to have a nervous collapse yourself?"

"I – I don't understand any of it or why I have to go on after everything that's taken place tonight. Why should I go on?"

"Listen to me, Maxwell Nash. If you want to find the answers to all of those questions, then you pull yourself out of this and find them. You're not going to find them in your pillow, so you'd better start looking elsewhere. I'm always looking." She smiled and adjusted the blanket before proposing, "I'll make you a wager. I say you'll figure it out first; you lay your odds on me."

"Whatever you say. It doesn't matter."

Walking towards the doorway, she called back, "You go on because you have to. Later, you'll go on because you want to."

When Max woke again it was dark.

"Milo? Milo, where is Nora?"

A soft snore was his brother's only response.

"Miss Nora be gone, Mista Max."

His head still throbbing, Max pushed himself up and looked at Moses, who was standing shirtless in the doorway.

"I know she's gone. Where is her body?"

"Funeral parlor. Dey gon' keep her dere 'til you well enough ta see to her. I tol' dem dat it would be a couple a days."

"I wish it were a couple of lifetimes." Max reached for the glass of water that Teal had left on the nightstand beside his bed and asked, "What do you think I should do? Louise says I should resign for the term."

"Missus Louise gots a mind of her own. She be a strange one, but she ain't no crazy woman. She jus' knows what it takes fer her ta get by."

"So, you think she's right?"

"I think you should do like she say. Den, you go back and finish at the college. Den, you go on to medical school. Dat's important."

"But what about Milo? I can't simply leave him here alone while I go off to study medicine. He'll only be twenty or so. He'll still be in college. I should leave him alone and go off?"

"Won' be alone. Teal and I, we be here wit' him, even when you go 'way. If dat's what you wants. Teal, she can stay like she was supposin' to, doin' de housekeepin' an' all. Me, I gots me a job workin' with the other coloreds at the Flemings, though I think dat'll be changin' in light of all dis. I wonder what Missus Mary gon' do. Don' matter. I'll be findin' work somewheres else if I have ta. Jus' be here when I ain't at work, be here fer you and him." He pointed at Milo and added, "He's always been a handful, dat one. He gon' need someone 'round to be guidin' him, a man who's been livin' a lot longer than seventeen years."

"But you wouldn't mind? I mean, being stuck out here with us and Teal?"

There was a flash of white teeth in the darkness.

"Case you hadn't noticed, I kinda got partial to Teal. She got more school learnin' than me, but she ain't had no man that she'd like to waste her time wit'. I gots dis feelin dat she might be changin' her mind in dat area. Me, I wouldn't mind dat myself."

"But what if it doesn't work out that way?"

Another flash of teeth.

"If she an' I don' get along, den we tolerate each other. If we do…."

"Just like that?"

"Just like dat. It be done."

Interlude

The bed was calling to Daniel. His eyes felt gritty; he was stiff from sitting in the same position; and it was now 3:00 in the morning. However, he felt "wired," not tired. He was also ravenous. The pizza was long gone.

Daniel lifted the receiver from its cradle. A not-so-chipper voice asked, "Can I help you?"

"Um, yeah. What's available from Room Service at this time of night?"

"There's a card by the phone that lists our selections. We should be getting a doughnut delivery shortly. Would you like some sent to your room when they arrive?"

"Two dozen. And some coffee."

Collapsing onto the couch, Daniel flipped on the television. He quickly scanned the channels, passing two shopping networks, several infomercials, a Spanish soap opera, and more B movies than he could count before clicking off the set. The truth was that he didn't really want to watch anything. He simply wanted a break from the journals. What had been an interesting examination of Max's childhood had turned into a study of the life of Job.

Tap, tap, tap.

The young, pregnant girl stood in the hallway holding his doughnuts and coffee.

"Hello, Celeste. Why the long face? Still having a rough night?"

"Uh-huh."

Daniel reached for his billfold then said, "I keep forgetting that I took my wallet out of my pocket. Let me take those." He accepted the boxes and the coffee and walked over to the little table before telling her, "Hold on just a second. Now, where did I put it?"

Lifting it from the bed, he removed the tip and passed it to her. Her face reddened when her stomach growled loudly.

"Want a doughnut? I have more than enough." He grinned and said, "I'm sure I have too many, but I didn't want to put in another call again for a while. I figured they'll keep for the rest of my time here."

Celeste gazed longingly at the boxes on the table.

"It *is* time for my break, but…." She looked back at Daniel and said awkwardly, "I shouldn't, like, stay in here, I guess. I mean, you're a guest of the hotel, and I work here and all."

"I won't tell your boss, and I won't try anything. I'm a married man."

She seemed unconvinced.

"Look, you're welcome to take some and go if you want."

Celeste hesitated for all of two seconds.

"I'll stay for a few minutes. If you don't mind, I mean."

"Have a seat."

The Krispy Kreme doughnuts were fresh and delicious. Daniel and Celeste ate in silence for a minute until she said, "Like, I hope this isn't too rude or anything, but what *are* all these books? I mean, there are tons of them."

Daniel sipped his coffee. Did he really want to tell her? Why not? He'd probably never see her again. Even if he did, what difference did it make?

"My father died not too long ago. These are his journals. I didn't know until the night of his funeral that he was my biological father." He sighed deeply and said, "It's complicated."

"Were you mad at him when you found out?"

"I was thrilled. I was also really angry and resentful. I'm sure he knew that was how I'd react. That's why he wrote these. He wanted to explain."

"What about your mother? Why did she wait to tell you until after he was gone?"

Pulling a tissue from the box in-between them, Daniel wiped at the sugar on the side of his mouth. As he squeezed the tissue into a tight ball, he said, "My mother, my biological mother, died when I was ten. Her husband, the man I thought was my father, well, he was…let's just say that he wasn't so nice to either of us. I was thankful to be alive when my real father took me in. The funny thing is, he didn't even know when he decided to take me that I was his son. Or so my adoptive mother says. I suppose I'll find out soon enough. That's why I came here this weekend. I have to know."

"So, you were happy to be adopted? They were good parents?"

"Yes, they were. I was lucky. You never know who you'll get when people take you in. Or at least that's what my friend Jamie says. He had some bad experiences in foster care."

"Like what?"

Realizing that the girl was probably considering putting her unborn child up for adoption, Daniel hastened to say, "I'm sure that most adoptive parents are great. If you want to adopt a child, then you should want that child. It's not like somebody shows up at a couple's doorstep and dumps a baby into their arms."

The girl nodded, looking more downcast than ever.

"You want to talk? I've seen a lot in almost forty years."

"My break's over. Thanks for the doughnuts."

"Sure."

She hurried out, pulling the door shut behind her. Daniel took the remainder of his coffee and the next journal over to the bed. Propping himself up against the headboard, he flipped to the first page and got back to work.

Daniel,

I am quite certain that you have no desire to hear about my years of immersion in academia. Suffice it to say that I did return to school in the spring, that I attended LSU (as it is called today) and earned a Bachelor of Science degree in 1934. When I departed for New Orleans to attend the Tulane School of Medicine in the fall of that year, I left Milo in the capable hands of Moses and Teal, who had married in the summer of 1931.

My first two years at Tulane were devoted to a general study of medicine and proceeded uneventfully. When it came time for me to select a specific discipline, I chose psychiatry, an area I had become fascinated with since that time of tragedy in 1929. I wanted to understand the human psyche and to help those who were troubled without traumatizing them further with what I saw as deterrents to recovery such as the common method of institutionalization and overmedication. It was during this time of intense focus that I met the person who was to become my closest friend, Isabelle Fernberg. My introduction to her provided me with a partner of sorts. But I jump ahead of myself. At any rate, this is where I will begin again.

Now, close this book and get some rest. You will be too tired to make heads or tails out of this, and that defeats the purpose, doesn't it?

Max

Smiling, Daniel laid the book on the nightstand. He put one of the pillows aside and plumped the other one before resting his head on it. Then, he switched off the lamp and went to sleep.

Tap, tap, tap.

Daniel jerked awake and tried to focus on the digital clock next to the bed. He turned the knob on the lamp, squinting and blinking at the brightness, and stumbled towards the door.

"Yes?"

"It's me."

"Celeste?"

Quickly turning the lock, he opened the door. Celeste stood in the hallway wearing street clothes and a jacket.

"I – I'm sorry. I shouldn't have come. I didn't mean to wake you up." Backing away, she added, "Never mind."

"No, it's not a problem. I didn't want to sleep long anyway." Stepping back, he gestured for her to enter. "I take it you're off-duty?"

"Permanently." She began to cry and announced, "I quit."

She followed Daniel to the little round table where they'd eaten the doughnuts earlier that morning. He helped her off with her jacket and draped it over one arm of the couch. Then, he sat facing her and said, "What happened?"

"I couldn't do it," she sniffled. "I've been feeling sick all the time since the beginning. It's been so hard just to keep up with school. I get okay during the night, but, like, it starts all over again in the morning. That's why I got a job at night. I thought maybe it would be better. But it's not."

"Have you seen a doctor?"

"Uh-huh. They did some tests. That was when I found out that it's a girl. She's okay. He said that sometimes people have it like this the whole nine months."

"So, why are you trying to work? If you're so sick, then shouldn't you be resting?"

"My father said it would teach me to be responsible, that if I was going to do *this*" – she pointed towards her stomach – "that I should see what the rest of being an adult was like." She tore out a handful of tissues from the small box. "What am I going to do? My boyfriend and I did it for the first time this summer. He's on the football team, and I'm a cheerleader." She laughed mirthlessly. "I know what you're thinking: the dumb jock and the airhead. But it's not like that. We're both honors students. I'm planning to be an engineer. Or at least I was. Now, I don't know what to do."

"What does he want?"

"He doesn't know either. He asked me to marry him, but we both know that we're too young. But neither of us wants to give her up. But we don't really see how we can, like, make it work. How can we go to school and have a baby? We're only seventeen. We'll be starting college in August. She won't even be six months old."

Daniel thoughtfully rubbed at his chin.

"Do you have kids, Mr. Nash?"

"My son is five."

"What's his name?"

"Kristopher."

She blinked, surprised.

"My boyfriend, his name's Christopher."

Daniel smiled and shook his head.

"Must be a nice guy then."

Celeste smiled and nodded. Daniel rose and went over towards the sliding doors that led to the balcony.

"What about your parents? And his? What do they say about things?"

Her smile faded.

"My parents said that they've raised their children and that they're not going to start all over again. His parents…well, his dad's been real sick for, like, two years with leukemia. They don't have the money to help, and all of their time is spent trying to keep Chris's dad going. I'm just worried about *her*," Celeste continued. "What if she gets adopted by somebody mean? Or, like, they abuse her? Remember that Lisa girl who was killed in New York by her adoptive dad? That was horrible. Maybe if I could meet them and make sure they were all right. Do you think I could tell?"

Daniel knew he should try to reassure her, but he couldn't lie. If there was one thing he'd learned throughout his lifetime, it was that often more harm could be done by being civil than by being direct.

"Tell me what kind of a person you think I am."

Startled, the girl looked questioningly up at him.

"Um, okay. I mean, you seem like a nice person. I mean, you've been really good about being kind to me and letting me talk. Taking an interest."

"Suppose I told you that I was an alcoholic."

Her jaw dropped.

"You? But you seem so normal!"

Daniel couldn't help but grin.

"Thank you. I'm working on it." He turned his chair around and straddled it, leaning on the back with his arms. "Anyway, the thing of it is that I'm not actually an alcoholic, but I could have been and you never would've known. My father-in-law was a substance abuser many years ago, and nobody around him knew except his closest friend. I don't want to turn you off on adoption. I think you are too young to get married. You do everything you can and hope for the best."

"What would you do?"

"I honestly can't say. I'd have to think about it for more than a split second. You've had several months to stew over it, right?"

She smiled sadly.

"You'd never give her up, would you? You'd do whatever it took to keep her."

"Celeste, I…I don't know. My thoughts on the subject are a little muddy."

"I don't understand."

"My wife, she almost died when our son was born. He almost died, too. No more children for us. We'd always talked about having more than one. Sarah's great with kids, and I think I'm a good father. But I can't risk losing my wife. So, when you ask me if I'd ever give up my daughter if I were in your shoes, I'm inclined to say 'No'. But I'm coming at it from the perspective of a man who's been denied that option, not a seventeen-year-old boy with his whole life ahead of him. Who knows what I'd do?"

"I do," she said firmly. "You'd keep her."

Celeste got up and went across to retrieve her jacket.

"I'd better let you get back to your dad's books. Thanks for listening. Merry Christmas, Mr. Nash."

"Wait, I –"

But she was gone, her blonde hair flying behind her as she ran out of the door.

Daniel considered going after her. And what if he caught up to her? Then, what would he do?

He found that he was more than ready to return to the past. Frustrated, he grabbed the notebook he'd been reading before and fell back onto the bed.

Chapter Four: Good Women

"Miss Fernberg? If you could drag yourself away from your notes for a moment, I'd like for you to explain to the other students about the character-disordered man you've been observing."

The petite Isabelle Fernberg lifted her platinum blonde head and deliberately closed her notebook.

"I am sorry, Sir," she said in her heavy German accent. "Your last lecture was so riveting that I had the uncontrollable urge to go over those notes once more."

There were snickers from the other students.

"I would very much like to tell you and the rest of the world about this man, but if I am not mistaken, our class time is over for today. Perhaps another time?"

The elderly professor glanced irritably at the clock on the wall behind him.

"So I see. First thing next lecture then. Dismissed."

The students collected their belongings and began to file out of the lecture hall. Max retrieved his satchel and walked towards where Miss Fernberg was gathering her papers.

"I'd stay away from her, Nash," whispered one of Max's roommates.

"Why?"

"Because there's no place for a woman in medicine," muttered a fellow student. "Well, unless it's as a nurse."

"You think women aren't as intelligent?" Max asked seriously.

"Some of 'em are," admitted the roommate. "They just don't have the same constitution as men. A woman will go to pieces in a crisis. Not a man. He can put all of his emotions aside."

"Women are fine as nurses," put in another classmate. "They only need a man to direct them."

"You're a bunch of Neanderthals," Max declared. "I pity your future female patients – and your future wives."

The men laughed gaily at this and slapped Max affectionately on the back.

"You'll see," his roommate called over his shoulder.

Max hurried out of the classroom and tried to catch up with Miss Fernberg. By the time he managed to locate her, she was leaving the building.

"Wait! Miss Fernberg, I'd like to speak with you!"

"Why? So you and your cronies can have some more fun at my expense?"

"Never."

She stopped and glared imperiously at him before commanding, "Speak, then."

Suddenly, Max was at a loss for words.

"Well, Mr. Nash?"

"I – I've been wanting to talk with you for quite a while."

"So, why haven't you? Is it because I'm a woman or because I'm a Jew?"

"You're a Jew?"

She actually dropped her satchel. She pointed to her chest.

"*F-E-R-N-B-E-R-G.*"

Max took her hand and placed it on his own chest.

"*N-A-S-H.*" He paused, then added, "I'm a Catholic man myself. Does this mean that you won't associate with me?"

The woman began to giggle; then she laughed.

"Come, Mr. Nash. We had better not be seen in public together. Tongues will flail."

"Wag."

"As you like." She hurriedly stooped down to retrieve her bag before he could pick it up and asked, "Do you have any more studies today? No? Good. Let us take the trolley downtown. There is a place I know where we can talk undisturbed."

It was a German restaurant tucked away behind a courtyard that faced Bourbon Street. Paintings of waterfalls and dark forests decorated the stone walls.

"Do you like German food, Mr. Nash?"

"Max."

"Do you like German food, Max?"

"I must confess that I've never really tried any. Oh, I did have German potato salad once at a church function."

"Maybe I should order for you."

"By all means. How long have you been in the States?" Max asked, as he sampled the dark beer the waiter had brought for him.

"More than ten years. And you?"

"I came from England to America with my parents and my brother when I was seven."

"A long time. Do they still live in the States?" Isabelle asked pleasantly. "Or did they return to England?"

"I lost both parents and my sister in 1929. My brother still lives in Baton Rouge though. That's where we settled when we crossed the Atlantic." He took another swallow of his beer and prodded, "What about you?"

"Pittsburgh, Pennsylvania. I have an aunt remaining there."

"Do you think you'll go back after you get your medical degree?"

"I hope so. My fiancé would be disappointed if I did not return."

"I expect he would."

"Do you have anyone waiting for you?"

"Other than my brother? Let's see. Moses and Teal. They're watching over Milo and the house while I'm at school. Then, there's Louise and Samantha, the mother and daughter who live next door. I also left behind old school chums."

He unfolded his napkin and draped it across one leg, as the waiter approached with their food. Isabelle smiled and nodded with satisfaction.

"There is someone I would like for you to meet."

"Miss Fernberg –"

"Isabelle."

"Isabelle, I've only begun to know *you*. I'd prefer not to be paired up with someone at this point in my life. I don't have time. My studies are quite consuming."

"You are like me. You spend too much time on your studies. However, I have a good reason to devote all of my waking hours to my work. It helps to fill the void while I am away from Jacob. You do not have such an excuse." She took a bite of her cabbage and said slyly, "I have been watching you for some time, Max Nash. You are too serious. You need something in your life, a kind of diversion. What is the saying? All work and no play makes John a dull boy?"

"I believe that 'Jack' is the correct name."

"Case in hand."

"Point," he corrected automatically. "I'd like to meet your friend, but not now. Perhaps another time? For instance, after my medical boards?"

"*You* are a fuddy-duddy." She smiled and pointed the tines of her fork in his direction and added, "But I do like you."

"I like you, too. I've noticed that we seem to have similar interests and opinions, at least where psychiatry is concerned. There's too much barbarism in this field for my taste."

Isabelle said, "It is good to know you, Max."

"And I you, Isabelle."

"My friend, her name is Gwendolyn by the way. I think you would be perfect for each other."

"I really don't –"

"Someday."

"Someday," he agreed. "Now, tell me all about this man with the character disorder."

One afternoon a year after they'd become friends, Isabelle and Max were scheduled to attend a lecture by a leading local psychiatrist on the latest approaches in treatment of patients with acute dementia. Isabelle arrived at the lecture hall five minutes early. She expected Max to be waiting for her, but he wasn't.

After ten minutes, she stomped into the auditorium and flopped down into a chair. Five more minutes elapsed. Finally, Max crept in and took a seat in the back next to her.

"Where have you been?" Isabelle growled under her breath. "You are very late. It is not like you."

"Sorry."

Narrowing her eyes, Isabelle placed her hand on his knee. He stared unseeing at the speaker and didn't acknowledge her touch.

"Max, what is it? Is something wrong?"

He nodded.

"Let us go." Leading him out of the auditorium, she drew him over onto the grass and gently ordered, "Tell me."

"I – I can't."

"This is me. Isabelle. Not only am I your friend, I am a damn good psychiatric student. Don't you dare say you *can't*. You *won't* maybe, but not you *can't*." She took his hand and directed, "Walk with me. I have that book on criminal psychology that you wanted to borrow. I will get it and make you some coffee."

He allowed her to lead him to her small apartment. Despite their year-long friendship, he had never been there, nor had she been to his rooms.

"It's so…empty."

"I like it that way. I prefer simplicity. Look at my furniture. Clean lines. No clutter. My brain is clear when my environment is in order."

"I see."

"Take off your jacket and sit. I will get the coffee."

"Isabelle, I don't want any coffee."

"Then tell me what is troubling you."

"You recall meeting Samantha Robichaux? Remember when you drove to Baton Rouge with me for Milo's commencement?"

"The young girl? Your neighbor's child? Yes, of course." Her lips parted with her sudden apprehension, and she asked, "What has happened?"

"She wandered onto the road and was struck by an automobile."

"Oh, poor little thing! But why was she on the road?"

"The cat."

"The cat?"

"Her cat, Figgins. Milo said that he was old and that he'd gone out into the street. It was nighttime. I suppose the girl decided that it would be safe for her to cross and bring him back." Max clenched his fists and swore, "Damn Louise!"

"The mother? Why do you curse her?"

"She used to send Samantha out after the cat whenever she wanted to…whenever a man was there with her."

"Shhh. You know good and well that the mother is not quite right psychologically. You've said so yourself several times in the past. She would not intentionally send the child to her death. Imagine the guilt she is feeling at this moment."

Isabelle put her arms around Max and patted him on the back. He placed his hands on her shoulders, then lowered his head and rested it on top of hers.

"I don't know why this has upset me so," Max muttered. "It's certainly an upsetting thing, but I feel the loss so profoundly. When I lived in Baton Rouge, I saw her almost every day, that's true. I came to expect her waiting in the bushes. It became a game for us to see how quickly I could locate her. Since I've been at medical school, I've hardly seen Samantha. Milo took over my role in the daily hide-and-seek. I would expect to be sad about her death, but why do I grieve so deeply?"

"The loss of youth. The loss of innocence, perhaps."

"The loss of my sister."

"Perhaps. The injustice of it all, a harmless girl taken so young and so violently."

"I must go back for the service."

"Would you like for me to come with you? I know that your brother will be there and Moses and Teal, but I will accompany you, if you wish it."

"I do." He rubbed his cheek against her blonde hair and murmured, "I am so alone, Isabelle. Or, rather, I am lonely. There is a difference, I must concede."

"I am lonely as well, my friend. Jacob is so far, and a letter does not give one much comfort or companionship. I am glad that you and I are friends." She pulled back slightly and stared up at him then raised a hand to stroke his cheek before breathing, "My friend."

Max brushed his lips across hers. Isabelle instinctively drew back at first; then she ardently returned his kiss.

As the pre-dawn light filtered in through the windows, Max lay in his friend's bed and focused on the ceiling above him. Beside him, Isabelle sat up and swung her legs over the side of the mattress. Max admired the beauty of her naked back, even as he felt the shame well in him. He reached out and laid his left hand on her hip. Isabelle stiffened but didn't draw away.

"We should not have done this," she said quietly.

"I should have been stronger. Moses once told me that it's a man's responsibility not to force a woman to be with him."

"You did not force me." Reaching down to the foot of the bed, Isabelle picked up her robe and slid it around her shoulders then insisted, "I am equally to blame."

"I don't think it would be wise for you to come home with me at this time."

She shook her head and twisted around so that her face was in the shadows, and the pale light shone faintly on her platinum hair.

"I do not love you, Max. Not like…not like this."

"Nor I you. We're best friends, not lovers."

"And can we continue on as before after tonight? How can I look Jacob in the eye and not be ashamed? I have been faithful to him for four long years. Here we are, a month before our studies are completed, and what do I do? I succumb to lovemaking with my closest friend."

Max got up and began to dress in the dimness of the bedroom. He turned away, lest Isabelle see the truth – that he still desired her.

"I had better go. I must let the administration know that I'll be at the services. Maybe when I come back, things will look brighter."

"That is my wish also."

The funeral for Samantha Robichaux was unconventional. Max had expected no less. Louise had dressed her daughter in a long, white nightdress. The service was held at the gravesite at night with only a handful of people in attendance. Among them were Max, Milo, Teal, and Moses.

"She died at night, so her spirit should pass on into the other world at night," Louise explained to Max, as they stood on her porch the next morning. "The nightdress they put on her, it was just like the one she was wearing when it happened. Maybe it will make her feel safer when she gets there."

"Louise –"

"It's been so quiet here without her."

"Louise –"

"Don't worry about me, Max. I can take care of things. You know that I can look out for myself. Samantha's still here with me in spirit, even if her flesh is gone."

"If you need to talk with someone, then I'll be available in the near future."

"I know where to find you."

"I'll be home permanently soon. If you'd like to meet with me on a regular basis, we could arrange it."

"Thank you for coming, Max."

And, with that, she walked into her house and closed the door.

"I'll look out for her until you get back," Milo assured his brother. "Don't worry about a thing, except finishing that blasted education of yours and taking those awful boards."

"And you? You're supposed to be finishing your advanced degree in horticulture. What about your thesis and the need to defend it?"

The brothers smiled at each other in the rising heat of the day.

"You'd best be gettin' back to Nawlins!" Moses sang out from the driveway. "Dey gon' be wondrin' where you at!"

"I've packed you a nice basket of sandwiches, tea, and cookies," Teal informed him, as she handed Max a small hamper that was alarmingly heavy. "You'll be home soon enough."

Max went back to New Orleans, to the stress of his relationship with Isabelle Fernberg, his studies at Tulane, and what lay beyond. By the time he returned home, his platonic friendship with Isabelle had been restored, but she'd ended her engagement with Jacob.

"Come to Baton Rouge with me," Max had told her. "We could start a practice together. What does Pittsburgh hold for you, if you and Jacob aren't together?"

"Memories," Isabelle sighed. "I will do as you suggest."

"Where Miss Isabelle gon' stay?" Moses inquired, as he helped Max to unload his and Isabelle's belongings in late August. "She cain't stay here. You wants to be 'spectable, don' ya?"

"Milo takes the train to California in two days. I won't see her in a boarding house. She can stay here until she finds an apartment of her own."

"Use yer head," grumbled Moses. "You too old to be actin' like dis. You be twenty-six. I be fifty-eight. I been smarter den dat since you was seven."

"I suppose you have. But where else could she stay?"

"She can stay with me."

Louise stood in the bushes that lined the driveway.

Samantha, Max thought. *She looks just like Samantha.*

He quickly turned in order to hide the tears shining in his eyes.

"I'm all alone, Max," she said pleadingly. "At least let me talk with your friend. She seems nice enough. If she's willing to put up with my eccentric lifestyle, she's welcome to stay as long as she likes. I won't disturb her."

"Of course you can talk with her. I'll send her over as soon as we have our things out of the car."

Not smiling, she nodded and disappeared back into the trees.

"I assume you will want me to warn Isabelle about the impropriety of living with Louise?"

"Don' know Miss Fernberg dat well, yet. It be yer job to do."

As they sat together on the porch swing after dinner, Max asked nonchalantly, "Well, how was Louise?"

"She was fine."

"Have you made a decision? I must warn you that she has a parade of men going in and out of that house. I'm inclined to say that you may be in for a rather daunting experience should you accept."

"The woman says that is all behind her for the time being."

Max glanced sharply at her and asked, "What does that mean?"

"She is expecting."

"Are you certain?"

"Quite. She asked me not to tell anyone, except you. Not yet, she said. So, you must promise not to tell a soul."

"But who is the father?"

Isabelle shrugged and suggested, "Perhaps she does not know. Who can be sure of how many partners she has had?"

"And you don't mind staying with her?"

"I must admit that I am fascinated by her. She does yearn for some meaningful companionship, no matter where it comes from. I can give her that. I would like to study her as well. I don't mean to be macabre. I do not wish to be totally clinical. However, maybe I can help her and this poor child that she will bring into the world. Maybe this child will have a better chance than the first."

"You idealist, you."

"Well, that is settled."

"For now," he muttered.

"What about our psychiatric practice? How are we to go about it?"

"I thought we were planning on combining our resources to rent an office."

"Not that. I mean, we have already agreed upon an amount that we can pay. We will do our work with the hospitals and build our clientele. But where do you think we should have our office? You are the one from this city. What do you think would be the best location?"

"Downtown. There are so many office buildings. We should pick one that has many other businesses in it."

"Yes. That way no one can be accused of seeing a psychiatrist." She sipped her iced tea and remarked, "It is a pity that there is such a stigma attached to our profession. We can do such good. Most people, in my opinion, are in need of psychotherapy at some point in their lives."

"I intend to work on that, Isabelle. Changing the perception of psychiatry in the modern world."

"It sounds like an excellent title for a journal article."

Max stood and picked up his glass in a salute to his new business partner.

"Tomorrow I'd like to spend some time with my younger brother. Once he's on the train Wednesday, we may begin our search."

"Agreed. Do you think Moses would mind helping me to move some of my things over to Louise's house in the morning?"

"I'm sure he'd be delighted," Max chuckled. "And so would I. I know that 'tongues will flail' if you stay here."

Isabelle grinned up at him, lifted her glass of tea, and said, "To us and to our new business venture. Certainly, we shall succeed."

"Gloriously, I'm sure."

Interlude

Clusters of muscles in various locations in Daniel's body began to spasm. Dropping the notebook, he held onto the bed. He hurriedly twisted sideways and planted his feet on the carpet. Rising awkwardly, he hobbled around the room, trying to ease the charley horse in his right leg and the muscle spasms on his left side and between his shoulder blades.

Swearing furiously, he made his way in a circular pattern around the hotel room. He fervently wished that his wife were there with him. She always seemed to know exactly how to rub the offending muscles when his body seized up like this.

Truth be told, he simply wanted his wife with him, period. He wanted to stop reading, to lie in the bed next to her and slip his fingers into her long auburn curls and feel her smooth skin beneath him. He derived such great comfort from wrapping his arms around her and feeling her sigh contentedly as he embraced her small body with its wonderful curves. That lower lip that stuck out when she pouted….

Daniel stopped himself, one hand on the phone. He couldn't call her. He had to finish this journal odyssey or at least as much of it as possible by the following morning.

But the pain was still there. He went to the bathroom and carefully stripped off his shirt, fumbled with his jeans, and then struggled to slip off his briefs. Back hunched, he turned on the tap in the tub and let it fill as high as he dared. Then, he ground his teeth against the pain and managed to climb into the hot water.

The web of scars across his torso darkened slightly as he soaked. He remembered how alarmed Sarah had been the first time she'd seen it happen. He'd had to reassure her that it was normal for him.

He knew that she hated those scars, even as she accepted them as an integral part of his body. She'd told him that they didn't bother her, except for the fact that she remembered where they came from and that made her angry. Sometimes, when she was particularly upset – which had been quite frequently in the last two months – she would spend an inordinate amount of time kissing him along the lines of those scars as they made love. He wasn't sure why she did this, and it didn't matter. It appeared to calm her, and it certainly was not unpleasant for him. Her tongue....

Stop it, Daniel thought. *You aren't going to call. You're going to get rid of these damned cramps and go back to those books.*

When the bath had cooled, he drained the tub and refilled it with more scalding water and massaged his leg and side. Finally, as the muscles relaxed, he began to breathe a little easier.

"I might as well bathe while I'm in here," he muttered, picking up the small bar of hotel soap and one of the washcloths that was stacked on the edge of the bathtub. He soaped his body, rinsed, then drained the water and refilled the tub one last time.

He emerged dripping and relatively pain-free and reached for a towel. As he dried, he caught a glimpse of himself in the full-length mirror that was on the back of the bathroom door. He stared at his own reflection.

He was almost six feet tall. Not much taller than Max. Perhaps as tall as Warren? His graying hair had once been completely black. Like Edith's?

Daniel decided he'd have to take a closer look at the picture he'd seen of the Nash family on the night of Max's funeral. He'd only taken a cursory glance that time, not knowing that the couple and their two small boys were actually his grandparents, his father, and his uncle.

All of them were dead now. He wondered if there was a picture of Nora anywhere. And what about the mysterious Gwendolyn, Max's first wife who had yet to appear in the journals? Were there photos of her as well?

He would have to ask his adoptive mother, Lillian.

Suddenly, he wanted to call Lillian and tell her about what he'd read. Did she know all of this? Had Max told her over the years about his early life? Certainly he must have. They were not the sort of couple who kept secrets from each other.

Yet, they'd withheld it all from him. He was trying to keep an open mind about the matter but was finding it difficult. The knowledge that they'd denied him this past until now chafed at his reason.

His mother, his real mother, had kept it all from him, too. What were her motives? He'd thought that it had been the two of them against the world in the years before she'd died. Now, he wondered.

Walking back into his room, Daniel withdrew a pair of clean underwear from his overnight bag. After slipping it on, he slid back into his jeans and donned a fresh shirt. He didn't bother to tuck it in.

He cast about the room for another place to sit. He had already tried the chair, the couch, and the bed. His only other choices seemed to be one of the chairs at the little dinette set, the chair on the balcony, or the floor. He ruled out the balcony for the time being. It was chilly, and he'd just come out of the bathtub. He wasn't ready to stretch out on the floor. So, he went back to the bed to pick up the journal.

There were only two pages left in that notebook. He stood next to the bed and finished them, smiling at Max's concise description of Milo's departure, the opening of the three-room psychiatric office on Third Street, and the observation that "*My career began to build up steam at a tremendous pace, as did Isabelle's. Life was hectic, yet routine, and I was enjoying myself immensely. That is, until February 27, 1939, when Louise Robichaux passed away due to complications from childbirth. For on her deathbed, Louise confessed to me something that few in this world have known.*"

Daniel slammed the book shut and hastened to find the next journal. For a few moments, he couldn't locate it, and he panicked.

"Great. Another damned secret. Now, I'll never figure it out!"

Then, he saw something out of the corner of his eye. There was a journal on the floor in-between the dresser and the couch. Breathing a sigh of relief, he pulled back one of the chairs and sat at the table. He looked at the remaining box of doughnuts then at his watch. He might as well order some coffee and breakfast before he got started. He could eat the rest of the doughnuts as a snack later.

While he waited for his two large coffees and his Country Farm Breakfast, Daniel forced himself to get back to his reading. The curiosity about Louise Robichaux's secret was too much to contain.

Chapter Five: The Innocent

"Tell us, please," Isabelle urged when the doctor stepped out of Louise's bedroom. "What is the news?"

"There's nothing I can do. She's lost too much blood."

"But if we get her to a hospital –"

"No, Dr. Fernberg. There's no time for that. She's minutes away from drifting peacefully to her death. I wouldn't take those few minutes she'll have with her child from her so dispassionately." As Isabelle wiped at her eyes, the physician added, "Dr. Nash, she wants to speak with you. Don't tarry."

Max went quickly into the bedroom. The curtains had been drawn tightly across the windows. Louise lay so still in the bed that he wondered if she'd already died. Next to her, the baby stirred and opened its unfocused eyes.

"Louise?"

"Thank you for being here," she murmured. "I need to talk with you before…before I die. You must promise me that you'll take care of my girl."

"I'll see to it that she's placed in a good home and will make sure that she's well cared for and loved."

"Thank you." She reached out and grasped his sleeve, twisting the material tightly in her hand then said urgently, "I'm going to tell you something that I haven't told another living soul, not even Isabelle, bless her. You must swear to me that you'll never tell anyone about this. Do you swear it?"

"Louise –"

"Swear it!" she demanded. "I don't have time for you to hesitate."

"I swear it," he said soothingly. "Shhh."

"The baby, I want her named Millicent. I want you to call her CoCo, so no one knows or figures it out."

"Figures what out?"

"That she's your niece."

Max gazed down at the baby, who was squirming in her mother's arms.

"But…but if that's so, then Milo should know, especially if you…since you…."

"You swore to me. He doesn't need to know. His life isn't here. Your brother will never marry or settle down and raise a family."

"Milo is no tramp."

"No, but his heart is forever young. That was one of the reasons we…."

Louise closed her eyes and seemed to float into unconsciousness. Within a few seconds her eyes opened again, and she tried to focus on Max.

"Please, don't tell Milo. Take care of our child. She'll be unbalanced like me, I fear."

"You can't possibly know that. She'll be fine."

"No," the woman insisted. "There's something not right about her, my beautiful girl. You'll see to it that she's raised by someone who won't be bothered by her differences?"

"I will raise her."

"Thank you, but no. I want her to have what Samantha never had. She needs two parents. Please, do as I ask."

"As you wish."

"Good. Call the doctor and Isabelle in now."

He hurried to the door and summoned them into the room.

"I've asked Max to take care of my daughter. I've given him my reasons, and he's accepted my request to be her guardian. You will…you'll be witness to it."

Max almost smiled at the shock on their faces.

"Of course," Isabelle assured her. "Whatever you would like."

Louise sighed and kissed her daughter's cheek.

"Isabelle, would you open the drapes? I want to see the stars."

"I'm afraid it's a cloudy night," the doctor gently told her.

"I can see the stars," Louise breathed. "Do you see them, CoCo? One of them is for your sister, Samantha. Now, one will be for me. We'll shine so brightly…."

Interlude

Daniel hastily closed the journal and put it aside. He got up and began to pace the room.

"This is crazy," he muttered. "You know that this kind of thing happens and that it happened a lot more frequently in the past than it does today. What's the big deal?"

The "big deal" was that Sarah had almost bled to death before his eyes. While he'd held her during the emergency delivery of their son and afterwards as the doctors had frantically tried to get the bleeding under control, Sarah had cried hysterically against his chest. Sarah never allowed herself to cry in front of anyone if at all possible, not even family. If she was hysterical in front of strangers, she must have been even more terrified than he. She needed for him to be strong, so he'd put his own fear aside.

Just like my grandfather did with my grandmother when Milo and Alyce were born.

It was not his or Sarah's fault, the doctors had said. They should be thankful that their first child had survived the premature birth. They shouldn't risk another pregnancy. The next time, they might not be so lucky.

Sarah and Daniel were thankful. They were also heartbroken. For two years afterwards, they'd discussed the possibility of working with specialists in an attempt at a healthy pregnancy. Deep down, however, they knew that their arguments were theoretical. After Daniel had a particularly bad nightmare about losing Sarah during a second birth, they'd finally agreed on sterilization.

And here was Louise Robichaux, dead as a result of similar complications to those Sarah had experienced. She had died, holding the baby in her arms.

Daniel shook his head at the irony of it. Little Millicent Robichaux was his cousin. The woman he had known as CoCo Genevieve for the last twenty-some-odd years was Max's niece.

Crazy Mrs. Genevieve, as Sarah used to affectionately call her when they were children, was now revealed as a relative.

Daniel wondered how Louise had known that something would be wrong with the newborn CoCo. Maybe all of her free-spirited ways had made her more in touch with herself and the world around her. Maybe it was because of her family history of mental instability. Perhaps she had just guessed correctly.

Did CoCo know that Max was her uncle? Had Max ever told Milo that CoCo was his child? There was only one way to find out.

But before he returned to his reading, there was something Daniel needed to do. He picked up the phone and dialed the number to the old Nash home.

"Hello?" a small voice answered.

"Hello, Kris."

"Daddy! Are you done with your work, yet?"

"Not yet. Remember, I told you that I'll be home sometime tomorrow, even if I don't get it all done. Are you having fun at Grandma Lillian's?"

"Yes! Mommy and I made mud pies this morning!"

"Sounds like fun. Maybe you can show me how. I've never made a mud pie. Did it taste good?"

"You don't *eat* it, Daddy! You pretend."

"I see. Is Mommy around?"

Daniel held the phone away from his ear as Kris called out loudly, "Mommmmy! It's Daddy!"

There were footsteps, then Daniel heard his mother say, "I'll take that, Kris."

He pictured his sixty-year-old African-American mother taking the phone from his son and placing the receiver against her ear. Her hair had turned gray over the past few years, and she said she saw no reason to dye it. He smiled as she spoke his name.

"Lillian? Hi. What is it?" His pulse quickened as he asked anxiously, "Where's Sarah?"

"Sarah's fine, Baby. It's just that she and Tristan are in the process of trying to fix that part of the railing on the porch that's been rotting. You know the one I mean? They're right in the middle of placing a bracket or something, so she asked if I could talk with you until she came. Do you mind?"

"No, of course not. Is she being careful about her arm?"

"Now, you know her arm is doing fine. Enough time has passed since that dish broke and she got that gash. And I know she tore her stitches after the Thanksgiving dinner, but she's been doing very well about not tearing them again. She did tell me that she felt guilty about being gone to the hospital to have it sewn up when your father died, but she honestly shouldn't feel that way. There was nothing either of you could have done, even if you had been here."

What Daniel knew was that the injured area on his wife's left arm was healing nicely and that she was due to have the stitches removed the following week. He also knew that it still got extremely sore when Sarah overdid it. She was not the type to complain. No one else would know if she were hurting. Well, no one else but her father.

As if she'd heard his thoughts, Lillian said, "Tristan would never let her help him if he thought she was in pain."

Daniel heard a door open and close and then some mumbling in the background.

"Oh, here they are now," Lillian told him. "Before I hang up, are you doing well? Are you eating?"

"Way too much. Lillian, I'm only here for a couple of days. I'm fine."

"Are they…are the notes being helpful? I never read them, you know. Is he explaining things?"

He had the sudden urge to ask her whether or not she knew that CoCo was his first cousin. Instead, he said, "Yes. No. Both, I guess. I haven't even gotten to his first marriage, yet. I hope I can finish this weekend."

"Well, you call back if you want. I love you, Baby. Here's Sarah."

He heard the receiver being handed to his wife.

"Hey, Daniel."

The tension and the irrational fear in Daniel were immediately washed away. It was amazing how the sound of her voice could instantly make him feel more at ease. She was both his cushion and his rock, a beautiful rose that was soft and fragrant on the outside but had a filament of concrete supporting every petal.

"I thought I'd call to say that I love you," Daniel offered.

There was a pause.

"Daddy, would you mind talking for a minute while I go to the home office phone?"

The receiver was passed once again. Daniel envisioned his wife, who was only five feet tall, passing the phone to her father, who was six foot seven. They had the same auburn curls and hazel eyes with black flecks in them, but that was where the physical resemblance ended. Sarah was delicate and pale, while her father had his father's Lakota Native American features and skin tone. But their personalities were very much the same.

"Hello, Dan."

"Hey, Tris. How's it coming with the porch?"

"Really well. The damage isn't too bad, but I'm glad we're taking care of it now. If it had continued on like this, Lillian might have been looking at replacing the whole porch."

"Wish I were there to help. Is Sarah taking it easy?"

"She has been. She seemed to be tiring a few minutes ago, so I told her that was all we'd do for this morning. I might come back later to work on it some more."

There was a *click* as Sarah picked up the phone in Max's home office.

"I have it, Daddy."

"Later, Dan."

"Bye, Tris."

Once Tristan had rung off, Sarah said softly to her husband, "Tell me what's wrong."

"Nothing," he replied. "I simply needed to hear your voice."

"Liar."

He sighed resignedly and admitted, "There's so much here. Max is giving me so much background, and I haven't made it to World War II, yet. There are minor revelations and major secrets and murder –"

"Murder!"

"Not Max murdering anyone. His sister was killed by a family friend."

"I didn't know he had a sister."

"Two. And there's more. I just…."

He wanted to tell her all of it, but he wasn't sure if he should right then.

"Do you want Daddy to bring me over there?" Sighing, she declared, "I wish I could still drive."

"No, I only needed to hear your voice. I only…." He hesitated then admitted, "I'm glad Max documented everything, but I am having a really hard time not resenting him for keeping it all from me. I want to understand why he did it and to know about him and my mother."

"Lillian's a nervous wreck," Sarah whispered. "It's good that we're here with her. Daddy and I are trying to talk her into going out to eat tonight at The Great Wall. Regardless, Lillian and I are supposed to go to the mall to do some Christmas shopping while Daddy takes Kris to the Arts & Science Center."

"Did you bring his letter to Santa with you?"

"It's in my purse. By the way, Santa didn't get a letter from you. Is there anything special you want?"

"Peace of mind."

"Santa doesn't do too well with intangibles like that."

"Then it doesn't matter. Tell Santa anything would be fine."

"You're no fun."

"And you are? What do you want Santa to bring you?"

"Something totally impractical."

It took Daniel a moment to recover himself.

"You? Impractical?"

"Shocking, isn't it? I am trying, though. Is Santa going to help me in my quest to be less structured?"

"Santa will do his best." He glanced at the journal on the table and said, "I should get back to work. Have fun with Lillian."

"I'll try. After everything that's happened to us in the last couple of months, I'm still so anxious off and on. I really needed to hear *your* voice. Call me tonight if you want."

"Okay. I love you."

"I love you, too."

Daniel was lowering the receiver when he heard his wife say, "And Daniel?"

"Yes?"

"Try and get some sleep."

"I will."

He went back to the book.

There were two more handwritten pages that explained how Max had placed CoCo with a wealthy, middle-aged couple from his church who had never been able to have any children. They were close friends and had agreed to allow Max to be an integral part of CoCo's life.

Daniel sighed and went in search of the next journal. With horror, he realized that there were no more. He went back to the boxes that had held all of the notebooks he'd already read. He checked the sides of the boxes. Nothing. He checked the tops of the boxes. Nothing. He checked the bottoms of the boxes.

MAXWELL NASH. CARTON #1 of 6. #454.
MAXWELL NASH. CARTON #2 of 6. #454.
MAXWELL NASH. CARTON #3 of 6. #454.

"Damn it all."

Daniel removed the phone book from the drawer in the nightstand and flipped through the pages until he came to Palmentier, E.J. He dialed, hoping against hope that his friend and attorney would be home.

"Hello?"

"Elmo, it's Dan."

"Hey, Dan. What's up?"

"I've got a problem. A big problem. You know those cartons of books that my father left for me through your law practice? Well, it seems I've only got three boxes out of six. Can you find the others?"

"What do they say?"

"Maxwell Nash. Carton number one, two, and three of six. Number four-fifty-four."

"That sounds like the number of one of our storage places. I doubt if I'll be able to track it down today since it's after noon on Saturday. Why don't you meet me at the office Monday after you get off from work, and I'll have them for you?"

Daniel was disappointed, but he hid it as best he could and agreed to meet the lawyer Monday evening. He checked his watch. It was 1:30, two and a half hours past check-out time.

Great. Now what should I do?

His wife and the rest of his family would be eating at The Great Wall at 7:00. He still had more than five hours. Daniel decided to reread some of the journals he'd already gone through in order to make things clearer in his mind. He set the alarm on his watch for 6:00 p.m. then pulled out one of the earlier journals. He was quickly asleep, waking with barely enough time to leave and drive to the restaurant.

Despite the crowd at The Great Wall, his forty-eight-year-old father-in-law was easy to spot. His height made it difficult for him to be lost in any crowd. Half Irish and half Lakota, he was an oddly handsome man with striking features, the auburn curls that fell past his shoulders when unbound, and the hazel eyes with black flecks. Daniel loved him as if her were his father and considered him a great friend. It had been Tristan who'd saved his life almost twenty-five years earlier.

When Daniel had first met Tristan Maes, the man had often worn his long hair loose. As the years had passed and his architectural career had flourished, he'd begun to wear it tied back with a black cord daily. He declared that he would never cut it short and that it was a good barometer of how sincere and accepting other individuals were. Daniel could not imagine him without it.

He pushed through the throng and came up behind his unsuspecting son. Kris jumped from side to side, his golden hair made more luminous by the dark gray coat he wore. They'd always wondered where the blonde hair had come from. Now, Daniel thought of Warren and Nora and their golden curls.

"Boo!"

The little boy squealed with delight as his father scooped him up and lifted him into the air.

"You're finished already?" Tristan asked incredulously.

"Nope. I finished three boxes. I discovered that the law clerk didn't give me the other three. Elmo's supposed to track them down. I'll meet him at his office Monday after work. So, I've got an extra night at the hotel and no reason to be there. You think you and Vaughn might be interested? I know Will's studying for his semester finals at his friend's apartment, and Katie's at that high school dance. You won't have kids at home tonight."

"Why don't you and Sarah take a night off? Would you like to spend the night with Grandma Vaughn and me, Kris?" The older man tickled his grandson before adding, "We'll ask your mother when she gets here."

"Would that be okay with you, Kris?"

"Yes! But what about Ralph? Could he come, too?"

"I don't know about that," Daniel said slowly. "They may not want to babysit you and an enormous, drooling black Lab. Grandma Lillian's had him at her house all day, and I'm sure she's ready to send him back home. He's probably filthy, Tris."

"No, it's okay," Tristan assured him. "Kris, you and I can go get Ralph on our way back to the house. If he's filthy, we'll clean him up before we take him home."

The threesome inched forward as the line moved marginally.

"Daniel?"

Sarah. Yes, the hair and the eyes were the same as Tristan's. However, whereas Tristan was naturally tall and thin, Sarah was petite and had wonderful curves. While she was concerned that she'd developed too many curves since the birth of their son, Daniel disagreed. He loved her full breasts and the shape of her hips and backside. She worried that the few pounds she wanted to lose would never come off. Daniel didn't think she needed to lose any weight. In his eyes, she was perfect.

It didn't matter to Daniel that his wife was visually impaired. She had Stargardt's, a form of juvenile macular degeneration that had slowly caused her central vision to deteriorate over the past sixteen years. She'd adapted well and used her peripheral vision to its fullest extent. Although she did have difficulty reading print, seeing certain things even with the help of magnification, and could no longer drive, no one would have guessed that she was partially blind simply by looking at her. He wouldn't have cared if they did. It wouldn't have changed how he felt about her.

He had the sudden and all-encompassing urge to make love to her right there, right then. He pushed the idiocy of it aside and watched her break through the crowd, followed closely by her stepmother and Lillian.

Once she stood in front of him, he hugged her tightly and gave her a quick kiss then put his lips close to her ear and whispered, "I didn't get it all read. They didn't give it all to me, so I'll have to get the remainder of it on Monday. But I've still got the room. Tris said he and Vaughn can watch Kris. Do you want to come back with me? I want to talk to you about things alone."

"You know I will," she whispered back.

As they broke apart, Lillian clucked in disapproval and concern.

"Daniel, you haven't slept at all, have you?"

"I did sleep. So there."

"Don't sass your mother," she admonished, but she was smiling slightly.

The African-American couple standing nearest to their group stared unabashedly at them. Daniel knew exactly what they were thinking. Lillian knew it, too.

"You should be ashamed of yourselves, staring like you are," she said in a huff. "Yes, my son is white, and I'm black."

"I believe the proper terms are 'Caucasian' and 'Afro-American,'" Tristan said with a wink. "Well, people say, 'African-American,' but that means somebody who is recently from Africa who's now an American."

"Hogwash!" Lillian exclaimed. "He's white, and I'm black. He's approaching middle age, and I'm just plain old. He's trim, and I'm not. What difference does any of it make? Why people feel the need to label each other to death is beyond me. No matter what you call it, that's no reason to be impolite and gawk at us in a public place."

The couple turned away and pretended that the incident had never occurred.

"I'm not half Indian anymore," Tristan continued. "I'm half Native American."

Vaughn Maes stepped nearer to her husband and took his hand before asking, "Have they come up with a new name for those of us who are of pure Irish descent?"

"We Native Americans might call you Glowing Skin with Deep Red Hair. After all, you do have the palest skin and the darkest red hair of anyone I've ever seen."

"Is that why you married me?" she laughed. Glancing at her son-in-law, Vaughn said, "You do look tired. Are you still reading? Will you rest tonight?"

"Okay, let me say this once again so I don't have to say it any more. I didn't get to finish because the law firm didn't give me all the material. I'll pick up the other boxes of notebooks on Monday. Yes, I'll rest tonight because I have one more night at the hotel. Sarah and I are going to go over there, and I promise I'll get some sleep."

"I volunteered us for babysitting," Tristan said sheepishly. "Sorry, Lillian. I didn't mean not to give you the opportunity."

"Don't be silly. I babysat last time. I don't want to deprive you of our grandson's company."

The hostess called for them and led the group to a long table near the buffet.

"I want Phoenix rolls!" Kris announced. "And noodles!"

"You may have both," Sarah said patiently. "Hold your horses, and I'll go with you to the buffet."

"I'll take him," Daniel offered. He felt as though he needed to be near his son in the worst way. "C'mon, Kris."

Daniel walked haltingly behind his child as they made their way down each side of the two, long buffet tables. He supervised as Kris got his Phoenix rolls and lo mein noodles, and he himself filled his plate with small portions of General Tso's Chicken, cheese-filled wontons, fried rice, and pan-fried sweet potatoes.

"Someday, I'm going to try the other three dozen or so dishes on the buffet," he commented, as he returned to their table and sat next to his mother.

"You say that every time, and you always get the same things," she scolded playfully. "As long as you eat, it doesn't matter to me what you choose. When we first brought you home, it was so difficult for you to get anything down. It was such a relief once you were finally able to enjoy food again." She looked pensive for a moment then forcibly brightened and said, "Tristan and Sarah did a wonderful job working on the porch today. Tristan, I was meaning to ask you about the post...."

"I'll be up for hours," Sarah groaned, as they climbed into the car an hour later. "Why do I feel so stuffed when we go there?"

"Because you can't resist those wontons."

"What about you? You must have had five."

"Seven, and I loved every bite." Sobering, he said, "I'd like to stay up anyway."

"I know. Let's get back to the hotel so we can relax and talk."

"I was proud of you. You didn't even say that you had no toothbrush or change of clothes."

"How impractical of me. I think that's progress, don't you?"

"Definitely." The leather seat groaned as he leaned back. "How was the shopping? Did you find everything we needed for Kris?"

"All except the Lion King tent. Oh, and I got your mother a really pretty cameo brooch that actually looks like it has the profile of a black woman on it. You remember how she said she's always wanted one but could never find one, so I thought that would be nice."

"I'm sure she'll love it. You didn't happen to see anything you liked while you were at it, huh?"

"I completely forgot to look. I'll let you know."

They arrived at the hotel, and Daniel led Sarah upstairs.

"It's cozy," she told him as she slowly scanned the room. "What's the view like?"

They stood together on the balcony and watched for a while as the cars went by. Daniel knew that Sarah couldn't see much of the hotel surroundings. The night was cloudy and extremely dark, and her night vision was poor. In order for her to see anything well, she needed good lighting.

Finally, Sarah turned, hurried inside, and rubbed at her arms in an effort to get warm.

"You're not cold?" she asked with a shiver.

"Not too bad. Come here."

He planted his hands on her hips and bent low to kiss her. She automatically lifted her arms and slid them around her husband's neck. As she did so, Daniel slipped his cold hands under her sweater.

Sarah squeaked and tried to push away from him.

"You rat! Your fingers are freezing!"

Daniel laughed and held on securely to his wife.

"It's not so bad," he insisted.

"You had your fingers on that metal railing! They're like icicles!"

Between her flesh and the knit of her sweater, his hands were beginning to warm. He stooped down to kiss her again, and she stopped arguing. He moved forward slowly, guiding her so that she didn't fall while walking backward as they got closer to the bed. Conscious of her injured arm, Daniel carefully lowered her back onto the mattress. Within minutes, their clothing was scattered on the floor, and their bodies joined together in the familiar heat of physical desire and emotional need.

Afterwards, Sarah lay warm at last in Daniel's arms. She listened quietly, letting her hands caress and calm, as he told her about what he'd read in his father's first three journals. When the story of what he knew was complete, she sat up slightly and looked down at her husband, her auburn curls teasing the skin of his stomach.

"So, CoCo is really your cousin? I wonder if she knows. Do you think you should tell her?"

"I'm not going to tell her anything, not until I read the rest of those journals. Maybe Max will let me know if she ever found out."

"Stranger things have happened." She cupped her hand against his cheek and said, "Your grandfather was named Warren. I wonder if your mother named you Daniel Warren because of that or if it was a weird coincidence. She might not have known."

"I hadn't thought of that. I wish that I had the other boxes. I want to know how close my mother and Max really were. Was it a fling or something serious?"

"You only have one more day to wait until you can get the rest of the boxes."

Tracing the line of her collarbone with his thumb, Daniel murmured, "I'm glad you're here. I needed you here."

"Relax," she said, as she straddled his hips. "Try to think about something else."

"Such as?"

"I'm sure something will come to mind."

She bent forward and began to trace the lines of his scars with her mouth. Daniel reached down, slipped his fingers through her curls, and concentrated on the movements of her hips and her tongue. For the rest of the night, he thought of nothing except his wife.

Part Two

The Consequences

Chapter One: Redirection

"I'm so sorry, Dan," Elmo Palmentier, Attorney-at-Law, offered then frowned and threw down the pen he'd been fidgeting with during his explanation. Picking up the pen, he unhappily tapped it on his mouse pad and continued by saying, "This fire at the storage place has been devastating for the firm and the clients who were affected. I'd have told you about it Saturday, but I was under the impression that the boxes of effects had been kept in one of the units that didn't burn."

Daniel nodded numbly at the man, who'd been his neighbor and friend for several years. Palmentier was about his age and height, but the man was much heavier and had bushy blonde hair and brown eyes.

"I'm afraid I wasn't aware of the contents of the cartons," the lawyer admitted. "Your father merely requested that we safeguard it all for you. Why in the heck they put half the boxes in one unit and the other half in another is a mystery to me. Is it something that the firm might be able to replace or could we perhaps help you to locate a replacement?"

Daniel pushed the envelope across the desk. He watched the lines deepen in Palmentier's face as he read Max's letter.

"Words can't express how much I regret what's happened," Palmentier said grimly. "We see people pass on such inconsequential things. They're not inconsequential to the owner, but the loss of Aunt Vera's broken tea kettle or Grandpa Bob's warped fishing pole is laughable compared to this." He leaned back in his expensive ergonomically correct office chair and said, "In light of the circumstances maybe Lillian would be able to disclose the information contained in these manuscripts."

"Max never showed the journals to her, although she knew of their existence. I know she can fill in some of the past for me, but she and Max were together for only about thirty years. Max was eighty-two when he died. I have no idea how much he shared with her about his earlier life." Daniel stood and asked, "How in the hell am I supposed to unearth the missing pieces? Elmo, I didn't even know that he was my real father until the night of his funeral! Those diaries, all those years that he spent painstakingly recording his story –" He broke off, gritting his teeth and blinking back tears. The frustration he felt was almost overwhelming as he went on, "Can you imagine what it's like to be so close to solving the mystery of your life and then have your chance snatched away at the last minute?"

"Dan, we've been neighbors and friends for a long time now. The injustice of this situation is mind-boggling. Don't believe for a minute that I don't care or feel awful about it."

"It's not your fault. There's not a lot I can do about it, is there? What, I could go after the security guard at the storage place for leaving his cigarette butt burning in a trash can or I could sue the makers of the faulty sprinkler system?"

"You could," the man replied with a sardonic smile. "Many people would. I know it's not much comfort, but the firm's already working on that." Palmentier leaned forward, began to flip through his Rolodex, and then offered, "May I make a few suggestions? Talk to Lillian and see what she knows. Then, speak with Isabelle Elenstraub. After all, she was your father's closest friend and professional associate for half a century. Surely, she must have some insight into the events that he wanted to expound upon. Also, let me contact one of the private investigators we retain from time to time. Who knows what he might uncover?" Palmentier pulled out a card from the file and reached for the phone and added, "The firm will pay the tab. Can you stay a second, and I'll see if I can get through to the P.I. so that you can set up an appointment?"

"You don't have to do this, Elmo."

"It's the least I can do." As he dialed the number on the card, he asked, "How is Lillian holding up?"

"As well as can be expected. It's going to be rough this first Christmas. Max died November 24th. It's only December 12th. With everything else that's happened, our holiday spirit is down the tubes."

"Sarah's doing better? My wife said she ran into her and Kris taking your dog for a walk last week, and she felt that Sarah seemed withdrawn. I hope –" Motioning for Daniel to wait, he said into the receiver, "Hello, Carson. Listen, I've got somebody in my office who needs your services. He's a friend and a client. No, that's not a contradiction in terms. Anyway, do you have time for another case, or are you too swamped? Great. The firm will be paying you. Yeah. I'll explain later. His name's Dan Nash. Okay, here he is."

Daniel accepted the phone and put the receiver to his ear.

"Carson Zerangue here. When do you want to get together? Is Friday good for you?" There came the sound of papers rustling, then Zerangue said, "Hm. I've got to be in St. Francisville all morning; then I have an appointment in Zachary and one in Baker. If you don't mind my meeting you at your house, we can do it that evening. If you'd prefer, we can schedule it for another day when I can meet you at some other location."

"No, Friday evening would be fine."

"You mind if I ask about the nature of the investigation? It doesn't matter if you want to wait to tell me. Elmo doesn't call me unless it's important. Still, I like to have some idea as to what I'm getting myself into – divorce, custody battle, murder."

"None of the above. I don't know how you'd categorize it. I suppose you could say that I want you to help me investigate my past."

"You an amnesiac?"

"At times I wish I were."

"'Nuff said. Give me directions to your house."

Daniel did so, struggling to attempt a summary of recent events.

"I'd rather you take your time and explain everything nice and slow," the detective told him. "It'll help me to build a file so I can do my job. See you Friday."

Daniel handed the phone back to Palmentier. Once the lawyer had replaced the receiver, he asked, "What'd you think?"

"I get this weird image of a grizzly bear, combined with Old Saint Nick."

"You're not far off. He's good, a retired police detective from the New Orleans P.D. He's very thorough," Palmentier added reassuringly. "He's one of those guys who isn't content with dates and names. He wants to figure out the real story. I gather that's what you want?"

"Yeah. Thanks, Elmo."

"Thank me when you know the truth. Now, tell me about your wife. Is she better?"

Daniel sighed and fell back into his chair.

"Some days are worse than others, but she's getting there. The last few weeks have been hard on both of us. I've been going through a tough time for a while, trying to deal with things about my childhood that I haven't resolved. I know that watching me struggle with it has put a strain on her."

"I didn't know. Are you okay?"

"Sarah finally put her foot down and insisted that I talk to a professional or else. I don't know how beneficial that's been. I guess I should try another therapist. The only other one I'd worked with was Max."

"There are lots of listings in the Yellow Pages, not that I'd necessarily recommend letting your fingers do the walking for something as important as this."

"I agree. Anyway, I was starting to work on that when she lost her new job. I think that hit her harder than she could have ever anticipated. You know she's dealt with the partial blindness thing for sixteen years. Except for not being able to drive for the last few years, she's adapted with no real problems."

"So, what happened?"

"Her new employer was aware of her disability but said it didn't matter. Turns out it did matter, and that was that. They lied to her about the job duties and fired her without even trying to make things work. It's a long story. I'd rather not get into it any more today, but it makes me furious."

"It sounds as though they didn't give a damn."

"They didn't, the bastards. You know how Sarah is, Elmo. She's smart and organized, and she works hard at whatever she does."

"What about the job she held before? She was a valued employee for years managing that bookshop."

"Tanner Edwards wanted her back immediately, but he'd already hired somebody to fill her position."

"Maybe that person won't work out."

"She didn't. Nobody could run that bookstore like Sarah did. She and Tanner were a team for so long. If the other opportunity hadn't been so promising…." As if clearing out the cobwebs,

Daniel shook his head back and forth and said, "It doesn't mean a thing. Tanner called last night to ask us to come to the store for a party on New Year's Eve. He's shutting down. With all of those book warehouses, his small shop can't compete anymore."

"What about other job prospects?"

"She's too shell-shocked at the moment. And have you ever tried to get a job without being able to drive? The bus service sucks. There's no route anywhere near where we live. Maybe if I hadn't had to take off so much lately, then I could arrange to take her to interviews. What then? We had a system going when she worked at the bookstore. How would we manage it now?" Picking at a piece of lint on his pants leg, he admitted, "Personally, I don't think she can handle the stress of trying to coordinate that right now. She hurt her arm last month, and it was like the last straw."

"So, all that was going on with you and her when your father died."

"Yeah. I knew Max's death was coming. We all did." He gestured to the letter that was lying open on Palmentier's desk and said tiredly, "But none of us anticipated this. Stumbling across the truth about my parentage on the day that we buried him was a lovely touch, wouldn't you agree?"

"Dan –"

"Sorry." Raking his fingers through his hair, Daniel lowered his left leg and said, "Enough of that. Are there any other documents I should sign or look at today? It's getting late, and we both need to be heading home."

"I think we covered the estate stuff at the meeting we had with you and Lillian at the end of November." Palmentier folded Max's letter and passed it back to Daniel with the words, "I'm glad you're taking care of the estate business. Your father knew what he was doing when he left you in charge. Your mother is a wonderful woman, but she really doesn't have the inclination for business matters."

"She's said that herself many times in-between telling me that I should stop swearing and wear my coat more often when it's cold outside."

"I can't comment on the coat business, but I wouldn't exactly call an occasional 'hell' or 'damn' serious swearing. Not nowadays. Have you added the 'F,' 'G,' and 'S' words to your everyday vocabulary?"

"It doesn't matter to Lillian. Whether it's 'hell,' 'damn,' or 'Jesus Christ,' it's more swearing than should be allowed."

"Take care, Dan. If you want to talk, you know where I live. Attorneys are frustrated psychiatrists at heart."

"I'll remember that. Thanks."

By the time he got to his car, Daniel's teeth were chattering. Once more, he'd forgotten his coat at the office. He was relieved that Lillian was nowhere around.

He drove past the darkened shops and the lighted windows of the houses that lined the streets on his way home. He could see the outlines of Christmas trees with multi-colored lights in some of the living rooms where the curtains hadn't yet been drawn. Holiday wreaths and wire reindeer littered porches, roofs, and lawns.

As he pulled into his garage, Daniel glanced at his watch. It was 6:30. Maybe he'd made it home in time for dinner. Something certainly smelled good. He unlocked the door to the kitchen and hurried inside.

"Daddy!"

Kris rushed forward and threw himself into his father's arms. Briefcase in hand, Daniel shifted the boy's weight and hoisted him up.

"Did I miss dinner again?"

"Nope. Mommy made it later so it'd be hot when you got home. It's chicken something. It smells real good!" As they entered the kitchen, Kris pointed to a large covered pot on the stove then continued, "And that one is the spaghetti."

"Where are the rolls?"

"In the oven."

"Looks delicious. Where's Mommy?"

"She got sauce on her dress, so she had to take it off. I'll go get her."

As Kris scampered towards the back of the house, Daniel put down his briefcase and stuck his half-finished Coke into the refrigerator.

"The Prodigal Husband returns for dinner. Haven't I heard that story somewhere before?"

Closing the refrigerator door, Daniel asked expectantly, "Aren't you going to kill the fatted calf and throw me a party?"

"Would you settle for lean chicken and some noodles?"

They met in the middle of the kitchen. Daniel slid his arms around his wife's shoulders as she took his face in her hands. He bent low to kiss her, moving his right hand up her back and into the tangle of that curly, auburn hair.

"How was it? What did Elmo have to say?"

"I'll tell you when Kris is out of earshot."

The cooking timer began to beep, so Sarah broke away from him and hurried to the stove.

"Would you mind setting the table while I get this ready?" Stirring the noodles, she added, "If you remember how to set the table, that is."

Kris came up next to his father and held out a piece of construction paper. Daniel accepted the drawing and squatted next to the child.

"What is this? It's really cool."

"There's Rudolph. And that's Charlie, Santa's dog. He protects the sleigh and helps Santa Claus." He looked up at Daniel and asked, "Will you be home for dinner on Christmas Eve?"

Daniel sensed Sarah looking at him from her position in front of the stove. He rubbed at his chin.

"I've missed being here at dinner, lately. There's been a lot I have to do at work and…with other things this fall. Sometimes, grown-ups have to do things they don't want to do. They have lots of responsibilities. Soon, I think I'll be able to get back to my old schedule. Then I can be here for almost every meal at night. How would that be?"

"Yay!"

"Go wash your hands, Kris," Sarah directed. "It's almost ready."

Daniel tacked the picture to the refrigerator and moved close behind his wife. Wrapping his arms around her, he said quietly, "It's all gone. Every page was incinerated in a blaze at the storage warehouse."

"All of it?" Sarah gasped. She put down the fork in her hand and tried to twist around to face her husband.

"Don't. I'm having a hard enough time keeping it together as it is." He broke away from her and went to set the table then added, "We're having company for dinner Friday night."

"Who?"

"A man named Carson Zerangue. He's a private investigator Elmo recommended. The firm is going to pay for his services so that he can help me sort things out."

"What's a private vestigator?" Kris asked, as he returned to the kitchen and hopped up into his chair.

Daniel hesitated, unsure as to how he should explain.

"A private investigator is a person who helps other people do research on things," Sarah told her son. "Do you know what research is? No? Well, research is when you have to find something out and look in different places." Handing Daniel his plate, she went on, "Sometimes, you can find what you need in a library or at the place where they keep important papers. Other times, you have to talk to people. A private investigator is someone who does those things for you when you don't have time or you don't know how."

"What will he help Daddy find out?"

Sarah took her seat, looking questioningly at Daniel. *I'll stall him*, her eyes seemed to say. *You think of something.*

"Don't forget to put your napkin in your lap," she instructed. "How was the party at school today?"

"It was fun." Kris continued, as though they'd never changed topics by asking, "Daddy, what will the man help you find out?"

Stabbing a piece of his chicken with his fork, Daniel remarked as casually as he could, "There are things I need to know that I don't remember or never knew."

"What kind of things?"

"Take a bite, Kris," Sarah prodded. "I think Daddy would rather talk about it after dinner."

"How was your day, Sarah?" Daniel asked, eager to change the subject.

"I washed several loads of clothes, dusted, mopped the kitchen, cleaned the bathrooms, and took the dog for a long walk. It was quite thrilling, as I'm sure you can imagine. At least I got a lot accomplished."

"That's good. Speaking of the dog, where is Ralph?"

"Did I mention that I mopped the kitchen floor?"

"Is he that filthy?"

"Not at all, but when I put him out so I could mop, he wanted to stay in the yard. You know how he loves the cold."

"We can get him in later."

"What about your day?"

"Work-wise it was uneventful but hectic. We did have a huge staff meeting in the afternoon. I was wondering if I'd get out in time to go to Elmo's. It was worthwhile, though. My boss has been focusing on restructuring for so long that we needed to regroup. Everyone seems pretty happy with the changes, and things are going well there."

"Can I be finished?" Kris asked impatiently after a few more minutes of eating and talking. "I've already told Daddy about my day and want to go play trucks now."

Sarah looked dubiously at her son's plate.

"One more bite of each thing," Daniel declared. "Then take your plate to the sink."

"When you're finished, will you tell me what kinds of things that man will help you with?"

"Sure," Daniel told him. "I'll be there soon."

After Kris had wandered off to his room, Sarah and Daniel gathered their plates and glasses and placed them on the counter.

"What are you going to say?" Sarah whispered.

"I don't have a clue. A half-truth. He's only five. I don't know how much he'll understand. Hell, I still don't understand."

"Daddy!"

Kris ran into the kitchen with his pajamas in hand.

"I have to go to sleep. Santa comes to school tomorrow!"

Sarah went over to the boy and checked playfully behind him.

"Is this my son? I don't think so. My son never wants to go to bed early."

"Well, he looks like our son. I guess I'll have to go ahead and bathe him until the real Kristopher Nash comes back."

He followed the child to the bathroom. Sarah heard the water for the bath being drawn. Once the dishes had been loaded into the dishwasher, she quietly tiptoed into the darkened hallway and leaned against the wall near the bathroom door.

"So, Mr. Zerangue will find the papers you need?" the child asked.

"I hope so," Daniel replied.

"Can he help me find my football?"

"Probably not, but Mommy and I can. Where was it the last time you saw it?"

Relieved, Sarah went back to the dining room to wipe off the table.

Kris was sleeping soundly within the hour. Sarah and Daniel sat together on the couch, and Daniel reviewed everything that had transpired during the meeting with the lawyer.

"If Max would have told me in the first place, none of this would be happening."

"He thought he was doing the right thing. Maybe he was. How do you know until you find out what really took place?"

"I don't. The only thing I know is that you look exhausted. Let's do something impulsive and go to bed early for a change."

"How remarkably radical."

Neither of them moved.

"Was it a good day or a bad day?" he asked.

"It was another day. We'll see what tomorrow is like."

Chapter Two: A Good Man's Search

Carson Zerangue reflected that it had been a great day. In the morning, he'd reunited two girls who'd been separated at birth. Immediately after lunch, he'd located a deadbeat dad who was three years behind on his child support payments. Later in the afternoon, he had uncovered proof that the wife of a distraught client had been secretly going to Weight Watchers, not having a weekly tryst with an old boyfriend.

Days like this were rare, he conceded. However, it was a stellar way to wrap up the most prominent pending cases before the holidays. The rest of his current load was routine and could be handled quickly and easily by visiting the Clerk of Court office, the city's mortgage records room, and the State Library. In short, it could wait. He didn't want to spoil the mood. He could get to it all next week or even after Christmas.

The only difficulty he could foresee for the remainder of the day was that he would be early at the Nash home. Maybe he could swing by Books-A-Million on the way and find that new suspense novel he wanted in hardcover.

Carson studied his reflection in the window as he walked towards the front door of the store. He was five nine with sandy brown hair and brown eyes. Although he remained muscular with each passing year and worked out daily with weights, he needed to drop about thirty pounds. Of course, he had needed to drop about thirty pounds for about twenty years now. At least he wasn't getting any bigger.

Wandering around the store, he found the desired novel and tucked it under his arm. He hated to pay so much for a book, but he'd been waiting for this one to come out for a long time. It could be an early Christmas present to himself.

As he headed back to the front register, Carson passed the oversized model of the train engine that was positioned at the edge of the children's section. Three little girls sat in the engine. Two were totally absorbed by a video about a red dog getting ready for

Christmas. The third was engrossed in an oversized copy of *How the Grinch Stole Christmas*.

The detective stopped in the reference section and observed the children for a few minutes. As he watched, a small boy laboriously climbed up onto one of the seats. In his hand, he grasped a padded book that was shaped like an angel. He shook the book, and a jangling sound echoed in the air.

"Christmas witout a chile, dat's a sad Christmas, yeah," Carson's Cajun mother had always said. "*Mais*, dere's not a Christmas dat goes by dat I don' t'ank God for my boys. We lucky, yeah."

"Lucky and poor," Carson's older brother would declare. "We'd be luckier if Daddy had him a steady job."

"Fishing's steady," their father would reply, nonplussed. "Feeds us, yeah. It gives us enough to allow for you to go to school, so's you can do more wit' your life."

Carson's brother would roll his eyes and –

"Can I help you?"

Carson shook himself back to the present and looked at the young female clerk.

"No thanks. It's time for me to check out."

He averted his eyes from the contented children in the engine as he passed by. His would be a sad Christmas, indeed.

He drove lazily towards the Nash home. He would still be early but not terribly so. There was no place else he needed to go and no errands left to run. He hoped that his client would be home from work.

After he emerged from his unassuming beige sedan, Carson leaned back in and grabbed his briefcase and cellphone. Straightening, he scanned the front of the Nash house. It was a ranch-style red brick home with green shutters and white trim. He estimated that it was perhaps fifty years old. As a light rain began to fall, he hurried along the walk and up the steps to the front door. Once there, he rang the doorbell twice. A petite, hazel-eyed, auburn-haired woman greeted him with a cautious smile.

The private investigator considered himself an excellent judge of character. His own intuitive nature had served him well throughout his career. Sometimes, he could tell at a glance the sum of a man's integrity and personality. If not, then it was only a matter of minutes.

Now, he got his first look at Sarah Nash. She wore a deep purple dress, small gold hoop earrings, and a tiny gold cross on a delicate chain. Her wedding band and engagement ring were of fine quality but were in no way ostentatious. Her smile was pleasant, and yet she was reserved. It was as if she was talking with him but thinking of something else at the same time.

Interesting, he thought.

He liked her immediately.

"I hope you didn't have any trouble finding the house. Won't you come in?"

"Thanks. Mrs. Nash?"

"Please call me Sarah."

He nodded and said, "Call me Carson."

As he lumbered into the Nash living room, he said, "Sorry I'm early. It didn't take me as long in Baker as I thought it would."

"No problem. May I take your coat and your briefcase?"

"Coat, yes. I'd rather keep the briefcase close."

Sarah gestured for him to take a seat on the couch and said, "Daniel will be home in fifteen or twenty minutes. Would you like anything to drink? I have apple juice, milk, water, and Coke."

"How old's the kid?"

"Five."

"Hm. Don't think I've had apple juice in forty years. Why don't I give that a go?"

"Be right back." From the kitchen, Sarah called out, "I hope you like lasagna."

"I wasn't expecting you to feed me. I don't want to put you out."

"You're not. Even if you were, I would still feed you."

He took the opportunity to quickly check out the room. It was a fairly standard, middle-class living room. A couch, a recliner, and a rocker faced a coffee table and an entertainment center filled with the television, CD player, stereo, books, movies, and the like. Flanking either side of the doorway that led into the kitchen were two enormous bookcases, crammed with novels and photo albums. Plants and candles adorned shelves and corners. Nothing looked particularly new or particularly old, but it was all arranged tastefully and purposefully.

Sarah returned to the living room and handed Carson the glass of apple juice. He watched her settle into the rocker that was facing him as he took his first sip.

"You mind if I ask you a few things while we're waiting on your husband?"

"No, not if you don't mind me asking *you* a few things."

He grinned and said, "You tell it like it is, huh?"

"For better or for worse."

"Ask away."

"Everything will all be kept confidential?"

"Yes, ma'am."

"You'll do whatever it takes to help us?"

"Yes, ma'am."

"How long have you been doing this kind of work?"

"I was a detective for the N.O.P.D. for twenty years. I've been on my own for ten."

"Is there anything you think I need to know or do?"

"Uh, I'm fifty-four; my hair is starting to thin; and I used to be a fullback at LSU way back when. I also like walks in the rain and beer by the fireplace."

Sarah smiled broadly.

Good, Carson thought. *She's not quite as tough as she'd like to be. There's something different about the way she looks at things though. Wonder what's up with that?*

"Thanks for your candor." Still smiling, Sarah asked, "Now, what do you want to know?"

"First of all, you got pictures of some of the people we're gonna be talking about? I don't want to go over them with a fine tooth comb right now, but I'd like to take a look to get them in my head before your husband starts telling me about this person or that one."

He walked behind her into the hallway, where track lights illuminated both walls.

"This is our picture gallery. Let's see. Here's a picture of the family. It's about two years old. That's Daniel."

"You mean the tall, black-haired guy to your left?"

"Yes. The little boy is our son, Kris."

"Who's that guy? The thin giant on the right?"

"My father, Tristan Maes."

"Him?" He leaned closer for a better look and muttered, "Yeah, I can see it in the hair and the eyes. The lady next to him must be your mother."

"Her name's Vaughn. She married my dad when I was eight."

"Your mother still around?"

"She died when I was six in a hit-and-run accident."

"My sympathies."

"Thank you." She pointed to a young man who closely resembled her father. "And that's my half-brother, Will, and there's my half-sister, Katie."

"He looks a lot like your dad except with brown hair and eyes, and she does resemble your stepmom."

"Max is standing next to Katie. He was Daniel's father."

"Maxwell Nash, respected psychiatrist. Died November 24, 1994. Funeral services held at St. Joseph's Cathedral. Survived by his wife, Lillian; one son, Daniel; one daughter-in-law, Sarah; and one grandson, Kristopher." In response to Sarah's incredulous stare, he said, "I do my homework. The obits are part of the job." He touched the glass and asked, "Who's the black lady?"

"Max's wife, Lillian."

To Sarah's surprise, Carson didn't raise his eyebrows or appear shocked, the two most common reactions.

"How long were they married before he died?"

"Twenty-five years."

"You got a picture of your husband's biological mother?"

"One."

It was a faded black-and-white photo of a young woman cradling a baby, presumably her son. Her skin was so white that it almost shimmered in the image. She had angular features and a small mouth with thin lips.

"Do you know her full name?"

"Assumpta Tessa Downey Samuels."

Carson studied the woman again, then asked, "Do you have a picture of your husband's father as a young man?"

"Here. He was thirty, maybe."

Squinting at the image, he noted the black hair, beard, and moustache. The man's eyes glittered like onyx.

Carson went back to the informal family portrait Sarah had shown him and found Daniel Nash once more. His expression was his mother's, but it didn't seem as though he had inherited any of her physical attributes. His hair and eyes were as dark as his father's but weren't exactly the same.

"Most likely I'll need to get copies of all of these and some others, too. It helps to jog people's memories when they can put a face with a name. Depending on whom I'm talking to, I need to be able to describe the person at the time they would have known him or her."

"Tell me what you need, and I'll have them copied."

"That'd be a help. By the way, where's the kid?"

"With my mother-in-law. We couldn't really talk openly with him around. Why don't we go back to the living room? It shouldn't be much longer."

Sarah joined the detective on the couch this time.

Progress, he thought.

Carson withdrew a notepad from his briefcase and said, "Okay, then. I'm going to go down the list of the people I saw in the pictures. I want you to tell me what they do. It gives me a better idea of how to deal with them."

"But you didn't see everyone. There are friends who are as close as family that we didn't look at."

"We'll get to them. I'd rather cover the family first."

"Fire away."

"Tristan Maes."

"Architect." She hesitated then asked, "Is that what you mean?"

"That's fine. Past accomplishments?"

"I could give you a list of architectural awards…."

"Nah, that's good. How about past problems?"

She shuffled some magazines on the coffee table.

"Nothing that pertains to Daniel's situation regarding the journals."

A little red flag went up in Carson's head. He tucked it into a corner for future inquiry.

Enough with that line of questioning. She's gonna become uncooperative if I press her.

"Why don't we stick with occupations," he suggested. "Vaughn Maes."

"Homemaker and artist."

"What kind of art?"

"Painting and sculpture."

"Will Maes."

"Vet student."

"Katie Maes."

"High school student."

"Maxwell Nash."

"Psychiatrist."

"Lillian Nash."

"Homemaker."

"Sarah Nash."

She seemed to struggle to formulate a description. They heard the garage door mechanism grind. A car door slammed; then the kitchen door opened and closed. Daniel entered the living room still carrying his briefcase and a half-finished Coke.

"Carson Zerangue?"

"The one and only."

Daniel stooped low, put his left arm around his wife, and kissed her tenderly, first on the lips and then on the forehead. The kitchen timer began to beep, and Sarah hurried off in that direction saying, "There's the breadsticks. If you want to freshen up…?"

"That'd be nice," Carson said.

"It's the first door to your right. Your plate will be ready by the time you're done."

He came to the table and found his place at one end. The plate was loaded with lasagna, breadsticks, and some sort of marinated vegetable salad.

"Mm. Looks delicious. Italian food's my favorite."

"Sarah loves to cook," Daniel informed him. "Lucky for me since I can't even boil water properly."

"*Bon*!" the detective exclaimed, after taking a bite of the lasagna. "I'm not used to *home-cooked* food that tastes like this. Fast food or frozen dinners is my usual fare. I'm no chef."

"I'm very blessed," Daniel put in. "Although maybe I wouldn't have to work out so much if she were terrible in the kitchen."

"How long have you two been together?"

"Together?" Daniel contemplated the question as he broke off a piece of his breadstick then finally answered, "About a quarter of a century. Married? About ten years."

"You want to tell me the specifics of why you need my services?"

"If you don't mind, I'd rather wait until after we've eaten."

"After dinner's good," Carson agreed. "You mind if we stay at the table? I see that your wife's made coffee. I'd love some, but I can't juggle coffee and the notepad at the same time."

"Fine by me."

So, they sat at the table with their coffee. Carson retrieved his pen and notepad and started to scribble even before he began asking questions.

"Why am I here?"

Daniel took a sip from his steaming cup then replaced it on the saucer and said slowly, "I…want you to find out where I came from and the story of my past."

"How come you don't know it yourself? Or, rather, tell me what you do know."

"I find that I don't know much anymore. Up until last month, I can tell you what I thought I knew."

"Start at the beginning."

"I was born on March 12, 1958. I thought my father was Zachary Samuels. My mother was Assumpta Samuels."

"Where were you born?"

"Baton Rouge."

"Which hospital?"

"I've no idea."

"Where did you live in the city?"

"I don't remember the exact street address. I've never had a desire to go back. Sarah's father or Jamie Nesser, a friend of ours, could tell you. The place was Sammy's Bar downtown. My parents and I lived upstairs."

"Were your parents from Baton Rouge?"

"My mother was from Echo, Louisiana. To my knowledge, her father was her only other living relative. He died a couple of years before she did. Thanks," Daniel said to his wife, as she refilled his already empty cup. "Anyway, Samuels was from Baton Rouge. He never mentioned any relatives."

"When did your mother die?"

"1968."

"Cause of death?"

"Peritonitis."

"Caused by what?"

Raking his fingers through his graying black hair, Daniel said, "Undetermined causes, according to the hospital."

"And according to you?"

"Samuels beat her regularly. I'm certain that the lethal internal infection was a result of one of his attacks."

"Did he assault you?"

"Not until after she died."

"How soon after?"

Silence.

"How soon?" he persisted.

"The next day."

His expression unchanged, Carson jotted down a series of notes before asking, "How long did it continue?"

"Until I was twelve."

"What happened then?"

"He beat me worse than he'd ever beaten me before."

"So, you called for help?"

"Actually, no. I showed up a couple of miles away dazed and bleeding at Sarah's house. Tristan and Jamie did what they could for me while the ambulance was on its way. Then the paramedics took me to the hospital where the doctors performed emergency surgery. They didn't expect me to live."

"Let me back up here. How'd you know Sarah and her father?"

"I had met them downtown earlier that summer. Tristan knew I was being abused. He was trying to get someone to remove me from the apartment, but no one was listening. He'd given me his address in case I ever needed a safe place to go."

"So, you're at the hospital, and you survive. What then?"

"Tristan and Jamie knew Max and Lillian. Max had helped Tristan and Jamie before, so they asked him to help with me. Lillian was Max's housekeeper at the time. They weren't involved romantically at that point. She came to the hospital to do what she could and ended up petitioning to adopt me. She said she knew that God had sent me to her."

"You sound doubtful."

"Lillian is a devout Catholic. Max was too. Sarah and I were both raised Catholic, but I'm really an atheist and she's an agnostic. We've remained members of the Catholic faith because of our families and so our son will have some sort of religious background."

"I see." The investigator scribbled more notes then continued, "After you went home with Max and Lillian, what then?"

"Samuels had been arrested and had surrendered all of his parental rights. Max and Lillian decided to get married and adopt me. I started school at St. Aloysius. I got better. It all took some time."

"And then?"

"I went on to Redemptorist High. Afterwards, I got my Bachelor's in Economics at LSU. I started working for a local bank. After Sarah graduated from college, she and I got married and eventually had Kris. I got my M.B.A. I work in financial services and love my job. Things were going all right until the beginning of November."

"Elmo explained that some important journals Max Nash had left for you were destroyed in a fire. He said you've had a rough six weeks or so."

"We've been through a lot. Sarah lost her new job recently. That's opened a whole other can of worms. It was blatant discrimination against someone who's visually impaired."

I knew it, Carson said to himself.

Turning to Sarah, he asked, "What's your condition called?"

"Stargardt's. I don't have central vision. Everything in the center is sparkly. It's a form of macular degeneration."

"My mother had the age-related kind," the detective told her. "You seem to have adapted better than she did." He returned to his notes and prompted Daniel, "What happened after the firing?"

"Sarah hurt her arm then re-injured it on Thanksgiving Day. That night, Max died. The night of the funeral I found out from Lillian that Max was my biological father."

Carson laid down his pen and asked, "How in the flaming *hell* did that happen?"

"Seems a little far-fetched, huh?" Daniel said soberly. "Unfortunately, it's not."

Chapter Three: To Tell the Truth

"So, your adoptive father was also your biological father?" Carson said. "And you had no idea until after he was dead?"

"None. According to Lillian, after Max's first wife died of some immune system disorder, he was devastated. He turned into more of a workaholic than he'd been before. On top of his private practice, he accepted a friend's offer to teach some classes at LSU. The workload proved to be too much, even for him. The friend, who was the head of the department, set it up so Max would have a student assistant. He ended up with a girl named Tessa Downey."

"Not Assumpta?"

"No. My mom went by Tessa then, I guess. For whatever reasons, they got involved emotionally and sexually."

"How old was your father?"

"Forties." He paused and said, "From what I know, sleeping with a college student wasn't typical behavior for Max. He was always a very ethical person. Lillian considered it an error in judgment, especially for that time period. You know, people would have been even less accepting of any sexual relationship outside of marriage, much less one between an older man and a college girl."

"More of an error in judgment than a professional white man marrying a black housekeeper in Southern Louisiana ten years later?"

Daniel grinned and remarked, "It's all relative, isn't it?"

Carson grinned back and said, "Extremely. So, Max and Tessa are having this illicit relationship. How long did it take her to get pregnant?"

"I think Lillian said they'd been together for about six months or so when Max came home from some conference and found the letter from Tessa telling him that she was pregnant and that she didn't want to ruin his life with the scandal. He tried to find her but lost hope after two years."

"How'd he find out in the end that you were his kid?"

"It was after I was living with him and Lillian. I'd never known why my mother died; no one had ever told me. He was checking into it at my request. Some medical professional he'd contacted happened to read him the full name on the records. It didn't take much for him to piece it all together – my date of birth, the use of her given name, and the fact that she'd married soon after he came home to find her gone. I guess he could imagine what had happened and why he hadn't been able to locate her."

"It must have been a crushing blow to know that he'd been living in the same area and had never been able to find you."

"Lillian said it was. He didn't say anything to her until after they were married. She says nobody else knew about it, not even Isabelle."

"Isabelle?"

"Dr. Isabelle Elenstraub. She and my dad were friends and colleagues for half a century. Lillian said that was probably the only thing Isabelle never knew about my father." He rose and refilled Zerangue's empty mug and confided, "I'm sure it was a worse thing for Max to know what kind of existence Mom and I had endured and what kind of life we could have had if my mother hadn't run away. She would've been alive, and I'd have been whole and functional."

"You seem functional now."

"Thanks. I have a wonderful wife, a great kid, caring family and friends, and a job I enjoy. That doesn't mean I don't have some serious shit going on in my head all the time. Hell, I don't even remember a lot of my childhood. My greatest revenge against Samuels is that I didn't grow up to be an abuser."

"From what I've seen over the last thirty years, that's an outstanding accomplishment in and of itself. How's the day-to-day stuff?"

"I've got a lot of emotional baggage. That's why figuring out this mystery is so important to me. If I could let go of even some of it…."

Carson nodded to himself and said, "Let me tell you the direction I'd like to take with this investigation. First, if Sarah wouldn't mind compiling a list of the names and addresses of all the people we've spoken about tonight, then that would be a great start. Add to it anyone either of you can think of who might have any information about Maxwell Nash or his past. I'm going to do some checking at the records office Monday and get back with you about the list. Then, I'll begin to interview the people and see what kind of responses I get. That may lead to something. We'll see how things go. I want to be as thorough as possible for you. Let me know if you stumble across anything else. I'll give you my cell number."

"Sounds good."

"One more question. Do you know why Dr. Nash never mentioned any of this to you before he died?"

Wordlessly, Daniel went to his briefcase and removed the envelope containing his father's letter. He passed it to Zerangue, who removed it and read it carefully. The detective let out a long, low whistle.

"I'd like to read the journals you do have if that's okay."

"I don't care. I don't know that there's a lot we need to know about before 1940. Max was pretty thorough."

"I'm not doubting his ability to write it all down. It might give me a clue as to anyone else I should interview or what other places I might want to investigate."

"We'll give you whatever we can. I want to know the story of my parents' relationship and why my mother married that son-of-a-bitch Samuels."

Carson slipped the pen into his shirt pocket, then pulled it back out, and asked, "Do you know your father's birthdate?"

"April 12, 1912."

"And your mother's?"

"I – I'm not sure."

"And the date of her death?"

"December 19, 1968. Next week, it will be twenty-seven years."

"Just in time for Christmas," the private investigator muttered and folded the top of the notepad over. "It's no wonder that you're an –"

The phone rang. Sarah moved across to the wall phone and answered, "Hey, Lillian. Oh. How high? Oh, great. You don't mind? Thanks." Replacing the receiver, she sighed and said, "Kris is running fever. It's not high, only ninety-nine point five, but you know how that goes. Lillian's bringing him home."

"He's prone to chest infections," Daniel explained. "Sometimes, his fever spikes."

"I'll be getting on then. We'll talk next week."

"Thanks, Mr. Zerangue."

"You'd better get used to calling me Carson." Taking his cup of cold coffee to the sink, he added, "As for the work, it's what I do. I like to do it. It's interesting, and it helps people. It's good when you can have both in your career."

Daniel and Sarah stood outside in the frigid night air and waved goodbye to Carson Zerangue. As his taillights faded down the street, Lillian's champagne-colored Camry came into view. She pulled up into the driveway, and Sarah hurried to get a blanket, while Daniel unbuckled their sleeping son and carried him inside. Lillian locked the car doors and followed.

"Do you need me to stay? I would have kept him at my house, but I have the Catholic Daughters meeting I'm hosting in the morning. I can cancel it."

"It's only a slight fever," Daniel said. "We'll give him some medicine and some Children's Tylenol, and I'm sure it'll be fine. You go home and get ready for your company tomorrow."

"You let me know if he gets worse."

"We will," Sarah called out softly from down the hallway. "You go home and get some sleep."

"Only if you're sure." She brushed a piece of thread from Daniel's sleeve and asked, "How was the man?"

"I liked him," Daniel admitted. "He'll be starting on the case right away."

"Good."

She walked to Kris's room. The child was already dressed in his pajamas and was sleeping in his bed. Kissing him lightly, she repeated to her daughter-in-law, "Call me if anything changes."

Once Daniel had shut the door behind Lillian, he locked it and went to his son's room.

"Is his fever still the same?"

"Yes, thank goodness. Maybe we'll luck out this time. He hasn't been sick in five months. I hope this is as mild as it looks."

As if in response, Kris coughed several times. Dismayed, Sarah said, "I hate to wake him, but we should try and get the medicine into his system."

Their son half-woke at his parents' gentle insistence.

"Here, Sweet Pea," Sarah crooned. "This will make you feel better. Take a sip of the water to wash it down."

He did as he was told then lay back against his pillow.

"Daddy, are you scared?" He asked drowsily.

Concerned, Daniel placed a hand on his son's forehead to see if his fever had risen that quickly. The boy continued to feel only moderately warm.

"Scared of what?"

"Scared of your first daddy."

Daniel's breath caught in his throat. Kris had always believed that Max and Lillian were Daniel's only parents, and he and Sarah had not thought it necessary to enlighten him until he was older.

"What do you mean, Kris?"

"Grandma Lillian and I were talking about swimming, 'cause Amanda goes to a pool in her own backyard. Amanda says her daddy doesn't wear a shirt in the water. I asked Grandma how come you never take your shirt off, and she said that you had another daddy before Grandpa Max and that he hurt you a lot. Will he come and hurt me, too?"

Lowering himself onto the edge of the bed, Daniel said soothingly, "Never, Kris. He wasn't my real daddy, and I haven't talked to him in over twenty years."

"Why did he hurt you?"

"Because he was a very bad man."

"You would never hurt me, would you?"

Daniel swallowed the lump in his throat that threatened to choke him. He was trying rather unsuccessfully to swallow the anger that was about to render him speechless.

"Never, ever."

"Is it really terrible on your tummy? Is that why you don't want people to see?" Kris persisted. "Does it still have pain?"

"If I don't exercise, then my body hurts. I have scars, like when you cut your lip and it made a scar. Understand?"

"Can I see your scars?"

"Maybe when you're older."

"Did you cry when you got hurt?"

"Yes, I did."

Kris pulled the covers up around his neck and asked, "Will you and Mommy stay with me until I go to sleep?"

"Sure."

"Are the windows and the doors locked?"

"Yes," Daniel said firmly. "You're perfectly safe."

The combination of the decongestant and the Tylenol took effect within minutes. The moment Daniel was certain Kris was sleeping, he leapt from the bed and stalked towards the front of the house. Sarah darted out after him, moving quickly but quietly in an attempt to keep up with her husband.

"Daniel, wait!"

"I'll be at Lillian's."

He hadn't been this enraged about anything since he'd been a child. He drove too quickly and too recklessly all the way to the house. Screeching to a halt in the driveway, Daniel threw the car into Park and wrenched the key from the ignition. Jumping out, he slammed the car door behind him and stormed to the back door.

In his anger, it took him three tries to insert the key into the keyhole. Finally, he unlocked the door and charged into the kitchen, just as Lillian flicked on the lights.

"Daniel! What on earth?"

"Why did you do it?" he cried, as tears of frustration and rage welled up in his eyes. "You had no right to tell Kris about my scars!"

Lillian asked calmly, "What was I supposed to do? Lie? I thought you were upset that we lied to you before."

"He's five years old! He's too young to even comprehend what happened and why!"

"You tell me what I could have said," she retorted belligerently.

Daniel was dumbfounded. This was not his mother talking. This was insanity.

"You could have told him that I get sunburned easily on my shoulders," he replied evenly. "You could have told him that everybody has a different way of doing things."

"That wouldn't be the truth."

"Goddamn motherfucking son of a bitch! Do you remember what the truth is, Lillian?" His fingers tore at the buttons of his shirt. "Do you?"

"Daniel! Don't you use language like that! Don't you take the Lord's name in vain!"

Flinging his shirtfront wide, Daniel yelled, "Do you remember this, *Mom*? You think Kris needs to know about this kind of horror and fear at his age? Damn you for taking his sense of security away!"

He ran from the house, his shirt unbuttoned, his feet thudding on the concrete steps. When he got to the Mazda, he roughly twisted the key in the ignition then sped back down the long drive that extended to Highland Road. A half a mile away, he pulled into the empty parking lot of the Victorian Doll Mansion and shut off the engine. Then, he pounded the steering wheel until the side of his hand throbbed. Finally, raw and shaken, Daniel drove home.

Sarah hovered in the doorway as he pulled into the garage. Daniel wanted to tell her what Lillian had said. His lips parted, but Sarah placed her hand over his mouth and silenced him before he could begin.

"Don't," she whispered. "I called Lillian. She was extremely curt about the whole thing. Something's not right."

"How could she?" he groaned, as his wife took his hand and pulled him through the house and into their bedroom. "What could have possessed her?"

"Maybe it's Max's death and the fact that she's all alone in that house."

"You don't believe that any more than I do."

"No," she admitted. "Maybe she's gone crazy with grief."

"Possible, but not likely."

"She could be trying to teach you some sort of a lesson."

"Like this? She's always been firm but unfailingly kind."

"I know it's ridiculous. I'm at a loss for an explanation. Could it be something medical? Maybe she had a stroke or something?"

"She's not slurring her words or anything like you see on TV. It has to be something else." He rubbed gingerly at the sore side of his hand and asked, "How is Kris?"

"Sleeping comfortably. No more fever."

His wife eased off his shirt and placed her hands on his shoulders. She began to knead the knotted muscles. Daniel stood still and tried not to think about the episode with his mother.

"It's no use! I can't get it out of my head." He slipped off his shoes then absently unbuckled his belt and let his pants fall to the floor. "Maybe she *is* losing it," he muttered, as he strode into the bathroom and jerked the blue toothbrush from the holder. As he unscrewed the top of the tube of toothpaste, he added, "I wonder what else she's said to Kris."

"I was thinking the same thing while you were gone," his wife confided, as she donned an old-fashioned cotton nightgown that was accented throughout with delicate lace. She began to brush her hair; then she stopped and said, "I think we've done an excellent job of giving Kris that 'normal' life that we never had when we were kids. What if she goes into detail about you and the abuse? What if she tells him about Daddy's problems? There are so many issues she could bring up."

"Jesus H. Christ," Daniel swore softly. "This is a nightmare."

Sarah got two tissues and returned to the bedroom to stuff them under her pillow should she need them later. Then she came back to the bathroom to brush her teeth, while Daniel slipped into a t-shirt and boxer shorts.

When she climbed into bed, Daniel was already tossing and turning in agitation. Propping herself up on one elbow, Sarah laid a soft palm on her husband's chest.

"Tomorrow we can call Isabelle. She's an M.D. She can go see Lillian and give us some input," Sarah suggested. "We can take it from there."

She slid her hand down and then up under the t-shirt he wore. Rubbing in a circular motion, Sarah lowered her head and kissed her husband on the jaw.

"Take off your shirt," she commanded.

Daniel wearily shut his eyes.

"For once in my life, I don't feel like sex."

"Let it go, Daniel. You're always in charge when we're in bed, which is fine. You know I like it that way. Will you do as I say this time, since I'm asking?"

Crossing his arms, he reached down, grabbed the edge of his shirt, and pulled it up and over his head. As he did so, Sarah pushed back the covers, got out of bed, and removed a box of matches from the top dresser drawer. She lit the candle that rested on top of the bureau.

Moving around to the other side of the bed, Sarah knelt on the mattress and tenderly kissed the few small, round burn marks on the upper part of Daniel's back. Then she crawled over him and sat looking down at her husband in the flicker of the candlelight.

"Sarah –"

"Shhh." She bent forward and began to stroke the scars on his torso with her fingers, her lips, and her tongue and murmured, "Be quiet now."

There were so many lines, some pink and some red, some raised and some flush with the rest of his skin. Daniel collected some of Sarah's curls in his hands as she continued her ministrations. Slowly, they both began to unwind.

Once she'd doctored every scar, Sarah lay with her head in the crook of Daniel's arm. He pulled her small body closer against him and murmured, "That was nice. Different without the sex, but nice."

"It's so cozy like this."

"You stay here. I'll check on Kris, let Ralph in, and blow out the candle."

He rose and walked in the chill of the house to his son's room. The child didn't appear to have a fever at all. Relieved, Daniel straightened the covers; then he went to the kitchen to open and close the door for Ralph before locking the deadbolt. The Labrador wanted to play, so Daniel pulled his rope toy for a few minutes before returning to the master bedroom. There, he blew out the candle and washed the dog slobber off his hands before returning to bed. Then he kissed his sleeping wife and drifted off into the bliss of nocturnal oblivion.

"Daddy? Daddy?"

Daniel came to in a panic. He had done on that night what he'd not done in over five years. He had forgotten to put his shirt back on before he went to sleep. The one night that Kris had been so concerned about his father's scars….

"What is it, Kris?" Daniel groped around in a fruitless search for his shirt and asked, "Is something wrong?" The cotton teased his fingertips, and he snatched at the shirt and thrust his arms into it as he persisted, "Are you okay?"

His son held up a stuffed dog and announced, "Elliot's hungry."

He wasn't awake, Daniel realized with a jolt.

"Why don't you let me take you back to bed; then you and Elliot can eat a big breakfast soon?"

Without another word, the child wandered out of the room and returned to his bed. Daniel followed after a few seconds to make certain that the boy was actually asleep. He was. Mercifully, there was still no fever. Daniel tucked Elliot under the boy's arm and went back to his room.

"Is he all right?" Sarah whispered, as her husband wormed his way under the covers once more. She was facing away from him and hadn't stirred throughout his exchange with Kris.

"I didn't think you were awake."

He slipped his arm around her and brought his knees up so that his cool thighs rested underneath the warm flesh on the back of her legs. Drawing in the faint rose scent that clung to her skin, Daniel tried to think of anything except how close he'd come to having Kris see his naked chest.

"You know what a light sleeper I am," she said quietly. "I could tell by the way Kris was talking that he wasn't awake. I figured if I stayed down, he might go back to sleep."

"He did. No fever."

Sarah reached around and laid her left hand on his leg.

"Relax. He won't remember getting up or seeing you like that."

He knew that his wife was right, but Daniel lay awake for the remainder of the night and wondered if he would ever be able to relax again.

Chapter Four: For Every Action...

Slightly before 7:00 p.m. the following Monday, Dr. Isabelle Elenstraub stood on Sarah and Daniel's front porch. When she rang the doorbell, Ralph began to bark excitedly. Kris's delighted face appeared in the window before he flung open the door.

"Aunt Isabelle!"

He threw his small arms around her, as Ralph danced in circles in the living room. The house smelled deliciously like warm bread and cheese.

"Hello, Kris," Isabelle greeted him in her thick German accent. "It is so good to see you." Reaching down to pat the dog on the snout, she added, "You, too, you rapscallion. Come, I will give you your treats."

"He won't leave you alone until you do," Sarah remarked, poking her head through the kitchen doorway. "I don't know what it is about you. He doesn't expect treats from other visitors."

"I am special."

"Yes, you are." Lowering a bowl of salad onto the counter, Sarah gave the elderly woman a hug and added, "Happy holidays."

"And to you."

Heading toward the pantry, the psychiatrist retrieved a box of dog treats and withdrew two biscuits.

"Sit, Ralph."

The dog's rump went down, and she passed him first one treat and then another.

"Good dog!" Kris applauded.

"Hello, Isabelle."

"Daniel," she beamed, as he came across the room. "How magnificent to see you!"

"I'm really glad you could come." As he leaned down to hug the diminutive therapist, he whispered in her ear, "How was it?"

"Patience," she whispered back before releasing him.

"Mommy made crawfish cheese bread," Kris announced excitedly. "After dinner, we're going to decorate the Christmas tree!"

"Being Jewish, I have never decorated a Christmas tree," the older woman confided. "It sounds lovely."

"Normally, we put up the tree right after Thanksgiving and decorate it immediately, but we couldn't this year because of…because of Max's death," Sarah admitted. "It felt so odd."

"Next year," Isabelle said encouragingly, as she patted her lightly on the back. "But doesn't the tree die if you put it up at Thanksgiving?"

"It's not a live tree. Kris has a lot of allergies, so we bought the artificial one four years ago. It's held up well."

"It looks real!" exclaimed the little boy.

"I cannot wait to see."

A half hour after dinner, the decorating began. The carefully packed ornaments were gingerly unrolled from their tissue paper cocoons. When all of the lights and baubles had been hung, Daniel accepted the delicate angel from Sarah and lowered it onto the top of the tree.

"Are you ready?" he asked dramatically.

Suddenly, the room was blazing with the sparkle of white lights, sheer gold bows, and brilliantly illuminated ornaments. Sarah spread the tree skirt around the stand then proceeded to pick up the loose tissue paper that littered the floor. Within minutes, the storage boxes had been taken back up to the attic.

"Did you like it, Aunt Isabelle?" asked the little boy.

"That was beautiful," she assured him. "Thank you for letting me share the experience with you." She lifted her large purse and rummaged around in its fathomless depths before withdrawing two articles and stating, "This is for you, and this is for your parents."

Kris accepted the two small boxes and ran to his mother, who said, "You so didn't have to do this."

"I wanted to. Humor me."

Kris painstakingly peeled the tape from his box. When the paper had been pulled off, he removed the lid and cried, "Money! And a train! Look, Mommy! Daddy, it's a train!"

Sarah removed the fifty-dollar bill then eased the porcelain Lennox train ornament from the foam.

"Really, Isabelle. Whatever possessed you?"

The woman merely smiled and asked Kris, "Where on the tree would you like to hang the ornament?"

"Where everybody can see it the best! The middle!"

"What do you say to Aunt Isabelle?" Daniel prompted.

"Thank you!"

"You're quite welcome."

"Open the other one, Daddy!"

Smiling slightly, Daniel took the package from his wife's hand and tore at the wrapping with exaggerated gusto. Kris giggled at his antics and hopped from one foot to the other in anticipation of what might lay within.

Inside there was a small card that had been inscribed in a florid script.

Mr. and Mrs. Daniel Nash have been invited to spend a weekend at Butler Greenwood Plantation, St. Francisville, LA.

Call us to make your reservation.

Must be used by December 31, 1995.

"It's too much!" Sarah protested.

"Way too much," Daniel concurred.

"Nonsense. What else should I do with my time and money? I have few living relatives, no children, and no grandchildren. I don't even have a cat. I decided that life was too short not to use what God has given me to bring joy to others. If anyone deserves some quiet time away, it is the two of you. You have always given very thoughtful gifts to me each Hanukkah. Make me happy and simply say thank you. No arguments, please."

"Thank you," they said in unison.

"Wonderful. You must swear to me that you will use it before it expires."

"We will," Sarah promised. "You know, we've never been to St. Francisville? Isn't that a shame? We're only forty-five minutes from there and we've never been."

"It is lovely," commented Isabelle.

"Oh, there's one box I forgot," Daniel mumbled, going back to the garage as the women continued their conversation.

"I'm glad that you were here for the tree putting up, Aunt Isabelle," Kris interrupted. "I know that you don't believe in Jesus, but you said you liked it anyway."

"Who said that Aunt Isabelle doesn't believe in Jesus?" Sarah asked nervously.

The child squeezed his eyes tightly closed as he tried to remember exactly what it was he'd heard.

"Aunt Isabelle is Jewish, so she believes that Jesus was a good man, but not as good as some people think." Kris opened his eyes, looked directly at his mother, and said, "It's *Daddy* who doesn't believe in Jesus."

Daniel stopped in the dining area. Ironically, he was holding a box marked "Nativity Scene" in bright blue marker. Carefully placing the box on the floor, he asked, "Who told you that I didn't believe in Jesus?"

"Grandma Lillian," the boy replied matter-of-factly.

"Grandma Lillian is wrong!" he growled.

"Daniel –" Sarah began.

"Well, she is! Kris, Jesus lived almost two thousand years ago, and he changed the world. That's a fact. How could I not believe he existed?"

Confused, the child chewed on his lower lip and twisted a piece of string that was dangling from his shirt.

"But why would she say it if it wasn't true?"

"Once in a while older people are forgetful or mixed up about things," the psychiatrist interjected, as she took the little boy's hand. "Would you do me a great favor and show me your room? My husband and I were never blessed with children, and I always enjoy seeing a room filled with toys and books."

"I have a fish of my own in there!" he announced and proceeded to lead her down the hallway.

Daniel went out the back door and stood on the porch. Sarah counted to ten and then counted ten more. Then she went out after him.

He was leaning against one of the posts, his arms crossed, one hand tucked tightly under each armpit.

"I keep thinking this can't get any worse," he told his wife.

"Things can always be worse, but they could certainly be much better," she conceded.

There was a light tapping on the screen door behind them.

"Kris has fallen asleep on the floor," Isabelle said as she emerged from the house. "One minute, he was showing me his book on the time of the dinosaurs. The next minute, he was sleeping."

"Isabelle, what's going on with Lillian?" Daniel asked. "Is she losing it?"

"I am more inclined to think that there is a medical cause behind this erratic behavior. She was not quite herself when we had dinner last night. She was the one who introduced the topic of your altercation, and she spoke plainly of how right she was and how wrong you were. It was very disturbing."

"What kind of medical cause?" Sarah asked. "She's only sixty. Look at you. You're in your eighties, and you're spectacular."

"How gratifying to hear that! How wonderful to have such a compliment, considering that I am shrinking more and more each year. If I live to be one hundred, I will be three feet tall."

"Even if you were, you'd still be splendid."

"Thank you, Child." Sobering, she shifted her attention back to Daniel and said, "Your mother needs to be examined by a physician. I do not think it is Alzheimer's or senility. However, her perception of acceptable boundaries has been altered."

"What would cause that?"

"Several things. It could be a chemical imbalance or a hormonal one. A tumor is a possibility, although I find that an unlikely scenario." She lowered herself onto the weathered porch swing and said, "More than likely, she has had a slight stroke."

Daniel looked at his wife, who looked away.

"Sarah suggested that to me Friday, but Lillian's always been healthy as a horse. I'd never suspect stroke." He eyed the doctor suspiciously and asked, "What made you consider it?"

"Your father used to lay out her blood pressure medication every night before bedtime. He is gone, so I wonder if she is not taking it regularly anymore." When Daniel appeared startled, she asked, "You did not know?"

He shook his head and clamped his lips together tightly.

"How long has she had high blood pressure?" Sarah asked in a small voice.

"Four years. No, maybe three."

Daniel gripped the cold post with his fingers and absently pondered whether or not the numbness in his digits was due to the icy metal or the shock of Isabelle's disclosure.

"What else haven't they told me? And how can we make her go to the doctor? What are we supposed to do? Should we tell her that she needs to take her pills and that we think she might have had a stroke?" He slapped his palm hard against the pole in frustration. "When could she have had this stroke? Friday when Kris was with her? A month ago?"

"In the first place, *you* do not tell her anything. Your emotions are much too near the surface on this. You came close to being explosive only minutes ago."

Daniel continued to stare into the gloom of the evening, but the muscles in his neck tensed visibly and his shoulders stiffened.

"I commend your ability to control what must be an overwhelming urge to perform some act of verbal or physical violence. However, I worry that you will not be able to keep your strength up should this drag on or should you have another face to face confrontation with your mother."

"I'm dealing with things just fine."

"Truly? I saw the way you looked at your son when he was twirling the stray piece of thread in his fingertips. For an instant, you saw yourself as a boy, yes? And what was your first impulse?"

"It was fear," Sarah breathed. "He wanted to make Kris stop."

Daniel gently took his wife by the shoulders and asked, "How'd you know that?"

"Because I felt it, too."

"There is no need for either of you to have this fear," the woman insisted. "As a child, Daniel had a propensity for fidgeting and focusing on things such as shoelaces, bits of string, or various miscellany in order to redirect his attention from whatever negative thoughts or feelings he might be experiencing. What Kris was doing tonight was not an anxious reaction to your demand. He was absently fiddling with the thread, nothing more."

Daniel replayed Kris's stance and attitude in his mind. He nodded quickly then said, "I'll accept that. What about Lillian? If I can't talk to her, will you?"

"I was thinking more along the lines of Tristan."

"Daddy?" Sarah broke away from her husband and sat on the swing next to Isabelle. "But why?"

"Call it intuition. If it works, call it good psychiatry. I will telephone your father when I return home tonight. The sooner Lillian is examined by her physician, the better." Although she touched Sarah's hand, it was Daniel she addressed next. "May I inquire as to why you asked whether or not Lillian could have suffered the stroke or whatever it was a month ago? Was there an episode then as well?"

Sitting heavily in the rocker, Daniel said, "Something she told me the night of Max's funeral. I accepted it completely when she said it. Now, I'm wondering if it's all made up."

"Daniel, you can't be serious," Sarah declared. "After the letter?"

"The letter doesn't substantiate all of Lillian's claims."

"But what else could it be?"

The therapist stood abruptly and stated, "I am lost. What letter? What claims?"

An owl hooted from the back of the yard in the ensuing silence. Ralph rapped on the bottom of the screen door with his paw and was let out. A slight breeze blew up and stirred the wind chimes Daniel had given Sarah for her last birthday, right before their stable life had begun to disintegrate.

"Lillian told me the night of the funeral that she'd had a husband and daughter who died before she accepted the job as Max's housekeeper. She also told me that Max was not only my adoptive father but was also my biological father. I know you're going to say that it's crazy, but it's not. She said Max had left me an explanation and that she didn't know anything except the bare essentials of the story. But it fit, Isabelle. It fit with my mother and the times and –"

"I do not doubt that she told you the truth," Isabelle replied, distractedly resuming her seat next to Sarah. "I do not doubt it at all."

Daniel jerked back as if he'd been stuck with a hot poker. "You…knew?"

"I did not know that Max was your biological father. I did sense that something was terribly wrong way back when, but I did not know exactly what it was at the time." She cocked her head and stared blindly into the darkness, as if she were calculating something in her mind then said, "It was 1957. You were born in 1958, were you not? I do not understand. It would not be like Max to let his child…and to let you be hurt like that?"

"According to Lillian, he didn't uncover the truth until I was already living with them."

"But how? How did your mother…?"

Daniel took a deep breath and decided that he would have to be brief, at least for that night.

"Max was married before."

"Yes. Gwen and I were great friends. There was not a bad bone in that woman's body. She was a good wife and would have been a good mother, if she had been able to have a child. On her deathbed, she mentioned that as her only regret in life."

"I didn't even know Max was a widower."

"Gwen was his life. He became obsessed with his work after her death, even teaching classes at the university." Her eyes widened as realization dawned and she asked, "It was someone he met at the university?"

"My mother was evidently a student assigned to help him."

"But Max's student assistant was named…ah, Tabitha was it? And your mother, if I recall, had a very different sort of name."

"Max's assistant was called Tessa Downey."

"Yes, precisely!"

"And my mother's first name was Assumpta."

"Now I remember."

"She had a strong dislike for Assumpta. She and Max had this intense relationship. When she got pregnant, she left to avoid ruining his reputation."

"And went back to using her first name to avoid discovery," concluded Isabelle. "Oh, Daniel. How awful. And for her to marry that evil man on top of it all!"

Sarah pushed with her feet so that the swing went back and forth then said, "There's something I haven't understood in all of this. How could you not know, Isabelle? For years, you were Max's best friend and colleague. You saw him all the time. Wouldn't you have known?"

"My Jacob was beginning to have his heart troubles not long after Gwen died. I was rather preoccupied with my own concerns, and Max seemed so busy. I am afraid that I neglected our friendship and only saw Max at the office." She rubbed her hand against her head, as if to force her brain to decipher what she'd learned and then admitted, "I find it hard to accept that Max would have become sexually involved with a student. He was such a moral man. Having illicit relationships with young women was not – How do you say it? – his style, no matter what the circumstances."

Daniel contemplated exactly how much more he should say at this point.

"Max left me a bunch of journals to explain everything and why he didn't tell me once he found out who I really was."

"Marvelous. I would be curious to see them myself."

"I would be, too. I have the ones that range from 1912 to 1939. The rest were destroyed in a fire last week."

"No…no copies?" she stammered.

"None that I can find."

"What do you plan to do?"

"A private investigator is working on it as of Friday. I'd appreciate anything you can tell me or him."

"Of course. What do you need to know?"

"Everything. Anything. Whatever you can tell me about Max, Lillian, Gwen, Max's brother, my mother, Max's parents, his sister. Anything. Another perspective might be helpful."

"I still cannot believe it," confided the therapist. She rose and went over to where Daniel sat in the porch rocking chair and confided, "I did meet your mother once, shortly after Jacob began to have cardiac problems. She was a lovely girl, full of life and wit. I am sorry."

In a maternal gesture, she reached out and drew the backs of her fingers across the hair near his right temple.

"What was Max like as a young man?" Daniel asked quietly.

"He was much the same as he was in later life. He was dignified, brilliant, and caring. He was quite a handsome, strapping man. It wasn't until…well, now that I know, it wasn't until after the time that he knew your mother that he became rather portly. Even so, he never appeared overweight somehow, merely large."

"Is there more?"

"There is as much as you would like to know. I would be pleased to sit with you and reminisce about my friendship with Max. I have nothing to hide from you. It is your right to know about him." Laying a hand on his shoulder, she said, "But for now, I must go. I am an old woman, and I find myself exhausted by all of this. I have told you the pertinent facts that I can recall. I would be happy to tell you about it in much greater detail another time. Perhaps you can come and spend the day with me now and again, and I can prattle on about the good old days. You may find it useful and illuminating."

"I'd like that. Do you mind if the private investigator calls you? His name's Carson Zerangue."

"As I said before, I will tell him or you anything I can. Give him my number, by all means." She briefly enveloped Daniel in her thin, but surprisingly strong arms and said, "I will telephone Tristan when I return to my apartment. We will take care of things. You will see."

Chapter Five: To and Fro

Carson grumbled all the way down Third Street. It was cold. It was sleeting. His bursitis was acting up. There was less than a week until Christmas, and Tristan Maes was working late on the site of a building reconstruction that was part of the Downtown Redevelopment Project.

Carson arrived at the site entrance and peered through the icy rain in search of the man. It didn't take him long to spot Maes standing under an overhang on the front of the building. He had to be one of the tallest men the detective had ever seen outside of a professional basketball arena.

Tristan turned slightly and pointed out something to a man standing beside him. The man nodded and then walked in that direction, pulling up the collar of his windbreaker against the cold and damp. Tristan scanned the clipboard in his hand; then he made two tick marks. He was so intent on what he was doing that he was unaware of the detective's presence until the investigator came up alongside him.

"Tristan Maes? I'm Carson Zerangue. We spoke on the phone."

"Good to meet you," Tristan offered, as he lowered the clipboard and extended his hand. "I appreciate what you're doing for my kids." The architect grabbed an extra hard hat, passed it to Zerangue, and said, "We don't want anything to fall on your head. Put it on, and I'll take you someplace warm and dry."

"That a promise?"

"I even have some day-old coffee."

"Lead on."

He followed the man around various concrete beams and steel poles. They slipped through a side door into the shell of the building. Work lights were hung in strategic places to give off enough illumination for those passing through to see a few feet in front of them. Eventually, they arrived at a heavily carved door.

"Just let me leave this inside; then we can head for the trailer," Tristan told him.

The detective followed him into a partially completed room. A bulletin board was suspended on one wall. Tristan removed one of the sheets from the clipboard and tacked it on the left side of the bulletin board.

They re-emerged into the rain and hurried to the trailer. Both men peeled off their wet outer garments and hung them on a coat rack to steam near the heater.

"None of the comforts of home," Tristan said apologetically.

"Says who?" Carson asked, as he tossed his hat on a worn green chair. "I grew up in a trailer smaller than this one." He accepted the proffered mug of coffee and took a gulp before saying, "Mm. Just like Mom used to make."

"I'm so glad I could oblige." Tristan sat in the chair behind the desk and warmed his hands on his own mug then breathed, "It feels good to sit."

"Correct me if I'm wrong, but I thought architects drew up plans and gave contractors the work to do."

"Some do. I prefer a hands-on approach, especially with reconstruction where there are structural questions and design applications that have to be addressed on a daily basis."

"You usually work after 5:00 the week before Christmas?"

"I thought it might be better to meet here. My wife's parents are in for the holidays. The house is sort of packed with people, suitcases, and presents."

"They don't know about any of this?"

"My youngest child doesn't, no. My wife and her parents do. So does my son."

"Why not tell your daughter?"

"Katie can't keep a secret to save her life. She'd be the one to accidentally blurt everything out to my grandson."

"Your folks come for the holidays, too?"

"My folks have been dead since 1960."

The detective studied Maes as he took another gulp of his coffee. Sarah Nash had to be about thirty, so Tristan must be at least in his fifties. He didn't look it.

"I'm in my late forties," Tristan volunteered. "Sarah's in her early thirties."

"Young," Carson remarked, leaving it open as to whether or not he meant father, daughter, or both.

"Look, don't pussyfoot around. I want to cooperate with your investigation. If you want to ask me a question, just do it."

"I see where she gets it from."

"What?"

"Your daughter. She's damned direct."

"That she is."

Carson set the mug down and reached for his notepad and a pen.

"I know you want to get home. Then again, with your in-laws there, maybe you don't."

"I love my in-laws. Jim and Helen have had a farm in Mississippi for over forty years. They're great, loving people who've treated me like their son and Sarah like their granddaughter since I met and married Vaughn."

"Your daughter gave me a recent picture of them in the photos I asked for. They look like a nice, older, gray-haired couple. He's still in shape, probably from all those years of farming. Your mother-in-law's in pretty good shape as well."

"I want to get home to them and the rest of the family, but I believe in doing things right or not doing them at all. You and I can talk as long as you need."

"Then we ought to get along real well." The investigator scrawled the date and Tristan's name at the top of the sheet and then asked, "Would you give me some brief background info on yourself? Hit the highlights. Then we can move ahead to Dan Nash."

"I was an orphan at fourteen, married and a father by sixteen, widowed at twenty-three, graduated from college and re-married by twenty-five."

"Anything out-of-the-ordinary about your life?"

"You mean besides everything I've just told you? Jesus, you're good."

"I was with the N.O.P.D. for twenty years. It takes a lot to shake me up."

"Hm. Anything else unusual…." He paused then said, "Not that I can think of." He gave Carson a sardonic smile and then added, "Unless you take into account that I'm a recovering alcoholic and drug addict."

So that's what the daughter didn't want to tell me.

"How long you been clean?"

"Sixteen years."

"Any slip-ups?"

"That was the slip-up. I became an addict after my first wife died. That was how I met Max Nash."

"Tell me about that."

"I'd been using for a few months, going downhill fast. My best friend, Jamie, had been trying to get me to stop."

"Is that Jamie Nesser? He's on the list your daughter and son-in-law gave me."

"That's him. Anyway, one night Sarah called him. She was sick, and I was unconscious. I'd been drinking and using drugs and had overdosed. Jamie hurried to the house and got us help. He spent days at the hospital worrying that we wouldn't pull through. That's where he met Max."

"What was Dr. Nash doing there?"

"Meeting Isabelle Elenstraub for lunch."

"And?"

"Jamie was pretty desperate for help and spilled his guts to Max once he found out that Max was a psychiatrist. Max and Isabelle intervened and kept me and Sarah together, despite the Family Services people's attempts to take Sarah away from me. When Sarah and I got out of the hospital, we even lived with Max and Lillian for a couple of months. They became sort of surrogate parents to all of us."

"Did Dr. Nash ever talk with you about his past or Dan's paternity?"

"I'm sorry to say that I didn't really ask him much about his background. First he was my psychiatrist; then he became my friend. You got the impression that your life was more interesting than his was when you talked to him. He did tell Sarah once that he was from Cornwall, but that was about it."

"Lillian was the same way. It was as if they didn't have a life before they befriended us, and we were too wrapped up in the present to badger them for details about their pasts."

"Tell me about what Dan was like when you first ran into him."

"If you were N.O.P.D., then you've dealt with kids like him. The first time we saw him, he was cleaning out the backroom of his father's bar. There was a dark bruise on his cheek and fear in his eyes. The next time we passed by, his lip was split. I talked to Max about contacting Social Services. I didn't have the best relationship with them, as you can imagine. Before he could get any real response, Dan showed up at our house, beaten like nothing I'd ever seen."

"And afterwards? Once he recovered?"

"You know how kids are. Physically, he healed quickly, although I'm sure his scars were a constant reminder of his previous life. He still struggles with it emotionally every day. He's overcome a lot."

"So have you."

"One day at a time," Tristan said amiably. "I was drug and alcohol-free for nine years before I had a relapse. I don't take anything for granted. Once an addict, always an addict." He traced the rim of his mug with the tip of his middle finger. "Max was a great guy and a great psychiatrist. In large part, I owe him my sanity. But about this whole cover-up regarding Dan's past, I know nothing."

Carson stood and rubbed at his aching shoulder.

"You've helped a lot tonight, although I'm sure I'll have many more questions as this case progresses. If you think of anything, give me a call." He passed him a business card and added, "Sometimes, people recall minute details when they get to thinking about things."

"Have you talked with anyone else, yet?"

"Dr. Elenstraub. I got some solid dates, a tale of immigration, and another story of what a wonderful man Dr. Nash was. Elenstraub's husband was having cardiovascular problems at the time that Nash was sleeping with Miss Downey, so she was unaware of their relationship. She did have an encounter with the younger Mr. Nash's mother."

"She did?"

"Yeah. Not much to say there, except that it gives me another perspective on the woman and makes me more curious than ever to figure out what in the name of God happened. I may be calling you back off and on to substantiate facts."

"Anytime."

Carson slipped on his jacket and opened the door. Then he went out into what was now a light evening drizzle. He'd taken three steps away from the trailer when he decided to go back.

Tristan had risen and was sorting through some papers on the top of a filing cabinet. Surprised at the investigator's return, he came towards the door with the papers in hand.

"Did you forget something?"

"Yeah. I forgot to ask who it is that you don't want me talking to about this."

The papers *thwacked* the wood on the desk, as Tristan tossed them down and said, "Lillian Nash."

"Why not?"

"She's been behaving strangely since Friday. Isabelle thinks she might have had a slight stroke. What if it's true and she gives you unreliable information? Or what if she's volatile? She's definitely not herself from what Dan, Sarah, and Isabelle told me. If her blood pressure is giving her trouble…."

"That'll be up to me to sort out, won't it? I'm a private investigator, for Christ's sake. I don't take anything at face value. You think I'm going to believe anyone's story until I've checked it out? People lie or tell their own versions of the truth all the time. Plus, if I see the lady's getting upset, I'll back off. Give me some credit, will ya?"

"Fair enough. Anything else?"

"Can you tell me where in the hell Zachary Samuels's bar was? It would save me a lot of time."

"If you can wait for about ten minutes, I'll take you there."

Carson waited.

"Sammy's was closed down after Dan's father…uh, Zachary Samuels was arrested," Tristan told the detective as they crossed the street fifteen minutes later. "It was a restaurant for a while, but it got revamped into an adult bookstore. Here it is."

Carson splashed through a puddle and read the sign that had been painted on the window in yellow letters: *The People's Choice in Adult Materials.*

"I bet the other businesses in the neighborhood are thrilled."

"I don't think they have to be concerned." Tristan tapped lower on the glass and instructed, "Look."

Underneath the store name in smaller print was painted: *Open daily from 8 p.m.-5 a.m.*

"Whoa. Real high-class establishment. Too bad it'll be another hour before it opens."

A muffled ringing began to emanate from Maes's long, black overcoat. Reaching inside, he pulled out a cellphone and clicked it on. A faint voice, rapid and unintelligible, could be heard in the stillness of the street.

"No!" Tristan exclaimed.

The sharpness of his tone made Carson tense immediately. He watched the man listening to whoever was on the other end.

"Which one?" Tristan asked the mysterious caller. "I'll phone Jamie and meet you there."

Gesturing for the private investigator to follow him, Tristan took off in a trot back the way they'd come. Carson jogged after him. Without a word to the detective, Tristan cleared the screen, pressed a number, then put the phone back to his ear.

"Jamie, meet me at Our Lady of the Lake. Vaughn called and said that CoCo Genevieve went next door to take Lillian some Christmas cookies and found her unconscious in the garden. Yeah, I know. I was supposed to go to her place tonight to try and talk her into seeing a doctor." Drawing the phone away from his mouth, he said urgently to Zerangue, "That's my Cherokee near the corner. Damn! Where are my keys?"

When the alarm had been deactivated, the detective automatically pulled open the door on the passenger side and climbed in. He didn't know when he and Tristan Maes had arrived at the conclusion that he should come along to the hospital, but they were obviously in agreement on the subject.

As Tristan drove the Cherokee through the evening traffic, he said, "I was afraid something like this would happen."

"Not your fault, Mr. Maes," Carson said in a practical attempt at consoling the man.

"Look, call me Tristan. I know you're calling my son-in-law and daughter by their first names, so you might as well get used to doing it with all of us."

"Only if you do the same with me."

Tristan nodded. He parked in the Emergency Room lot, and the two men hurried inside. A receptionist informed them that Mrs. Nash was in Intensive Care and gave them directions. They walked down a long, white corridor that was accented by various pastel stripes. They emerged at a waiting room that was outlined in glass and bordered by a low wall filled with plants. Escalators ran down to the first floor.

"Can't anything ever be easy in these places?" Tristan groaned. "I thought she said we'd see the Critical Care Waiting Room in front of us when we came around. This is the waiting room for surgery. Did we take a wrong turn?"

"Not as far as I can tell."

Several unproductive turns later, they accidentally stumbled through the correct door. The enormous waiting room was crowded with people. One man snored loudly in a high-backed chair. A young girl lay listlessly across a loveseat. Clusters of men and women dotted the floor area. Some looked as if they'd been camped out for days. Newcomers sat in unwrinkled clothing.

There were two people huddled in the far right-hand corner of the room. Carson recognized the woman with the deep red hair as Vaughn Maes, Sarah's stepmother. The blonde man must be Jamie Nesser, Tristan's long-time best friend.

"How is she?" Tristan quietly asked his wife, as he drew up beside her.

Vaughn wiped at her eyes with a frayed tissue and shook her head.

Her husband put a long arm around her shoulders and asked again, "How's she doing?"

"We don't know," Jamie answered. "Sarah and Dan are in there with the doctors now."

"Where's Kris? Not here, I hope."

"He's at our house," Vaughn sniffed. "Mom said she would cook dinner with Katie. Dad and Will offered to stay and distract Kris."

"He knows?"

"He was playing in the backyard when CoCo's husband called. Dan didn't hear Kris come in while he was talking on the phone. Kris heard enough to know that Lillian is in the hospital. He's scared."

"I don't blame him. I'm scared, too."

"Who's your friend?" Jamie asked.

"Dan's P.I. Carson Zerangue, this is my wife, Vaughn, and my closest friend, Jamie. Carson's –"

"Daddy?"

They all turned to see Sarah standing in the doorway. It was then that Carson knew there was no hope for Lillian Nash.

Chapter Six: You Say Goodbye

Sarah came towards the little group and gave Tristan a tight hug. The detective marveled at how small the woman appeared when she stood beside her father. The top of her head barely reached his chest.

She wore jeans, a pink sweater, and a shell-shocked look that Carson recognized immediately as the reflection of bewilderment and hopelessness that comes with knowing nothing can be done but to wait for the inevitable. He wondered if she would tell the others how bad things were or if she would leave that up to the doctors or her husband.

Vaughn asked, "Will Lillian be okay?"

Sarah shoved her hands down into her pockets and looked out at the dark sky framed by the long row of windows. She shook her head.

"She…she won't?" Vaughn stammered.

"The doctors said she suffered a massive stroke. They did a CAT scan to confirm it. Her internist told us that there's no chance for recovery. She's…there's no brain activity. She'll never wake up."

The others were obviously stunned. But Carson wasn't stunned at all. His grandmother had died of a stroke twenty years before. He knew the drill.

"Where's Dan?" Jamie asked thickly.

"With her. Normally, visitors can go in during three periods of the day, but the doctor told the nurses to let in whomever we pleased. They only allow two people at a time in patient rooms, so I said I'd come out here and let each of you go in. She's in the third one on the left."

"I don't know if I can," Vaughn said, shredding her tissue into tiny pieces.

"The least we can do is tell her goodbye," Sarah said angrily. "I've already told her."

Tristan led his daughter over to one of the loveseats and sat next to her. His wife stayed where she was next to Jamie and wiped at her cheeks. No one noticed when Carson exited the waiting area and went to find his client.

Daniel stood facing the narrow window with his back to his mother's hospital bed. He wore his work clothes – dark blue shoes and pants, a gray shirt, and a patterned tie. He'd probably just arrived home when the call had come.

Lillian Nash lay still and unresponsive. The machines beeped, whirred, and whooshed, echoing loudly in the small room.

"I'm sorry," Carson said sincerely.

Startled, Daniel turned his head to see who'd spoken. He nodded to the private investigator then went back to looking out of the window.

"I'd talked with her this morning," Carson continued. "I was supposed to meet with her tomorrow at noon."

Lightning flashed so brightly that Carson was temporarily blinded. Daniel didn't flinch or shut his eyes.

"Do you want me to suspend the investigation?"

"No."

"You're the boss. I want to talk with CoCo Genevieve."

"CoCo's not all there."

"How long has she lived next to your parents?"

"Close to forty years."

"And how old is she?"

"In her fifties. Read the journals. Nobody except Sarah and I know that she's also my first cousin. I'm not certain she knows it herself."

"I definitely want to question her."

"Her husband's name is Jean-Paul. If he has a problem with it, tell him to call me."

The detective sensed someone behind him. It was Jamie Nesser, waiting to enter the room. Carson moved in order to allow Jamie to step forward, but he didn't leave altogether. Instead, he leaned one shoulder against the wall outside of the room where he could still see what was happening and, more importantly, listen.

"Hey, Lillian," Jamie murmured. "It's me."

"Do you really think she can hear you?" Daniel asked tightly.

"Stop me if you've heard this one before. A boy goes into a hospital, see. He's been beaten by this vicious S.O.B. and is as close to dead as you can get. He actually dies a couple of times on the operating table, but they bring him back. Anyway, when he's in the pediatric ICU, he's unconscious but his heart is racing real fast. And then, this stranger, a psychiatrist's housekeeper, comes in and starts talking to the kid and holding his hand, and guess what? His heart rate slows down. So, she makes up her mind to stay with the boy until he comes out of it. And what do you know? He does."

The lightning flickered, but not so brilliantly this time. Daniel lowered his head and closed his eyes.

"Just tell her what's on your mind," Jamie suggested. "Like this: I love you, Lillian. You've been a good friend to me and Chloe and the kids. I'm gonna miss the way you always used to whack my hand with that wooden spoon whenever I'd go to taste the food before it was ready. I'm gonna miss the way you used to scold me for making bawdy comments in front of…well, in front of everybody. You're the best."

Jamie wiped at his eyes with the sleeve of his shirt as he walked unseeing past Carson. The investigator remained outside the door, a guard against…what? He wasn't sure.

Vaughn came next. A few whispered words and a sluice of tears accompanied her brief good-bye.

Finally, there was Tristan. He halted a few feet from the door. Carson pushed away from the wall, unsure as to whether or not he should say something or offer some assistance. Tristan waved him back and shook his head. Then, he squared his shoulders and went in to the third room on the left.

Carson peered into the room once again and reminded himself that he wasn't eavesdropping. He wasn't being nosy. He was doing research, evaluating how sincere these people were about their close relationships and their desire to help one another.

"I tried Isabelle again, but she still wasn't home," Tristan said. "Jamie's going to run over to her place in a while and make sure she's okay. I know we shouldn't worry but…."

"No, that's a good idea."

Tristan went to stand next to his son-in-law and reached up to touch the cold glass in front of them.

"I know what tomorrow is," he said plainly. "It's been almost twenty-seven years to the day since your mother died."

Daniel stretched out his arm and splayed his fingers next to Tristan's on the smooth surface. "At least no one will beat me afterwards. There's some consolation in that."

"Dan, you've found it easier to talk to Jamie about the experiences you've shared with the abuse. You and I have spoken on just about everything else. I want you to talk to me about this when you feel you can. I'd appreciate it if you'd let me bend your ear, too."

Daniel let his hand drop back to his side and said, "I will."

Tristan sadly viewed Lillian's still form and said, "If only I'd gotten to her this morning, but she told me she had to go to the store, and we could meet tonight. Stubborn to the end." The corners of his mouth twitched ever so slightly. "Don't give St. Peter too hard of a time, Lillian, and keep a light burning in the window for me."

"You believe that St. Peter's up in Heaven waiting for her and that she'll keep watch for you until you knock on the Pearly Gates?"

"Don't be disrespectful of her or me," Tristan said calmly but firmly. "She envisioned it that way, so I can do her the courtesy of acknowledging her convictions."

"Are they yours?"

"Not here and not now."

"I have to know what you believe!" he said in an almost desperate tone of voice. "Do you think there are angels and devils? Is there some God looming all around us?"

The man looked thoughtful for a time then said, "I think we're all connected and that we go on after we die. Whether or not there's a Heaven or Hell I don't know. I do believe there's a power greater than all of us, but I doubt I'll grasp it's magnitude in this lifetime." Placing a hand on Daniel's shoulder, he suggested, "Tell me what you think. Is there a God? Is there an afterlife? What happens when we die?"

"When I died as a kid, there weren't any white lights or welcoming messiahs. I wish I could believe in all of it, Tris. It would make my life easier to trust that…to…." He broke off and shook his head before admitting, "Dead is dead. That's all I've seen. It may not be fluffy clouds and harp music, but at least it's an end to suffering."

"Then don't put it off any longer. She needs some peace."

Daniel went over to Lillian's side. He lifted her smooth, limp hand and stooped down to kiss it.

"Go on, Lillian. You deserve to die with dignity. All I can say is thank you for everything. I love you, Mom."

As the two men walked back in the direction of the waiting area, Carson heard the high-pitched scream of the machine as Lillian Johnson Nash ceased living. He was ashamed by his own surprise and saddened by the fact that when Lillian died, any information she knew about her son and his background had gone with her to the grave.

Carson had permitted himself to become very attached to this case, more attached than he normally afforded. He wanted to take a step back. He'd tried to buy himself some time to regain his detachment by suggesting that he suspend his investigation, but Daniel hadn't given him the answer he'd expected.

Carson didn't want to be the one to tell that group of family and friends in the waiting room that Mrs. Nash had died. So, instead, he ducked into the men's room to collect his thoughts. He emerged fifteen minutes later and found Daniel and Sarah alone in the center of the throng that inhabited the waiting area.

Sarah was sitting in her husband's lap, her arms draped around his shoulders. Neither of them cried, although Sarah's eyes seemed to be shining with tears. It was touching, the way they sat, the way they grieved in silence.

"I want to meet with you as soon as possible."

Carson turned to face Jamie Nesser.

"Yeah?"

"Yeah. I don't know that I'll have much to add, but he –" Jamie nodded in Daniel's direction "– needs some answers soon. Life's been a bitch for him, but he's stayed a good man. I don't want to see that change."

"But you're worried it will?"

"Aren't you?"

Chapter Seven: I Say Hello

A hospital worker came over to Daniel and proceeded to explain the procedure for release of his mother's body to the funeral home. Sarah detached herself from her husband and walked towards the doorway of the waiting room. She ignored the others, regretting that she should leave her husband alone to deal with the arrangements, yet knowing that she had no other choice. If she was going to protect her own psyche, then she had to leave.

She wandered aimlessly throughout the hospital, accessing the elevator and randomly pushing buttons, getting off at whatever floor happened to await her when the doors slid apart. In some rooms the people laughed and joked with recovering relatives. In others hushed voices uttered words of encouragement. A woman cried and asked for more pain medication. A child spun round and round in circles as he waited for his mother to buy a bag of chips from a vending machine.

At one point, Sarah stopped to examine the wares displayed in a darkened gift shop window. Amid the dolls and candles, there was a book on the display table. The title hinted at a detailed account of one traveler's experiences as he circled the globe. The cover of the book was littered with images of brilliant flowers from various locations. Something was familiar about that book, although Sarah was certain that she'd never read it before. It was irksome not to be able to satisfy that nagging feeling of recognition.

Sarah shrugged it off and turned left at the next corridor. About thirty feet in front of her, she spotted stained glass doors that appeared to lead into another hallway. Intrigued despite her current mental lethargy, she went through the doors and continued down the hall. She could see more stained glass further ahead. The images extended down a smaller corridor. She halted in front of one huge section of glass and tried to study the patterns in the dark of the stormy evening.

Suddenly, there was a rapid fire of lightning flashes, and the purples, greens, whites, and reds came alive. Jumbled leaves and plants and figures of men filled the corridor. The beauty of it was enticing even though she wasn't able to see everything because of her damaged vision.

A door lay in front of her. She automatically pushed through the entrance and was greeted by a mosaic of Christ. She'd stumbled into the chapel.

Sarah glanced nervously around the octagonal room. She appeared to be its only occupant. Large, stained-glass panels adorned four of the walls, perhaps North, South, East, and West. On each of the other four walls there were three smaller, stained-glass selections, depicting whom or what Sarah wasn't sure.

She took a seat in one of the empty pews. There was total silence in the room, an eerie calm that was slightly unnerving. The statues of Mary and a man who might have been Jesus or St. Joseph stared kindly but reprovingly at her. Not wanting to look anywhere else, Sarah looked up at the wooden beams that crossed the ceiling in a huge, wagon-wheel shape.

The storm outside intensified, and the wind began to wail around the corners of the building. Sarah brought up her knees and wrapped her arms around them, being careful not to put too much pressure on the tender spot that remained on her injured arm. She laid her cheek against her knees and closed her eyes, telling herself that it was silly to be afraid just because she was alone in a deserted area of the hospital with a tremendous thundershower raging outside.

There was a loud *clack* behind her, as the door to the chapel slammed shut. Sarah jerked but refused to open her eyes and give in to the wild pounding of her heart. She strained to make out the sounds of the stranger dipping his fingers into the Holy Water and walking towards the altar, towards where she sat.

Sarah opened her eyes as an older man sat in the pew in front of her and turned to face her. The man wore the clerical collar of a priest. He was balding with a fringe of gray hair, and wire-rimmed glasses shielded his bright blue eyes.

"Are you in need of anything?" he asked with a gentle smile.

"I – I don't think so," Sarah stuttered. She lowered one leg to the floor and suggested, "I should go."

"Why? You're not disturbing anyone. Sometimes, people come into this room and sit all night in these benches." The priest draped one arm over the back of the pew and introduced himself as Frank Randall.

"Sarah Nash."

As she reached out to shake the man's hand, the sleeve of Sarah's sweater drooped down, revealing the bright pink scar on her arm. It gleamed wickedly in the dim light, and Frank Randall quickly fixed his gaze on her face in an obvious attempt to avoid staring at the healing wound.

"Is there something I can help you with?" he persisted. "Would you like to tell me what brought you here tonight?"

"The stained glass."

"I beg your pardon?"

"I saw the stained glass windows, and I came down the hall to investigate. That's a very sneaky way of luring people here, you know. Baiting the sinners with pretty pictures isn't fair."

Father Randall's laughter echoed in the emptiness of the church.

"You're a sinner with a sense of humor, I see."

"One might as well be honest about it."

"True," He sobered and said, "But seriously, the glass may have brought you here, but you stayed, didn't you? You look…unwell."

"I'm sure I do. We've been upstairs for hours; I'm upset; and I haven't eaten anything since noon. What time is it now? 11:00?"

A huge boom of thunder interrupted their conversation. They sat silently and listened to its rumble roll off into the distance.

"My mother-in-law died tonight," Sarah began quietly. "She had a stroke. My father-in-law died last month of heart failure. I didn't want him to die, but he'd been in poor health for a few years. At least he was older. Lillian was only sixty."

"My heart goes out to you."

"Thank you. I should be on one of those pathetic talk shows. Or, better yet, I could be a case study for some psychiatrist doing research on hopeless causes."

Randall rubbed thoughtfully at his chin and admitted, "I don't perceive you as a hopeless cause. You appear to be the type of person who perseveres."

"I'm tired of it. I want to give up, but I can't. Everybody's depending on me, as usual."

"Take a vacation from it then. Try depending on *them* for a change."

"I've tried it before. I'm not very good at that."

"As a nun I once knew used to say, old habits die hard."

"That's awful!" she said as she flashed a smile.

"I know the pun is bad, but it got you to smile."

Clack!

"Sarah?"

The priest tried not to gawk at the towering form of Tristan Maes. The man stood silhouetted by one of the great stained-glass windows. It glowed with an otherworldly light behind him as lightning struck somewhere close by.

"My father," Sarah said to her new acquaintance. "I guess the arrangements have been made." As she rose to leave, she added, "Thank you for the company."

"If you want to talk again, please call the hospital. They'll put you through to my voice mail or beeper. I'm a 'floating priest' at the moment. I have no parish. The bishop likes for me to go where I'm needed."

"You have a beeper?"

"We have to be available for emergency baptisms or last rites."

"My mother-in-law?"

"No. Another priest was on call earlier tonight."

With a final nod to the priest, Sarah went to join her father and took his hand. They left the chapel and returned down the colorful corridor back towards the main area of the first floor of the hospital.

"I didn't want to interrupt," Tristan told his daughter as they walked. "Who was that?"

"A priest who happened to come in while –"

She stopped so quickly that Tristan's hand came away from hers. He went back to where she stood and saw with trepidation that her face was completely drained of all color.

Bending down until she was eye-level with the traveler's book on display in the gift shop window, Sarah stared open-mouthed at its cover. Tristan squatted next to her and gently touched her wrist.

"Honey? What is it? Is something wrong?"

She lightly touched the glass, drawing her finger around in delicate circles as if she were tracing the outlines of the flowers on the cover of the book.

"It's the book."

"The book?"

"It must be a reprint."

"Sarah, what are you talking about? *That* book?"

"Let's just leave it alone for tonight. I'm so tired."

They walked past the decorated Christmas trees and down brightly lit hallways until they arrived at the Emergency Room entrance. Vaughn paced in agitation near the desk. Daniel leaned against the doorframe, his arms folded across his chest and anxiety dancing in his eyes.

"Where have you been?" Vaughn demanded. "I've been worried sick."

Knowing his wife's propensity for becoming overly agitated in times of stress, Tristan deflected the question with a question of his own.

"What happened to Carson?"

"Jamie said he'd give him a ride back to his car before swinging around to Isabelle's." Daniel pushed his shoulder away from the wall and said, "We'd better go. It's close to midnight. I'm ready to be away from all this."

Kris ran to his mother when they arrived at the Maes's house. He cried in the pitiful fashion of young children who've lost something precious to them or who've seen great disasters unfold before their eyes. Daniel was reminded of a picture he'd once seen of a small girl in some war-ravaged country who had witnessed the destruction of her family's apartment building. He knelt down beside his wife in the hallway and reached out to touch his son's hair. The boy threw his arms tightly around his father's neck and cried harder.

Daniel carried Kris into the living room and sat in the large, well-padded chair near the fireplace. Sarah had named it "The Comfy Chair" twenty years earlier when it had first been delivered to the house. It seemed to have a supernatural ability to relax anyone who reclined in it. Daniel suspected it wouldn't work for him that night, but maybe it would help him to comfort his son.

The boy cried himself to sleep in Daniel's lap. As he watched, Vaughns' mother, Helen, crossed the room and sat down on the edge of the hearth so that she could be closer to him. She placed a hand on Daniel's right knee and said consolingly, "Is there anything Jim or I can do?"

"No, Helen. But thanks for offering."

Daniel looked down at his son. He took his finger and traced one golden eyebrow. The urge to crush the child against him and never let him go was a powerful one, but he settled for kissing Kris on the forehead, laying him on the couch, and covering him with an afghan.

He helped Helen up, and they walked arm in arm to the kitchen where Sarah, Tristan, Vaughn, Will, and Vaughn's father, Jim, were filling cups of coffee. Will stepped forward to briefly embrace Daniel and clapped him on the back. They nodded to each other; then Will walked out and slowly climbed the stairs to the second floor.

Jim, ever the stereotypical gentleman farmer, extended his roughened hand to Daniel. When Daniel took it, Jim pulled him closer and put his arm around Daniel's shoulder for a moment.

"She was a fine woman," he said.

Daniel agreed and thanked Jim for his kind words.

Helen handed Daniel a cup of the steaming coffee. He went to one of the empty chairs at the table and slumped disconsolately in it. Helen and Jim joined him and Vaughn at the table, while Tristan and Sarah remained standing near the counter behind Daniel.

"When did Katie fall asleep?" asked Vaughn.

"About an hour and a half ago," Jim replied. "You know how she wears herself out when she's in that hyper mode."

"It can be tiring, yes. Sarah, you look pale. Why don't you sit down?"

"I'm okay," she said, swaying slightly. "I –"

Daniel was instantly alert and out of his chair. He had his hand around her back before her father had raised his own to catch her.

Coming back to consciousness, Sarah slowly opened her eyes. She was lying on the bed in her old room. That was the only thing her brain could fathom for the moment. That and the fact that she was going to throw up.

She made it to the bathroom just in time, the acrid taste of the recently ingested coffee burning her throat. She gasped for breath and felt a cool cloth being drawn across first her forehead then her cheeks and finally her mouth.

Her stomach heaved again, oblivious to the fact that there was nothing left to be cast out. A paper cup of water was brought to her lips. She swished the water around in her mouth and then spat it into the toilet. She held out her hand and was rewarded with the desired tissue.

Her muscles quivering, Sarah leaned against the tub and felt the cool porcelain under her hands. She lowered her cheek, pressed it against the edge, and sighed.

"Better?" Tristan asked.

Fighting against a recurrence of the dry heaves, Sarah tried to take shallow breaths and turned her face so that the other cheek could be cooled.

"Where's Daniel?"

"Taking a call. It had something to do with moving Lillian's body to the funeral home."

He went to wet the washcloth in the sink. Bringing it back to his daughter, he held it out in front of her. She accepted it gratefully and placed the cloth over her throat.

"What about Vaughn, Helen, and Jim? I'm surprised Vaughn's not hovering."

"Oh, she'd like to be. She wanted to call an ambulance when you fainted, but Jim dissuaded her. Helen's helping her get Kris to bed."

"Bed? But we have to go home."

"Not tonight. You're going to stay here. Jim went to let Ralph out and to feed him. You can go home tomorrow."

"But where will everybody sleep?"

"You and Dan can sleep in your old room. Will can stay in his bed. We'll stick Kris in the trundle in there. Vaughn's going to sleep in the other twin bed in Katie's room. Jim and Helen can take our bed, and I'll sleep on the couch."

"Daddy, you can't! You're too big to stretch out on the couch."

"I'm not going to stretch out. I'm going to pull out the sofa bed and curl up on that. I think if I bring my knees up I can sleep comfortably on the diagonal, thank you very much." Judging that she was sufficiently recovered, he reached out and pushed a strand of hair behind one ear before saying, "They've got specialty clothing stores for big and tall men. Maybe I could start a specialty furniture line." He deepened his voice and said, "Come to Tristan's Big and Tall Furniture Outlet where, when we say you'll have gigantic savings, you can bet on it!"

She half-smiled at him. Her stomach twisted, and her throat was irritated. Her soul craved the oblivion of a deep, dreamless sleep.

"Daddy, I need you to do something for me tomorrow. I know it sounds crazy, what with everything that's going on, but it's important to me."

"What is it? Not that I won't do it if I can."

"I need for you to go back to the hospital and buy that book in the gift shop. I'll pay you back."

"Of course, but I'm not taking any money from you." Tristan opened his mouth to ask her why she wanted the book, closed it, then asked, "Do you want it gift-wrapped?"

"No. No, it's a gift, but I don't need it wrapped."

He helped her to bed then watched her sleep for the next quarter of an hour. His little girl, this woman. It was a thought that made him mourn and marvel. She seemed so young when she slept, all of the seriousness of life and the pain of the past washed away for a time. If only those things could stay gone when she awoke.

In the early hours of the morning, Tristan rolled off his square prison and climbed the stairs to check on his family. He knew that they were safe, but he needed to *see* that they were safe. Maybe then he could get some rest.

Will slept on his back, one arm dangling off the side of the bed. His LSU shirt was pulled awkwardly around his chest, and the shorts he had on were torn at the hem on the left leg. His hair was crushed against his head on one side. The covers had been kicked off.

Kris lay on his stomach, a small wetness directly under his mouth. He was almost sideways on the trundle. Tristan carefully eased him straight until his head rested on the pillow once more. The child mumbled in his sleep, as his grandfather searched in the tangle of sheets and blankets for the stuffed tiger that Will must have pushed under the boy's arm. As Tristan replaced the animal, the mumbling stopped, and Kris settled back into calm sleep.

Jim and Helen slept holding each other. This surprised their son-in-law, although he wasn't sure why. Did he really imagine that older people only shared a bed for sleep and not for intimacy or comfort?

Katie shifted again and again in her bed, as active in sleep as she was in wakefulness. Tristan pitied any partner she might have in the future. She and her husband would either need a king-sized bed or a wall of pillows between them.

Tristan walked around to the other side of the room and lowered himself onto the edge of the twin mattress where his wife rested. The dark red hair was braided to prevent knots, and the moonlight glowing through the shade bounced off of her exposed white throat and face. She was as beautiful and delicate to him as any legendary court lady of King Arthur's day.

A sound sleeper, Vaughn didn't stir as her husband ran his thumb around the curve of her eye and stroked her slender throat. He touched the rounded part of her shoulder and moved down the length of her arm to her fingers. She moved when he drew the digit across her right breast and hip but showed no sign of rousing.

It's so easy to love her like I used to when she sleeps, he thought. *I wish I could still love her that way when she's awake. I wish things were like they used to be.*

Tristan leaned forward and lightly kissed her. Then he headed for his older daughter's room.

He was shocked. Sarah, who had never liked to be touched when she slept or was injured or sick, was firmly pressed against her husband. Daniel sheltered his wife near his chest, his arms wrapped protectively around her, his fingers laced through her auburn curls.

As Tristan watched from outside the doorway, Sarah began to turn in her sleep, put her hands against Daniel's chest, and tried to push away from him. He woke at once, the whites of his eyes visible even from Tristan's hidden vantage point. He murmured Sarah's name, and she came to with a jerk and a tiny cry. Brushing the hair away from her face with his fingers, Daniel spoke gently to her. Within sixty seconds, she was asleep again. Her father wondered if she'd ever truly been awake.

Tristan was torn between what he wanted to do and what he should do. He stood on the landing for several minutes watching Daniel continue to lovingly rake Sarah's hair with his fingers. When Daniel lowered his head back onto the pillow, Tristan took that as his cue. Now was the time to either return downstairs or step into the room. He crossed the threshold, surprising both Daniel and himself.

"Does that happen often?" Tristan whispered.

"She's only had these little nightmares since she hurt her arm. Well, since everything. Afterwards, she actually sleeps deeply for a while. Paradoxically, I haven't had a nightmare since the week before Max's death. Strange, isn't it?"

"And she lets you hold her like that?"

Daniel's teeth flashed white in the darkness.

"I keep thinking that I'm dreaming a nice dream and that I'll wake up any minute. It's great to be able to hold her like this when we sleep and not just when we're awake."

"Speaking of holding, are you holding up okay?"

"You shouldn't ask me that. I was doing a damned good job of not thinking about things."

"Sorry."

"Don't worry about it." He sighed then said, "I am tired, and the prospect of attending a parent's funeral for the second time in a month is *not* appealing. But it could be worse."

"At least no one will beat you afterwards?" Tristan asked, repeating Daniel's words from the hospital. "There's some consolation in that?"

"Go to bed, Tris. I'm sure some new disaster will await me tomorrow."

Disturbed and uneasy, Tristan went instead to the kitchen and brewed a fresh pot of coffee. Darkness was giving way to the haze of the coming dawn. He slipped into his shoes and put his coat on over the sweatpants and sweatshirt that he'd worn to bed. Then, he took the black coffee outside and sat on the top step of the porch.

After about ten minutes, Daniel came out through the back door, dressed in his work clothes from the previous day. Coffee cup in hand, he planted his backside on the step next to his father-in-law. They listened to the small noises of the pre-dawn morning and sipped from their mugs as they waited for the new day to begin.

Chapter Eight: The Most Unlikely Places

"Just let me know if you want another beer," Jamie said, as he drained the remnants of the bottle in front of him.

Carson glanced over the pages of notes he'd taken over the last two hours. Jamie had been right when he'd said that he didn't have much to contribute in regards to the mystery of Daniel's parentage. The man did have a lot to say, most of which the investigator had already heard in one form or another from Daniel, Sarah, and Tristan.

"I have another question, but it's not about Dan's paternity. Well, it might be. One never knows in these cases."

"And that question is?"

"At the hospital the other day Tristan made a remark about Dan's being able to talk with you regarding shared abuse. Can you clue me in on what that's about?"

"Me, I could have been a poster child for the perils of foster care. Some of my foster parents were nice people. A lot of them weren't. I have a few scars. Nothing like Dan's, but it doesn't take many cuts, burns, or bruises to make you understand. I don't talk about that with many people, but I told Dan about it when they first brought him home. I wanted him to be aware that he wasn't the only one. He and I used to spend time together and talk about it. He could open up to me and I to him."

"You still speak on it?"

"Not as often, but we have our talks. You feel sort of…cleansed afterwards."

"They have groups for that now like Alcoholics Anonymous. I guess they've got groups for everything in today's world."

Jamie nodded then admitted, "Dan and I've been debating for a while now on whether or not we should go to one of those meetings. I've been thinking about it more in the last few weeks. I'm not enough for him. Dan's seeing a therapist, but I don't sense that the guy's doing that great of a job." Sighing deeply, he continued, "And Sarah…Sarah's been walking a fine line herself, lately. She's the one who tries to take care of everybody else and everything on her own."

"Except herself," Carson observed. "At least that's the way it seems to me."

"Well, it's been one tragedy after another. At least when there's a moment between each blow, you have a chance to catch your breath. When the belt doesn't pause, you can't collect yourself enough not to lose hold of rational thought." Jamie grasped the neck of a fresh beer and admitted, "Something has to give soon. We're all likely to be a little irrational if this keeps up. Tristan and I have been family for thirty-five years. In the beginning, it was him and me, and that was it. It's a pretty lonely way to live, let me tell you. But then came Sarah's mother and then Sarah herself. And after her mother's death, there was Max, Lillian, and Vaughn – as well as my ex-partner, Chloe, and our friends, Halley and Benjamin. Benjamin died of cancer, and Halley's moved away. Chloe and I split permanently the week after Max died and don't talk much unless it's about our kids. But back then we were all one big family. It didn't matter if it was blood that bound us or misfortune or love. Just like any family, when one person is in pain, then the others are affected by his suffering."

"Understood," Carson said, as he pushed back his chair and rose to his feet. "Look, I'll be there in the morning for the funeral."

"I don't think it would be good for you to come to the house afterwards. Nothing personal, but that should be our family time."

"Actually, I was planning to go next door after the service. Mrs. Genevieve's husband has agreed to let me talk with her, but only if she's not too distraught."

"Are you this involved in all of your cases?"

"I like to be thorough."

When CoCo Genevieve greeted Carson the next afternoon, it took great effort for him not to laugh. CoCo was attired in violet silk pajamas and wore bright gold slippers. Her head was wrapped in a silver silk scarf. Her arms and neck were weighted down with bangles and chains of all kinds, and a ring adorned each of her fingers. Her face was red, and her skin was puffy under the eyes.

"Afternoon, ma'am."

"Whatever you're selling, we don't want any."

"CoCo, dat's de man I tol' you 'bout, yeah."

Jean-Paul Genevieve was dressed in stark contrast to his wife. He wore blue jeans and a denim shirt. A simple gold wedding band was the only piece of jewelry in view.

"You come on in. Your name's Zerangue? You Cajun?"

"Used to be. Not so much anymore."

They walked through mountains of newspapers and magazines. Jean-Paul cleared a spot for the detective on the couch.

"You don' talk like you Cajun."

"I been gone from home a long time. The way I talk got corrupted."

"I been gon' a long time, too. I still gots me some family down dere dat CoCo and I go see every Sunday. Keeps me pure Coon Ass."

Giving him a lop-sided grin, Carson whipped out his notebook. If he got to chatting with the Cajun about back home, he'd be there all day.

"I don't want to keep you long," Carson insisted. "I know this is a sad time for everyone who knew Lillian Nash."

"Why is your first name Carson?" CoCo asked from her perch on the arm of a chair. "Why not Pierre or Michel or something more Cajun French?"

"I was named after a World War II buddy of my dad's, a friend of his from New York who got killed during a ground attack." He lifted his pen and said, "Now, if you could –"

"Were there a lot of mourners today?" CoCo asked seriously. "There were so many for Max's funeral, and it was such a nasty day for that one, not clear and sunny like this morning. I wish I'd been there."

"Now, Chere, you wasn't feelin' too good dis mornin'."

"No, you're right. I wasn't. Maybe I should go over there now, though."

"CoCo, let de man ask you what he want. Den we'll see."

She looked expectantly at Carson and asked, "What do you want to know about me? What if I don't want to tell you?"

"I'm not going to ask you about your medical treatment by Dr. Nash."

CoCo nodded, seemingly enthralled with this new line of conversation.

"How long did you know Maxwell Nash?"

"My whole life, although I spent the first years of it living with the people who raised me. I saw Max at least once a week from the beginning. Oh, not because I was crazy back then; I was only a baby at first. Today, they would have called a child like me ADHD. But that wasn't why I saw him."

"Why then?"

"Because he was my uncle."

"You knew."

"Of course. For as long as I can remember I've known it, although I swore I'd never tell it to anyone, not so long as Max or Milo were alive. They're dead now, aren't they?"

She glanced at her husband as if for confirmation. He nodded.

"Who told you this? Max or Milo?"

"Milo never did figure it out and with me looking just like him, playing right under his nose whenever he came home for a visit." She adjusted some of the bangles on her right arm and said, "He wouldn't have made a good father, even though he was a nice enough man. He wouldn't have known what to do with a child, especially someone like me."

"Now, CoCo," Jean-Paul said. "You a treasure and a pleasure, Chere. I ain't sayin' dat you be so easy sometime, but dere's notin' not to love."

To each his own, Carson said to himself.

"So, if Max and Milo didn't tell you, then who did? Isabelle Elenstraub?"

"She didn't know either, I don't think. No, it was Teal. She said that my father would sneak over here after supper and not come home until dawn. Teal knew."

"Teal. Mr. Nash's original housekeeper?"

"Yes. Moses knew, too. I heard Teal telling him once that even a fool could count and that Milo wasn't a fool, just a man who was too much his own person and no one else's."

"So, you knew Max, Milo, Isabelle, Teal, and Moses from infancy?"

"Yes."

"How about Gwen Nash?"

"She was a grand lady. Sometimes when she was sick, I'd play in her room. Teal used to try and shoo me out, but Miss Gwen would smile and tell her to let me be and say that she liked the noise and distraction. She used to keep candy in her bed jacket pocket and give me a piece every time I came. I always keep candy with me like she did. Would you like a piece?"

"Sure."

Carson accepted the obviously ancient piece of candy she offered him and asked, "Mind if I take it with me for later? I have another appointment tonight."

She smiled sweetly at him and said, "I'm so glad you like the candy. My friend, Tessa, she used to like that particular one the best."

"Tessa?"

"Tessa Downey."

His face must have registered his shock because Jean-Paul asked, "You feelin' all right?"

"I'm not sure. How…how did you know Tessa Downey?"

"Jean-Paul and I had gotten married in January of 1957. We decided to move back here to my mother's house. We didn't have much back then, did we, Jean-Paul?"

"No, ma chere, we did not. But den, we don' have much now either."

"The place had been rented out for seventeen years. We moved in four days after the wedding. January 15, 1957. I met Tessa on January 31, 1957."

Carson raised an eyebrow at the mention of these specific dates, but Jean-Paul hastened to say, "CoCo has a mem'ry for dates, numbers, and game show questions, and she ain't never been one to lie, yeah."

Scribbling furiously, the investigator paused long enough to gesture for the woman to continue and asked, "Can you describe Miss Downey to me? What'd she look like? What'd she act like?"

"She was beautiful! Tall and that white, white skin. Her hair was a light red and frizzy – not like Vaughn's, so dark and shiny – and she had some red freckles on her nose. And she had almost no lips! I had never seen anyone with lips so thin. She used to tease me and say that maybe someday she could have my lips, but only if a bee would come up and sting her twice on the mouth."

For some reason, this statement conjured up an erotic image in the detective's mind. There was a flash of Tessa Downey in a filmy white dress standing in a field of flowers and calmly offering her mouth up to a passing bee.

He cleared his throat and shifted uneasily on the couch.

"Uh, yeah. So, she was attractive. What was her personality like?"

"Fun. She was fun. She could make jokes that would have entertained any person with a reasonable amount of intelligence and good humor. She was smart, too." CoCo shut her eyes and turned herself inward, evidently trying to recapture that long-lost time in her life. "She loved to do fun things like take her shoes off and splash around in the creek. She could even get Max to do that sometimes. Max had never been one to run around in wild abandon. I doubt if he even did things like that as a child, but Tessa could get him to enjoy that and other things."

"Such as?"

"Jean-Paul worked a lot off-shore then, so I was here by myself. He never would let me drive, which is probably a good idea between you and me. So, I'd be here alone a lot. That's how I saw Tessa so much back then. That's how I could know what was going on between her and my uncle."

"Such as? Did she tell you about their relationship or did you see things that would lead you to believe that it was serious?"

"Both. When Max would be taking care of business things, Tessa would take a walk and come visit with me. She wasn't much older than I was, so we'd drink a Coke and talk about our lives. It never bothered her that I wasn't quite right in the head. She knew that I needed company, so she came. She was my friend."

"And she told you about them? What did she say?"

CoCo slid from the arm of the chair into its seat and sat cross-legged facing him. For a moment, he envisioned her as a genie.

"Tessa'd say that Max was so kind, smart, and handsome. She'd say that she loved and admired him. She'd say how good he was in bed." She rested her chin in her hands and confided, "He and Gwen couldn't do it, you know, not after the first one."

Puzzled, Carson echoed, "The first one?"

"The first baby. You know that Miss Gwen was sickly?"

Carson nodded.

"They'd found out they were having a baby and were so happy for a few months. Then it happened. I must have been around ten. Well, one Saturday after it happened, I overheard Moses talking to Max, and Max was telling him that they couldn't risk it and that she was too weak to ever try to have another child. She'd die for sure. So, they couldn't…you know. Max and his wife were very Catholic, so they didn't believe in artificial birth control. Plus, it wasn't very reliable in those days anyway."

"Mrs. Genevieve, I'm going to ask you for your opinion. Please don't get angry. I'm only trying to uncover the truth. Do you think your uncle ever had an affair or visited prostitutes during the time between then and the first Mrs. Nash's death?"

"Max?" she chuckled. "Max was way too moral and in love with his wife to do something like that. But I bet that's why he fell in with Tessa. Miss Gwen was gone; Teal and Moses had gone to live with one of Moses's nieces; and there was Tessa, who was pretty, witty, and practically throwing herself at him. Plus, she was full of energy, something Miss Gwen had never had, poor woman. Why wouldn't he want to be with her, no matter what the consequences?"

"You said you saw them together at times?"

"Mostly going to and from the house. Tessa didn't tell Max that I knew about them. She didn't tell anyone else either. She said she felt like they were all alone and safe in this little cocoon at his house. Oh, she was so in love and so happy. I did almost tumble over them one day when I was walking in the woods behind the house."

"What were they doing?"

"It was a powerful thing they had between them, and I don't only mean the sex, although that seemed mighty good when I saw them. No, it was more. If only she'd stayed with him."

"Can you tell me about the last time that you saw Miss Downey?"

"Max was out of town at some meeting of psychiatrists, but I saw her coming up his drive on foot. I went over and found her crying in the kitchen. She had the prettiest pink dress on. I can still see it so clearly."

"Ma'am, I really do need to know what happened."

"Well, I'm telling you. When I asked her what was wrong, she said, 'Oh, CoCo! It's horrible. There's a baby.' And then she cried harder. I said, 'Why is it horrible? I thought you and Max loved each other? Now, you can have his baby, and you can be a family.' But she told me no, that it would destroy Max's career and his life and that she loved him too much to let that happen. What she wanted didn't matter. She wanted the baby so much, but she said maybe it would be better if it were never born." CoCo's hands fluttered up like butterflies and covered her mouth. "Oh! You won't tell anyone I said that, will you? That sounds gruesome, and I know she didn't mean it."

"I won't tell anyone about that. What did you say to her?"

"I was worried that she would, you know, do something rash. So, I told her to talk to Max about it, that he would know what to do. He had always helped me to know what to do. She nodded and didn't cry so much, and she asked me if I'd leave her alone so that she could think on it. She hugged me, and I left. I never saw her again."

"Did you ever ask your uncle what happened to her?"

"Well, I wasn't supposed to know in the first place, but he got to looking so haggard over the next few months that I worried. It made me very sad. Max and Miss Gwen had wanted to have a baby and couldn't have one. Here was Max's chance to have a child, and Tessa was gone. I used to wonder about her and the baby. I worried that they were living on the streets in poverty. I used to look for her whenever Jean-Paul and I would go out to places."

"Did Miss Downey ever mention any other men she might have been involved with, either before or during her relationship with Dr. Nash?"

"Like…?"

"Zachary Samuels."

"Dan's father?"

Carson kicked himself mentally.

"I tol' you she never forgets anythin'," Jean-Paul said, chiding Zerangue.

"You can't mean…but that would be…but Max…." She looked frantically around the room for a solid answer to her vague mumblings.

Carson looked to Jean-Paul for guidance.

"She's no tattle-tale. Neither am I. Tell her."

"Dan Nash has good reason to believe that Maxwell Nash was his biological father. I'm assisting him in his attempt to verify this."

"So, Max found him after…after…what that terrible man did to him…after…." She thrust her hand forward, frustrated by her inability to discuss Daniel's near-death experience. "Tessa is Daniel's mother? But why didn't Max tell him about their affair? And why did Tessa marry Zachary Samuels? Didn't she know what kind of man he was?"

"That's what we're trying to find out. You've given me more help than anyone else so far, with the exception of Dan Nash himself. I thank you."

CoCo proudly drew herself up at his compliment and smiled.

"So, Dan Nash is my cousin?" she asked in disbelief. "Does he know?"

"He found out last week," Carson confided. "But he wasn't sure if you knew."

"Do you…do you think it would be all right for me to call him and for me to tell him more about his mother? There's lots more about the things she said and the way she acted. She was so fun."

"I think he'd love to hear it all, although maybe it'd be wise to give him a few days."

"Yes," CoCo said. "Yes, you're absolutely right. You give good advice, just like Max used to."

"I'd better shove off. Here's my card. Call if you think of anything else that might be relevant. I'm sure I'll be calling on you again."

As Carson started his car, he reflected that truth sometimes lies in the most unlikely of places.

He wished fervently that he could interview Teal and Moses, but both of them had died in the 1970s. An inspection of Assumpta's LSU records had shown nothing of real value, simply Tessa Downey's dates of attendance. Other documents had verified the immigration story, business transactions, graduation dates for Max and Milo, and a marriage license for Maxwell and Gwendolyn Nash, among other minutiae. That left three main avenues to explore: hospital records regarding Daniel's birth, a trip to Assumpta's hometown, and the locating and interviewing of Zachary Samuels.

Carson reminded himself that it was December 21st. People would be busy, harried, and possibly traveling for the holiday. He had best wait a few days to follow up on his leads. It was Christmas after all, and he deserved a break, too.

However, Dan Nash wasn't getting any breaks, and he thought tiredly. And Carson sensed that what Jamie Nesser had said was right on target. Nash needed some relief after thirty some-odd years of hell or he would snap.

He liked Dan and his wife. Truth be told, he liked all of the people involved. They'd climbed a lot of mountains and had remained decent folks throughout it all.

Carson called an old N.O.P.D. friend and asked him if they could meet and talk over a couple of beers. Instead, they met at the Waffle House and stayed for three hours.

As he worked on his fifth cup of coffee, Carson's friend asked, "What the fuck is wrong with you? You haven't been this depressed since…since I don't know when."

"Ah, it's this case I'm on. It's really bringing me down."

"What's the scoop?"

"You know I don't kiss and tell."

"Talk to me, Man."

"The client's a good guy in spite of all this terrible shit that happened to him as a kid. His life's been falling apart, lately. He's lost both parents recently, and there are some major secrets unfolding as a result. The wife has been dealing with his problems and some of her own."

"And that ain't helping anybody."

"Right. Now, I've got to interview the man who abused my client when he was a boy."

"And you don't want to talk to the asshole. Who would? But you know you have to. You think I liked talking to the families of victims when I worked homicide? It liked to kill me, but if I didn't do it and do it right, then somebody else who maybe wasn't so considerate might take up the job. That's not what I wanted. I don't think that's what you want either. You want to help this client, just like you want to help all of your clients."

"This is different. I've gotten too close, but it's too late to throw in the towel and tell them to get someone else. These people are depending on me."

They sat without speaking for a few minutes before his friend offered, "I know this case is weighing on your mind, but that's not what's bringing you down to begin with. It's your little girl, isn't it?"

"Yeah, I guess so. It's Christmas for God's sake, the third Christmas in a row that I don't know where she is."

"She's all right, Carson."

"Yeah, sure."

"You'll find her and that good-for-nothing ex-wife of yours soon."

Carson stood and withdrew some money from his wallet to cover the bill and the tip.

"I gotta go," he told his friend. "You take care."

"You, too."

As Carson drove home, he listened to the strains of the Eagles version of "Please Come Home for Christmas" playing on the radio. He detoured to Albertson's and bought a six-pack of beer and a box of holiday cupcakes. It was going to be a long, long night.

Chapter Nine: Acts of Kindness

Daniel was finding it almost impossible to concentrate. He'd insisted on coming in to work, but he was so distracted by thoughts of his parents, the estate, the investigation, and his wife and son that he conceded he was not being very productive.

Penny, his administrative assistant, brought him one innocuous document after another approximately every ten minutes. She lingered in the room each time. Circling anxiously, she knitted her brows with his every movement and pause.

"For Christ's sake," he growled after two hours of her hovering. "Will you leave me alone? You don't have to bring me any more papers. If you want to spy on me, then just do it, all right?"

Wordlessly, she backed out of the room and pulled the door shut behind her. Fifteen minutes later, the sound of knuckles rapping on the wood disturbed Daniel's futile attempts to read a report regarding one of his best client's accounts.

"Penny, I told you to leave me alone!" he barked, tossing down the sheaf of papers in his hand.

"I told Penny to take a break."

Hunter Brachman walked in authoritatively and sat in the chair in front of Daniel's desk. He'd been promoted to department head the year before at the tender age of thirty-three. He was knowledgeable in the field of finance and had always been good at dealing with people, whether they be his clients or his employees.

Daniel looked askance at Hunter, feeling like a schoolboy caught in the act of teasing a new student.

"You've got the poor girl in tears, Dan," Hunter said. "She thinks you're the greatest boss in the world. You know that. She's only concerned. You didn't have to snap at her." He casually folded his hands across his chest and asked, "Do you realize that when Penny first applied to this company, the Human Resource people didn't think she'd stand a chance of being hired? Then, when you chose her to be your assistant, they were laying bets on how long the shy girl with no self-confidence would last. You treated her with respect, and she's been here for over two years. She's become an extremely competent employee because you're a good boss. Or at least you were until this morning. My assistant found her sniffling at the water cooler, and Penny blurted out the whole story. So, here I am."

He sat waiting – not asking, not telling, just waiting.

"What do you want, Hunter?"

"I want you to tell me what's going on with you. You're one of my best employees. You do your job well, and you never hesitate to pitch in and help other folks in the office, even when you don't directly benefit from it. You come in on time and stay late when it's called for. Up until the last month and a half, you've hardly ever taken off time from work. I remember when you had the flu last year, but you didn't miss a day. Just between you and me, I would have preferred it if you and your germs had stayed at home, but I admired your determination to do your job."

"Thank you," Daniel said morosely, knowing that Hunter was leading up to something unpleasant.

"You're not doing your job right now, Dan. Last month when your wife was fired you took a little time off. Not enough. Then your father died, and you didn't even miss a day."

"It was Thanksgiving, Hunter. We had the Friday off anyway and –"

"Your mother died Tuesday, and you took off yesterday for the funeral."

"I'll make it up with comp time."

Hunter shook his head and said, "You're missing the point. Do you think that I care about the leave time? I checked with Human Resources before I came in here. Do you know how much leave you have?" He paused for effect then said, "Fifty-six days not counting a decent amount of comp time. They also informed me that you've been turning in leave slips for an hour each Wednesday when you leave early, but you always stay an hour later the next day so they pitch the slips in the trash. What are you saving the time for?"

"I'm not saving it for anything."

"When's the last time you and Sarah took a vacation? You planning some major surgery? Unlike my assistant, I doubt if you'll ever need six weeks off for a hysterectomy."

"I got into this business late, remember? People usually start a serious career in the investment industry in their twenties, not their thirties. I feel like I need to push a little harder. I *need* to work, especially at this time."

"You've recently lost both of your parents. That would be tough for anyone. It's the Friday before Christmas. That would be harder on anyone."

"I can handle it."

"Maybe you can. Can Sarah? I've bumped into her three times at Wal-Mart, lately. Once she was with her sister and the other two times she was with her brother and Kris. She looks…I don't know…stunned." He sighed and continued, "And you…I don't know what's going on with you, Dan. Whatever it is, you're not yourself. Your work is suffering. I want you to take some time off."

Daniel stood hastily, pushing his chair back as he rose.

"Hunter, I can't do that! Who'll take care of my clients?"

"I'll divvy up your load."

"We have Monday and Tuesday off for the holiday and –"

Shaking his head, Hunter stood and walked around the desk until he was in front of Daniel.

"That's not enough. Everyone will get off at noon today. You can stay until then, but then I want you to take off for at least thirty days. Use the comp time first. Check in with me. Providing I feel you're ready to return, you'll come back after that and pick up where you left off. If not, then you can take more time. I don't care if you have to take some leave without pay. I want to keep you here but not like this. You're doing us and yourself a disservice at this point."

"Don't I get any other choices?" Daniel asked sullenly.

"You can quit."

Daniel glared at Hunter and kept his mouth firmly closed.

"Good. I don't want you to quit either. Merry Christmas. I'll be talking with you."

Daniel watched him go. He checked the time: 11:42. He clenched his hands into fists and ground his teeth for as long as he could stand it. Then he forced his hands and mouth to go slack and walked over to the door.

"Hey, Moneypenny!" he called out, using the familiar nickname he'd given her shortly after she'd been hired. "Would you come in here for a minute?"

At the sound of his using the nickname, Penny's face lit up brighter than the tiny tinseled tree she'd placed on the corner of her desk. She came into his office with an uncertain smile.

"I'm sorry, Penny. I didn't mean to yell at you like that. I'm really tired right now. As a matter of fact, I'm going to take a month off to get my head together."

No longer, I hope, he added silently.

"Hunter will probably assign you to help the other advisors while I'm out. They're going to be dividing up my clients until I come back."

"I'll do everything I can to keep things straight while you're gone."

"I know you will." Attempting to repair any hurt feelings he'd caused earlier, he asked, "Do you have any special plans for Christmas?"

"Well, yes," she said blushing. "You know the guy from the computer department I've been dating? He asked me to marry him last night. We're going to tell our parents on Christmas Day."

"Penny, that's great. I'm happy for you. He seems like a really nice guy, but you tell him that he better treat you right or he'll have to answer to me."

She stepped forward, gave him a hug, and said, "Merry Christmas. I baked some Magic Cookie Bars for you and the family. It's my grandmother's recipe."

"Magic cookies?"

Daniel felt the blood drain from his face and hoped that Penny hadn't noticed. As it was, she was too busy retrieving a large, gold box filled presumably with the cookies.

When he'd read his father's journals, he'd assumed that "Magic Cookies" was simply a colloquial name given to the Nash children's favorite treat. He had no idea that it was an actual type of dessert.

He accepted the box from Penny. Curiosity got the better of him, and he undid the ribbon and peered at the cookie bars inside. Daniel lifted one to his lips and tentatively took a bite.

"They're wonderful."

"You really like them? There's not too much coconut?"

"No. I've always wanted to try Magic Cookies."

"Well, they're Magic Cookie Bars. I think Magic Cookies are something different. Chocolate with sugar or something."

"Oh. Well, maybe. These are delicious, though. Thank you, Penny." He took another bite then said, "I have something for you, too."

It was a dark blue sweater that had knitted black cats climbing all over it. Each cat had a red ribbon at its neck. Penny, who loved cats even more than she loved James Bond, adored it.

"Sarah picked it out," Daniel admitted sheepishly. "But then I'm sure you already knew that. I'm no good at picking out things for anybody but Sarah."

He experienced a sinking feeling, as he realized that he had yet to purchase a Christmas present for his wife.

At noon, Daniel slipped into his coat and took his briefcase and the enormous box of treats to his Mazda. After staring at the concrete post in front of him for a few minutes, he stepped out of the car and headed for the street. He wasn't sure where he was going, but maybe the cold air would clear his muddled brain. Perhaps he would stumble upon a Christmas present for his wife.

He was halfway up the steps of St. Joseph's Cathedral before he realized it. He halted then forced himself to climb the rest of the way and enter the old Gothic-style church.

Daniel had been there the day before for his mother's funeral. The church appeared deserted now, except for a lone worshipper emerging from the confessional. Daniel picked up a bulletin that rested on a side table and read the line:

The Sacrament of Reconciliation will be celebrated every day this week from twelve to one as we prepare ourselves for the coming of Our Lord, Jesus Christ.

It was 12:54.

He stepped into the side of the confessional reserved for the penitents. Then he pulled and locked the door behind him. The little panel covering the screen that separated the priest and the parishioner slid back with a *crack* and a shadowy blob was visible through the thick mesh in-between them.

Daniel struggled to recall exactly what one was supposed to do in Confession.

"Bless me, Father, for I have sinned. It has been nineteen years since my last confession."

His cheeks burned with embarrassment at this, and he was grateful that the priest couldn't see him. Even though Daniel had never truly believed in the sacrament, he didn't want to incur the priest's disapproval. He wasn't sure why this mattered to him, but it did.

"I can't remember what I'm supposed to do next."

"Do you recall the Act of Contrition?"

Tightly squeezing his eyelids together, Daniel summoned the words he'd been taught by Assumpta.

"Oh, my God, I am heartily sorry for having offended You, and I detest all my sins because of Your just punishment. Um, I firmly resolve with the help of Your Grace…to avoid sin…no…to sin no more and avoid the near occasion of sin. Amen?"

The priest chuckled then said, "That's pretty good after nineteen years. You'd be surprised at how some people butcher it. Now, what can I do for you? Why have you come here today after such a long absence? Not that I'm complaining."

Daniel checked his watch.

"Father, it's 12:59, and –"

"I've got nothing waiting for me this afternoon, save the proofreading of next week's bulletin. You're here, and that's more important. Now, what's troubling you?"

Daniel opened his mouth to tell the priest about his argument with Lillian. He wanted to explain to the man how guilty he felt over his anger regarding his father's concealment of his true paternity. He wanted to talk of the helplessness he was experiencing in regards to his wife and her distress. He wanted to tell him about what had happened at work only an hour before.

Instead, he exhaled a sob, which was rapidly followed by a series of sobs. Try as he might, the force of the tears was too great to contain. Months – no, years – of vigilantly combating fear and anger were giving way to an uncontrollable sense of the futility of his defensive maneuverings. He wrapped his arms tightly around his stomach and fought to catch his breath.

Suddenly, the lock on his side of the confessional was turned back and the door swung open. Daniel became aware of the presence of another person in the little closet-like room. Strong hands gripped his shoulders. He pried his eyelids apart and saw the priest kneeling in front of him with consternation and compassion in his expression.

The man was older than Daniel, perhaps fifty or sixty. He was balding and wore wire-rimmed glasses that covered bright blue eyes.

"It's all right, Son. The Lord is with you, and so am I."

The priest held him as a father would his crying toddler. Daniel's entire body seemed to hurt from the surface of his skin to the muscles deep underneath. He eventually quieted, and the older man loosened his hold and eased him back against the wall of the confessional.

Daniel sat, exhausted and listless on the wooden bench. He longed to be at home in bed with Sarah. Whenever he had the worst of the nightmares, she would calm him with her voice, her touch, and the comfort of her naked skin against his.

Would it work this time? he thought dully. *This isn't a nightmare. This is something that's never happened before in my life. My life. Most of that's been a waking nightmare.*

The priest left the confessional, returning quickly with a handful of tissues and a small cup of water. Daniel reclined against the dark wood behind him, too dazed to accept what the man offered. Finally, the priest wiped at the wetness on Daniel's cheeks and brought the cup up to his lips, tilting it so that the water teased his tongue. Then, the man put the back of his hand against Daniel's forehead, checking to see if fever was to blame for his current state.

"My name's Frank Randall. Come with me," the priest said with authority. "You need rest. The staff's gone for the day. Here, let me help you."

He half-lifted, half-prodded Daniel until he stood upright, although he leaned heavily on the older man. Daniel paid little attention to their surroundings as he was guided through the church and into a sparsely furnished room that was painted a soothing shade of blue. He was helped to a large chair and almost collapsed into it.

When Randall handed him a glass filled with a dark, red liquid, Daniel pushed it away.

"It's only red wine. It hasn't gone through the Transubstantiation, yet. I haven't prayed for it to be transformed from wine into the blood of our Lord as I do in Mass." When Daniel continued to hesitate, he added, "You look as though you could use a stiff drink, but this is all I have to offer."

He held out the glass a second time, and Daniel accepted it. He drained it in four large gulps, feeling his chest burn as the alcohol descended. He continued to hold the glass in his hands and let the wine soak into his system.

Daniel dozed, waking with a start an hour later. He clutched at the air in front of him, trying to catch a glass that was no longer there.

"It's on the desk," Randall told him. "You were restless. I didn't want to leave you. Do you feel better now…?"

"Dan Nash." He gave a half-shrug and asked, "Am I better?"

Like his wife, Daniel preferred being direct. Unlike her, he could not click that mental switch and become unobtrusively manipulative. Subjugated to a disruptive home life from birth and then to repeated physical assault, Daniel had survived by keeping his mouth shut and his eyes lowered as much as possible. For twelve years, he'd stayed alive by not talking, by not saying what he really felt.

"Thank you," he said finally. "I'm sorry I've put you out."

"I'm a priest," Randall replied. "Priests are supposed to be emissaries of God. Do you think Christ would have left you alone in the confessional? Do you think the Blessed Virgin would have done any less? I daresay she would have wiped at your tears with the hem of her veil. In that light, holding out tissues and a cup of water is almost laughable."

"I'm not laughing, am I?"

"Before, you wouldn't drink the wine until I told you that it hadn't been transformed into Christ's blood, yet. Why did it make such a difference to you?"

Daniel fingered a thread that hung from the arm of the chair and said, “I don’t believe that it *becomes* Christ’s blood, no matter how much you pray over it. I never have.”

It was the first time he’d ever said it aloud to anyone but Sarah, although he’d thought it many times before.

“I disagree with you, although I don’t think now’s the time for a theological argument. If you truly don’t believe then the wine would merely be wine, and you could drink it with impunity, correct?”

“This sounds like a theological argument to me.”

Randall smiled at Daniel and said, “It’s only an observation. You can make of it whatever you wish.”

“You want the truth? I want to believe in God. As it is, I don’t believe in anything.”

“You wear a wedding ring.”

“Yes.”

“Then you believe in marriage?”

“A person can’t win with you, can he?”

“It’s not a game, is it? This is your life we’re talking about and your soul.”

“If we’re going to have a serious talk about my soul, then I need another drink.”

Randall went over to a side table and poured wine into two large glasses. The men drank silently for several minutes before Randall asked, “Are you going to tell me about it?”

“I guess that’s why I ended up in here, so I might as well. My adoptive mother died Tuesday night. It was the day before the twenty-seventh anniversary of my biological mother’s death. My father died last month. My wife….”

He took a sip from his glass and stared vacantly at one curved leg of the desk. Unperturbed by Daniel’s hesitation, the priest drained the small amount of wine that remained in his glass and waited.

“She’s always taken care of everyone, especially me. Not that I haven’t been there for her, but I guess I needed more taking care of emotionally. I had a pretty horrific childhood, and it left me on shaky ground. Sarah’s an expert at handling things. She’s carried me through time and time again. Lately, though….”

“Perhaps now it’s time for you to return the favor.”

"You don't think that's what I want, what I'm trying to do? But I'm not doing so well myself."

"So I see. Maybe we could pray together and ask for the Lord's guidance?"

The anger Daniel felt was searing and instantaneous. It was also impossible to conceal.

"Such fury." The priest shook his head then asked, "What led you to this?"

"When I was a boy, my mother used to pray and pray," Daniel explained. "She used to say that God would deliver us from the violence that my stepfather inflicted upon her. I didn't know he was my stepfather, you understand? I didn't know that until last month. I thought the monster was my natural father." A scowl of hate contorted his features as he said, "God delivered her all right. She finally died as a result of my stepfather's attacks. Then he started in on me."

Daniel licked his lips, tasting the tang of the wine and remembering when he'd tasted blood there instead.

"Deliver us from evil, isn't that what the Lord's Prayer says?"

A stark memory suddenly engulfed him, as vivid thirty years later as it had been on the day it had happened. Zachary Samuels had his fingers wrapped tightly around Assumpta's arm. Her shirt was torn, and there was a blue-black bruise on her face. Her husband was screaming unintelligibly at her, but Assumpta's eyes were fixed on some point beyond his left ear. Daniel could hear her voice, low and clear, as she recited again and again:

"Our Father, Who art in Heaven, hallowed be Thy name. Thy kingdom come; Thy will be done on earth as it is in Heaven. Give us this day our daily bread, and forgive us our trespasses, as we forgive those who trespass against us. And lead us not into temptation, but deliver us from evil. Amen. Our Father, Who art in Heaven…."

"The Lord's Prayer does include that," the priest confirmed. "If you remember, it's also said in the Mass. Deliver us, Lord, from every evil, and grant us peace in our day."

"I've never known peace."

"You have to want to be spiritually and emotionally healed. It must start with forgiveness."

"Forgiveness? For whom?"

"Many people, I'd suspect. If your life's been so troubled, then I'd expect you harbor anger against those you feel were responsible for your pain." He glanced at his watch and admitted, "I have to go. While you were sleeping, I received a call for my services. I'd like to meet with you again, although the next few days are booked because of the Christmas services. How about lunch next Tuesday? Noon at the Black Forest?"

Although he was, as always, leery of trusting outsiders with the story of his past, Daniel felt a definite desire to open up to this man. He didn't care if the man was a priest or a therapist or a blues musician. He was comfortable in the older man's presence. There was an air of simple wisdom and compassion around Frank Randall that his psychiatrist lacked.

Too much detachment on the therapist's part, Daniel reflected. *Necessary detachment, I'm sure. But wouldn't the same apply to the priest?*

"I didn't think priests did the lunch thing. I thought you talked to people in church or in offices like this."

"I may be an emissary of the Lord, but I don't share His almighty constitution. I find that it's better to discuss things such as this when food is involved. People are more inclined to relax when there's a po-boy or a pizza around to distract them."

"Okay. I'll be there."

"You harbor anger in your heart against certain people. These are the people you must forgive. Make a list of forgiveness, so to speak. Bring it with you to lunch. Then we can talk."

It was only as Daniel rose to go that he realized he was still wearing his coat. He looked down at himself, the trappings of the real world forcing reality into his brain.

"What time is it?"

"Almost 4:00."

"Jesus H. Christ. Sarah's probably wondering where in the hell I am." Red snaked up his neck and flooded his cheeks as he muttered, "Sorry."

"I've heard much worse." Randall lowered his glass onto the desk and casually asked, "Your wife's name is Sarah? I believe I may have met her at the chapel at the Lake Tuesday night. An attractive woman in her late twenties or early thirties? Auburn hair? A scar on her arm?"

"Yeah, that's her. Too weird." Daniel swallowed the last of his wine and asked, "How was she with you?"

"Very tired in mind and body. She does need for someone to take care of her. What do you think it would take to help the two of you right now?"

"A miracle," Daniel replied, only half-joking.

Randall smiled, lifted his empty glass, and offered, "To a miracle, then."

Chapter Ten: Returning the Favor

"I have off until the beginning of February," Daniel said in conclusion.

Sarah lay beside him in their bed. The house was cool in the early morning chill, and Daniel was content to lie next to his wife in the small pocket of warmth created by the bedclothes and the heat of their bodies. The familiar faint scent of rose was in her hair and on her skin. He laid his hand on her thigh, enjoying the feel of the soft flesh under his palm.

"And you're going to go to lunch with Father Randall on Tuesday?"

"Mm."

"You're not going to stop seeing the psychiatrist, are you?"

The tremor in her voice made him open his eyes and look down at her.

"I'm worried you'll quit and get worse. I don't think I could take it if that happened."

"What about you? You went to that woman therapist one time, and you didn't go back."

"I didn't like her. Her style wasn't for me."

"I've been seeing my current therapist for several weeks, and I don't think his style is for me," he admitted. "Maybe you should come to lunch with me and the priest on Tuesday."

"Maybe." Then, "Sometimes, I get so afraid for you."

Daniel was touched by how small and pale she seemed. How vulnerable she appeared, even in this tiny cocoon of warmth. Moving awkwardly within the tangle of sheets, blanket, and comforter, Daniel gathered her up against him in a rush of protectiveness mingled with love and desire that unsurprisingly led to sex.

He lay on his back afterwards, and Sarah slept resting on top of him, her chest against his waist and her head near his heart. He fingered her curls and tried not to move or make any noise.

Daniel was gradually beginning to understand how profoundly his personal struggles had affected his wife. She'd given of herself so completely when he'd battled the nightmares and the memories. How many times had she comforted him in the darkness as he'd told her about the things that no one else had ever known? He had inadvertently given her the burden of understanding what he'd endured, and in response she had willingly taken on the role of primary healer.

Physician, heal thyself?

Sometime after 7:00, Daniel heard Cookie Monster's voice coming from the direction of the living room. Sarah stirred in his arms then tried to push herself up.

"Go back to sleep," he ordered softly.

"But Kris –"

"Kris is fine."

She lay silent beside him for a time. Then she said his name softly.

"Hm?"

"What are we going to do with the house on Highland?"

"Put in a security system. Once people know that there's no one living there, it won't be long before someone tries to rob the place. I was thinking about calling an alarm company Tuesday morning."

"And after that?"

"A part of me wants to never see it again. Another part of me never wants to let it go." He wrapped his arms more tightly around her and asked, "What do you want to do with it?"

"It's not my house."

The laughter rumbled under her right ear.

"It's as much your house as it is mine. You actually lived there before I did. You married a Nash, and your son is a Nash. Do you want to live in it?"

She didn't answer, but Daniel felt a tear drop onto his chest and slide down his left side.

"We'll think about it later," he murmured. "It's not going anywhere." Forcing himself to sound cheerful, he said, "Let's shower and get Kris dressed. It feels like it must be really cold outside. Looks like this year you'll get one of those cold Christmases you like. We won't be wearing shorts like last year.

Anyhow, they must have the fire lit at Cracker Barrel. We can go there for breakfast."

"Daniel, I can make breakfast here."

"Will you stop for once in your life? I know you *can*. Right now, you *don't need to*."

When they arrived at the restaurant, the parking lot was crammed with cars. People were sitting in the rockers on the long porch. The little Nash family hurried towards the door and the warmth inside.

"While you and Kris look around the store, I'll put our name down on the waiting list."

Nodding, Sarah took their son's hand and began to wade through the crowd.

Five minutes later, Daniel made it to the head of the line and gave the hostess his name, the number of people in his party, and their non-smoking preference. Then he scanned the room in search of his wife and child. They weren't in the candy area, which was adjacent to the hostess stand. As he passed through it on his way towards the toy section, he picked up a Lindor Ball, one of Sarah's favorite treats. She and Kris were not in the candle area, nor were they looking at the toys. Peering around Coca-Cola sweatshirts and giant white pitchers in round basins, he spotted them near the center of the store. Sarah was attempting to see the price tag on a porcelain baby doll.

"Kris, can you see how much this is?" Daniel heard her ask, as he drew up behind her.

"Um, two thousanded ninety-nine dollars."

She smiled and said, "I think there's probably a dot in-between there somewhere. Thank you, Sweet Pea. That was a very good try."

The boy caught sight of his father and spun around, narrowly avoiding contact with a huge Christmas tree which was decorated with glass ornaments.

"Daddy! Look at what I found! Do you think that Santa could bring it to me?"

He held up the old-fashioned toy. Two dogs were attached with pulleys at each end. There were small, red wheels on the corners and a string at the front. As Kris demonstrated, when one pulled the string, both dogs went alternately up and down as if they were racing.

"I think it's charming," Sarah said enthusiastically. "Much better than a video game."

"I agree. Santa's elves love to make these old kinds of toys. I bet if you leave a note, then Santa might find an extra one in his sack for you."

"Really?" Kris asked, wide-eyed.

"Really," Sarah concurred. "When we get home, I'll help you write a special letter."

Pulling the dog toy slowly in a wide arch, Kris watched with fascination as the dogs rose and fell. Daniel put his arm around Sarah's shoulders and held out the Lindor Ball.

"Here's something to tide you over until they call our name. I know how you love these. Milk chocolate on the outside. Creamy, soft milk chocolate on the inside. Guaranteed to be better than anything else you've ever tasted. Better than sex, even."

His wife giggled and unwrapped the chocolate ball and offered him a bite before popping it into her mouth.

"Mmmm," she moaned, closing her eyes as she savored the taste. "That was fabulous."

"Well, now I know what to get you if I ever get a headache and don't want to make love."

"I can think of one time in your whole life that you haven't been ready to make love and that was last week."

He bent low in order to kiss her, the sweet residue of chocolate on her lips and tongue.

Someone standing to Daniel's left cleared his throat in disapproval. Daniel turned quickly, ready to tell the man exactly where he could go. He was startled to see Father Frank Randall's smiling countenance.

"Good morning, Dan. And Sarah! So good to see you again. I thought that stern *harrumph* would get your attention. I didn't want to interrupt but did want to say hello."

"It's so good to see you," Sarah said with a wave of her hand and a smile. "It's nice to see you again, too. Have you already eaten? Would you like to join us?"

"I wouldn't want to intrude on your breakfast."

"You wouldn't be intruding at all," she said graciously. "Even priests have to eat."

"So I informed your husband yesterday."

Daniel never ceased to be amazed at his wife's talent for being able to control her emotions at a moment's notice. When they were alone or when she was with her father, Jamie, or Helen and Jim, she was fragile and anxious. Yet, when their son was present or when she was conversing with others, the mask of acceptable emotion veiled her fear.

The sound of breaking glass made them all turn. Kris was staring at the pieces of a small crystal ornament that lay at his feet. He looked up shyly at his parents, the string of the dog toy gripped tightly in his hands, and said solemnly, "I didn't mean to break it. I'll pay for it with my allowance."

"Stay there, Kris," Daniel warned. "You might cut yourself on the glass."

He went forward and reached down to lift the boy away from the shards on the floor. An employee came hurrying over with a pan and a brush.

"Daddy and I know it was an accident," Sarah told her son. "If we pay for it this time, will you watch more closely next time?"

"Yes, Mommy."

"Good." She hugged her son then released him and straightened as they heard, "Nash. Party of three. Nash. Party of three."

After explaining the addition to their party and removing Father Randall's name from the list, they were led past the enormous fireplace and seated at a table near the wall. Kris immediately pounced on the peg game that had been placed next to the sugar.

"I'm hungry, Mommy."

"I wonder what you could want," Sarah teased. "Could it be…turnip greens?"

"No!" he cried laughing.

"Could it be…biscuits and gravy?"

"No!"

"Ham steak with mashed potatoes?"

"No!"

"Then, it must be…French toast!"

As she said the last two words, Sarah reached out and tickled her son, who squealed with laughter. Moments later, they sat back panting and giggling as their waitress approached.

"Welcome to Cracker Barrel. I'll be your – Mr. Nash?"

Daniel looked up from his menu and said in surprise, "Celeste? Hey, how's it going? How long have you been working here?"

"One week. It's much better here, and, like, my dad has chilled a little."

"That's great. I'm happy for you."

Realizing that Sarah, Kris, and Frank Randall were all being politely quiet and confused, Daniel decided that now was as good a time as any for introductions.

"Celeste, this is my wife, Sarah, our son, Kris, and our friend, Frank." Turning to the others, he explained, "Celeste was working for Room Service at the hotel where I stayed recently."

"My first and last day," she said with embarrassment. "Look, I don't, like, want to hold them up in the kitchen. Can I get you something to drink while you look at the menu?"

"I think we all know what we want," Daniel assured her. "We can order now."

"That would be cool. Ma'am, what'll you have?"

"The Old Timer's Breakfast with fried apples and bacon as my selections and my eggs over medium. I'd also like some coffee."

Celeste turned to Kris.

"And you, Sir?"

"French toast and hot chocolate!"

"Okay. And you, Father?"

"I'll take Grandpa's Country Fried Breakfast with the chicken fried steak and hash browns. Orange juice, too."

"And you, Mr. Nash?"

"Grandpa's Country Fried Breakfast, but I want chicken fried chicken instead of the country fried steak and apples instead of the hash browns."

"And to drink?"

"Black coffee. My wife can have all of my cream and sugar. She'll probably still need more."

"Probably," Sarah agreed dryly.

"I'll be right back with your drinks. Thanks."

As she headed for the kitchen, Frank Randall shook his head sadly.

"A high school student, I take it?"

Daniel nodded.

"She seems like a nice young lady," remarked the priest, as he unrolled his napkin and laid his silverware out in front of him. "Especially in today's society, it's an all-too-common situation to see teenaged pregnancy."

Oblivious to the men's conversation, Kris asked his mother, "Did you like that doll, Mommy? It was a lot, wasn't it?"

"Yes, I liked it, but not so much," Sarah admitted.

She paused in order to accept her coffee from Celeste and waited until the girl had moved on to another table before adding cream and sugar to her cup. Her husband and the priest had ceased their discussion before Celeste's arrival and were now busying themselves by sipping their own beverages. Kris happily slurped at his hot chocolate, receiving a gentle reprimand from Daniel in the process.

"Mommy, how come you didn't like that doll so much?" the child inquired. "I thought girls liked dolls."

"It didn't look like a real baby. Plus, I didn't like that its eyes were painted closed."

"When you were a little girl, did you have one that the eyes were painted closed?"

"I never had a doll like that when I was a little girl. I had a Barbie doll and some stuffed dolls."

"How come you didn't have one like that?"

"Because my daddy and I didn't have the money. Even back then, nice dolls were expensive." Helping Kris pour more hot chocolate into his cup, Sarah added, "One of my friends had lots of nice dolls. There were babies, girls, and ladies in different outfits. We used to play with them when I'd go to her house. One time, she even let me bring one home for the night. Her mother was furious."

"What's furriess?"

"Furious. Very angry."

"Why was the lady so mad? Did she think you wouldn't take care of it?"

"That must have been what it was."

Their food arrived, and it took several minutes for Celeste to sort out who had what and where to place it on the table. Eventually, she figured it out, and the diners were able to eat.

"Did you have a favorite doll at your friend's house?" the priest asked casually, as he cut into his chicken fried steak.

"Several. She had tons of them. It was fascinating. Some of them, their eyes were open but when you laid them down the eyes would close."

"How many did she have?" asked Daniel.

"Oh, a couple of dozen."

"Did you want all of her dolls?" Kris asked with interest.

"No, and I didn't need them. There were more important things we had to have. I would have been happy with a baby doll in a nice cotton and lace gown and a girl doll in some old-fashioned clothes. But I never cared much for the lady dolls."

In a moment of clarity Daniel realized that every year for the last ten years, Sarah had purchased and donated a doll for the girls and a baseball glove for the boys for the annual Christmas toy drive at their church. The dolls she bought were certainly not as expensive as the ones they'd been discussing. The drive organizers instructions were clear. Nothing fragile or expensive could be donated.

So, she'd bought the prettiest plastic dolls she could find. He remembered her standing in the toy aisle at Target the previous year. Her curls were pulled back into a ponytail, and she was picking up each box, scrutinizing the plastic faces, the hair, and the clothes. She'd tilted the boxes of the prospective gifts back and forth to see if the eyes closed when the doll was laid down to sleep.

Of course, he hadn't known that was what she was doing at the time. He'd merely thought the painstaking process was her way of ensuring that the lucky child would have a decent present. Now, he knew that there was so much more to it than that.

Chapter Eleven: Evasive Maneuvers

"– that the team would win, Daddy?"

It took Daniel five frenetic seconds to make sense of what his son was talking about before he could answer.

"Well, that's who I hope will win the Super Bowl." He wiped his lips and folded his napkin next to his plate. "C'mon, Kris. Why don't we make a pit stop at the bathroom?"

"But I don't have to go!"

"You never have to go," Sarah said reprovingly. "It's not good for you. Go on with Daddy."

"But Mommy –"

"Try."

With a long-suffering sigh, the child slid off his seat and accepted his father's hand.

"We won't be long," Daniel called back, as they edged their way around a waitress. "I hope."

The line in front of the hostess was still thick with hungry people, so Daniel swung Kris up into his arms. The feel of the child's body was unimaginably reassuring to Daniel, the slight weight both soft and solid near his chest. He lowered Kris to the floor when they arrived in the bathroom and led him to the handicapped stall.

"Daddy, why do you always have to go in here?"

"I don't when I'm alone, but I won't leave you outside the door while I go. Some stranger could grab you. These are usually bigger than the regular stalls, so we can go in together." Reaching under the child's arms, he lifted him up until his feet were planted on the top of either side of the toilet seat. "Go for it."

"But I don't have to! Really!"

"Try," he said firmly, echoing his wife. Then, "See? It never hurts to try."

Annoyed at being proved wrong, Kris stuck out his lower lip and leaned against the wall to wait for his father.

"I have an idea," Daniel said, as they washed their hands. "It's about Mommy's Christmas present…."

Returning to the restaurant, they resumed their seats and joined in the current discussion concerning the importance of

Christmas traditions. Periodically, Kris would giggle for no apparent reason, then Daniel would smile mysteriously.

"What's the deal with you two?" Sarah asked. "Am I missing something?"

"It's a guy thing," Kris said with a somber expression. "You wouldn't understand."

The adults laughed uproariously at this, surprising Celeste as she delivered their bills.

"Thanks, Celeste. That was great."

"You're welcome, Mr. Nash. Thank you all for being patient with me."

"Have a merry Christmas," Sarah said to the girl. "And a happy New Year."

"You, too."

"God bless you," added the priest, as he laid his utensils neatly in his plate.

"Bye!" Kris sang out, as Celeste hurried back to the kitchen to pick up another order.

They walked single-file through the restaurant and into the store towards the cash register. Daniel insisted on paying the priest's bill despite his objections, stating that it was the least he could do in light of what had happened the previous afternoon.

"Oh! I forgot my keys on the table!" Sarah cried. "I'd better hurry."

Daniel chuckled and shook his head, making the priest look questioningly at him.

"She hasn't had her keys out of her purse yet this morning. She can't drive; she's partially blind," he explained, causing the man to look startled. "Hard to tell sometimes, isn't it? She's very adept at adaptation."

"Therefore, she went back to the table to …?"

"To leave the girl some extra money, I'm sure. Whatever she can spare."

"Is she always this good at hiding her true feelings?"

"Always." Then, realizing what the man had said, Daniel asked, "You can tell?"

"You must remember that I met her before, when she was not interested in or not able to be quite so 'on guard'." He smiled mischievously at Daniel and admitted, "Being observant and able to read people's emotions is a benefit of the job. If you'll recall, I also noticed you two here in the store before you noticed me. I'm sure her guard was down a fraction or two, although a complete stranger would most likely not have noticed anything amiss."

"What do you think?"

"She needs time – and you." As he reached into his pocket for a handkerchief, he asked, "Have you worked on the list?"

"Not yet."

"Don't forget it Tuesday."

The temperature had dropped several degrees outside. The Nashes said goodbye to Frank Randall. Then they ran, shivering to their car.

"How much did you leave her?" Daniel asked after they'd climbed into the Mazda.

"Twenty dollars more. I hope you're not upset."

"Why would I be upset?" He twisted and leaned forward, putting his hands behind her head and drawing her closer before murmuring, "My wife cares about people and wants to help them."

"Ewwww!" Kris cried, covering his eyes with his hands as his parents kissed. "Gross!"

"I'll drop you off at Tris's," Daniel said, buckling his seatbelt. "I told Kris I'd take him to the bookstore. You think you could get your dad or Vaughn to help you with that errand?"

They both knew he was talking about returning to Cracker Barrel to buy the wooden toy for their son.

"Somebody will get me to the library," Sarah nodded.

Unbeknownst to her husband or anyone else, Sarah actually did intend to go to the library. Once Daniel had dropped her off at her parents' house, she found that no one was at home, save for her brother, Will. She asked him whether he would mind taking her back to the restaurant and then to the Goodwood Public Library.

They pulled into the parking lot of the library before noon, the old-fashioned toy safely stowed away in the back of Will's car. After receiving directions from the man at the front desk, Sarah approached an office to the right and tapped on the glass of the door. Will, who had agreed to peruse the shelves, stood off to one side of the room and watched his sister enter the office. He moved closer as she withdrew a large book with a flowery cover and held it out to an older woman who was wearing a long dress dotted with so many flowers that it rivaled the book jacket in Sarah's hands.

"I didn't know if anyone in this area would be here today," Sarah admitted.

"Normally, I wouldn't. My sister and her husband and their three obnoxious children are visiting for the holidays." The woman grinned and said cheerfully, "And me with all this work to do. Now, what can I do for you?"

"I – I have this book that I want to return to the library."

"I don't think this is one of ours. There's even a price tag still attached to it." Paper ruffled as the woman flipped the pages so that she could view the inside of the book. "And there's no bar code."

"Well, I found it at a bookstore, but I'm afraid it is one of your books. My mother checked it out from the library over twenty-five years ago and never got to return it."

"It was lost?"

"No, she was killed, and the book was damaged beyond repair. My father didn't even know about it, and it got thrown away. When I saw it in the shop window, I thought that maybe it should be put back into your collection. She really enjoyed it."

"Let me fill out the donation card. Would you like the donation made in her honor? We put a sticker in the front that says *Donated in Memory of.*"

"That would be great. Her name was Emma Maes. M-A-E-S."

Will had heard enough. He strode over to the stacks and pretended to be engrossed in the first book he found. Shortly thereafter, his sister laid a hand on his arm.

"We can go now. I'd appreciate it if you wouldn't spy on me again like that, Will."

"Who said I was spying?" he asked innocently.

"Oh, come off it! I changed your diapers and rocked you to sleep as often as Vaughn or Daddy. I watched you take your first steps. I was there from the beginning. My name was the first thing you said."

"If I recall correctly, I was told it was 'SaSa.' That could have meant anything."

"You were pointing directly at me when you said it."

"Okay, okay. I was spying. I'm sorry. I apologize. I was curious and worried about you."

"Don't, Will."

He couldn't tell if she meant that he didn't need to worry about her or if she didn't want him to dredge up an unpleasant topic.

"Wanna get some lunch, *SaSa*?"

"I'm not very hungry after the breakfast I had, but I'll go with you and have a Coke."

As they passed through the front doors of the library, Will reached out and touched his sister's shoulder. She stopped and turned to him, waiting.

"Why didn't you just give the original book to Dad to return?"

"I was planning on it when I found it in her book sack, but the pages were all stuck together with blood, and I didn't think they'd take it like that. So, I put it back where I'd found it and went to throw up for a while. Daddy thought I'd caught a virus from one of the other second-graders."

She pivoted and walked towards the car, but Will stayed where he was, watching her. She was so petite, his big sister. One would never be able to tell just by looking at her how strong she really was.

By the time they reached La Madeleine, the lunch crowd had already come and gone. Thankful for the lull, Sarah decided on coffee and chocolate cake, while Will selected a large chicken Caesar salad and a Coke.

"You should get more than that," Will chided. "That's not a very healthy lunch."

"Thank you, Dr. Maes. For your information, I didn't have a very healthy breakfast either. It was delicious, though." In mock defiance, she broke off a piece of the cake and delicately inserted it between her lips and said, "Mmmm."

"You're making me hungry for it, and I've barely even started my salad."

"You'll have to get a piece for dessert."

Will proceeded to devour his lunch while his sister sipped her coffee and savored her cake.

"Sarah, can I ask you a question?"

"You can ask me anything you like. Whether or not I'll answer…."

"What was Dad like before?"

"Before what?"

"I don't know. Before."

Sarah sighed and crumpled the napkin that she held in her hand. Tossing it down onto her empty plate, she asked, "When? You have to be more specific, Will."

"What was he like when your mother was alive? Was he different than he is with Mom?"

"You mean did he love my mother more than he loves yours?"

"No, I'm sure when you love more than one partner in a lifetime, it's different with each one. What I'm asking is how was *he* different?"

She paused to carefully consider her next words then said slowly, "It wasn't like he hadn't already had a tough time, at least after his parents were killed in that car wreck. But he was happy with MaMa and with me and with Jamie. He was…well, I can't explain it."

"Why not?" he asked intently. "What's the big secret? I know that something happened in Dad's past, and I don't mean the substance abuse. I know all about that. He's open about the fact that he was an addict and a drunk after your mother died, but I can sense that there's more. Why don't you talk about it?"

Sarah wasn't surprised by her brother's question. She was surprised that he had waited this long to ask.

"There's a lot that we don't talk about, Will. There's a lot that you don't need to know."

"I'm not a little boy anymore, Sarah. I'm in college. I deserve to be told."

"You deserve to stay happy and ignorant."

"That's not for you to decide," he said, his temper beginning to flare. "Whatever it is, I can handle it. I'm a mature adult. It can't be that bad."

He thought he was prepared for any answer that she could have given him. What he was not prepared for was her hollow, bitter laugh.

"No, you're right. It can't be that bad. It can be worse. It can always be worse. Take it from one who knows."

"Sarah –"

"Please don't ask me to tell you about it. Even after all these years, it's still painful for me to talk about it all. I love Daddy so completely, but I hate some of the things that he did. I won't tell you."

"But that's not fair!"

"As your big sister, I need to enlighten you on something." Emphasizing every word, she said, "Life's not fair."

"How can you deny me a part of my family history?" Will asked. He lifted her right hand and wrapped his fingers around hers. "I can't picture Dad going out to try and make somebody – especially *you* – suffer. You're closer to him than Katie and I will ever be. Not that we're not close, but it's different with you. There's a bond that I can't quite pinpoint and –"

"It's a moment," his sister interrupted.

"What?"

"The thing you want to know about. We share a moment, a horrible, awful, mind-numbing moment. You think you understand, but you can't even begin to comprehend what our lives were like. You say that you know Daddy was an addict and a drunk." She rested her left hand on top of their intertwined fingers and said tiredly, "It's such an abstract idea for you. I can't tell you about the incident, but if you want to know about the rest, then that's fine. You want to know what he was like when he was drinking or using? The stuff he can't remember or isn't aware of? Would that satisfy your curiosity?"

"I can tell you about how a seven-year-old girl who's trying to deal with her mother's death is also trying to cope with her father's addiction. How he'd forget to go to the store sometimes, so there wouldn't be enough food. He would pass out before he could tuck me in bed or read me a story. I used to try not to get my clothes dirty, because he was too stoned to go to the laundromat on a regular basis. Do you want to know about how I got sick because of his addiction?"

"Sarah, I had no idea that –"

"Or would you rather hear about his relapse and how the sixteen-year-old girl tried to keep up the pretense of normality by herself for months on end? I paid the bills when Daddy was too high to be concerned about insurance, phone service, electricity, or house notes. Things hadn't been so good between him and Vaughn, and I worried that they would split up, especially if she found out about his relapse when the both of you came home from your summer at Grandma and Grandpa's farm. Whenever I found the stuff he was using, I'd pour it down the drain. I cleaned him up and put him to bed more nights than I care to recall, when he was incapable of performing the most basic of daily tasks. I loved him and worried about him, even though I despised what he was doing to himself and what he was putting me through."

She drew her hands back and rested them in her lap. Will stared at his plate and poked at his last piece of lettuce with the tines of his fork.

"If you want me to go into more detail I can sit here for hours and regale you with gory stories of addiction, neglect, illness, and insecurity. In the end, I can tell you what came from it all. One, I became a very responsible person. I learned to take care of myself and everyone else. Two, Daddy did get help and has been clean for a long time. Three, he totally betrayed my trust."

She reached up and rubbed at the bridge of her nose, an unconscious gesture Will had seen repeated frequently for as long as he could remember.

"How can you talk about it all so calmly? You sound so…detached."

"I built up a wall," she said matter-of-factly. "There was no way that I could handle what happened when I was sixteen, and there were other factors, other threats to a world that had been remarkably stable for eight years. I decided that I couldn't let myself be hurt any more. Lately, my defenses have been compromised."

"You even talk like a soldier."

"I'm scared to death. It's like the ground is crumbling underneath my feet, and I can't stop it."

"Could you talk to Dad about it? Maybe he could help you work it out."

"You don't think Daddy knows? People who survive things together stick together, even when they've hurt each other. I forgave him a long time ago, but I can't forget. It's my problem. I don't want to talk with him about it. He blames himself enough as it is, and rightly so. We can't change the past."

"So what do you do?"

"Keep going. Take lots of deep, cleansing breaths. Try to maintain a sense of humor in the face of adversity. Try not to be envious of others who've been fortunate enough to lead more normal lives."

"Like me?"

"Forget about it, Will. Be content, and leave it alone. Let the sins of the fathers lie dormant."

"Anything else?"

She leaned forward, her expression deadly serious and said, "Never, ever, ever use drugs or drink to excess. I can't do it again. It would kill me."

That night, Will lay awake and stared out of his window at the stars winking in the clear winter sky. He'd been unwilling to ask his sister for more details about her life with their father. He had told himself that he wanted to spare her from the pain of her memories, and that was true enough, but now he realized that he'd been trying to spare himself, too.

All in all, William Maes had enjoyed a happy childhood and adolescence in upper-middle-class America. He knew that his parents didn't have the greatest of marriages, but they were devoted to their children, their grandson, their close friends, and to Helen and Jim. Both of them had been present at countless school functions, dance recitals, and varsity sporting events. It was an almost idyllic world for a child.

It hadn't been idyllic for Sarah.

Will heard the footsteps as his father went downstairs to the kitchen. He waited then followed and listened as Tristan filled a coffee filter with grounds and then placed it in the coffee maker. Water was drawn from the tap and poured into the machine. The switch was thrown and brewing began. A chair was pulled back and then all was quiet, except for the gurgling sounds of the Mister Coffee.

"Dad?"

His father laid his book down on the table. It was Virgil's *The Aeneid.*

"You couldn't sleep, Will? Me, neither. I thought I'd do a little reading. I figured maybe it would take my mind off things."

"Things?"

"Your sister and her husband. Max. Lillian. Things." He shrugged and tugged at the chair next to him before asking, "You want to join me? I made a lot of decaf coffee. I don't think I'll be able to sleep any more tonight. You know how it is when I get these bouts of insomnia."

Once they were both seated at the table with steaming mugs of coffee in front of them, Tristan asked nonchalantly, "You want to tell me what I did? You've been different with me ever since yesterday afternoon. Was it something I said?"

Will gulped a mouthful of the hot coffee, scalding his mouth and tongue in the process. He cleared his throat and said, "I took Sarah to the library. You remember that book she asked you to buy at the hospital? Well, she gave it to the library."

"Why? I mean, I don't care if she wants to give it to the library, but why?"

"She told the woman that her mother had checked it out before she died and that it never got returned. When I asked her how come, she said that when she found it the pages were…were stuck together with blood."

His father's face registered first shock then understanding.

"It must have been in Emma's book sack," he mumbled, as if talking to himself. "I couldn't look through it and had put it on the back porch to throw away with the garbage the next morning. So, Sarah found it. No wonder she was sick that night."

"I took Sarah to La Madeleine for lunch," Will continued uneasily. "We talked a bit. I asked her some stuff, questions I had."

"Did she answer them?"

"At first, no. Then, some. She told me to leave well enough alone, but I pressed her. She didn't really say a lot. She would have said more if I'd persisted, but I couldn't do it. She…."

As he searched for words to explain his concerns, his father reached across the table and placed a hand on his arm.

"I know. You don't have to say it. Just tell me what's on your mind."

"What happened between the two of you when I was little? What was it? That was the one thing Sarah couldn't talk about."

"She didn't say anything?"

Will hesitated.

"She told me that you were messed up while Mom and I were at the farm with Grandpa and Grandma. She told me what she did taking care of you and how she felt that summer, but she practically begged me not to ask her what brought it all to a head."

"Did she tell you how she felt afterwards?"

"I – I don't want to hurt you, Dad, no matter what you did."

"The truth, Will."

"Sarah told me that you betrayed her trust to such a degree that it changed the way she interacted with people. She likened it to erecting a wall for protection."

Tristan rose from the table and poured himself a second cup of coffee. Returning to his seat, he said quietly, "I hit her."

Certain that he hadn't heard correctly, Will asked, "You what?"

"I hit her. I broke her nose."

Will gaped at his father.

"But you…you'd never hit anyone, especially not one of us."

"I did. Sarah had had enough. She'd stayed out all night. I was frantic with worry, but what was I going to do? Do you think I'd call the police knowing I was high?"

"What did you end up doing?" Will asked quietly.

"I went out looking for her. It was probably not the most rational decision I've ever made. It's amazing that I didn't get arrested myself as out of it as I was. It would have been better for both of us if they'd locked me up that night.

"By the time Sarah came home, I was coming down off a high. We argued about where she'd been and what she'd done. During the argument, I hit her. I didn't even know I'd done it until I saw her on the floor. God, she was totally hysterical. I wanted to call the cops, but she begged me not to. I'd never seen her like that before, and I've never seen her like that since. My poor little girl."

"You were high and didn't know what you were doing."

"Don't make excuses for me," Tristan snapped. "I was thirty-two years old. I'm a very large man, and your sister is so small. Of course, I didn't see it at that moment as it was happening. Addicts are totally self-centered. All you care about is the next high. That nearly cost me my sanity and Sarah's love. I can honestly say that I wanted to die for some time after that. If it hadn't been for Max, Jamie, Benjamin, Lillian and your mother, I would have killed myself. If it hadn't been for Daniel, I think Sarah would have given up."

"What brought you out of it?"

"I swore I'd never drink or do drugs again after the first time, and I went back on my word. I *had* to recover. I *had* to prove to her that she could trust me again. I've been trying to prove it to her ever since. If it takes until the day I die then fine. I deserve that.

"Your sister and I have always been so very much alike. The punishment for my indiscretions has been knowing what I've done to her, not once but twice. I could say I was young and sick and unstable during those times, and all of that would be true. It's still no excuse. I was the parent. I was the one who was supposed to protect her and take care of her, not the other way around. I don't want the result of my stupidity to be the ruination of her life. I can only hope that she'll forgive me someday."

"But she does forgive you. She said it at lunch this afternoon. Yesterday. She said that she forgave you."

"She forgave me," Tristan said slowly. "Thank you, Will."

"For what?"

"For the best Christmas present I could ever hope to receive from anyone: redemption."

Chapter Twelve: The Element of Surprise

The dead leaves from the trees swirled down, circling around Daniel. He was sitting in the desolate garden next to his parents' home. The icy wind was biting at his ears, nose, and fingers, but he felt none of it. He was so lost in thought that he was certain that nothing could disturb him.

"Do you come here often?"

CoCo Genevieve stood on the path that led towards the gate. Daniel smiled at her from where he was sitting cross-legged on the cold ground under the Japanese magnolia tree. She came forward, halting about ten feet from where he sat.

"How are you?" CoCo asked. When he hesitated, she reached out and touched a branch on an azalea bush as she told him, "There used to be a tree here, a crape myrtle. It was a big old thing. I used to climb it when I was small. One time there were ants all over it, but I didn't see them until it was too late. There were tons of them. How I bawled! Teal smeared me with some slimy stuff; then Miss Gwen insisted that I be put to bed with her. It was nice snuggling under the covers with Miss Gwen, drying my tears like she was my own mother. She didn't even mind the ointment rubbing off on her quilt. I used to pretend that I was her daughter. I used to wish that she'd get better, so I could come here and live with her and Max, Teal, and Moses."

"Didn't you like your foster parents?"

"Oh, they were moral people, and they took care of me just dandy. But I *belonged* here, and I knew it."

It was only as she sat next to him that Daniel noticed her choice of clothing for the day. She wore a purple scarf, three gold chains, large silver hoop earrings, a mood ring, leopard skin pants, a white sweater with zebra stripes, and black shoes.

Pretty tame for CoCo, he thought.

"I like your outfit today," he told her.

"Thank you, Deary. I saw it on television that animal prints are back in style. Jean-Paul likes them. It must be because he likes to hunt."

"Must be. Maybe you could redo your whole house in animal prints."

"Don't think I haven't thought about it. The other night, I wore this fake chinchilla coat to bed, and he was wild for it!"

Daniel's explosive laughter was swallowed in a barrage of wind gusts. The blasts of cold air stung his tear-filled eyes and chilled his lungs. He felt CoCo press a tissue into his hand and asked, "Why don't we go in the house? Unless Jean-Paul will get worried about you."

"He's in Lafayette for the day. Some part that needed fixing before it went out on a rig. Things still have to be fixed whether it's Christmas Eve or not. He said he won't be back until late tonight or maybe even tomorrow morning. The extra money will be good. There's lots of overtime on holidays." Allowing him to pull her up, she added, "What about you? Won't Sarah wonder where you are?"

"I told her I was coming to the house for a while. She and Kris were going to spend the morning baking Christmas treats."

They huddled together, as they walked arm in arm towards the back of the house. Daniel's fingers were numb, and he dropped the keys once before successfully unlocking the door.

"Brrr!" CoCo shivered. "I think it's colder in here than it is out in the yard." Hugging herself, she suggested helpfully, "Maybe we could go back to the garden."

"No, hang on a minute. Let me switch on the heater." He hurried down the hallway to the thermostat calling back, "I shut it off last week, since nobody was here."

A warm blast of stale air shot out from the vent in the kitchen. CoCo instantly relaxed and sighed with pleasure.

"Why aren't you wearing a coat?" Daniel asked, removing his leather jacket and vigorously massaging his ears and nose.

"Because I didn't feel like it. Besides, you're the one who doesn't ever wear a coat. Why *are* you wearing one?"

"Because I felt like it. Do you want something to eat or drink? Coffee, maybe?"

"You look very nice today," CoCo said with a smile. "I like that sweater. Milo used to have one like that, cream-colored cable knit. He never wore jeans, though. He preferred khaki pants."

"Why didn't he wear jeans?"

"Too restricting, he said. Now, you sit right there and let me make you some hot cocoa. Lillian taught me how to make it exactly as she did."

She went to the pantry and removed a box of chocolate squares, a tiny brown bottle, and a small white can.

"I am sorry that I couldn't go to the funeral, Dan. Was there a good turnout? Did the priest do a good job?"

"Yes, there was a good turnout, although there weren't quite as many people as there were at Max's. And yes, the priest gave a nice homily."

"Well, I didn't expect there would be as many people," she admitted, her voice muffled by the cabinet door. "Max had all of those professional types there and those former patients and those Knights of Columbus men. A-ha!" Triumphantly, she brandished the saucepan she'd been searching for, then she placed it on one of the burners of the stove and continued, "But Lillian was so active in Catholic Daughters, I knew they'd all come. I hear her sister, brother-in-law, and their children were all in bed with a horrible stomach virus. What a shame, not to be able to come to the funeral. I wish I could have gone, but I was too upset. I was the one who found her unconscious, you know."

"I know."

"I never thought about it before, but I missed Lillian and Max's wedding. Jean-Paul and I were staying in Corpus Christi for some job he had that month, and it slipped my mind. Was it pretty?"

"Yeah, I guess it was. We had it in the garden."

"What did they wear? Where did they stand?" CoCo asked, breaking squares of chocolate into the saucepan.

"Max wore a brown suit. Lillian wore a suit, too, but it was a woman's suit with a jacket and skirt. They stood under the Japanese magnolia."

"Oh, Nora's tree."

"Nora's tree?"

"He planted that in her memory years after Nora died. It's held up well, hasn't it?"

"If Max planted it after she was killed –"

"No, no," she said distractedly. "Not Max. Milo was the one who planted that tree. Your mother always loved it. She and your father used to make love there; she liked to watch the petals move in the wind. Sometimes, the petals would flutter down on them."

"Lillian told you that?" Daniel asked in disbelief.

"Now, I didn't say Lillian, did I? Lillian would rather be caught dead than do something improper in public, although I think she kind of liked to be improper in private." She dropped the spoon she'd been holding onto the counter and raised her hands to her mouth then exclaimed, "Oh! I didn't mean that she'd rather be caught *dead*."

"I got it, CoCo."

"Didn't that investigator fellow tell you anything?"

"Actually, he has been keeping me updated. He did tell me what you said about knowing my mother, but I didn't connect it when you were talking about my parents making love." His face colored, but he merely shrugged and asked, "They really did love each other?"

"Your mother used to say that under that tree was their favorite spot." She lowered her voice and said in a conspiratorial tone, "But I didn't tell Mr. Detective that part. He doesn't need to know everything."

"CoCo, I meant did they love each other in a spiritual sense?"

"They did, and don't you ever think differently." Picking up the spoon, she gestured towards the table and commanded, "You sit down, and let me finish this."

Daniel obediently returned to the table, turned a chair around, and straddled it. He rested his arms on its back and silently watched his cousin make hot cocoa.

"It won't bother me," CoCo said suddenly, as she poured the steaming cocoa into two mugs.

"What won't?"

"If you want to go on like before. We can keep on being neighbors and not cousins. I know full well that I'm a little off in the head, Deary. I don't want you to feel obligated to acknowledge me." She placed a mug on the table in front of him and took the seat to his right before saying solemnly, "All I ask is that you don't sell this place – at least not until after I'm gone. I know that's selfish, but my uncle and my father lived here. And my aunt and my grandparents, even though I never had the good fortune to know them. I never had much in this world, but I had my house to live in and this house to come to. Please, don't take it away from me. The thought of strangers coming in here and moving in all of their things is atrocious!"

Daniel inhaled the steam from his cocoa, and then he took a small sip.

"Just like Lillian's."

"I told you! Didn't I?"

"Yes, you did." He took another sip, larger this time, then said, "CoCo, you're my last, living blood relative besides my son, and I don't care who knows it. We're family. Because of all this subterfuge on everybody's part, we've lost years that we could have spent getting to know each other better. I don't want to waste any more years."

"You mean it? But what about Kristopher? Children are impressionable. That's what they say on those talk shows. What if I embarrass him?"

"I'm sure *I'll* embarrass him at times as he grows older. He'll still love me. I'm sure he'll love you."

"That's right. If I can be crazy Mrs. Genevieve, why can't I be crazy Cousin Genevieve?"

"Cousin CoCo."

"Cousin CoCo. That sounds nice. Could I play with him sometimes like Miss Gwen used to play with me? Jean-Paul and I never had any children. I didn't want to pass any more of my mother's family genes on to anyone else, but I do like children. You could stay with him and me or Sarah could. Would that be all right?"

"That would be fine," he assured her. "What are y'all planning for Christmas? Maybe you two could come over."

"Really? Nobody would mind?"

"Really."

"I'll have to talk with Jean-Paul about it. I think we were planning to go down the bayou tomorrow. They sort of expect us.

Jean-Paul's family is fun. They roast a pig and make ethnic things like blood pudding and tasso. It's tasty."

"I'll take your word for it," Daniel said dubiously. "How about today? You could call Jean-Paul or leave a note. Then you could have fun this afternoon here in Baton Rouge and fun tomorrow in wherever it is that Jean-Paul takes you."

"Fun! That's it."

"What's what?"

"I have something for you." As she felt in her pockets, she asked, "What about the house? Will you save it?"

"I'm thinking that maybe I should sell both houses and start over in a new place," he confided, raking his fingers through his hair. "I need to take your request into account. It's partially your house, too."

"No," she said, still rummaging in her pockets. "When Milo died, Max gave me the money from his house in Washington. I asked for some of his things, too. This is your house." She stopped her search momentarily and gripped his hand then said, "Oh, dear. I'd asked you not to sell it, but I don't want you to keep it and be sad. Just think about it for a while. Don't act rashly."

"That's good advice."

"Thank you," she said proudly. "Here it is!"

Resting her arm on the table, CoCo slowly unfurled her fingers and revealed a small, silver pin adorned with a tiny bird of some kind.

"It's a hummingbird," she explained. "I thought you might want it. It took me two days to find it."

Daniel accepted the delicate pin and fingered it gently.

"Thank you, CoCo. It's very attractive."

"Your mother gave it to me when we were friends. It was on her scarf, and I admired it. She took it off and gave it to me one day. She loved birds."

"She did?"

"Finches were her favorites. There were so many different kinds of them, ones I'd never even heard of. She knew all their names, where they liked to live, and what they ate. One day, she said she'd have a gigantic birdhouse and put out lots of food so that she could watch them and listen to them twitter away."

The slight weight of the pin was like an anchor in Daniel's palm.

"Why, CoCo? I think I understand why she left, or why she thought she had to leave, but why did she marry Samuels? From what I know and from what Carson's found out, he was the antithesis of everything she was. Why would she let him hurt her so much?"

"She was pregnant with no husband and no job. Maybe she thought it was the only way she could keep you. Maybe she really did fall in love with your stepfather. Maybe he was good to her at first, and then he changed. Maybe Tessa wasn't as self-assured as I thought she was. It could be all of those things or none of them. I wish she had confided in me about her plans or called me afterwards to let me know that she was well. I looked for the both of you for years and years every time we went out."

"I appreciate that."

"It wasn't just because you were my cousin. It was because you should have had more. Don't blame her too much for making the wrong decisions."

He closed his fingers around the pin. Slipping it into the pocket of his jacket, Daniel said, "I try not to blame any of them, but that's a lot harder than it sounds. I want some kind of resolution or restitution. I want to know why. Is that so unreasonable?"

"It's human."

"You're very wise, CoCo."

"Maybe I should have a talk show. CoCo's Corner or Chat with CoCo or something. Speaking of CoCo, would you like some more cocoa?"

By the time they arrived at the Nash home, six dozen cookies had already been baked and stored for the next day's festivities. Sarah was spreading fudge in a pan, and Kris was helping Tristan to crack pecans to top off the fudge.

"Grandpa had to come help with the cracking," Kris explained. "Mommy and I couldn't break them. It made Mommy's arm hurt."

"Oh, Kris. It wasn't that bad."

Daniel went over to his wife and pried her fingers off of the pan. Lifting her left arm, he examined the scar.

"Daniel, it's nothing. It was sore. That's all."

He smiled and bent down to kiss it.

"That's like in the Addams Family!" Kris giggled.

Daniel noticed CoCo standing awkwardly near the door that led to the garage.

"Kris, you remember Mrs. Genevieve?"

He glanced at Sarah then at Tristan. His father-in-law nodded and smiled.

"Well, I have a surprise. She's also your cousin."

Hopping down from his chair, the child rushed over to CoCo and threw his arms around her zebra-patterned middle.

"Cousin, I have a fish. Do you want to see?"

"I'd love to see! Does he have a name?"

He drew her out of the room and down the hall. They could hear the child's voice as he pointed out things of interest throughout the house and then listened as CoCo began to read him a story.

"I'm glad you brought her here," Sarah whispered.

"Me, too," Tristan agreed. "Where's Jean-Paul?"

"Working. He won't be back until later tonight or early tomorrow. Then they're supposed to go 'down the bayou' for some stuffing wrapped in cat gut or some similar food fit for a Christmas feast."

"What a shame we have other plans," Sarah said merrily. "I'd love to try that."

"Tragic," Tristan chimed in.

Daniel picked up a large chocolate chip cookie that was shaped like a star and decorated with green-and-red icing. He bit into the cookie, made what Kris liked to call "yummy noises," then went to the refrigerator and removed the milk jug. As he poured himself a glass of milk, he asked, "So, what's for lunch?"

"Lunch?" Sarah glanced at the clock on the stove and asked rhetorically, "It's 1:15 already? I thought it was more like 11:00. I haven't even *thought* about lunch, and everything's all over the counter and in the sink." She stared at the mess as if willing it clean and then said with obvious frustration, "By the time we get all this straight, it'll be 3:00."

"Maybe Dan could make lunch," Tristan teased. "He's such a help in the kitchen."

"Hey, if you want to be eating food that tastes like it's been in the trash for three weeks, then I'm definitely your man. Even if I was a good cook, if Sarah can't get to the sink, what makes you think that I could?" Picking up another cookie, he leaned down and kissed his wife and then called out, "Kris! CoCo! When you're finished, come see!"

"What's the plan?" Tristan asked curiously.

"I'm going to take them to Brew-Bachers and pick us all up some food. You think you can spare five minutes to wolf it down before returning to your culinary tasks?"

"I think I could manage," Sarah promised.

"Okay, one chicken pasta salad coming up. Tris, how about you?"

"Hm. Catfish po-boy, no lettuce."

"Got it."

Kristopher and CoCo were both delighted to go for a ride in the car, and the trio soon set off for the restaurant.

"I hope he can handle it," Tristan remarked. "CoCo can be erratic sometimes."

"Daddy, you know she's harmless."

Sarah opened the refrigerator and stood contemplating what exactly was the best way to rearrange the food so that she could squeeze another pan of fudge onto the shelf. Her father watched her calculating the amount of space needed. She shifted a Tupperware container filled with mushrooms and a Corningware dish that contained rice dressing. Satisfied, she came back for the pan on the counter and slid it neatly onto the shelf.

"There!" She pushed some of her loose curls away from her face and said, "I guess I better wash some of these pots and pans, so I can start again after we eat."

"How about if I dry?"

"That would be great. I could use them right away if they're already dry. It would make things go more quickly. Are you done with the nuts?"

He walked back over to the table, held up the bowl, and asked, "Is that enough?"

"Plenty. Thanks. That yellow towel in the second drawer is good for drying. It's kind of big. I usually let these drip dry, so it might be buried under some other towels."

They stood together at the sink. Sarah scrubbed the pots and bowls clean then rinsed them and passed them over to her father. She was rinsing a colander when Tristan said, "I had a talk with Will this morning. He told me about your lunch yesterday."

Tristan braced himself for his daughter's reaction, uncertain as to whether she would become angry, sad, or defensive. No matter what she did, he vowed to be prepared, to remain calm. He hadn't realized how sorely his vow would be tested.

Chapter Thirteen: A Slap in the Face

Sarah's movements slowed, but she didn't stop what she was doing as she asked, "Did you and Will have a good talk?"

"I suppose," Tristan said as he swiped at the bottom of the pot. "I told him about what happened. He said that you forgave me. Is that true?"

Sarah rinsed her hands and turned off the tap. Turning to her father, she said, "Of course, I forgave you. You didn't know?"

He shook his head.

"I forgave you," she said firmly.

"Do you love me?"

"You know that I do."

"Then trust me again, Sarah. I don't want you to go on like this. It's been long enough. Isn't there anything I can do?"

"Daddy, that was eons ago. After the first few months, things were good between us again, weren't they? We went back to our normal – abnormal? – symbiotic relationship. I'm not aware of too many fathers and daughters who are as close as we are."

"Except for the insidious underlying lack of trust."

"I trust you. If I were about to get hit by a train, I have no doubt that you'd throw yourself in front of it to save me, just like I would do with Kris. If I asked you for anything and you had the power to give it to me, you would. That's not trust?"

"You don't trust that I won't hurt you again. You don't trust that I won't break my promise."

Going back to the dishes, Sarah said, "I don't know what we can do about that. When it first happened, I wanted to hit you back. I wanted to wait until you were distracted and unprepared. Then, I wanted to hit you with all of my strength. Not that I could have done much damage, but I wanted to wound you as deeply as you wounded me and in the same fashion." As she worked on a particularly tough stain on a cookie sheet, she added, "I doubt I could have even reached you."

Tristan accepted the cookie sheet and began to wipe it dry then proposed, "Why don't you try it now?"

Laying down the sponge, she asked in disbelief, "What did you say?"

"Hit me. If you can't reach my cheek, then hit me in the stomach or something."

"Daddy, I don't think I really could do it. Maybe when I was sixteen and it was all so fresh in our lives, but now? Do you think that this is something Max would approve of?"

"Max is gone," Tristan reminded her. "I'm winging it. Hit me."

"You're crazy."

"No, I'm not. It may make you feel better. It would most certainly make me feel better." Throwing the towel over the faucet, he said, "C'mon, Honey. It's worth a shot."

"No way."

Tristan stepped forward and wrapped his left hand lightly around her arm. Then he began to speak of how things had been and how they should be. He continued to talk, but Sarah wasn't listening anymore. She saw her father not as he was in the present but as he was sixteen years before. His hair was a tangle. His clothing was stained with dirt, grass, and sweat. His pupils were huge. He had gripped her arm so tightly that he'd left five dark bruises where his fingers had been.

Sarah thought of the argument, the only shouting match they'd ever had. She could once again feel the rage and the frustration. Tristan was destroying himself, and he was forcing her to watch. Being his child, she felt she could do nothing else but aid and abet him.

It had been a shock to see her father raise his hand then bring it down. She'd seen it coming, the image of it crawling forward in slow motion, but she hadn't been able to block it or turn away. He'd crushed her before the back of his hand ever made contact with her face.

Sarah came back to the present. She blinked and stared at the white imprint of her hand that remained on her father's cheek. Her palm stung with the aftershock of the slap.

"Daddy, are you okay? I'm so sorry. I didn't mean to do it. Did I hurt you?"

"No, I'm okay. I asked you to do it, remember?" he reminded her, as he rubbed his hand against his reddening cheek. Then he smiled down at his daughter. "How do you feel?"

"My hand's kind of sore."

"That's not what I meant."

"I feel…relieved," she admitted.

"Me, too," he agreed, as they embraced.

Tristan had lied. She'd hit him with surprising force, and it had hurt him. It wasn't the physical pain that he thought of, though. It was the fact that if his petite daughter could strike him that hard, how hard had he struck her on that terrible morning? It wasn't just their difference in size that bothered him. He had been larger than she; that was true. But he had also been high, panicked, and angry. It was a wonder that he hadn't done more damage.

"Daddy, don't do that."

"What?"

"Start thinking about it like that."

Sighing, he pulled back and held her away from him. He opened his mouth to once again tell her that he was sorry. The garage door mechanism began to whir.

"I know you like I know myself," she said quickly. "You don't have to say it anymore."

She smiled and stretched up to give him a peck on the cheek.

"Help me to get at least one more pot done before they come in," she urged. "We can finish the rest afterwards."

As he entered the kitchen, Daniel looked askance at Tristan's red cheek but merely smiled back at his father-in-law. As Kris, Sarah, and CoCo gathered around the table to unpack the bags of food, he asked, "Why are you so happy?"

"Your wife slapped me as hard as she could."

"Somehow I don't think I'd be smiling if my son did that."

"I asked her to. Amateur psychology. I think it worked."

Daniel nodded, shook his head, then threw his hands up in resignation.

"I give up. Tell me later, Tris."

"Get Sarah to tell you."

From the table, Sarah said, "We've got it all set out. Daniel, would you bring some Cokes over here so we can eat?"

The doorbell rang.

"I'll get it," CoCo cried. "I've got it!"

"Mrs. Genevieve. Hello."

"Mr. Zerangue! Oh, it's good to see you again! But don't you have a life?"

"CoCo, that's not polite," Daniel admonished with a smile as he came forward to shake the detective's hand.

"Well, maybe. It's the truth. It's Christmas Eve, for goodness sake. Isn't that what they say in the song? So be good for goodness sake."

"Come on in, Carson. You know, CoCo may not be the soul of tact, but she's right. You should be taking today off. It *is* Christmas Eve after all. Don't you have family at home?"

"A good cop never rests until the job's done."

"I know I told you I didn't want you to cool it with the investigation, but I didn't intend –"

"Hey, this is just the way I work."

"Why don't you join us for lunch?" Sarah asked from the doorway. "We have plenty of food."

"No, thanks; I already ate. I just needed to talk to Dan here about something. It can wait until after lunch though. I'll come back in a while."

"Nonsense," CoCo chided. "You can sit and talk with us."

"Do you like Coke?" Kris asked, taking the private investigator's hand. "We only got Classic. Mommy and Daddy don't like any other kind."

"Me neither. That'd be fine, if you all don't mind."

"This is fun," Coco said, as they finished their lunch. "But I think I'm getting a bit tired. I think I should go home. You won't be upset, will you, everyone? Mr. Detective?"

"How about if I drive you home, CoCo?" Tristan offered. "That way, Dan and Carson can have their talk."

"But Grandpa!"

"Then I can come back and spend some more time here."

"But Grandpa, can I come, too? I wanted to go somewhere!"

"Where, Kris?" Sarah asked, puzzled.

"I can't tell you or Daddy. *Please*?"

"You can tell me about it in the car then we'll see," said Tristan.

"Okay. Wait here."

He hopped up and started for the doorway, but his mother called out, "Kris, what do we do with our plates when we leave the table?"

The child returned to his place and picked up his paper plate and plastic cup. After the plate had been disposed of and the cup had been placed in the refrigerator, he darted out of the room. He hurried through the kitchen with his football bank concealed in plain sight behind his back.

"We're going out of the front door, Kris," Tristan reminded him. "Go get your coat on before we leave."

"Keep him out of trouble," Daniel joked. "With that much money, who knows where you'll end up?"

As he collected his own paper plate, napkin, and glass, Tristan assured him, "I'll avoid the arcade, but I don't know if I can keep all those little five-year-old girls at bay. Ready, CoCo?" As he slipped into his coat, he added, "I'll be back to help you finish the dishes, Sarah."

"I may have to start without you. You can help me with the next go-round."

When the front door slammed shut, Daniel rose to help Sarah clear the table. She shook her head and urged, "You go ahead and talk. I'll take care of this."

Nodding, he turned his attention to the detective and asked, "Did you find out anything new?"

"Yeah. First of all, I went to your mom's hometown. There's not much to it. A few people in the vicinity did remember your grandfather. They basically said he was a decent man and a hard worker. He came over from Ireland when he was a teenager. He married a poor Italian girl, who died when your mother was born. Your grandfather raised his daughter by himself. He really loved his kid. Everybody agreed on that."

"And Mom?"

"Assumpta was a tomboy growing up. As she got older, she took an interest in all things feminine, but she still had that tomboy streak in her. Her dad didn't seem to be too big on discipline. I heard the word 'wild' more than once in regards to her."

"Did these people know much about my mother after she went away to school?"

"Not a lot, unfortunately. One old lady told me that your grandfather was so proud when your mother went off to college. He only had a fourth-grade education, although those who knew him said he was very smart and had a real head for numbers. He knew his daughter had brains, and he wanted her to have an advantage in life by going to college."

"Some advantage it turned out to be. Anything else?"

"Not about him."

"What, then?"

"I've located your stepfather."

Sarah lowered the pan in her hand into the sink and came back to the table.

"Where?" Daniel asked hoarsely.

"Same place downtown. He never left."

"But the bar had to close," Sarah insisted.

"He may have lost his liquor license, but he didn't lose his property. It appears that he inherited it from his father. The place used to be a –"

"If you say a store called Nash and Company, I'll shoot myself," Daniel growled.

"No. It used to be a bordello. A discreet one, but a bordello nonetheless. It was owned by Zachary Samuels' father. I couldn't find any records on his mother."

"She was probably employed at the bordello," Daniel suggested.

"That would be my assumption. Anyway, after the bar was forced to close, your stepfather leased the property out while he was in jail. The restaurant that had moved in didn't do too well, and, by the time he got released, they were shutting down." He took a sip from his Coke and added, "Samuels had been barred for life from ever receiving another liquor license, so he opened an adult bookstore on his property. The records indicate that he's still the owner of the building. The business license is registered in his name, and he lives at the same address. I'd like to interview him."

Daniel sat tight-lipped and rigid in his chair. Sarah stared down at her hands.

"What's your objective?" Daniel asked. "What do you hope to find out by interviewing him?"

"Whenever possible, go to the source. Hostile subjects may not tell you a thing. Then again, lots of them like to brag. Some get angry and rant and rave. You can actually find out a helluva lot that way, if you've got the stomach for it."

"And you do?"

"Any good P.I. has to."

Daniel sat silently pondering Zerangue's suggestion. Sarah kept her mouth closed and watched the light glinting off the diamond of her wedding ring. She didn't want to influence her husband in any way. This wasn't her decision.

"I want to protect my family. I don't want him to know that I'm in town, what my name is, or where I live or where I work. Can you talk to him without revealing that or making him curious?"

"I've been doing this for a long, long time. You learn how to handle it. You lie about your true intentions. Sometimes, you lie about your identity and get them drunk, and they open up to you. Then, you go home and take a shower and try to wash away the stink of being that close to them." He set his empty glass down in front of him and said seriously, "I need to know what sort of a man I'm dealing with, not that I don't have some idea. After everything I've unearthed about Zachary Samuels, I feel like I can tell you exactly what kind of scum he is. But if you have anything else that might help me to go in better prepared, I'd appreciate it if you'd share that with me. Is there any other example you might give me of his behavior or demeanor?"

Rising, Daniel grasped the edges of his sweater. Sarah bit her lip and clenched her fists, but she didn't try to stop her husband as he lifted first his sweater and then his t-shirt over his head. He placed both of them on the table and stood without speaking, letting the man see his scars.

Zerangue didn't avert his eyes. He had seen worse on the force. Not many times, but he had seen worse. Of course, those people were usually covered with a sheet, waiting for the coroner's van to come and take them away.

"Sarah's the only person besides my doctors who's seen these since 1970. Well, Lillian saw them not long before she died. I don't want anybody using this as a topic for discussion, either within or outside of our family circle."

"Understood. When I told you that everything would be kept confidential, that meant *everything*." Folding his hands across his chest, he said, "Thank you. That took guts."

"Did it help?"

"Yeah, it helped."

Zerangue left the Nash home and drove back to his apartment. He had planned to see Zachary Samuels that evening, but after viewing Daniel Nash like that, he couldn't do it. He needed to act detached and cool with Samuels. If he went right away, that would be impossible.

Chapter Fourteen: A Merry Little Christmas

"Are you surprised, Mommy?" Kris asked excitedly. "Doesn't she look real? The lady said that she's supposed to be six minutes old, and she has gold hair like me."

"I think that was six *months* old, Kris," Daniel corrected. "If she were six minutes old, I doubt she'd be sitting up."

"She looks so real!" Katie exclaimed. "Where did you find her?"

"At the Doll House!" Kris said proudly, as he waded through the wrapping paper that was scattered across the Maes's living room floor. "There's tons and tons of dolls there. There's boy dolls and girl dolls and men dolls and lady dolls and things for them to wear and carry and sleep in and play with!"

"The Victorian Doll Museum," Daniel mouthed to Katie. Then, he asked his wife, "Do you like her? Is it the kind of doll you were talking about? I never realized that there were so many different kinds of dolls in the world. If she's not the right one, we can return her."

"She's perfect," Sarah declared. "Her gown is so authentic. It looks like a traditional baby dress from the turn-of-the-century. What's her name?"

"The dolls come with names?" Jim scratched his head and asked, "Doesn't that take all of the fun out of it?"

"The companies have to give them names, Dad," Vaughn explained. "If they didn't, then how would the collectors keep them straight?"

"I guess so," he muttered.

"You can change the name if you want to," Helen assured him. "If you're a true collector, then you'd never take the doll out of the box. The moment you remove it, it loses some value."

"What's the point then?" Will snorted. "What little girl wants to own a doll that she can never play with?"

"I fully intend to take her out of the box," Sarah announced. "I think I'll do it right now."

Carefully lifting the cardboard flap, she eased the doll out. Vaughn handed her a pair of scissors, and she cut away the restraints that held the doll in place. Then, Sarah arranged the baby's limbs until they were positioned to her liking. She touched the soft curls of the "baby" who sat in her lap.

"So, what *is* her name?" Katie asked impatiently.

Daniel reached into the box and felt around for the certificate of authenticity then read, "Brianna Rachel."

"Well, I don't know that I would have put those two names together," Sarah admitted. "I do like both of them." She picked up the doll, looked at it appraisingly, and declared, "Brianna, I think I'll leave your name just the way it is." Replacing the doll in her lap, she said, "Thank you, Daniel. Thank you, Kris. I love it. Her."

"That's not all, Mommy! There's more!"

"Does Brianna have a twin?"

"Not exactly," Daniel replied. "But you're not far off."

Whereas Brianna Rachel was life-size, the doll in the other box was a miniature version of a little girl. She stood two feet tall and had auburn hair and green eyes. Lace petticoats showed from underneath her maroon velvet dress, and she wore stockings and suede shoes with tiny buttons on each side. Her neck was framed by a lace collar, and her curls were pulled back from her face with a maroon ribbon.

"Why, she looks like you!" Vaughn exclaimed, as her stepdaughter removed the doll from the package. "How adorable!"

"And watch," Daniel said, taking the doll from his wife's hands.

As the others looked on, he tilted the doll. By the time she was flat on her back, her eyelids had dropped down. She was asleep.

Sarah's expression was one of unmistakable delight, even as she said, "Daniel, you shouldn't have done this. The two of them must have cost –"

"Will you let me do something extravagant for you for once in your life? You said you wanted a gift that was totally impractical.

This is something you've wanted for a long time. It's obviously made you happy. So, enjoy it, and don't say anything else."

"What's this one's name?" Jim inquired with a twinkle in his eye. "Petunia Marigold?"

Daniel lifted the card and said, "Ugh. Almost as bad. Wilhelmina Octavia."

"Who on earth would give any child that awful name?" laughed Helen.

"You are in for a major name change," Sarah said pointing at the doll.

"What's her new name going to be?" asked Katie. "You could always call her Sarah since she looks like you."

Without disturbing the balance of the baby doll that still sat in her lap, Sarah reached around and raised the girl doll in front of her.

"Her name should be Emily," declared Tristan.

Everyone turned to look at him. He had been quiet throughout the entire presentation and examination of the dolls. He'd enjoyed watching his daughter open the boxes with such joy and had been pleased by what Daniel had done. He wished he'd thought of it himself.

"It has to be Emily," Tristan asserted. "Sarah and Emily."

Sarah smiled and agreed, "You're right. It couldn't be anything else."

"Why not?" Kris demanded. "I like Madison."

"When your mother was small, her favorite book was *A Little Princess*. When she was very young, I used to read her a chapter a night. When she got older, she read it herself. It's about a girl named Sara. Her father is forced to leave her at a boarding school far away from where he lives, but before he leaves, he buys her a doll that Sara names Emily. Emily helps Sara not to be afraid when things get bad in her life. Emily gives her comfort. Your mother used to re-read the book whenever she needed comforting."

"Daddy, how did you remember that? It was so long ago."

He shrugged and said, "It was your favorite book. We must have checked it out a hundred times from the library before I finally bought you your own copy for your…twelfth birthday?"

"Eleventh, I think."

"Well, I believe that Emily is a very appropriate name for her," Helen said, taking the doll from her granddaughter.

"Welcome to the family, Emily," said Will. "You, too, Brianna."

Kris giggled as his uncle pretended to shake the dolls' hands.

"I don't think there are any more presents to be opened, except for these two," Tristan announced. "Kris, you want to do the honors since they're your presents for your parents?"

The child ran over to his grandfather and took the two small packages over to where his mother and father sat next to each other on the couch. The wrapping paper was folded at odd angles, and the ribbons were half-tied. It appeared that an entire roll of Scotch tape had been used to secure the paper on the two boxes.

"Did you wrap these yourself?" Sarah asked. "What a good job you did!"

"You sure Grandpa Tristan didn't help you?" Daniel asked with a straight face.

"It was all me!"

Sarah fought her way through the tape and managed to open her box.

"Six Lindor Balls! Yummy, Kris. I'm going to have one right now. Thank you! Mmmm."

"You're welcome! Open yours, Daddy!"

Once Daniel had lifted the top of his box, he removed a handful of cotton balls and unearthed a silver whistle.

"Cool, Kris."

"In Tom and Jerry cartoons, Jerry always has one so that he can call Spike if he needs help. You can keep it with you and blow on it if you need help."

"Smart." Daniel raised the whistle to his lips and puffed. "You ought to be able to hear that across town. Thanks."

Vaughn leaned down and began to scoop up the paper around her feet saying, "It was a fantastic Christmas Eve celebration, but we'd better start picking up or we'll be late for Midnight Mass."

"But Mom, it's only 10:00," Katie pouted.

"Remember what happened last year when we got there at 11:15?" Tristan asked.

"Yeah, we had to park down the street and stand the whole time," Will said, shuddering dramatically.

"What time should we leave?" Jim asked.

"I'd say no later than 10:30," Sarah suggested. "Are we taking two or three cars?"

"Don't throw away any presents by accident!" Vaughn reminded her family. "I don't want to lose anything this year."

With a wad of tissue paper in his hands, Daniel took a moment to sit still and watch the others in their cooperative efforts at a hasty clean-up. He was having one of those odd moments when he saw the immediate world around him as if he were merely an observer and not a participant. The scene in the Maes' living room was normal and routine. For an instant, he felt like an outsider. The sheer wholesomeness of it was such a far cry from the Christmases of his childhood. He raked his fingers through his hair and then rubbed his eyes. He was suddenly very, very tired.

"No, no," Sarah was saying. "That can be recycled. Put it in this bag."

As he slipped the paper into the correct bag, his wife reached out and lightly touched the back of his head.

"Tired?"

He nodded.

"We could always go in the morning."

"Nah. I'd rather do it tonight. That way we can stay home and play with our toys after Santa comes."

"Well, as long as we're keeping our priorities straight," she replied in that unmistakably sarcastic tone.

He considered arguing with her, decided that he was too tired to put in the effort, and smiled instead.

"Okay, you two!" Jim called from the hallway where he was putting on his coat. "The rest of us are moving out. You coming?"

"We could meet there," suggested Tristan.

"Grandpa Tristan, I want to ride with you, too. Can I? Mommy, can I? Please?"

"Yes, you may, if it's okay with Grandpa."

Once the others had left, Daniel and Sarah quickly finished collecting all of the trash from the floor. Sarah left her husband stacking presents in the living room, as she made one final trip to the bathroom before church.

When she returned to the living room, Daniel was standing in front of the Christmas tree, staring up at the serenely smiling angel that hovered at the top.

"I'm ready," he said abruptly. "We'll be late."

They arrived at 11:15. They had to park their car two blocks away and hurry through the cold night air towards the beacon of light that flickered on and off as the front door of the church swung open and shut. All of the seats were taken, and the Nashes were forced to stand in the back near the door.

"Cold?" Daniel whispered.

"Freezing. Why did I wear a dress? My legs are chilled to the bone."

"Every year when it's cold, you wear a dress. Every year when it's warm, you wear a dress. Maybe next year you should wear pants."

"Then it'll be a hundred degrees for sure," she shot back.

Daniel unbuttoned the coat he was wearing. It had been Max's coat, lent to him by his father before the man's death. Although they had been similar in height, Max had been a much heavier man. The length was right for his son, but the material hung loosely around him. Daniel loved it.

Wrapping the coat around his wife, he folded the sides together so that he and she were both protected by the insulating warmth of the lining and the wool. Daniel rested his cheek against the top of Sarah's head and sagged slightly.

"Daniel?"

"I'm tired," he mumbled. "Just tired."

I've held up remarkably well this Christmas Eve, he thought. *No Max, no Lillian, no Assumpta, a new cousin, a hopefully temporary change in my work status, and a host of unanswered questions.*

He knew that his father and stepmother had done what they'd thought was right. However, he wondered how they couldn't have realized the internal damage Daniel had inflicted upon himself, the self-loathing he'd experienced whenever he thought of the supposed shared physical link to a man he considered to be inhuman. He'd agonized over how a man could father a child and then spend years threatening and then beating him. He'd worried that he had inherited a genetic trait that would make him more likely to beat his own wife and child. Max had known that, and still he'd kept silent.

Daniel listened to his wife's voice as she recited the prayers and responses that were woven throughout the Mass. She was neither overly enthusiastic, as was the man to their left, nor was she overly indifferent, as was the woman in front of them.

For his part, Daniel kept quiet. He didn't participate in the responses with gusto or say the prayers blindly by rote. He didn't say them at all. It was a habit that drove Sarah crazy. Even though her faith was not so strong, she'd always participated, partly in order to strive for a higher level of belief and partly for the sake of their son.

"I don't care if you don't believe!" she'd said more than once. "If you're going to come with us, then say the prayers. Kris doesn't understand why you don't. It makes him less likely to say them. He'll be confused. He looks to both of us for guidance. You're not setting a good example."

"You do too care if I don't believe, so don't lie to me or yourself about that. I can't do what you're asking. I'll go with you; I'll stand, kneel, and sit at the appropriate times; and I'll shake hands with the pastor on the way out. I can't do the rest, Sarah. I walk through every part of the Mass, except Communion. The only other thing I don't do is sing, but then I can't carry a tune anyway, so Kris doesn't expect me to sing."

"There's more to it than singing, standing, sitting, and walking," she'd say tartly. "If Kris asks you why you don't pray, what will you tell him?"

That Christmas Eve, Daniel didn't have to explain anything. He was leaning against the back wall, sheltering his wife in his arms. His son was somewhere else in the church. There were no seats available in the pews, so he didn't even have to sit or kneel at the correct intervals. He did give the Sign of Peace by shaking hands with those around him.

He drifted off to sleep for a time, dreaming hazy and fragmented images of his mother and Zachary Samuels. He awoke with a start to the music of the recessional. Sarah slipped out of his embrace and buttoned her coat as they left the church in search of family, friends, and a hopefully normal Christmas Day.

Chapter Fifteen: In Search of Norman Rockwell

"It's not polite to fall asleep during the Christmas service," someone said from behind him.

"Merry Christmas to you, Jamie."

"Fa la la la la, la la la la. You snored."

"Did not. If I snored, Sarah and I would be sleeping in different bedrooms."

Jamie grinned at the younger man and suggested, "We can talk more about that tomorrow when I pass by with the presents." Jerking his head to one side, he yelled, "Merry Christmas, Tris!!"

Daniel stuck his fingers in his ears and shook his head.

"You'll make me deaf. I guess I should be more tolerant on Christmas, right? Forgive them, Father, for they know not what they do and all that."

"Try not to be such a smart ass, Dan. Max and Lillian put up with your baiting them on religious issues because you were their son. All I did was help to save your life and be your friend. I won't put up with your crap, not when you're insulting my beliefs." When Daniel didn't respond, Jamie added, "I see a fellow biochemist I haven't spoken with in several months. See you tomorrow afternoon."

Daniel stood alone, angry, and chagrined in the middle of the throng. Searching for the faces of his family members, he caught sight of Tristan and Kris. Pushing his way towards them, he came up beside his father-in-law and took Kris into his arms. The child quickly slouched against his chest and fell asleep.

Daniel nodded to Tristan and moved away from him, walking back into the church. People were milling about, but the crowd was thinning as everyone headed for home. The pew nearest the altar was directly under a vent. It was one of the warmest spots in the church. Daniel shifted his son's weight so that the boy was perched on his father's right thigh. He looked down at his child then up at the crucifix. Then he shut his eyes and fell asleep.

Once again, he dreamed of his mother and stepfather. This time, however, the scene was unbroken. Preschool Daniel was standing in the corner of his parents' bedroom. His mother lay crying on the bed. There was blood on her clothing, but Daniel wasn't quite certain where it had come from. Samuels stood gloating over her as he buttoned his shirt in order to go down to the bar for the evening.

"You're *mine*, not his. You're *my wife*. You damn well better not forget it."

"You won't let me!" she cried. "I hate you!"

"You can fucking hate me all you want," he sneered. "You're mine. You have nowhere to go. You won't take my *son* away from me. Not like all the rest."

"I didn't take the others away from you," she insisted. "You took care of every one."

Daniel lowered himself to the floor. He knew what was coming. He hated to see his mother hurt. He prayed to turn invisible and slip out of the room, but nothing happened.

"It's your own Goddamned fault," Samuels said coldly afterwards. "You're responsible." His voice softened and he added, "I love you, Assumpta. If only you wouldn't provoke me. I don't want to hurt you. It's for your own good. Come on. I know you love me."

"I – I do love you, and I hate you."

"Daniel?"

A hand was laid upon his chest. Automatically, he reached out and caught a hold of it. Opening his eyes, he blinked in the bright light of the church.

Sarah stood in front of him. Although she appeared composed, her face was extraordinarily pale.

"Daniel," she said in a strained tone. "My arm."

He was tightly gripping her injured arm directly at the site of her scar. He instantly released her, apologizing profusely for inadvertently hurting her.

"It's already better," she insisted, as she took a seat beside him.

"Yeah, right."

"No, really. When I couldn't find you outside after a few minutes, I figured you'd come in here with Kris to keep him warm. The two of you looked so cute sleeping there like that."

"Was I making any noise?"

She eyed him warily and asked, "Why? What were you dreaming? Not one of those bad nightmares, I hope. It's been six weeks. It's been a nice respite."

"No, not one of the bad ones. Just a regular one. It was…one of those mundane things I guess I suppressed as a kid."

"What was this one about?"

She leaned her head against his shoulder as he told her. She laced her fingers with his and held his hand tightly as he spoke. When he'd finished, his wife disengaged herself from him and stood, bending to button their son's coat.

"What do you think he meant?" she asked. "What did he mean about your mother's taking away all of the rest? And her saying that he had taken care of it all?"

Daniel stood and hoisted his son into a better position. He and Sarah locked arms and walked through the now-deserted church towards the back door.

"I don't know. I do think…I think she really did provoke him that time."

"How could you say something like that?"

"I'm not giving you the typical abuser rhetoric that my stepfather was so famous for. I'm saying that on that occasion and others, she did provoke him. I was a witness to it, although I didn't understand it. Normally, she was terrified of him. I'm beginning to have an awful feeling that I know why she drew him into arguments those times."

"Would you care to enlighten me?"

"It's Christmas. I'm freezing, and I want to get home and put Kris to bed so Santa Claus can come. I want to hold you until he wakes us up." He glanced at his watch and said tiredly, "That'll be in about four and a half hours. I want to watch Kris open his presents and laugh and ask me how Santa got into the house when all of the doors and windows were locked. I'm looking forward to seeing his face when he finds the pieces of carrot that the reindeer left in the bowl on the lawn. I want for you and me to lounge around on the floor and let Kris climb all over us while we put together toys that don't have all the right parts or any instructions."

"A nice Norman Rockwell Christmas," she said with a melancholy tone in her voice.

During what remained of that night, Daniel slept fitfully, waking briefly several times each hour. Every short burst of sleep brought with it vivid memories of Christmases gone by.

"Daddy!"

Little hands pushed against Daniel's chest.

"Daddy, he came already! Wake up and see!"

"We're coming, Kris," he mumbled. "Let me wake Mommy; then we'll be there."

As his son danced impatiently next to the bed, Daniel kissed his wife and teased, "One would think you didn't get enough sleep or something."

"I'm up," she said, as she rubbed her eyes and reached for her robe. "I want to see what Santa brought, too."

Kris darted out of the room as his parents slowly climbed out of bed.

"Mommy! Daddy! Look! The dog toy! Just like at the Cracker Barrel! Look!"

They dropped to the floor and watched in delight as the child pulled the old-fashioned toy around the living room. Ralph proceeded to chase the toy in hilarious circles and bark continually.

"And a bike! Not a tricycle, a *bike*! Daddy, will you teach me how to ride it?"

"I'll try."

"How come you don't have a bike? Mommy has one, and she can't even see good."

"I never learned how to ride a bike. Nobody ever taught me."

Kris thought about this for a minute then turned to his mother.

"Maybe *you* should teach me how to ride."

"Maybe I should. Then we can both teach Daddy."

The rest of the presents were opened; then Kris made his annual journey to check the bowl of carrots.

"The reindeer were more hungrier this year," he reported. "There's hardly any left!" He held out the bowl to his father and exclaimed, "Look!"

"Wow. Only a few pieces. Why don't you give the rest to Ralph?"

Daniel watched his son feed the remainder of the carrots to the dog. Sarah came up behind her husband and slid her arms around his waist.

"Penny for your thoughts," she said, her voice muffled by his back.

"I could never have done that as a boy," he said, nodding in the direction of their child, who was now running around the yard in his pajamas, coat, and boots and throwing a stick for the Labrador.

"Done what? Wear that get-up? Have a dog? Run around like that?"

"Any of it. Damn it, we couldn't even have a normal Christmas!"

His wife walked around and stood in front of him, then she admonished, "It's Christmas morning. I thought you weren't going to do this, Daniel. What happened to Norman Rockwell?"

"Norman wasn't in my dreams last night."

Standing on tiptoe, she kissed him quickly then stepped back and said, "Anything I can do?"

"Later."

"Then let it go for a while."

She lifted her coat from the back of a barstool and slipped it on over her nightgown.

"What are you doing?"

"I feel really good for some reason."

"Ever since you slapped Tristan?"

"It was kind of liberating. Not that I'm not worried about you and everything else that's been upended in our lives, but I feel in control. That particular thread of insecurity is gone, at least for the moment. Maybe *you* should try hitting your stepfather."

Slipping his jacket over his t-shirt and pajama bottoms, Daniel said, "I'd be afraid that it wouldn't stop with a slap. I could never hurt you or Kris, but I believe that I could easily beat him to a pulp. I grew up to be bigger than he is, and I remember. I'm remembering more and more."

They went out the back door and came in twenty minutes later chilled and breathless. Daniel drank three cups of coffee in quick succession, and Sarah and Kris had two cups of hot chocolate each. Once they'd warmed themselves, Sarah insisted that they change clothes before lunch.

She was loading the dishwasher after their meal when the phone rang. It was Carson Zerangue.

"Merry Christmas, Mr. Private 'Vestigator!" Kris sang out at top volume.

"Kris, not so loud. I'm sure he appreciates your good wishes, but you don't want to make his ears hurt either. Let me talk, please." Daniel extended his arm and accepted the receiver. "Thanks. Carson? Merry Christmas."

"Merry Christmas to you, too."

Daniel sat up a little straighter on the couch.

"What's up? You sound…not right. Did you talk to him?"

"No. It's not that."

"You're not sick are you?"

Kris was playing on the floor with his new Lite Brite, but Sarah had overheard her husband's side of the conversation and was now hovering anxiously nearby.

"No. I'm not sick."

"He's okay," Daniel said quietly to his wife. "So, what's wrong, Carson?"

"Nothing's wrong *per se*. The holidays just aren't real exciting for us single guys."

Daniel heard the now-familiar sound of the notebook pages being flipped back.

"I'm going to go see Samuels tomorrow and start working on building up a line of inquiry. It may take some time, depending on how he responds to my approach. Anyhow, I wanted to ask you a question before I go. I'm sorry to do this on Christmas Day, but it won't take a minute."

Daniel sighed and said, "No problem."

"Did your mother have a nickname for her husband?"

"Yeah, she called him Sammy like everyone else."

"Thanks. I'll be in touch."

The line went dead, and Daniel clicked off the cordless receiver and put it down on the coffee table. Then he joined his wife and son on the floor and helped them with the glowing picture of a Christmas tree that held a star on top.

Chapter Sixteen: Stroll Down Memory Lane

When Daniel entered The Black Forest, Frank Randall was already seated at a small table in one corner. After greeting the priest, he took a seat and ordered a drink from the waitress as she breezed by. Once she'd departed, he gave the menu a cursory glance. Then he tossed it down in front of him.

"I always get the Reuben with the cold cabbage on the side," he explained.

"And I always get the Reuben with the German potato salad," replied the priest, nodding politely to the waitress as she came back and deposited Daniel's Coke in front of him. "I believe we're ready."

Once they'd placed their orders, Daniel asked politely, "Did you have a good Christmas?"

"Lovely. Every Mass was packed. In the evening, I spent time with my mother, father, my brothers and their families."

"Your mother and father are still living?"

Randall laughed and asked, "Do I look that old? My parents are in their eighties and are both in reasonably good health and of sound mind." Unrolling his napkin and laying out the silverware in front of him, he asked, "How was your Christmas?"

"It was…okay. We had a great time opening presents with the rest of the family on Christmas Eve. That night, we went to Midnight Mass, and I had this dream…."

He reviewed his dream as they waited for their food. He'd just begun to talk of the relatively peaceful Christmas Day when the waitress arrived with their plates. They lowered their napkins into their laps, and Daniel raised his pickle to his lips.

"I love watching Kris open his presents and play with everything. He gets so excited about it all. I like being able to give him that opportunity."

"And you weren't given that opportunity, I take it?"

"No. My stepfather told me from birth that Santa Claus was a crock and that kids got too much stuff as it was. He allowed Mom to buy two presents for me each Christmas, one ostensibly from him and one from her. She used to somehow buy a few more and hide them from him then put them under the tree in the bar while he was asleep and tell me that Santa was real after all and had brought me some more toys. I'd hide them in my closet and take them out one by one over the next month and a half or so. Somehow, he never caught on. She was taking a big risk by doing that, but I suppose she wanted me to have some kind of magic in my life."

"Do you think your mother and stepfather's overall behavior is what caused you to resent organized religion?"

"What do you think? My God, my God. Why have You forsaken me?"

The priest shook his head thoughtfully and took another bite of his sandwich. He chewed, swallowed, then asked, "Did you write down the list of those you need to forgive?"

"I didn't have to; it's pretty short. It goes like this: my mother, Max, and Lillian."

"What about your stepfather?"

Daniel said icily, "I could never, ever forgive him. I don't want to forgive him. That may be a very un-Christian thing to say, but then I'm not really a Christian, am I?"

"Let me tell you what the path to forgiveness entails. First of all, you have to recall the hurt. Then, you must feel the pain. Finally, you must let go of the hate or resentment or anger that is associated with that person and their actions. I know that's not an easy thing to do, but it's necessary if you aren't going to remain bitter."

"How can I let something like that go?"

"It's an extremely difficult thing to do. For some, it's virtually impossible. Yet, that's what God asks. That's what can heal."

"Maybe I should add God to my list of forgiveness. If He's really there, then how could He let things like this happen? If He's so all-powerful, then why doesn't He stop the misery?"

"God allowed free will for man and the angels. Without permissive will, we'd all be slaves. Not that omnipotent will doesn't lead to miracles at times."

"How can Man forgive terrible evil when it manifests itself?"

"By the grace of God we can forgive. We don't have to love our enemies, but we can pray for the salvation of their immortal souls."

"My stepfather can burn in Hell for all I care. I wish he would as a matter of fact. It would be a fitting punishment for torturing me when I was a child and for killing my mother."

"To wish for the loss of a mortal soul is the greatest hate a man can have. As long as he wishes for another's damnation, he can't truly be free."

"Frank, did you have a happy childhood? Were your parents good to you? Did you have a nice house to live in, decent clothes to wear, lots of food on the table, and family who loved you? Did you play ball in the street with your friends? Have a dog that followed you around the neighborhood?"

The priest raised his glass as the waitress passed nearby.

"Another refill, please."

"Well, Father?"

"My parents were strict, but they were loving. Our house was small but we were comfortable there. Every year, my mother would take me and my siblings to the department store to buy our school clothes. My father was a grocer, so we had good food. My friends and I *did* play ball in the street. Kick the can, too. And my dog's name was Buster."

"I think we're ready for our check," Daniel told the waitress as she brought the priest his Dr. Pepper. "That is, if you don't mind taking a walk with me, Frank? There's something I'd like to show you. It's not too far from the church, actually."

"A long walk will do me good. I think I need to work off that lunch. Just let me polish off this soft drink first."

Twenty minutes later, they stood across the street from the People's Choice Adult Bookstore. Daniel couldn't stand to look at the building. He stood with his back to it and faced the brick wall of the travel agency that was located on their side of the street.

"You see that building directly across from here?" he asked tightly.

"The one with the dark windows? Yes, I do."

"It's an adult bookstore now. It used to be a bar. Before that, it was a house of prostitution. My stepfather owns it. He inherited it from his family. That's where I grew up; our rooms were on the second floor." Dropping his head, he admitted, "I've avoided this place since I was twelve." Pretending to examine an advertisement for a trip to Cancun, Daniel continued, "It was a really wholesome place to grow up. There were bedrooms upstairs and a kitchen and a bathroom. Each bedroom had a closet, and there was one in the hallway. My mother and I never had good clothes or a lot to eat. I don't know what the man did with the money he made. Maybe he was a bad businessman or, conversely, he was a good one and invested it all."

The priest stood quietly and stared at the building as Daniel shut his eyes and debated about how much he wanted to tell the man.

"He never showed any affection towards me," Daniel said bitterly. "He was…indifferent until my mother died. Of course, he beat her up all the time and forced her to do all sorts of unpleasant things." Clearing his throat, he confided, "After she died, I used to hide in the closets or under the bed sometimes when he was after me. It was pretty stupid. As if he couldn't get to me. Still, your body reacts instinctively to some things. Fear can be a great catalyst or it can immobilize you."

"Did your mother ever standup against him?"

"She used to provoke him every so often. Every time she got pregnant, I suspect. The idiot never caught on. He'd get drawn into it, never stopping to think how uncharacteristic it was for her to talk back. He was really fucked up. *She* was really fucked up. She wouldn't kill his babies. She'd get him to do it for her. You can't imagine what he did to her whether she was goading him or not. You can't imagine how cruel he was to me and the scars he left on my body and in my head."

"It's a miracle you didn't become like him," the priest said quietly. "That's something that happens so often when children are abused or see a parent or sibling abused."

"My real father did help me to conquer those tendencies. He was a good psychiatrist. When I was first with Max and Lillian, I wanted to hit; I wanted to hurt. I wanted someone else to feel that pain. The first time I was with a woman –"

He stopped, and his face went crimson. He began to stride down the sidewalk in the direction of the cathedral.

"You think I haven't been with a woman?" Randall asked from behind him.

That stopped Daniel.

"You're a priest."

"I've been a priest since I was thirty-four years old. Before that, I was a journalist. I didn't realize that the priesthood was my true calling until I was almost thirty. You think that priests are celibate their entire lives?" He laid a hand on Daniel's arm and said, "Even if I had never known what it was like, you could talk with me about it."

"Part of the job?"

"Part of the job. Understanding even those things of which you have no knowledge."

Daniel shuffled his feet and manipulated the keys in his pocket.

"I was rough. Really rough. I mean, I didn't rape the girl or anything. She was more than willing."

"Not a virgin, I take it?"

"Definitely not."

"And did she complain afterwards?"

"She said she liked it like that, but I came to realize that I didn't. It felt like rape, even though it was consensual. That was part of the reason I broke it off with her. That, and the fact that I knew I really loved Sarah. I was being unfaithful to her, even though we'd never been physically intimate. I was in college, and she was in high school. I was involved in things on campus, and I got involved with that girl. I felt guilty when it was over, so I didn't call Sarah. That was the worst mistake I ever made. That was when her father was going through his relapse with drugs, and she was dealing with it all alone. If I had called her, then maybe I could have prevented things from deteriorating late that summer."

"Then again, maybe not."

Daniel scratched at his chin and resumed walking, this time with the priest walking beside him.

"And when you were finally together with your wife in the Biblical sense, as they say?" Randall asked.

"I wanted to know if I could love her without hurting her. She'd been hurt enough by others and by me. I found that I could, although it took some effort at the beginning to be forceful and gentle at the same time. Once I got the hang of it, then it was…I don't know. Beautiful."

"You and Sarah have known each other since childhood?"

"I met her and her dad not long before my stepfather pretty much beat me to death. Tristan saved my life, and Sarah saved my soul."

"She seems to be a perfect complement to you. Have you ever stopped to consider what a miracle that is? Right at your darkest moment God sent her to you."

"Right before my darkest moment, I happened to meet her and her father. I saw them again once, and Tristan gave me their address. I guess I stumbled there after that last beating, the one that almost did me in."

"And where would you have gone if her father hadn't given you his address?"

"I don't know. Maybe I would have stumbled to the police station or perhaps I would have stayed in my room and died."

"But instead you *did* meet Sarah and her father, and you *did* end up at their house. Through them, you inadvertently found your biological father. You also found in Sarah a partner for life. You think that it's all coincidence?"

They'd reached the steps of St. Joseph's Cathedral. Daniel sat on the top step, fingering a piece of yarn that was unraveling near the cuff of his sweater. Randall joined him and clasped his hands together between his knees.

"Chance," Daniel offered with a shrug. "Coincidence. Fate. Whatever."

"You won't even admit the possibility of a Divine influence?"

"Okay, let me think. God's going to sit around and let me suffer for the first twelve years and then intervene and try to make it up to me?"

"Perhaps at that point He felt that intervention was the only way."

"To do what? Save my soul?"

Randall smiled and said, "I can't second-guess the Almighty."

"So, He's willing to cut me some slack, but I need to forgive all of these people – my mother, my father, and my stepmother? Oh, I forgot. I should also forgive my stepfather. Did I leave anyone out?"

"Yourself."

"Me? What do I have to forgive myself for? Surviving?"

The priest stood and patted Daniel on the shoulder.

"I have to go. Think on it. If you're interested in continuing our discussion, then call me. Goodbye, Dan."

"But –"

"Call me," he repeated, as he walked towards the doors of the church.

Daniel watched him pull back the heavy door and step inside.

"That was a real dumb thing to do," said a gruff voice behind him.

Startled and confused, Daniel swung his head back around and stared into the eyes of Carson Zerangue.

"I can't talk to a priest? Is there some law about atheists talking to members of the clergy that I'm not aware of?"

"I wasn't bitchin' about your talking to the padre. I was bitchin' because for some asinine reason you decided to take a stroll down memory lane this afternoon. What in the hell did you think you were doing? You haven't been back to that building in a quarter of a century. Now, on the eve of my investigation of the place, you and the good Father want to loiter around across the street. What if old Sammy decided to look out the window and recognized you? Don't you think that would jeopardize my inquiries? Don't you think he might be suspicious when I start nosing around about his former life?"

"Come on, Carson. Do you think he'd recognize me after all this time? The last time he saw me I was a kid. Here I am, a grown man approaching middle age. You think he'd see my back from his window and say, 'Hey! That's Danny's back over there! Him, reading the travel posters and talking to that priest! I'd know that back anywhere!' Get off it, Carson."

"No, *you* get off it. If you want me to continue working on this, you stay away from that place unless I say otherwise. Next time you'll be wanting to go inside."

"Inside? I couldn't even look at the outside. I was making a point to the priest. Why would I have any desire to set foot in the building again?"

"You wouldn't be the first. Some people have a morbid curiosity that compels them to eventually return to the scene of the crime, so to speak. Others want to validate their memories."

"I think my scars are validation enough."

"Perhaps," Carson admitted, as he lowered himself down next to Daniel. "When the investigation is over, you might want to go back. Sometimes, it helps to bring a touch of finality to things."

"You think Samuels is still a danger?"

"I won't know until I talk with him."

Daniel reflected on this, saying nothing.

"I thought you had a therapist," the detective volunteered. "You decided to switch to the priest for counseling? Or have you seen the light?"

"I do have a therapist. He's been okay, but this guy is doing me a lot more good. He pushes me a little harder, makes me a little angrier, and confronts me with issues I'd just as soon avoid. He's good at it. Maybe he chose the wrong profession."

"Or he chose the right one."

"You'll call me as soon as you can and tell me how it went after you have your first meeting with Samuels?"

"Of course. Is there a time that's too late? I don't want to wake the kid by phoning once he's in bed."

"Kris could sleep through anything."

"Later then. I'll call after I get cleaned up."

"You want me to ask Frank to say a special prayer for you?"

"The priest? Nah. I got me a guardian angel already. You use those prayers for yourself. Depending on what I find out, you may need 'em."

Chapter Seventeen: Seeing the Light...And the Darkness

Carson sauntered into The People's Choice Adult Bookstore at 9:59. Clad in weathered jeans and a faded New Orleans Saints sweatshirt, he passed a hand over his hair, then wiped some of the grease that he'd applied to it off on one pant leg. Slipping a pack of Marlboros from his back pocket, he tapped out a cigarette and placed it between his lips. It hung suspended and unlit as he perused the pornographic material available.

Passing over the magazines that would normally attract a middle-aged, heterosexual American male, he selected some titles that, although perverse, would certainly make good fuel for lighting his fireplace. He wanted to make a distinct impression on Zachary Samuels.

The buzzer on the door sounded as a new customer entered. Carson automatically looked up. He was both startled and ridiculously pleased to see Natalie Perrealtos, a private detective who entered the store that evening, disguised as a prostitute.

She wore platform shoes, a leopard print mini-skirt, a black leather top, and a blonde wig. No one else would have recognized Natalie. But Carson had seen her use this costume in New Orleans when they'd been investigating a homicide case that involved cocaine trafficking. She'd worn it off and on for several weeks. It would have been something difficult for him to forget.

Carson buried his face in one of the magazines. It wasn't that he didn't want Natalie to see him here. He knew she wouldn't give him away any more than he would reveal her true identity. They were both too professional for that. He simply had to hide an enormous grin that was threatening to turn into a laugh.

"Hey!"

It was Natalie, standing at his elbow.

"Hey! I was talking to *you*, Mister! You think there's something funny about me?"

He lowered the magazine, all evidence of the smile eradicated from his face.

"What de hell you talkin' 'bout? I'm jus' tryin' ta pick out a magazine, yeah. You gon' tell me jus' what a beautiful lady like yerself's doin' in a place like dis?"

She batted her eyelids at Carson, making it difficult for him to keep the grin at bay.

"Some men like this kind of stuff. It, you know, adds, like, to the experience."

"*Mais*, yeah. I knows dat! An' yer name is –?"

"Sindy. That's Sindy with an S. Get it? Sin-dy?"

"I gets it. Maybe I can get it a little later, too?"

She thrust her Miracle Bra bosom at his chest and said, "I'm working now. Maybe in a while?"

"Where you be at?"

She lifted her head, put her lips next to his ear, and whispered her phone number. Carson gave her the slap on the backside that was expected, and Natalie casually picked up a hard core publication and tossed it on the counter in front of a gray-haired man of average height and weight who practically radiated an aura of evil.

"Can you hurry up, Sammy? I've wasted enough time here. My John's waiting."

"Always a pleasure, Sindy," he leered. "Good to see you back in the neighborhood. It's been a while. Seen Veronica, lately?"

"Aw, she moved out to Port Allen." As she handed him a ten-dollar bill, she added, "If you want to do her, you'll have to check out that club on Highway 68."

"I don't get over the river much," he lamented, as he gave her the change.

"See ya, Sammy."

"See ya, Sindy."

My cue, Carson thought. *Let's get this show on the road.*

He tossed the magazines on the counter, grateful to Natalie for giving him a good opening topic of discussion.

"She wort' it?"

"I wouldn't know," Samuels grumbled. "She won't take me as a client. Says she doesn't mix business with business. Bitch.

But she does give me some sales when she's around, and she refers people to me. That kind of shit."

"I be lettin' you know, yeah?"

"You do that. You new in town? I haven't seen you before."

"My cousin's sick. Nothin' I can do, 'cept sit 'round in dat dere Earl K. Long Hospital. Not doin' me no good to be mopin' 'round dere. My cousin, he tells me to get out and take care of his place while he's laid up. Not much dere, I'm tellin' ya. I don' know nobody. I don' wanna sit 'round an' stare at de four walls. I gots to have me some company." He glanced back at the door and said, "Now, I gots me a coupla hours to kill; den I'm gon' have me some company for a few minutes at least."

"Need a light?"

"Dat'd be good." Carson leaned forward, as Samuels removed a lighter from his pocket. "Name's Aucoin."

"Samuels. Just call me Sammy. Everybody does."

"You run dis place all by yerself? How you ever get some action in?"

"I got a kid who comes in here on Fridays and Sundays. That's when I have my nights out. Little faggot named Hamp."

"You like dose types?"

"Shit, no!" Samuels guffawed. "But it's good for business. I really get the queers in here on those nights. It moves a lot of material with that crowd when he's working."

"Dat's real smart."

Looking pleased with himself, Samuels nodded.

"I do pretty good."

"How long you been in dis here place?"

"All my life. I grew up in this building. It was a whorehouse back then."

"Who ran it? Yer mama or yer papa?"

Samuels howled with laughter.

"You Cajuns don't waste any time, do you?"

"Time, she's money."

"My daddy," Samuels informed him, as he rang up a video for a scruffy-looking boy who was probably under eighteen and definitely drunk.

"Yer mama was, ah, one of his ladies?"

"When it was called for."

Carson took a deep drag from his cigarette before saying, "Me, my papa was a fisherman. My mama, she done jus' 'bout every man 'round when he was out on de boat. I gots me a lot of brothers and sisters dat way. You?"

"If there were any, I don't know what my father did with them."

Carson felt the sudden urge to vomit. He forced himself to regain control of his mind and stomach in order to continue the conversation.

"You better off for it. Dey ain' nothin' but trouble. Jus' like kids. Me, I gots four of dem, an' all dey want is my money an' a place ta stay when dey ain' in jail."

"Yeah. I had me a son once."

"He died, den?"

"Nah. Long story. My wife's fault. I loved her, even if she was a lying whore. I just had to keep setting her straight. She was always testing me. I had to keep showing her who was the boss." He grinned maliciously and confided, "There were only three things that she'd listen to, and two of them were my fists."

Carson's mouth twisted into what he hoped was a vicious echo of Samuel's grin.

"My ex-wife, she was like dat, too. She'd be cryin' for me ta stop, tellin' me dat she hated me, den she'd be all fired up in bed afterwards."

"Yeah," Samuels nodded enthusiastically. "Exactly. They all want it like that."

"You know it. Look, I gots ta go, but I be back 'round. Lemme pay you fer dis, den I best be on my way. Sin-dy be waitin'."

"Enjoy her for me."

Carson made the long walk to where his car was parked. Once inside, he slumped back and reached for his cellphone. Natalie answered on the second ring and arrived at Carson's apartment as he was preparing to light a fire. He'd already showered and put on a clean pair of jeans and a clean flannel shirt.

"Some strange man called and told me to meet him here," the woman said when he opened the door. "Disgusting slob with greasy hair. You acquainted with him?"

"Never met the guy in my life. Actually, I was trying to reach some trashy hooker with a bad perm. You don't really look like her. She was blonde, and you're a brunette. She was tall, and you're not. You really her?"

"I can be whatever you want me to be," she whispered seductively. "That's what we do, isn't it? Become whatever we need to get the job done?"

Carson returned to the fireplace and handed Natalie a magazine.

"Make yourself useful and start tearing these up. I need the trash to stoke the fire."

"Ooh. Nice ones. What are you working on? Keeping the world safe from perverts?"

"Just giving a man some answers about one particular pervert named Zachary Samuels. It's obvious that you two have met before. What's the scoop?"

"What's to tell? You know the kind. He's mean as hell. He likes ones who put up a fight and knocks them around a bit before he does his thing."

"Is that what he did with this Veronica woman he mentioned? Maybe I should talk to her."

"Do me a favor and don't. She's not really in Port Allen. I told the creep that because I knew he'd never go over there to find her. I don't know where she is. Wherever she ended up, I'm sure she's happy to be away from Samuels."

"He was a regular John for her?"

"Once a week. She told me he paid her really well. You get what you pay for."

"You two were good pals?"

"We lived next door to each other when I was working on a drug case about six months ago. Veronica and I got to know each other during the seven weeks that I was living in the motel."

"Seven weeks! Damn. What kind of drug case took you seven weeks?"

"Corporate president's son. I made a great deal of money off that one. It sure as hell beats the usual deadbeat dads, affairs, and court records cases. The rich father wanted all the info I could find – associates, dealers, habits, girlfriends."

"And Veronica went out of her way to tell you about Samuels?"

"No. She knew that I frequented his store in the line of duty. His name came up one day, and she spilled her guts."

"What'd she tell you?"

She put her hands out near the now-blazing fire and asked, "Can we talk about something else? I want to get away from work now that I'm here."

"Natalie, my client is his stepson. He caused the kid's mother's death and nearly beat the kid to death as well." Carson leaned back and grasped the unopened beer on the coffee table. Handing it to his friend, he added, "This case has gotten under my skin more so than any case I've had in years. Please."

"Business before pleasure?" She opened the beer and took a swallow before exclaiming, "Oh, all right! Veronica said he used to do the same thing each time. Well, you know, vary it slightly, but basically the same thing. She had to pretend to be his wife, and she'd done something wrong. He'd kind of knock her around. It was pretty rough stuff. The jerk said that it was a good prelude to sex."

"All the wife-beaters say that."

"Veronica said he was dead serious about that, not just bragging. She inadvertently gave me a lot of information when I was on that case. I never thought any of this would be relevant. I almost told her I didn't want to hear it, but I thought that would be out of character."

"I'm glad you did hear it for the sake of my investigation."

"I'm getting tired of hearing it, Carson. Yes, our work can be interesting and exciting, but you know that it's mostly the seedy underbelly of the world that we deal with when we go undercover like this. I'm pushing forty. I'm thinking about subbing out this kind of work."

"I never thought I'd say this, but I've been thinking the same thing. When I was buddying up to Samuels tonight, I almost lost my lunch. The man is such a sleaze. You can't imagine what he did to the kid."

"Give me a few moments." She placed her beer on the edge of the hearth and admitted, "I'm sure that I can, but I really don't want to."

"Your friend Veronica didn't say why the wife put up with or participated in the relationship? That's the thing I can't seem to figure out. We've pieced together some of the past, but nobody can see why she ended up with Samuels or why she stayed.

"It's not that I can't understand her marrying someone. It was the fifties, and she was single and pregnant. She felt like she couldn't marry the father. But why Samuels? And how? She married him less than a month after she found out she was pregnant. She was young, pretty, and smart. She had a college degree."

"Smart women are abused just as often as dumb ones. Maybe he was good to her at first when she didn't have any place else to go. Or she actually loved the creep. Perhaps he reminded her of her father, God forbid."

"I'm hoping that Samuels might be able to clear up some of the mystery, and I hope it happens quickly. I don't want to spend any more time with him than I have to." He leaned back against the front of the couch and stretched out his arm then asked, "What kind of case are you on?"

"Extramarital affair. I finished up tonight."

"And?"

"The jackass has been with several of my streetwise women friends. I think a divorce and an HIV test will be in order for the wife." The woman moved over next to Zerangue and slid her arm around his waist before confiding, "I feel sorry for her. They have two kids. She hasn't worked outside the home since 1986."

Squeezing her shoulder, Carson muttered, "It's a damned shame. At least she knows the truth."

"Sometimes I wonder if our clients regret that they found out the truth," she said, as she stared into the flames in front of them. "Will the truth feed this woman's children next month? Will it pay her rent?"

"It may save her life or her sanity. Take my client. Everything in his past is over and done with. He accepts that. All he wants is some peace. He wants to know why. It won't affect his relationship with his mother or father or stepmother; they're all dead. But it will affect his relationships with his wife, child, boss, in-laws, and friends because it makes a difference to him. He needs to let go, but he feels like he can't until he's exhausted every avenue."

"This case really *has* gotten under your skin. I haven't heard you spout such pearls of wisdom since that case with the kid in Kenner."

"That little kid and his folks needed more from me than an official report. So does this client."

"Are you going to bring him to People's Choice?"

"Are you out of your ever-loving mind? Who knows what might happen? Samuels may pull a gun out from under the counter and shoot my client, or my client may lose it and attack Samuels. I wasn't even his victim, and I know I'd love to beat the living crap out of him. The scars that kid has.... You would have thought they would have faded after twenty-five years."

"That bad?" Natalie asked and shuddered slightly in his arms. "I thought we'd seen it all."

"You getting soft on me, Natalie?"

"You know I steer clear of the child abuse cases if I can avoid them." She hesitated and asked, "But if the client is stable enough to go there, it might do him some good. Disguise him, and give him a lecture on staying calm. Hamp will let you upstairs for twenty dollars, you know. You could take the client on one of Sammy's nights off."

"Hamp? You mean the man who works for Samuels? You can go upstairs?"

"You've been around the block too many times not to know what I mean. I'm sure that Sammy's aware of it. He must split the money with Hamp. Sammy would never take a risk like that himself."

"I wouldn't think so. He was in trouble with the law before for almost killing my client. If he were to be caught pandering...."

"Hamp takes the blame if the police ever raid the place at the wrong moment."

"So, is Hamp stupid or greedy?"

"Indifferent."

Zerangue got up and placed another log on the fire.

"You finished your case tonight, although I know you have to write up your report and talk to your client. You want to help me with mine? I'll pay you."

"Then I'd *really* feel like a hooker."

"So, you'll help?"

"Only if you're up front with me about the whole story. You know the rules."

"Yeah, I do. I'll have to get permission from my client. He'll probably want to meet you. This isn't something he shares easily."

"You think he'll want to go back?"

"He can't even bring himself to look at the building when he's in the area, but who knows? I can't believe I'm even talking about suggesting this. Still, the chance to go in and see if we could unravel this mystery is appealing." Zerangue frowned at Natalie and asked, "Did you have a good childhood?"

"Yes, I did. You've met my mom and dad. They have their faults, but they're okay. Regular folks. My sisters took ballet, and I took karate. We were all cheerleaders in high school."

"You? A cheerleader?" Seeing the scowl on her face, he hastened to add, "Not that you're not prettier than most other women. It's only that I don't picture you being part of that crowd. You're not the type."

"And how would you know if I'm the type or not?" she asked coolly. "I've known you for twelve years. We've worked and played together, but we've never been serious enough for you to make any judgments on what kind of person I was or am. You think you know so much about me, Mr. P.I.? Well, what if I told you that I loved being a cheerleader. It was fun, and it made me feel sexy and energetic?"

"The last time we played together, you were energetic enough for me," he said, rolling his eyes. "You're gonna do this old man in."

"Yeah, like you're so ancient. That's why I keep coming back."

"Well, I'm glad that you're enlightening me. So, go on. You were a cheerleader. Then, you were a cop. Now, you're a P.I. What about your sisters? What do they do?"

"One is a hair stylist; one is a housewife; and one is an investment banker."

"Diverse bunch."

"What about you? Happy childhood?"

"Happy enough. My parents were good to us. My brother was a troublemaker. When we were kids, it was mischief, but as he got older, he got to be a regular offender. He's been in and out of jail his whole adult life."

"Is that why you became a cop?"

"Nope. I became a cop because I wanted out. I didn't want to be a poor, happy fisherman."

"So, you opted for being a comfortable, lonely private detective instead?"

"Natalie, I asked you to marry me three years ago, and you said it wasn't the right time."

"You said you didn't want children."

"I'm too old."

"You and I both know that's not the issue. You're afraid that history will repeat itself. I'm not your ex-wife. Even if we were to split up, I'm not the kind of person who would steal out of town in the middle of the night and take our kid with me."

"I didn't think *she* was that kind of person either. I still don't get it. I was a good father. I had Angela every other week. I paid my child support on time. So, why take Angela away?"

"Is that what this case is about? Finding out why someone who appears to have sense and brains will stay with someone who puts her child at risk?"

"It didn't start out that way. Now, I don't know."

"You're worried that whoever your ex is with might hurt Angela?"

"What if it's someone like Samuels? The scars that he left on my client are terrible."

"Enough of that 'my client' talk. What is the guy's name? If I'm going to be working on this with you, then I can't go around saying 'your client' all the time."

"Dan."

"Much better. Am I going to get to see Dan's file, or am I going to be better off uninformed?"

"Once I get his permission to put you on, you can see everything. I don't believe he's going to object to your involvement."

The wood crackled in the fireplace. Natalie rested her head against Zerangue's knee, and he began to stroke her hair.

"Angela's all right, Carson. The police or FBI will find her."

"*I* couldn't even find her, and I'm her father and a private investigator! The other night I came home and the answering machine was blinking. I had this insane notion that maybe Angela had managed to somehow call me and tell me where she was. My heart started pounding; I actually thought I'd hear her voice. Of course, it was some blasted telemarketing message, and I was pretty crushed. It made me mad that I, of all people, can't locate my own child."

"Your ex learned all the tricks of the trade while you two were together. You worked enough missing persons cases for her to know what sorts of clues the police are looking for."

"What if Angela doesn't remember me? She was five the last time I saw her."

"How could anybody forget you?" she laughed. "Lord knows I've tried."

"Marry me?"

"Okay. Anything to get you to stop asking – if you don't rule out the kid issue."

"I won't rule anything out."

"Good."

"Well, Sin-dy, I'm bushed." As if to emphasize this piece of information, he yawned and stretched then murmured, "Would you like for me to escort you home or would you prefer staying here this evening?" He glanced at the clock and corrected, "This morning?"

"How soon do you want to get married?"

"What the hell? It's been years, and I never thought you'd actually accept my proposal. We can go to get the license tomorrow. As for the ceremony, that's up to you. Justice of the peace, minister, priest – whatever you want."

"We could go down to LSU and look for those evangelists who're always out to save everyone's souls. I'm sure we'll find Brother Barry and Sister Cindy in front of the Student Union building on campus. That's Cindy with a 'C,' of course. Wouldn't that be a trip?"

"Natalie, you know that Brother Barry converted Sister Cindy in the backseat of his car."

"For real?"

"That's what he said with the greatest sincerity the last time I was loitering out there on a case. She saw the light!"

"I bet she saw a whole lot more than that. Praise God, Brother!"

"Amen, Sister!"

Once the peals of laughter had died away, Zerangue asked, "So, what do you want to do?"

"Get the license tomorrow and find someone to marry us."

"And about this morning?"

"I think I would prefer it if you'd escort me home, kind sir. I know it's stupid. We've slept together so many times before, but it has been a while, and it might feel more…special if we wait until after we're married to do it again."

"Am I seeing a flash of the cheerleader in you?"

"The cheerleader in me would already have you in bed. This is the romantic in me. You'd better take a quick look. I only let that one out about once a year."

Carson grinned and told her, "I'll get my coat."

Chapter Eighteen: Confining Spaces

Daniel stood in his father's bedroom, wearing his father's clothes. As he studied his reflection in the enormous mirror, he muttered, "How in the hell did he keep Lillian from fixing these?"

The red-and-white flannel shirt had been Max's favorite for working in the garden during the winter months. Two buttons were gone. The cuffs were frayed. The pocket was missing-in-action.

The torn, brown workpants were long enough for Daniel, but the waist was much too big. He'd had to bunch up the excess as he'd fed a belt through the loops. The material at the knees was worn practically white.

Max's battered dock shoes were slightly too long. Daniel had put on two pairs of socks so that he wouldn't come out of the shoes every time he took a few steps. The ends of the laces had come undone.

The overall effect was perfect.

Amazingly enough, Daniel felt comforted by wearing the dead man's clothing. As he was swallowed by the large shirt and pants, it was as if Max's spirit had descended over him and wrapped his arms around his son. Some sort of unseen force surrounded him and gave him strength.

Daniel ran a finger along one ragged cuff. He would never get rid of these clothes. He would pack them away, along with one of his father's handkerchiefs, his favorite robe, and a tie Daniel had given him for his birthday the first year that they were together. Max had worn that tie at least twice a week until his retirement.

"Don't you look stunning?" Sarah remarked from the doorway. "I love that stubbly beard. Maybe you should skip shaving more often. It makes you look rugged."

"You're the one who looks stunning. I love that combination. You'd better not let CoCo see it. She'll be jealous."

"Yes, I thought that the orange cardigan was a lovely complement to the blue dress. The pink, red, and purple scarf added that special touch." Sarah pirouetted in the doorway and admitted, "I feel like a child, playing dress-up. Lillian's clothes are way too big for me. Do you remember this dress? I found it way in the back of Lillian's closet. I haven't seen her wear it since we were children. I wonder why not? This color was beautiful on her. I want to keep it when we go through her things."

"I want to keep these, too. I already have the coat that Max let me borrow before he died. I won't keep much else in the way of clothing."

"We should go through the house when Kris goes back to school. You'll be off work. We could get a lot accomplished."

He nodded distractedly as he tugged at a loose string on one shirt cuff.

"Are you certain you want to go through with this?" she asked seriously.

"Yes. Are you certain you want to come with me?"

"If you're going back to that building, then you're not going alone."

"What if the cops raid the place and arrest us for solicitation?"

"I don't see how two married people could be accused of soliciting sex with each other. It wouldn't take long to straighten things out. I'm willing to accept that risk if you are."

"I don't see as how I have a choice in the matter."

"When are we supposed to meet Carson and…what's her name again?"

"Natalie. At 9:00. We have three hours. What do you want to do?"

"How about if we start to pack the clothes in those boxes Lillian was collecting? The lady from that shelter we contacted called this morning and asked me how soon we could have them ready. It's been so cold this winter that she says people are desperate."

"Let's do it. I'd like to get it all out anyway. As long as Max and Lillian's stuff is hanging in the closets, I feel like they're not really gone. It's like they're on vacation or something."

"You get the boxes, and I'll start taking things off the hangers."

Daniel taped up the last carton before 8:15 and said, "We've got to get to Louie's Café if we're going to meet Carson and Natalie."

Sarah pointed her finger at each box as she silently counted.

"There are only ten cartons. It seemed like they had more clothes than that. I guess Lillian must have sorted through things a few years ago."

"I remember Max said something about families from Eastern Europe who had come to the States. They needed everything, so he and Lillian gave away clothes they hadn't worn in a while."

Daniel squatted down and maneuvered his fingers under the edge of one box. Grunting, he hoisted it up and placed it on top of another larger box.

"Maybe we could come back here tomorrow," he suggested. "At least here I feel like I'm *doing* something. It'll be Saturday, and we're not supposed to pick up Kris from that sleepover until after lunch."

"We could sleep here tonight," Sarah offered.

"I don't know if I'm ready to sleep here, yet. I don't know if I ever want to sleep here again." Lifting one of the smaller boxes, he handed it to his wife and asked, "Why don't we get started with moving these? We can decide about spending the night later. We need to get Ralph in before we go."

"We should bring him with us," Sarah giggled. "It would certainly add some spectacular effect."

"He's too well taken care of to belong to street people, although he would come in handy if I wanted him to attack my stepfather if he returns early."

"As if Ralph could attack anyone. Maybe he could lick them to death," Sarah said with a smile. She then frowned and asked, "You don't think Samuels will come back while we're there, do you?"

"Carson says it's unlikely."

"I'm still worried. What if he does?"

"I don't want to think about that or I won't be able to do it. I need to do this, Sarah. I have to."

The two detectives were sipping coffee at a back table in the diner when Daniel and Sarah shuffled in. As Daniel reached up to remove his knit cap, Zerangue stopped him.

"Leave it on at all times. You leave that scarf on, too, Sarah."

"Part of our disguise?"

"An integral part."

"You two look great in those outfits," Daniel joked. "Who can resist a man in torn jeans and a stained John Deere shirt and a woman in a hot pink skirt with fishnet stockings and a spandex top? Too much."

"Only the best of the worst for us," answered Natalie. "You didn't do so bad yourselves. You may have found a new talent."

"It runs in the family," Daniel told her, as he thought of CoCo. Sobering, he asked, "Can we go now?"

The detectives nodded, and they headed for Natalie's old minivan. Zerangue drove and parked it two blocks from the People's Choice Adult Bookstore. As they neared the building, he ushered them into an alcove that sheltered them from the blustering wind on the street as well as any prying eyes.

"Remember what we talked about. Follow our lead." He squinted at Daniel in the darkness and asked, "You still up for this? There's time to turn around."

"No."

Sarah lost all feeling in her left hand as Daniel squeezed it tightly with his fingers. She was glad for the cold. Perhaps the others would mistake her trembling for chills and not manifestations of fear and dread.

She stepped out into the street after Natalie. Daniel released his grip on her hand as she walked forward, and she sensed the tingle in her fingers as the circulation was slowly restored. By the time they reached the shop, her hand was no longer numb.

The heat was blowing full-blast in the bookstore. Natalie took Sarah's hand and led her around the shop, pointing out various magazines that 'Sindy' thought might be of interest. Sarah's face burned with embarrassment as Sindy rattled off some of the titles. For once, Sarah was glad of her vision problem. Not being able to clearly see the covers of the magazines, books, and videos was a relief.

"Hey, Hamp!" Natalie called out to the tall, skinny young man behind the counter. "How's it hangin'?"

"Oh, it's hanging too much, lately," he moaned. "There is a *dreadful* shortage of men around town!"

"Not in my area," Natalie teased. "I've got more than I can handle."

"Well, send some of them my way!" Hamp said. "Who's your friend?" Examining Sarah closely, he speculated, "One of your types?"

"As if you'd know," she retorted. "Nah. Her old man screwed her and left. For real. He took all of their money and moved out. She's been living here and there. She hasn't been with a man in six months."

Hamp leaned forward and said sympathetically, "It's the story of my life, Girlfriend. Too bad I'm not straight. I most definitely *would.* If you weren't underage, that is." He looked at Natalie and nervously asked, "She's not underage, is she? You can't just feed her to the wolves, even if she is desperate."

"You can't be picky on the streets, Hamp," Natalie admonished. "I'm trying to do the girl a favor and find her someone. She's got ten bucks saved up. If I find somebody, will that pay for a room upstairs?"

The man looked directly at Sarah and said, "I'm not supposed to let anyone up there without twenty dollars, but I tell you what. If you find someone, and he doesn't have another ten, then I'll let you go on up, poor dear."

Feeling nauseated, Sarah nodded and tried to look grateful. The buzzer sounded, and Carson swaggered in with his hand securely on Daniel's shoulder. Daniel seemed stiff but composed.

"Yo, Aucoin! It's me, Sindy! You remember?"

"Remember? How could I be forgetin' de udder night? One of de best times I been havin' in years! I gots a friend wit' me tonight, and he could use yer services. Can you help 'em?"

"How much does he have?"

Daniel slowly removed a folded bill from his back pocket and held it out to Natalie.

"Ten bucks? Hey, I'm no cheap thrill, Mister."

Hamp asked, "How about your friend? She needs a man, and he doesn't look *that* bad. Between the two of them, they have enough to go upstairs."

"Dat be a great idea!" Carson boomed. "We goin' upstairs, too, Sindy?"

"If you've got the money, Honey, I've got the time."

"It be Friday, Chere. Me, I got paid dis aftanoon. If I pays you de same as before, den I still gots me fifty dollars left. If I put dat in, will dat guarantee none of us be disturbed?"

"Hamp?"

"Oh, why not? Seventy dollars between the lot of you? Two hours. Longer, if nobody else comes in and asks to go upstairs."

"You'll give us a warning if somebody does that?" Sarah asked softly.

"You bet, Sweetie." Hamp looked at Natalie and warned, "Not too much noise, Sindy."

"Me? Too much noise?" Taking Sarah's hand, she began to climb the steps leading up to the second floor, calling back, "Let's move."

"Have fun, Girlfriend." Hamp made a sweeping gesture with his hands. "You, too, Gentlemen."

"T'anks." Carson shoved lightly on Daniel's back and urged, "C'mon. T'aint polite ta keep da lady waitin'."

Daniel went forward then balked at putting his foot on the lowest step. He stared down at it as if it were covered with asps. He raised his head and looked at his wife, who was standing with Natalie near the top of the stairs.

Behind him, Daniel heard Carson saying to Hamp, "Mus' be shy, yeah." Then to Daniel, "*Mais*, it's jus' like ridin' a bike. You be fine."

"I never learned to ride a bike," Daniel said flatly.

"You – you can go, if you don't want to," Sarah offered. "I'm sure they won't mind if I stay."

Hamp, who had been distracted by a paying customer, pretended to be absorbed in a stack of magazines he was removing from a box behind the counter, but it was evident that he was listening intently to every word. Cocking his head, he slowly reached for the scissors and snipped the plastic binding that held the stack together. He then proceeded to count the magazines four times.

Daniel finally uttered a hoarse "no" and began to climb. As he reached the step below his wife, she tried to take his hand. Wordlessly, he shook his head and urged her to continue up.

Natalie closed the door and locked it. Checking her watch, she said, "Okay. Two hours. That'd be 11:37."

Carson glanced at his own watch, as if for confirmation. He looked over at Daniel, who had one hand braced against the doorframe. The younger man's eyes were shut; his head was down; and his breathing seemed slightly labored. Carson rested his hand on Daniel's back in what he hoped was a reassuring gesture.

"You okay, Partner?"

Nodding rapidly, Daniel straightened and opened his eyes. Turning his head to the left, he said as steadily as he could manage, "There's a kitchen that way. The bedrooms are down the hall in the other direction."

"You're in charge of this part of the show," Natalie declared. "Where do you want to go first?"

Glancing from one end of the hall to the other, Daniel licked his dry lips and said, "The kitchen."

"All right. Natalie and I will start in on the bedrooms." Carson turned towards Sarah and reminded her, "If you move anything major, don't forget to put it back."

Sarah watched the two private investigators disappear through an open doorway. When she turned back around, Daniel was gone.

For a moment, her heart flip-flopped in panic. Then, she forced herself to relax. He hadn't gone past her or downstairs. The only other way he could have walked was towards the kitchen.

Outdated and dark, the area was nonetheless orderly and clean. Daniel stood across the room near a tiny window. Although faded curtains still hung there, the window had been sealed with some plywood and nails.

"Was it always like that?" Sarah asked.

"Sealed up? Yeah, but it used to be closed with aluminum foil, not plywood." He glanced around the room and said, "It's so much bigger than I remember. Except for a couple of the appliances, it still looks the same. Still just as neat, too. He was a neat freak. Everything had to be in its place."

"Including you and your mother."

"Exactly."

Daniel opened and closed cabinet doors, inspecting plates and glasses without removing them from their resting places. He took

Sarah's hand as he passed by and led her down the hallway. Pausing at the bathroom on the right, he flicked the switch and peered in. He walked a few more yards down the hall and then rapped on the door of what had once been his bedroom.

"We're not finished, but you're welcome to come in," came Natalie's voice through the wood of the door. "Or, if you'd rather wait until we've cleared out, that's fine, too."

Daniel turned the knob and went in with Sarah close behind. He stood stiffly in the center of the room and looked around. Carson, who was examining the contents of a drawer in the bedside table, paused to watch Daniel for a moment then went back to work. Natalie, who was investigating the closet, emerged rumpled and empty-handed.

"Anything out of place?" she asked, her eyes fixed on Daniel.

"The furniture's in the same position it was in twenty-five years ago. It's the same furniture and same old blinds. It's only my stuff that's gone."

He strode over to the closet. Then, he walked around the bed until he was near the windows.

"No aluminum foil or wood in this one?" Sarah asked.

"The building next door had a window on the second floor that was pretty close to the kitchen. This bedroom has a window that looks out on a brick wall. There's no need to hide anything from a brick wall."

He knelt and touched the wall under the windowsill. The others tentatively moved towards him and squinted at the faded wallpaper.

"You found something?" Carson asked hopefully.

"What? Oh. No. I was only remembering. I – He used to make me kneel on rice here. I had to hold my arms outstretched until I was no longer punished. I used to rest my fingertips against the wall when he was out of the room because my arms felt so heavy. That made it better when I had to pick up all the kernels of rice."

"Kneel on rice?" Natalie echoed. She had obviously never heard of such a punishment and exclaimed, "How sadistic!"

"I've heard of it before," Carson admitted. "They used to do it at my elementary school with the kids who were deemed incorrigible."

"Those were the days," Natalie grunted.

Sarah squatted on the floor and put her arms around her husband's waist. He seemed unaware of her touch but moments later said, "There's nothing else in this room. What time is it?"

Brushing his fingertips along his partner's elbow, Zerangue inclined his head towards the doorway and said, "It's 10:22. We're moving to the master bedroom."

"Sarah and I'll be there in a minute."

Daniel stood. Much to Sarah's dismay, he flopped back on the bed. With all of the will she possessed, Sarah didn't comment on the bedspread. Although it appeared clean, who knew what was on it? Not only had people been using it for sexual encounters, but what if they had lice or worse?

"He'll wash it every morning if there have been people up here at night," Daniel said, as if reading her thoughts. "Like I told you before, he's a neat freak. He doesn't like germs. Why he lets people come up here like this is beyond me. Either he's really broke or it's simple greed."

"Or perversion."

"A definite possibility." He motioned for her to join him and suggested, "Come see."

Reluctantly, she climbed onto the bed and laid her head against his chest. Despite his outwardly calm appearance, her husband's heart rate was rapid although steady.

"Look." He pointed at the sliver of sky that was visible over the rooftop on the other side of the alley and asked, "You see the sky up there? I used to lie here every night and watch the stars shining and winking in and out. My mother used to say that the stars had lasted for millions and millions of years. I figured if they could last that long, then I should be able to last in this place for eighteen years. Of course, that was before she died."

"You never told me that."

"I didn't remember it until tonight," he admitted. "I wonder how Carson and Natalie are doing in the master bedroom?"

"Why don't we go see?"

They found the two detectives on their hands and knees peering under the bed.

"Well?"

“Trashy magazines and a box of receipts,” grumbled Carson. “Nothing in the bureau or nightstand, either. Well, nothing you’d want to see.”

“Nothing that appears to tie in to this case,” Natalie mumbled. “Maybe in this closet. Any suggestions, Dan?”

He was staring at the bed with such a sad expression that Natalie almost put down the book in her hand and went over to him. A small shake of the head from Sarah stopped her, and she forced herself to turn back around and rifle through some papers in a box on the floor.

Sarah hovered near Daniel. She knew more about the things that had taken place in this room than anyone else in the world save for Daniel and his stepfather. She hadn’t been present during those terrible years, but the images Daniel had brought to life for her were present as she walked through the rooms.

“Bingo!”

Startled, Sarah, Daniel, and Natalie turned to stare at Carson. He’d removed an old, brown leather suitcase from the top of the closet. He stepped back so that the others could see what he’d seen upon opening it.

Daniel rushed forward and lifted the piece of paper on the top of the pile, as Natalie whipped out a notebook from the huge purse that she’d deposited on the floor near the doorway. She handed it to Carson, who clicked his pen into readiness and knelt beside his client.

“Your birth certificate?”

Daniel nodded.

“Which hospital issued it? I’ll be damned if I can find a record of it.”

“It doesn’t look official. It says it was a home birth. The doctor who signed the form is one Anthony Laucke.”

“Next.”

Carefully laying the paper on the ground, Daniel lifted a stack of letters that had been bound with string.

“These are from my mother’s father. His name is on the return address. What in the hell do we do about them? If we cut the string, Samuels will know that someone’s been in his things.”

"His loss. If he's stupid enough to rent out these rooms, then he must know that people will go through his belongings. He just doesn't expect them to care about this kind of stuff."

"Yeah, I guess," Daniel said. "I'll deal with it in a minute."

Placing the envelopes on top of the birth certificate, he reached in and withdrew a blue nightgown that had seen better days. The lace edging had yellowed, and the straps had obviously been torn and re-stitched several times. As if the satin of the fabric had scalded him, Daniel flung the nightgown into a corner, jumped to his feet, and stumbled back into the hallway.

A sudden *bang* made the others rush out after him. To Sarah's relief, the sound had resulted from the slamming of the closet door handle against the wall in the narrow hall.

Daniel stood in front of the darkened opening. Reaching forward, he moved a broom, a mop, a bucket, and a dustpan out of his way and walked into the closet. He scanned the walls, floor, and ceiling.

"This is the only place that seems to be *smaller* than I remember. I guess your imagination tends to distort things when you're alone in the dark."

"He used to lock you in the closet?" Carson asked hesitantly.

"No. I used to try and hide here every once in a while. Dumb, I know, but it bought me a couple of extra minutes now and again."

"You couldn't lock yourself in?" asked Natalie.

"There aren't any locks on any of these doors. I take it you never worked child protection," Daniel said blithely. "Even if there had been a lock, I wouldn't have dreamed of using it."

"Why not?"

"Say I had a lock, and I used it. You think I could stay in there forever? What do you think he would have done to me when I came out after disobeying him by not letting him beat me in the first place?"

The volume of his voice was rising with each sentence. Sarah approached him and wrapped her fingers lightly around his wrist.

"Daniel," she said softly. "Natalie didn't mean anything by it."

"Maybe that's what happened that morning he almost killed me," Daniel continued. "Maybe I tried to run, really run. I never have remembered."

"I only meant –" Natalie began.

Daniel drew in a great, gasping breath. Whirling around, he tore away from his wife and flung himself onto his hands and knees. Scrabbling around on the floorboards, he turned inside the closet.

"What is it?" Carson asked urgently. "You found something?"

"Playing a hunch," muttered Daniel. "I hope my hunch is wrong."

The foursome jumped involuntarily as three thumps emanated from the floor below the smaller bedroom. Carson checked his watch and swore, "Damn! 11:47."

"Someone's headed up," Natalie said in hushed tones. "We've got to get out of here."

"No!" Daniel protested. "Not yet! Just another minute!"

"We've got to get the hell out of here now," Zerangue insisted.

"Here!" Daniel cried, as he pulled up a loose board at the back of the closet.

Heavy footsteps could be heard coming up the stairs.

"Dan, we've got to go," Carson urged, grabbing him by the collar. "Now!"

"No!" He looked pleadingly up at the detective and said, "Two more minutes. Please!"

Everyone stared at the private investigator as he quickly debated the pros and cons of two more minutes. A large fist pounded on the door at the top of the stairs.

"You and Sarah stay in the closet," Carson ordered. "Natalie and I'll stall the next couple for as long as we can."

Daniel focused all of his attention on the space under the floorboard. He and his wife were crammed into the little closet, and the door was shut. His eyes strained to adjust to the darkness. He knew that Sarah would be virtually blind without good lighting. He also knew that if he didn't keep his mind on what he was doing he was going to lose it emotionally.

"All right! All right!" he heard Natalie say, just as his fingers closed on something made of paper. Whatever it was, it had been taped to the bottom of the loose floorboard. An envelope, he decided. Carefully peeling it away from the wood, Daniel slipped it through the front of his shirt, then tucked it into the waistband of his underwear. He'd replaced the floorboard and risen to his feet when he heard the all-too-familiar voice.

Chapter Nineteen: Blood on His Hands

"What the fuck took so long?"

Natalie cleared her throat and said hotly, "Sorry, Sammy. I guess I was enjoying myself a little too much, you know?"

"Yah," agreed Carson. "Good piece of ass here."

"Yeah, well, your time's up, according to Hamp. He might be soft enough to let you stay up here as long as you want, but I'm not."

"Whatcha doing home?" asked Natalie. "I thought you loved to stay out all night on Fridays."

"That's why you brought your John here? Don't make it a habit, Sindy."

"Was my idear," Carson said. "More fun in a store like dis den at my cousin's place."

Samuels paused, finally saying, "You're a man after my own heart."

In the blackness of the closet, Daniel's breath was coming in short, rasping inhalations. A long-suppressed, remembered feeling of terror and the threat of impending pain was extending its tendrils throughout his body. The sensation of being trapped with nowhere to run was bringing on an overwhelming sense of claustrophobia.

Sarah groped for her husband's face. His skin felt clammy. He was shaking.

"Shhh," she whispered in a voice so quiet that it was almost lost in the low noises of Daniel's struggle to breathe normally. "We'll be outside soon. Don't think about it. Kiss me."

"W-what?"

"Kiss me."

She slid one hand behind his neck and urged his head down towards her face. With her other hand, Sarah guided Daniel's right palm to her back. Automatically, he pulled her closer as they kissed. He pressed hard against her, trying with every ounce of strength he possessed not to black out.

Suddenly, the door was flung open, and light from the exposed bulb in the hallway shone in on them. Sarah blinked at the black spots that flickered across her field of vision. Daniel loosened his hold on his wife but didn't release her completely.

"Put the broom and the rest back in the closet before you leave," Zachary Samuels ordered. "Or use them to clean up after yourselves, if necessary. I don't tolerate a mess."

His jaw set, Daniel shielded Sarah from the man as they went past him. Grabbing the cleaning implements, he tossed them into the closet and slammed the door.

"Hey! I said I didn't tolerate a mess. Pick it up."

Daniel felt the eyes of the others upon him. In the part of his brain that dealt with irrational emotion, a voice was telling him to beat Samuels until he was near death, throw him into the closet, and keep him therefore a long, long time. The voice of logic was pressuring him to do what Samuels had said and spare himself, his wife, and the others from a situation that could be potentially dangerous.

"I said to pick it up!" growled Samuels. "You deaf or something?"

"Fuck you," Daniel said coldly. "Go back to Hell where you belong."

Samuels looked shocked, then pleased.

"Well, I'll be damned. It's Danny Boy, is it? I'm surprised you've got the balls to come back here. Still like to hide in the closet, I see."

Daniel pulled back his fist and punched Samuels hard in the face. Completely unprepared for the assault, the man tripped over his own feet and crashed to the ground.

Nobody moved. Then, Daniel turned towards his wife and motioned for her to walk around him.

Carson saw the attack coming but was unable to push Daniel out of the way in time. He yelled at the man to look out as Samuels came up surprisingly fast from the floor and punched his stepson full force in the abdomen. Sarah cried out her husband's name as he toppled over.

Natalie was on top of Samuels before Daniel hit the ground. Carson pulled his client to his feet and shoved him towards the stairs.

"Move! We'll be right behind you!"

Sarah and Daniel dashed down the hall, down the steps, past a confused Hamp, and out of the store. Carson and Natalie were only steps behind. It was sleeting outside, and they ran, slipping and sliding occasionally until Daniel suddenly veered off the main street between two deserted office buildings. Lurching to one side, he put a hand out to steady himself and vomited.

When there was nothing left in his stomach, Daniel stood, the weakened muscles of his legs threatening to give way. Sarah, who had been rubbing his back, edged closer in an attempt to support him. She was too petite to have truly carried him, but her small body did give him the anchor that he needed to stay upright.

"Can you make it to Natalie's van?" Carson asked skeptically.

"We're pretty close, aren't we?"

"It's over there," Natalie said, pointing to the tan minivan not far down the street.

Daniel nodded and tried to ignore the sweet and sour taste in his mouth. His throat burned, and his knees wobbled. Twenty feet from the van, he felt the uncontrollable urge to vomit again.

"I'll take a fever over dry heaves any day," he groaned. "Jesus H. Christ, now I'm dizzy."

"Delayed shock," Carson remarked. "We need to get in the van and get out of here in case anyone comes after us."

Natalie rolled her eyes at Carson and said, "Get real. Nobody's going to come after us, and Sammy won't call the police." She looked at Daniel and added, "But you're right about the shock. It's only going to get worse before it gets better."

The shaking began as they approached the van. Daniel's knees buckled, and he found himself kneeling on the cold, wet ground. He vomited again.

"I thought you didn't have anything left to throw up," Sarah said worriedly, as he sat back on his heels and wiped his mouth on his sleeve.

When Daniel remained silent and immobile, Sarah squatted beside him and tried unsuccessfully to make out what he was looking at in the dim light.

Carson trotted back to where they were and said, "Lemme have a look-see."

Daniel held out his arm so that the private investigator could see the shirt cuff more clearly. It was smeared with blood.

"Damn it!" Crouching next to Daniel he called out, "Natalie! Start the van! I think he's got some internal bleeding!"

Sarah's eyes widened, but she showed no sign of full-blown panic.

"I want to go to the Lake," Daniel said, as Carson and Sarah lifted him and hustled him to the van.

"The General's closer," volunteered Carson.

"No. The Lake."

Carson looked inquiringly at Sarah, who shrugged and nodded her agreement.

"Fine. Natalie, we're heading for Our Lady of the Lake Hospital. Hurry."

"I'm cold," Daniel said, and then all he saw was darkness.

Chapter Twenty: Dead Again

Someone was repeating Daniel's name over and over. He fought to open his eyes, but the lids felt weighted down. He needed to take a deep breath, but his lungs proved uncooperative. As he tumbled back into unconsciousness, Daniel wondered idly who had stuffed his nostrils with cotton balls and what exactly was stuck in his throat.

Time passed, and time stood still.

Someone laid a damp cloth across his neck and wiped his face with a wet rag.

"Don't cry," Tristan said gently. "You're safe now."

Don't cry? Am I crying?

He could hear the beeping of machines. One of them was making a sickening *click-hiss, click-hiss* sound. He could feel wires attached to his chest and tubes inserted into him in various locations all over his body.

Panicked, Daniel's eyes snapped open. Bags of fluid were suspended on poles beside his bed. Tristan's fuzzy image teased at the edges of his peripheral vision. His father-in-law bent low, reaching out to lightly lay a hand on the top of Daniel's head.

"I'm here. Sarah's down the hall talking with the doctors. She'll be back any minute."

Why can't I move? Daniel screamed silently.

"Try to get some sleep," Tristan suggested.

Sleep? How on earth can I sleep? Daniel wondered, even as the blackness overtook him and his eyelids gave way once again.

The next time he opened his eyes, the wires and tubes were still there, but the *click-hiss* sound and the hardness in his throat were mercifully gone. His vision remained less than perfect, and he continued to be unable to move easily.

Daniel turned his head stiffly to one side and encountered a pale wall. He slowly forced his head the other way until he found what he was looking for – his wife.

She was sitting in a preposterously uncomfortable position in a preposterously uncomfortable-looking chair. No, she wasn't just sitting. She was sleeping. Her right knee had been brought up, and her shoulders were hunched around folded arms. Her left leg remained rooted to the floor. Her hair was unkempt, and her face was as white as snow. Ludicrously dark circles outlined her eyes. There was something not right about the white shirt she was wearing.

Suddenly, he realized what it was. The shirt was enormous. She'd rolled up the sleeves to avoid having them cover her hands. The hem of the shirt hung so low over her jeans that it came down to her knees. It was one of Tristan's shirts.

Fear began to infiltrate Daniel's muddled brain. Although her sleeping habits had changed recently, Sarah had never, ever been able to sleep in an upright position for as long as he'd known her. That, combined with her appearance and attire, alarmed him more than the tubes and the wires.

The heart rate on the monitor picked up speed, but Sarah didn't wake. A red-haired nurse hurried into the room and came over to the bed.

"Hey! Hey! Relax," she said soothingly, as she glanced at the monitors. "It's all right, Dan. We need to slow your breathing and heart rate down a little. That's it. Don't fight it. Just relax."

"My…wife."

His voice was unrecognizable. The pain in his throat was sharp and far-reaching.

"I know it hurts," she said. "Let me get you some ice chips. Try not to talk as much as possible. Your wife is fine. Your father-in-law finally insisted that she either take a sedative and get some rest or go home. We don't normally allow people to stay in the first place, but she was very persuasive."

"What…day?"

"What day is it? It's Monday." She touched him on the shoulder and offered him several small ice chips from a spoon. "I'll page your doctor. Then, if you promise to lie still and wait, I'll go get someone who can explain everything to you. How's that?"

He nodded weakly.

"Hair…like…my…mother's. Beautiful."

"Thanks. You can take the Irish out of the bog, but you can't take the bog out of the Irish. That's what my great-grandmother used to tell me."

"My mother…was...half-Italian. Still had red hair."

She smiled and offered him the spoon a second time. He tried to refuse, but she persisted.

"No, a little more. Good. Now, the buzzer's right here in case you need anything."

Despite the brevity of their conversation, Daniel felt drained. He focused on his wife's sleeping form and watched the miniscule rise and fall of her shoulders. Within seconds, the rhythm had put him to sleep.

"Hello. Hello there. Dan, it's Dr. Beibee. Do you remember me?"

It seemed to Daniel that he hadn't moved or spoken at all, yet obviously he had, for Dr. Beibee said, "No, I didn't expect that you would. I was called in to do your surgery. Did you know that you had surgery? Dan? No? Do you remember being injured? You do. Is that the last thing you remember? No?"

"I…was…cold. Your…voice. You…talked to…me. Made me…feel better."

The surgeon smiled warmly at him and said, "I'm glad it did. I'm a firm believer in encouraging patients, even when they're under anesthesia or heavily medicated as you are now."

Removing a penlight from his white coat, Beibee leaned forward and shined the light first in Daniel's left eye, then his right. Nodding to himself, he replaced the light in his pocket as a nurse folded down the sheet.

"I'm going to check on your injured area. I apologize if my fingers are cold."

"Why…the tube? Why –"

He broke off, groaning as Beibee probed somewhere in his abdomen and a familiar pain came back to him.

"Sorry about that. The medication dulls the pain in general, but I know that had to hurt. You're healing well, but I want you to be extremely careful with this. It needs to mend correctly or it could lead to a host of other complications." He continued his inspection of Daniel's torso and answered his question by saying,

"As for the tube, we had to keep you intubated for a while because you were having some trouble breathing on your own."

"Don't…understand. I thought…my stomach…not my lungs."

The doctor pulled up the sheet. Bracing both hands against the rail of the bed, he looked down at Daniel and said, "I need to ask you some questions. I'll fill you in on what happened, but you have to agree to stay with me and tell me what I need to know."

"No…choice."

"In the last year, have you had any health problems that you haven't informed your doctor of?"

"No."

"How about before that?"

"No."

"Can you tell me your wife's full name?"

"Sarah…Elisabeth…Anne…Maes…Nash."

"Can you tell me who is the current President of the United States?"

"Bill…Clinton."

"Your favorite football team?"

"Packers."

"Good choice. Mine, too."

"What…happened?"

"Your wife and your friends brought you in to the Emergency Room a half hour after midnight on Saturday morning. Your wife informed the attending physician that you suffered a blow to the stomach and that you'd been vomiting blood. You'd been in and out of consciousness during the ten-minute ride to the hospital. She also told him that you'd been seriously injured in that same area as a child. It was determined that you were bleeding internally, and I was summoned to the ER. Your father-in-law arrived and gave us a more complete medical account of your previous hospitalization. We obtained your records from your internist. Your injury was, indeed, to the same area as before."

"He always…liked…to hit…there. Almost killed…me that…way. My mother…per – per –" Through the haze of morphine, Daniel struggled to formulate the correct word. "Pain…in her…stomach. Brought…her knees…up."

"Peritonitis," Beibee said soberly.

"What about…the tube?"

"We're not quite sure what went wrong," the surgeon admitted and frowned. "You were on the table, and the surgery was progressing well. Your vital signs were stable. Then, you flat-lined. We gave you epinephrine and that successfully restarted your heart, but your vitals wouldn't stabilize. Your father-in-law said that the same thing happened when you were a child."

"It did? I…can't remember…right now. Will…I recover? My wife…my son…."

"You're going to have to follow my instructions without deviation if you want to avoid seeing me again in the operating room. We don't need to discuss that now, though. I believe you've had enough medical talk for one day."

The next time Daniel woke, Sarah was no longer in the chair. He groped for the button that would summon the nurse, but was unable to find it. Gritting his teeth, he gave a mental shout at his muscles to lift him slightly to the right.

"Whoa! Whoa! Whoa! What in the flaming hell do you think you're doing, Man?"

Daniel reached out and awkwardly plucked at the front of Jamie Nesser's shirt.

"Jamie, where…is she?"

"She's in the cafeteria. The only way we could think to get her to eat something decent was for Vaughn to bring Kris up to the hospital. Sarah's been living on chips, candy bars, and Cokes for the last few days."

"I saw…her once. She…looks…too pale."

"Well, duh. She was up for about seventy hours straight, and she's been worried out of her skull about you. Of course, she won't admit that she's about to fall flat on her nose. She's damned good to have around in a crisis. You know that. She puts herself on hold and does whatever it takes to get the job done. Not that it didn't catch up with her when all that shit happened to her at work and then with hurting her arm before Max died."

"The nurse...said that…Tris made her…take a sedative."

"At least it worked. She slept for fourteen hours. The nurses have been pretty cool. They kept an eye on her, too."

"Kris. How…what does he think?"

"He knows that you got hurt in the stomach. He hasn't asked how, so no one has told him. Sarah's worried that he's going to start associating ambulances and hospitals with death because of Max and Lillian. Some social worker here at the hospital is supposed to meet with her today," Jamie said, as he dragged the chair over near the head of the bed and sat. "Kris wants to see you, but kids aren't allowed in this area. It's probably better that way. If he saw you like this, he'd freak."

"How close did…I come?"

"Pretty damned close. The doctors are confused, same as when you were twelve. They're investigating whether your body is unable to process anesthesia properly or if it's something else. Their supposition is that the anesthesia is what triggered the heart failure and all the other crap."

"Carson and…Natalie…were with us."

"They've been in and out here at the hospital. Zerangue's really pushing some leads and trying to get you more answers. I think he blames himself for what happened."

"Not…his…fault."

"That's what we told him. You're no kid. You knew the risks. It was your decision." Jamie leaned closer to Daniel and said darkly, "And don't you ever fucking do anything like it again."

"But I –"

"Will you shut up for a minute? Let me be selfish. I've had some practice in that area. You can't even begin to know what I felt when Tris called and told me what had happened. I had this flashback of you, lying on the kitchen floor of Tris's house with your broken nose and the ungodly bruises, cuts, and scrapes and your bloody clothes. To this day, I can't fathom how you made it from downtown to Tris's in the shape you were in."

"Jamie?"

"Yeah?"

"Back then…what was Samuels…doing when they went…to arrest him?"

"I believe he was drinking a beer and watching TV. Apparently, he thought you were still in your room."

"Do the…police know…what happened last…week? Are they…did Samuels press…assault charge?"

"No one's told you then. Samuels is dead."

"Dead?"

"A piece of something dislodged in his brain."

"Because…I hit…him?"

Jamie shrugged.

"That guy who worked for him found him dead when he went to bring up the night's receipts. Are you sorry he's dead?"

"No."

"Me neither."

"I want to…talk about something…else like…the envelope I found in the closet. Did Sarah open…it?"

"She thought you might want to do that yourself. It's in the bag on the floor over there. You want it now?"

"Yes. No." Shaking his head slightly, he said resignedly, "I have no choice."

Chapter Twenty-one: Choices

Daniel tried to coordinate his brain with his fingers in order to open the envelope, but the medication and the lingering weakness conspired against him. He handed it back to Jamie, who ripped it open and tilted it over. Something smooth and hard fell into Daniel's palm.

It was a yellowing oval pin. A thumbprint dominated its center. Two wings, two antennae, and two tiny feet had been added with a felt tip marker in order to make the shape of a bee. Underneath, in uneven letters, was the name DANIEL.

"I made it for Mom…when school started…a couple of months before…she died. I was…so proud of it."

"So was she, by the looks of it."

Daniel stared at the pin in his hand. His eyes filled with tears, as he closed the fingers into a fist around the small bee.

"Why, Jamie? Why did she…do that?"

Jamie stood and wrapped his hand around Daniel's fist.

"It sounds like she knew she was going to die."

"And she hid it in…the closet."

"I know."

"Because she knew that…I would be hiding in there…after she was…gone."

"I know."

"She sacrificed me to…to…to protect Max and to obey Samuels." Daniel shut his eyes, and tears slid down his temples. "How could a…mother do that to…her child? How could *my* mother do that…to *me*? She knew what…he was like. Of course, she loved…Samuels, Goddamn him. He'd hurt her, and…she'd cry. Then, he'd make love to…her, and she'd respond with…such love in her eyes even when he'd force himself on her."

"You were in the room?" Jamie asked. It was impossible for him to disguise the disgust in his voice as he added, "For real?"

"Sometimes. He made me…sit in the corner…when they were arguing…or…or not. I've…never told anyone that…before. Don't tell…anyone. Don't."

"I won't," Jamie assured him. He unfurled Daniel's clenched fingers and took the pin from his hand then said, "She was sick, Dan. He must have warped her sense of self or something."

"Or something," Daniel muttered. "How the fuck…how could she?"

A nurse appeared and informed Jamie that he would have to leave for a while so that Daniel could calm down and rest. Jamie nodded and looked at his friend. Removing two tissues from the box on the table, he wiped away the tears on Daniel's face.

"Sarah should be back any time," Jamie told him. He put his lips close to Daniel's ear and said, "You'll make it through this. Don't you give up on things. It'll all fall into place."

Daniel stared at the ceiling for a long time after Jamie left. He realized that there was one less wire connected to his chest. A doctor was talking about subdural hematomas to someone at the desk. One of the nurses was trying to trace the relatives of a critical patient. And the machines beeped on….

"Daniel?"

He jerked involuntarily. He hadn't even known that Sarah had come into the room.

"It's good to see you awake," she said, softly stroking his hair. "I was wondering if you were trying to avoid me."

"Never." He took her wrist, brought her hand to his mouth, and kissed the palm. "I love you."

Her lips were almost painfully soft against his.

"Kris?"

"He wants us to come home."

"We missed Tanner's New…Year's Eve party."

"Yes, we did."

"I'm sorry."

"What are you sorry for? Because the man who almost killed you before almost killed you again? You think that's your fault?"

"No. No. I'm just sorry we…missed the party. It would have…been good to see them all."

"Just about all of our friends have come by the hospital. Everyone's thankful that you're alive."

"How long do…I have to stay…in here?"

"Well, you've been in the Critical Care Unit since Saturday. You know people talk about how hospitals want to push patients out as soon as they come in. You must be a special case because they don't seem to be in a rush with you. Dr. Beibee said he'll re-evaluate you tomorrow afternoon. If you're still improving, then you might be moved to a regular room this weekend."

"Good."

"Jamie told me about the pin."

"I'm…not ready, yet."

"Later, then." She brought a spoon filled with ice chips to his mouth and told him, "Frank Randall's been here as much as his schedule's permitted."

"When did you…call him?"

"Saturday."

"When Saturday?"

"Daniel, I don't remember."

Reaching up with his left hand, he drew the backs of his fingers along her jaw.

"Tris called him to…do the Last Rites?"

She bit her lip then took his hand and brought it down against her chest.

"Do you know how many people care about you?" she asked. "So many people love you."

There was movement in the doorway. A nurse Daniel didn't recognize stood just inside the room.

"The social worker's here to see you. He asked if you'd mind talking in the family conference room we have to the right."

"No, I don't mind." She turned back to her husband and began, "Kris –"

"I know. Go see what the guy…says."

The social worker had several suggestions for dealing with Kris's questions and concerns. He was discussing a children's book that dealt with death and healing when the screaming started.

Sarah had heard those screams before, and she knew what they meant. She was out of the conference room in an instant. Rushing back to her husband's room, she walked in on utter chaos. Daniel was thrashing violently in the bed. A male nurse and a female doctor Sarah had never encountered were attempting to restrain him. Monitors were flashing and beeping wildly.

"Daniel!" Sarah called loudly in the tone of voice that had always brought him around during his worst nightmares. Placing both hands on the sides of his face, she said firmly, "Daniel! Wake up!"

He opened his eyes wide and immediately stopped struggling.

"Tell them to page Beibee!" the doctor shouted to the social worker, who darted out of the room towards the nurses' station.

"Focus on me, Daniel," Sarah said in an attempt to calm him.

She was desperately trying to stay calm herself as she heard the doctor and nurse beside her reviewing her husband's condition.

"It's over, Daniel. I'm with you."

"No," he shuddered. "No. Not…I know. No."

And then Dr. Beibee was barking orders at the rest of the hospital staff at his disposal. He came over to the bed and deftly began to examine his patient.

"Hello, Dan. How're you doing? They tell me you're having a rough afternoon." His hands probed Daniel's abdomen as he said, "Maybe we'll have a better evening."

Daniel reared off the bed as Beibee's fingers pressed on one side of his incision. The surgeon grimaced and rattled off a list of what he wanted done in the next five minutes. Sarah continued to try to soothe her husband in the midst of the pandemonium.

"I'm going to have to go back in," the surgeon announced grimly.

"But you can't!" Sarah protested. "Look at what's happened the last two times he's had surgery!"

"That may not happen again. If it does, then at least we'll be better prepared for it."

"But –"

"I don't have a choice. I think he has a rupture."

"Do you have family in the waiting room?" asked the social worker.

"My brother's taking this shift."

"Why don't I walk with you?"

"Thank you, but no."

"We're taking him now," Beibee said gently. "Wait with your family. I'm going to take care of Dan. I promise."

The social worker accompanied her to the waiting room, where they waited with her brother for news of Daniel's condition. Tristan, Jamie and Isabelle soon joined them. After what seemed like an eternity, Sarah was summoned to a nearby conference room.

She paced from one side to the other as she waited for the doctor. There was a couch against one wall in the small room. A chair faced the couch. Sarah wondered how many people had been given life-altering news as they had sat on that couch or in that chair.

She went to the window and tried to distract herself by watching the movement of a tree illuminated by one of the outside lights.

"Mrs. Nash?"

Without turning around, she asked, "Is it bad?"

"Why don't we sit?" suggested Dr. Beibee.

"Is he dead?"

"No, he's not dead. Please. Sit, and we can talk."

She looked over her shoulder at Beibee and asked, "Why are you being so nice and taking time with us? Don't you know that doctors are supposed to be arrogant, unfeeling clinical types?"

He smiled and admitted, "We're all arrogant to a degree, although many doctors prefer the term 'confident.' 'Clinical' is not necessarily a negative thing. As for 'unfeeling,' some doctors have to divorce emotion from their work in order to perform at their optimal level."

"But not you?"

"In some cases, yes."

"But not in Daniel's case?"

The surgeon sat in the chair and confided, "My niece died as a result of domestic violence four years ago. No one had suspected a thing. It became a prominent issue for me."

"It's a terrible thing," Sarah said, as she came over to the couch.

"Yes, it is. Monstrous when a child is involved. My wife and I have become advocates for awareness in the community since it happened in our family. I'd like to think that perhaps that's why it happened, that maybe some good will come out of it."

"Perhaps it already has. Will you tell me about the operation?"

"I'm afraid that we're back to where we were after surgery Saturday morning."

"He had the same problems as before?"

"Yes, he did. His heart stopped, but we were able to resuscitate him more quickly this time. We did some testing on his heart to make sure it hasn't been damaged by our efforts and those of the doctors when he was younger. Everything looks good, but I want a cardiologist to evaluate him as often as necessary until we're one-hundred-percent certain."

"What…what do you recommend now?"

"The same as before. However, I don't want to run the risk of re-injury. As he stabilizes, we have two options. One is to use sedation to keep him immobile. The other is to taper off the meds as we did this time. If we do that, the only alternative I can see is the use of physical restraints."

"Will it harm him to keep him sedated like that?"

"Normally, we don't like to heavily medicate patients for extended periods. But in certain cases, it's deemed necessary. We'd monitor your husband very closely."

"No restraints."

He nodded and picked up the clipboard. As he made a note in the chart, he said, "Your father told me that Dan's a successful man. He said that he's a good father and husband, that he has his M.B.A. and a job he loves. He also told me that he's lost both his father and his stepmother recently and has been trying to resolve some very troubling issues regarding his past and his abuse. Has he been receiving psychiatric treatment?"

"He was seeing a psychiatrist, but I think now he's talking with a…a friend who's a priest. And he talks with another friend who had some experience with abuse as a child. Nothing like Daniel's, of course."

Beibee stood and slid his pen through the clamp at the top of the clipboard before saying, "It would be a good idea for him to continue his talks with the priest and his family and friends, but he needs a psychiatrist. I can recommend one if you'd like."

"Thank you. How long will he be in Critical Care this time? How long do you think he'll be in the hospital?"

"We'll have to take it day by day. Would you like to see him?"

Back in the Critical Care Unit, Sarah once again took up her post at Daniel's bedside. She stared vacantly in front of her and listened to the *click-hiss* of the ventilator.

"Sarah? May I?"

She rose stiffly as Isabelle came into the room.

"Stay where you are," Isabelle directed. "You are tired. I merely wanted to see how the two of you were doing."

"Well, he's oblivious because they've got him heavily sedated. I wish I were oblivious. I hate seeing him like this. He looks like those people on television who're permanently on life-support. Every time I look at that tube and the tape around his mouth, it makes me scared."

"You must keep in the forefront that it is only temporary. Will there be any special orders when he is allowed to wake?"

"What you'd imagine. A special diet for a while and restricted activities. He'll have to wear one of those Medic Alert bracelets because of the way he reacts to the anesthesia. That'll be a trial, getting him to wear that. The nurses say that they're not all those ugly gray ones anymore, but he'll hate it anyway. He doesn't like to wear any kind of jewelry, except his wedding ring. He'll balk at a bracelet, no matter how manly it looks." With a sigh, she added, "I'm babbling. I'm sorry."

"Do not be sorry. It is a valid concern. We shall have to work on that with him."

"He'll have to do it," Sarah said decisively. "I can't live through this again."

"I do not know if he can either."

Chapter Twenty-two: Clarity

I know.

Those two words flashed in Daniel's head like a blinking neon sign.

I know.

Daniel floated. The only thing keeping him grounded was the hardness in his throat.

I know.

Occasionally, he would be surprised to discover that his eyes were open and had in fact been open for some time. His view of the ceiling never changed, but his wife would often be within his field of vision. Sometimes, he saw nurses he recognized. The surgeon came in and out, as did Daniel's internist and other medical personnel. Frank Randall visited, as did Tristan, Vaughn, Isabelle, Will, Helen, Jim, Katie and Jamie.

I know.

Jamie. Daniel urgently wanted to talk with Jamie.

I know.

People touched him, and he felt it, yet did not feel it. People spoke to him, and his ears could hear, but did not hear.

I know.

Gradually, the fog in Daniel's mind started to dissipate. Unable to move or speak, he began to become aware once more. He felt his wife's lips on his forehead. He heard Frank say a prayer. He smelled the antiseptic scent of the soap that the nurses used to clean his skin. He tensed at the prick of a hypodermic needle.

I know.

Daniel was twelve years old that miserably hot summer. That morning, he'd been charged with emptying the garbage that collected at the back door of the bar. On his third trip to the dumpster, he'd seen the dog.

A medium-sized mixed breed, the mutt had obviously come to the alley to look for a cool place to lie down. Its mouth stayed half-open, the tongue dripping with saliva as it panted. Daniel wondered when it had last found water since no rain had fallen in days.

Returning inside, he searched in the cabinets until he found a large plastic bowl. Placing some ice in the bowl, he filled it with water and carried it back outside. The mutt wagged his tail and danced around in anticipation of a drink.

Daniel lowered the bowl onto the ground and knelt to watch with pleasure as the dog lapped greedily. When the water was almost gone, the stray stopped and gratefully wagged his tail at Daniel. The boy ran his hand over the animal's back, thinking how nice it would be to have a pet of his own.

"I could call you George," he murmured, as the dog nuzzled against his leg. "And I would love you and hug you and –"

Suddenly, the dog skittered away, barking furiously. Daniel spun around and saw his father drawing back his foot in an attempt to kick at the animal.

Daniel called out for the mutt to run, and it didn't hesitate to obey. The dog scampered down the alley and out of sight.

Rough fingers slid in-between his neck and his collar, and Daniel was abruptly lifted to his feet. Without a word, Samuels dragged him into the bar and towards the stairs. As his father marched upwards, Daniel struggled to regain his feet, but Samuels wouldn't give him the chance.

When they reached the second floor, Samuels pulled him past the bathroom and the master bedroom. He slammed open the door to his son's room and pushed him against the wall.

"You want to waste time with a Goddamned stray? You were given a job to do! I won't tolerate your messing around when you're supposed to be doing your fucking chores! I won't stand for it, Danny!" He lowered his voice and said in a menacing tone, "Now, if you ask real nice, then maybe I'll forget about this, and we can both get back to work. Just say it."

Daniel considered his options. If he capitulated, then he might get off with a cuff on the head. If he refused, he knew that he was in for much worse.

"Fuck you," he said evenly. "Go back to Hell where you belong."

Samuels drew him away from the wall. For a moment, Daniel thought that he might be let go. Instead, his father adjusted his grip on the front of his son's shirt and slammed him back. Daniel saw stars.

Samuels was unrelenting in his attack. Daniel felt every punch to his already bruised torso. He heard the crack of his nose as his father landed a particularly forceful blow. His whole body sagged forward against Samuels's restraining hand, and the man released him, letting the boy slide down the wall.

The blood from Daniel's nose coated his left cheek as he sank to the floor. He swallowed hard in an effort not to moan. He was determined not to give his father the satisfaction of hearing him moan.

"You fucking think about this, Danny. Next time you want to disobey me, you think about the fucking consequences."

The toe of Samuels's boot sank into the flesh underneath the boy's ribs. Then, the man was gone.

Daniel lay curled in a ball, listening as his father went down the stairs and out through the back door. Then, all was quiet.

"Couldn't kick the dog, so you had to kick me," Daniel laughed weakly, as he pushed up on his hands and knees and inched his way towards the closet.

I can't call the police, he thought. *Dad'll come back and tell them it was a prank call. I've gotta get to Tristan's. Tristan will help me.*

He used an old t-shirt to wipe at the blood; then he methodically stripped off the clothes he was wearing. He reasoned that he had to change, or someone might see the blood on his shirt or his pants and bring him back home. He was cold anyway, despite the heat of the day. He chose a long-sleeved shirt, a pair of jeans, and a jacket with a zipper and a hood. Somehow, he managed to bend over to slip on his tennis shoes and tie the laces.

He half-walked, half-slid down the stairs. Knowing that his father would be returning via the back door, he zipped the jacket, pulled up the hood, and went out through the front.

Daniel knew Tristan's address as well as his own. He'd memorized it the month before when Tristan had offered him his house as a refuge in case of emergency. Well, this certainly was an emergency.

He knew where the street was, if not the actual house. He wasn't sure if he would be able to make the long walk. But if he couldn't, he'd die trying. He could no longer live in Sammy's Bar.

Daniel kept to the alleys and backyards as much as possible in an attempt to avoid detection. By the time he reached Cherokee Avenue, his legs were weak and his heart was racing. He wondered if his intestines were actually knotting up inside of him or if it was simply his imagination. The urge to vomit was impossible to suppress, and he bent over and threw up in the midst of some white azaleas. In an effort to catch his breath, he leaned against a tree and shut his eyes.

"Hey! You okay, Kid? You want a ride?"

A man on a Harley-Davidson motorcycle had pulled over near the curb. He looked Daniel up and down then frowned.

"I...I got into a fight," Daniel managed to offer. "I was trying to get home. You don't mind giving me a lift?"

"No, Man. Come here, and I'll help you to get on. You look like you're in pretty sad shape, Man. Who'd you have a fight with? Muhammad Ali?"

Within three minutes, they were parked across the street from Tristan's house. The man helped Daniel off the bike and offered to accompany him to the door. Daniel declined the offer, thanked the biker, and watched him ride away.

His shirt felt sticky underneath the jacket, but he wasn't sure if it was sticky with blood, sweat, or both. Weaving slightly, Daniel crossed the street and headed for the backyard so that he could knock at the back door and not draw any unwanted attention from passersby. He was almost to the gate when he noticed that his nose had started to bleed again.

When he reached the gate, he leaned against it for support. It swung open and he caught a glimpse of Sarah kneeling underneath a tree digging in the dirt with a small trowel. She saw him then and screamed. Tristan came running towards her, perhaps concerned that something had bitten her. Then, he saw Daniel.

He dashed forward and extended his arms as Daniel collapsed.

Safe, Daniel thought, as he listened to Tristan call out Jamie's name. *I'm safe.*

The air seemed to vibrate around him when Tristan lifted him from the ground. Daniel discovered that not only was he unable to open his eyes, but he also had no control over his limbs. His head fell back as they entered the house, and he began to choke on the blood from his nose.

He was quickly laid on his side in the kitchen. The tile under his cheek was smooth and cool. Sarah's tennis shoes squeaked on the floor as she ran to call for help. Jamie and Tristan were trying to remove Daniel's jacket and shirt. They succeeded in freeing one arm, thereby baring his chest. Then there was silence in the kitchen.

Jamie's fingers brushed lightly over the swollen purple area under his ribcage. Daniel stiffened and cried out.

"It's okay…it'll be all right…help is on the way." These were some of the things Jamie and Tristan said to him as they waited for the ambulance. They held his hand and touched him where there were no bruises or cuts. They watched him sink deeper and deeper into himself.

Then Tristan was gone, intercepting his daughter before she could come into the kitchen and see the battered, broken child on the floor. Jamie never left his side. The paramedics rushed in and hastily prepared Daniel for transport to the hospital. He heard himself scream; then he heard Sarah crying in another room. And then all was quiet.

I...know.

Someone was exploring his stomach with warm hands. Daniel reached down and felt for the fingers.

"Glad to see you with us again." Halting the examination, Dr. Beibee moved over so that Daniel could see him clearly and ordered, "Blink twice if you can understand me. Good. I was just examining your abdomen. Your body is knitting itself back together very neatly. We've been lowering the doses of morphine by degrees in order to give you time to heal. You still need to take it easy, but you should be out of the woods now.

"Listen, I want to take you off the ventilator. Here's what I'd like you to do. As I withdraw the breathing tube, I want you to blow out as hard and long as you can. Ready?"

Sarah took Daniel's hand. He hadn't realized she'd been in the room and squeezed it appreciatively. Within seconds, the tube had been pulled from his throat, leaving him coughing spasmodically.

"I want you to rest your vocal cords as much as possible," the surgeon told him. "Give them time to heal, too."

He nodded then looked at his wife.

"Love…you."

"I love you, too."

"Can't…sell…the house…on Highland, yet."

"Don't worry about that now."

"Jamie."

"He had to leave town this morning on business. He's been putting it off so that he could be here. We can call him if you want."

"It…can…wait."

Chapter Twenty-three: The Capacity to Forgive

For several days, Daniel did little more than sleep. Yet, now it wasn't a drug-induced sleep, and he woke each time feeling slightly stronger. Eventually, he was moved from the Critical Care Unit to a regular room where Kris was finally able to visit his father.

Daniel was released from the hospital the following week. As Sarah helped him dress for the ride home, she asked, "Which house do you want to go to – our place, the Highland house, or Daddy's?"

"Our house. I want to be home with you, our son, and our dog."

"Don't forget the fish."

"Is Tris coming to drive us?"

"No. He had a meeting that he couldn't miss."

"So, who –?"

They heard the brief rap of knuckles on the door before Jamie breezed into the room and said apologetically, "Sorry I couldn't get over here sooner. You almost ready to break out?"

"More than ready. I'm glad you're here. I've been wanting to talk to you."

"So I heard. Once I knew that you were going to pull through, I had to head out for that job in New Mexico. It was a short but productive consulting trip. A biochemist's work is never done."

"S'okay. I had enough visitors once I was released from Critical Care. With all the family, friends, and co-workers, I wasn't lacking for company."

"Yeah, a lot of them came to the waiting room while you were still in CCU. You know your boss, Hunter, seems like a really decent guy. And that girl, Penny, thinks that you're the best boss in the history of the world."

"Sarah said CoCo and Jean-Paul brought lemonade and sandwiches every day at the beginning."

"The lemonade was the best," Jamie admitted. "Those sandwiches left something to be desired. But when you're that hungry, who cares? It was nice of them. Has CoCo been by your room here?"

"No, but she's called at breakfast, lunch, and dinner every day. She says she just wants to make sure that I'm eating so I can get well."

Sarah pecked Jamie on the cheek as she walked towards the door.

"Hey, Princess, where you headed?"

"The nurses' station. I wanted to thank them for everything. I'll have to bake them something very special and bring it back later. Of course, I'll do the same for the CCU nurses. See you in a minute."

Once she'd gone, Jamie asked, "You need help with something?"

"My shoes. I can't bend for a while. You mind?"

As he knelt on the floor and fought to untie a knot in the laces of a tennis shoe, Jamie asked, "So, you ready for the recliner?"

"Some people might enjoy sitting there all day, watching QVC, but I'm not really looking forward to it. I'll be napping three-quarters of the time. Sarah'll bring me liquids and soft food. What's the fun of being at home all day with your wife if you're not allowed to fool around?"

"Whine, whine, whine."

"Jamie, Sarah will be gone for a while."

"I know. We can either watch the collectible doll show and the Craftsman tool hour, or we can talk. I don't know about you, but it's not a difficult choice for me."

"Me neither."

"So, what's up?"

"I remembered about that morning when I was twelve. I know what happened to me."

"Are you sure it wasn't a dream? You were on a bucket load of sedatives."

"It wasn't some hallucination. It was a memory."

"And you want to tell me about it."

"Yeah, I do."

Jamie listened patiently as the story was told. He asked no questions and volunteered no comments. Once Daniel had finished, he said, "You're glad you remembered."

"I don't know if I'd use the word *glad* to describe it. There's still so much of my childhood I don't remember and don't want to. However, it satisfies me that I've filled in some of the missing parts, but I keep replaying the scene in my head all the time."

"Did you tell anyone else?"

"Not yet. Frank Randall is supposed to come to dinner tomorrow night. I'm sure I'll talk with him about it. I'll be interested to see what he has to say about forgiveness when I'm done."

"And Sarah?"

Daniel shrugged, then grimaced at the resultant pain.

"I've upset her enough, lately."

"She knows something's wrong. She told me you've been…let's see…how did she put it?" Jamie hesitated then said, "She said you'd been 'distant' ever since you came to."

"She told you that?"

"Mm-hm. Has Zerangue gotten with you, yet?"

"He and Natalie went out of town to follow up on some leads. They're supposed to be back day after tomorrow. I'm too screwed up to care about that right now."

"A new shrink could help."

"I was thinking that Isabelle might take me on, even though she's retired."

"Good for you. God's brought you back not once, but three times. Don't waste the opportunity you've been given to live a happy, normal life. 'Live long and prosper' and all that."

"Modern medicine is what saved me, Jamie."

"Oh ye of little faith."

"If the shoe fits…."

"Yeah, well I got the damned knot out a while back, so let's see if this one does."

The following night Frank Randall did come to the Nash home for dinner.

"I haven't had homemade soup in way too long," he said with a contented sigh after the meal.

"It was a fantastic change from the gruel the doctors have been forcing me to eat," Daniel confided. "Not real solid, but much tastier than scrambled eggs."

"I liked the bread!" Kris declared.

"Well, I'm thrilled that everybody was satisfied," Sarah said, as she rose to clear the table. She kissed her husband as she went around his chair and took some dishes to the sink.

"Daddy, you promised that we could play Super Nintendo," Kris reminded his father. "Do you want to play, Father?"

"I'd love to, but I've no idea how to play Super Nintendo. What is the name of the game?"

"Megaman X."

"Sounds interesting. Perhaps I can watch and learn."

"Daddy and I usually play football or baseball, but he can't right now, so we play Nintendo or Go Fish or things like that."

"Thirty minutes, guys," Sarah warned. "Kris, you have to take your bath. We're running late, and tomorrow is a school day."

"But –"

"No buts. Hurry and show Father so that he can have a try."

Forty-five minutes and several games later, Sarah hustled Kris off to his bath, leaving the two men to continue their video battle. Randall conceded defeat a half hour after that, while Sarah was tucking Kris into bed.

"That was fun," Randall smiled. "I wish they'd had games like these when I was a boy."

"It is addictive," Daniel admitted. "We really have to make a concerted effort to limit Kris's Nintendo time. He'd play for days if we'd let him."

"I'd like to come back myself and give it another go." The priest laid his controller on the coffee table and asked, "How are you, Dan?"

"Glad to be alive."

"I understand that Zachary Samuels wasn't so fortunate."

"Nope. I guess there is some justice in the world. It is kind of ironic the way things happened. He beat my mother for years until he killed her. He beat me for years until he nearly killed me. Then, he hits me again, nearly kills me again. And I punch him once, and he dies. Maybe I should have punched him a long time ago."

"You don't mean that."

"Don't I? If anyone deserved to die, it was him. They said it was probably quick. He got off easy."

"Being bitter –"

"You think I'm bitter? You're damned right I'm bitter," Daniel said curtly. "Do you know what caused me to flip out enough to tear up all that nice work that Dr. Beibee had done? I remembered what Samuels did to me that day when I was twelve. Let me tell you about it…."

Sarah stood out of sight in the hallway and listened to the tale. As her husband finished his story, she heard him say, "You asked me before whether or not I could forgive my stepfather for what he did. I can safely say that the answer is 'no'. I can safely say it because he's dead, and I know that he can't hurt me or others anymore."

"What if you found out that Zachary Samuels had been similarly abused by his father, who had been abused by his father before him?"

"Samuels had a responsibility to stop the cycle just as I did," Daniel snapped.

"I'm merely pointing out that there's a story behind every evil deed in the world. I'm not suggesting that you wipe the slate clean and forget it ever took place. God's already judged your stepfather and your mother and your father and all of those who have passed on before you. He's examined their souls. Let Him handle things and release some of the burden from your own soul."

"Maybe that would work if I was certain that there even was a God to begin with."

"Let's say for the moment that there isn't. There is no God. Your mother, father, stepmother, and stepfather are gone, regardless. What purpose will continuing to be bitter serve?"

"No purpose whatsoever. That's just the way it is."

Randall sighed and smiled.

"You look tired. Sarah is exhausted. I do enjoy these debates of ours, but I think I should go. We can pick up where we left off soon. In the meantime, I brought a book I thought you might find interesting."

"C.S. Lewis?"

"Try it; you'll like it."

Sarah stirred in the hall and came into the living room in time to see the priest out. Once he'd departed, she began the routine she and Daniel normally performed together.

"It's 10:15," she said, as she let Ralph in and locked the back door. "It's way past your bedtime."

"Yeah, it is. I feel like such a rebel."

"I'll check the other doors and feed the fish. Go on and lie down. I'll be there in a minute."

Daniel waited for his wife to come to bed. The tasks she had to perform should have taken less than five minutes. When ten had passed, Daniel carefully got up and went to see what was taking her so long. He found her kneeling in front of the glowing fish tank in the kitchen.

"Sarah? Are you coming?"

"Why didn't you tell me?" she asked quietly.

Daniel placed his hand on the back of her head and said, "Because I knew you'd stew over it like I've been, and I wanted to spare you." Lifting his hand, he asked, "Are you sorry he's dead? Do you forgive him?"

"No and no. I don't really think Frank does either. I think he's attempting to get you to deal with it as best you can, and that's his approach."

"I won't even try to second-guess him. I'm too worn out from trying to second-guess everyone else. Whatever Frank's motives, I appreciate the effort. I enjoy our talks, too. I like being with him."

"I don't doubt it. He's so very much like Max."

Daniel blinked in surprise.

"He is, isn't he?"

Sarah rose, put the canister of fish food back on the counter, and asked, "How long are you going to go on with this quest to understand your parents?"

"You think I should abandon it?"

"That would be impossible, but I don't want it to consume you either."

"It won't consume me."

"It already has, not that I blame you."

"In the last two months –" Daniel began.

"We should never have gone back to the building," his wife interrupted.

"How can you say that?"

"How can I say it? As if simply being there wasn't emotionally draining enough, but going into that closet, seeing

Samuels, and finding the things we found…." She dropped her head and added, "Not to mention that I had to watch you being hurt and sick. Not being able to do anything about it was horrible."

"You don't think I haven't put myself in your place a hundred times over the last few weeks? It would have killed me to see you in the same situation, but I'm not sorry we went. The bastard's dead. That makes the whole nightmare worthwhile."

"I can't believe you!" Sarah cried, as she spun on her heels and headed for the back of the house. "You're so stubborn! I give up!"

"As if!" Daniel called after her, as he came slowly in her wake. "You'll be arguing with me about this same thing in an hour."

"I'll be asleep in an hour!"

By the time he got to the bathroom, she was pulling a long, cotton nightgown over her head. Her lower lip stuck out, and her cheeks were wet.

"Carson will be back soon," he said in a feeble attempt to stimulate conversation.

Sarah wiped at her eyes and nodded. She brushed her teeth then brushed out her hair. Not once did she look at Daniel or speak. When she came to bed, she turned her back to him and pulled the covers up around her chin.

The phone rang shortly before 8:00 the next morning. Daniel expectantly lifted the receiver, hoping that it would be Carson. Instead, it was his lawyer and friend, Elmo Palmentier.

"Hey, Dan. Look, about what happened…don't do that to me again. Handling the wills of both your parents is enough for the next sixty years or so. I don't want to have to be advising Sarah on your estate before then."

"A lawyer who doesn't want business?"

"I have plenty of business and the perfect number of friends. I don't need to be looking for any replacements in either department."

"If you're going to nag me like that, then I guess I'll have to oblige."

"Good. Now that we've settled that, I need to talk with you about something real important. I didn't figure you'd be up to coming into the office, so I was wondering if I could pass by on my way in to work."

"That'll be fine. Sarah's getting Kris on the bus as we speak. She'll be back any minute."

"I'll be there in fifteen."

"Liar," Daniel said to Elmo, as he walked in at 8:30.

"Sorry. The office called and –"

"Elmo, he's kidding" Sarah said. "You think we have anyplace else to go?"

"No, but I'm still sorry for being late."

"You lawyers are so anal-retentive," Daniel goaded.

"Unlike you investment types," Elmo retorted.

"Do you want some coffee?" Sarah asked the lawyer. "We also have tea."

"No. Thanks, though." Palmentier shifted uncomfortably in his seat and said, "I'd better get on with this and get to the office."

"That bad?" Daniel asked. "What's wrong? I don't think there's too much that could shock me anymore."

Chapter Twenty-four: Shock Value

"Zachary Samuels named you as the heir to his estate."

"Bully for him," Daniel said flatly, as Sarah sat in the nearest chair. "I don't fucking want it."

"His attorney is a man named Carmichael. He happens to work in our firm. Several of us were at lunch the other day, and Carmichael was griping about how a client of his named Samuels had died, and he was going to have to go through the motions of contacting the man's heir. I asked him for the name of the heir, and guess who it was?"

"He didn't have anyone else to leave it to, I guess. He must have made his will before I…before he…."

"You were listed by your adoptive name, Dan. Your current address was on file. According to Carmichael, Samuels provided it."

Daniel couldn't breathe for a few seconds. How many nights had he chided himself for being foolish about rechecking the locks on the windows in Kris's room? How many times had Kris played alone in the backyard? How many times had Sarah been at home by herself and left the door unlocked while she walked to the mailbox?

Thank God for Ralph, he thought.

"There's the merchandise from the store," Palmentier was saying. "The property alone is worth quite a bit now that the Downtown Redevelopment Plan is going great guns. There was some life insurance and a few investments. He left a decent estate."

"Decent," Sarah remarked dryly. "What an interesting choice of words."

"What a joke," Daniel muttered. "Even in death, he's going to torment me by saddling me with that damned building." He stiffly rose and began to pace the room then asked, "Elmo, will you deal with this other lawyer for me?"

"As much as I can. You'll have to take care of certain things yourself."

"Fine. As soon as it's possible, I want to liquidate all the merchandise in the store. I want Sarah and Carson to go to the building and get rid of all of Samuels's personal effects. Anything else they feel should be kept, they can bring it to me."

"And the building itself?"

"Whatever. I may sell it to the highest bidder."

"Good deal. Technically, it's all your stuff now, but Sarah can act as your representative if you're unable to go yourself. I just have to draw up the paperwork."

"Great."

Palmentier stood and slipped on his coat before saying, "Call me once you've talked with Carson, and we'll set it up. In the meantime, I'll get with your stepfather's lawyer on the rest."

Once their friend had gone, Daniel resumed his seat in the recliner and sat, mulling things over in his head. Had Samuels done this to taunt him from beyond the grave? Was there simply no one else to leave his estate to? Maybe he didn't want the estate to go to the government.

Daniel was so wrapped up in his thoughts that it took him a while to realize that Sarah was in the kitchen violently washing pots and pans in the sink. This was not a good sign. When she was angry or upset, she tended to do everything around the house a little more forcefully than was necessary. Tensing, Daniel went to the kitchen.

"Sarah?"

"Who says I want to go?"

"What?"

"You offered my services to Elmo without even asking me!"

"I need for you to go to the building. Who else would know what to keep and what to pitch?"

"What else is there besides what we found that night?"

"How do we know what there is? We might have missed something. Look at the board in the closet. Carson and Natalie were thorough, but we were in a hurry."

"If it needs to be done, who better to do it than Sarah?" his wife proposed angrily. "If you can't count on Sarah to do the dirty work, then who can you trust?"

"Sarah, I –"

"I can't do this anymore!" she cried. "I don't want to!"

"If you don't want to do it, then just say, 'No'."

"No!"

He hadn't expected her to call his bluff but recovered himself quickly and suggested, "Jamie could go with Carson."

She nodded and lessened the pressure on the sponge in her hand. Daniel came up behind her, placed his hands over hers, and then followed the movements as she cleaned a griddle in rhythmic, circular motions. The soapy water was warm, and the movement was soothing. As always, the scent of rose clung to Sarah's hair and skin.

"You'll get tired," Sarah said softly after a time. "You should sit down."

Truth be told, Daniel was slightly dizzy with weakness, but he was content for the time being, and he didn't want to leave that precious feeling behind just yet.

"Would you come with me to lie down?" he asked tiredly.

She placed their hands under the tap, rinsed the soap off in the tepid stream, then dried them with the towel. By the time she replaced the towel, Daniel's eyelids were drooping with fatigue.

He lay down on the bed, and Sarah covered him with the quilt that Helen and Jim had given them as a wedding present.

"I like Helen and Jim," he said sleepily, as he drew one finger along the stem of a quilted flower. "They've always treated you like you were their real granddaughter and not their step granddaughter."

"They have been wonderful," his wife agreed. "I always figured it was because I was their only grandchild for so long. They loved me from the beginning. They've always loved you as well."

"Yeah."

"Your mother loved you, too."

"Maybe. I love her and I hate her. But most of all, I pity her. I wish I could go back in time and stop her from leaving Max. I wish I could have the kind of happy childhood I'd always dreamed of."

Daniel fell asleep and dreamed of Jim and Helen's farm. Jim was driving a tractor. Helen was baking bread. He and Sarah were making love in an upstairs bedroom with the windows open to the spring breeze. It was as American as apple pie.

"Daniel?"

He resisted waking. He felt so strong and calm in the dream.

"Carson's here," Sarah said quietly. "Do you want me to tell him to come back later?"

He pried open one eye and looked at his wife.

"No. Just let me get my bearings."

"Carson looks half-dead. I doubt if he's slept much, lately."

"Doesn't sound promising."

She shrugged and kissed him.

"There's someone with him you might like to meet. Don't be too long."

Daniel grimaced as he came into the living room and saw his friend. The man looked positively haggard.

"You better not be looking like this on my account," Daniel chided him.

"Of course not. Natalie's been keeping me up nights."

"Sure she has. Look, I don't want you to drive yourself into the ground trying to make up for what Samuels did to me that night."

"I want to see this thing through. Unfortunately, none of my leads panned out – except for the doc here."

The man was undoubtedly elderly, but he was trim and fit. Almost as tall as Daniel, he exuded an unmistakable energy and intelligence.

"I'm Dr. Laucke. You probably don't remember me, but I remember you quite well."

"The doctor who certified my birth certificate? No, can't say that I do. That's newborns for you."

Laucke grinned and shook his head.

"I didn't just certify your birth certificate; I delivered you. I also treated your mother many times when you were small."

Daniel squinted at the man's face and tried to picture what he must have looked like thirty years before. Nothing came to him.

"I was very sorry to hear about the recent incident," the doctor told him. "I was also sorry to learn of your mother's death. Not surprised, but sorry."

"You knew he was beating her?"

"One thing at a time," Carson said. "Maybe we should start at the beginning."

"Once Daniel sits down," Sarah insisted.

He sat.

"I'd like to talk with the good doctor alone."

"Carson, maybe we could go out on the back porch," Sarah suggested. "There's really no place else in the house where we won't hear them."

Once they'd gone, Daniel gestured for Dr. Laucke to begin.

"I was called to the apartment over the bar early one morning by Mr. Samuels. He told me that his wife had been trying to have a baby all night while he'd been working in the bar, but she hadn't come down to tell him. She refused to go to the hospital, and he was obviously concerned. I must admit I was concerned, too. I didn't feel that a woman in the modern age should give birth without medical assistance available. So, I hurried over.

"Your mother had received no pre-natal care. Her husband told me that the baby was early. I encouraged her to go to the hospital, but she continued to refuse. She also kept insisting that Samuels leave the room, but he wouldn't hear of it.

"When you finally came, it was evident you weren't premature. You weighed almost eight pounds, if I recall correctly. Your eyebrows were formed, and you responded appropriately to stimuli. I explained this to Mr. Samuels."

"How did he react?"

"He paid me and asked me to leave."

"Did you?"

"No. I told him I couldn't leave until I'd finished my medical duties regarding my patients. I went back to the bedroom and told your mother that it would be foolish to remain. I could sense some sort of impending violence coming from her husband."

"But she wouldn't leave."

"She told me that you weren't Samuels's son, but she insisted that he wouldn't hurt you. He had sworn to her that he would never harm a child of hers while she was alive. She said he always kept his promises." The older man shivered and added, "I didn't care much for the way in which she said it. I threatened to take you from the home, but I had no conclusive proof of past or present abuse."

"Conclusive proof? You had inconclusive proof?"

"There were bruises."

"Let me guess. She fell down the stairs."

"It would have been extremely difficult for a woman to get those bruises by falling down the stairs. They were on the insides of her thighs."

"What did you do?"

"I gave her my card. I told her to come to me when she wanted to leave or if she needed medical treatment for herself or for you."

"And did she come to you?"

"Two weeks later. Then, two weeks after that. Then, she didn't come for six months or so. Each time, she brought you with her so that I could see you were unharmed. It became sort of an unspoken deal between us. I would continue to treat her, if she could show me that you weren't being abused. It would be incredibly difficult for me to have you removed from the apartment if you weren't the victim of abuse."

"How long did you treat her?"

"Off and on for four years."

"Why didn't you tell someone that he was beating her?"

"Things were a little different back then, Son. Domestic abuse was a very hush-hush topic in society. Women's rights weren't always a top priority in those days. Even if a woman charged her husband with beating her, a judge might chide her for being disloyal to her husband and send her home. If she left him, her children could be taken from her and given to her abuser."

"So, you saw her for four years. Why did you stop seeing her?"

"During those four years, I treated your mother for various injuries that resulted from her husband's attacks. I also treated her for six miscarriages. Each time she came in after a miscarriage, there were bruises. I –"

"You don't have to explain it to me," Daniel cut in. "I remember what he did. I was there some of those times."

The physician looked unnerved and stammered, "She – your mother came in to see me one afternoon. The bruises were there, but there had been no miscarriage. She wanted advice on how she could end the pregnancy herself. I couldn't – " He broke off and placed his hands on his knees before admitting, "I refused to help her. A doctor is supposed to save patients, not destroy helpless innocents. I told her that she was too far along at any rate. I pleaded with her to leave her husband, as I did at the end of each visit."

"Did she always answer the same way?"

"Yes, except for that time. Usually she said that she had nowhere else to go."

"And that time?"

"She said they loved each other and despised each other. She said she lived to please him. I asked her how murdering his children was pleasing to him. She said it didn't have anything to do with Samuels. It had to do with revenge. Besides, she argued, she didn't murder anyone; he did. I pointed out that she was in my office asking me to help her commit murder that day. I counseled her to seek psychological help and to remand you into the custody of the state. I told her that I'd take it to the police and damn the consequences. She became very calm and told me that if I'd had proof that I would have done something about it years before. Then she thanked me for my help and walked out. I never saw her again."

"Did you go to the police?"

"Yes."

"And the authorities did nothing."

"Correct."

They sat in the living room without speaking for some time. Finally, Laucke said, "I wish I could have done more. I wish I could say that your mother was the only patient I've ever treated who was being abused. At least today there are more programs and more opportunities for intervention through the legal system, shelters, and education."

"I appreciate your frankness."

"Mr. Zerangue said you wanted the truth, no matter how painful it was."

"No matter how painful," Daniel agreed, wondering how exactly his mother had aborted that particular child.

Later that afternoon, Daniel woke with a start to the sound of his mother's laughter. It wasn't her laughter, of course. It was Sarah laughing as she watched their son pulling the dog's rope toy. Ralph twisted on his back, growling playfully, his tail thumping repetitively on the floor. Kris was giggling uncontrollably as he maneuvered the toy like a snake that slithered just out of reach of the dog's mouth.

To laugh, play, and love without hesitation. It was all Daniel had ever wanted as a child. It was all he wanted as an adult. He wondered if such a thing was possible for him or if his past would always cloud his future.

Chapter Twenty-five: A Good Man's Reality

The man from the St. Vincent de Paul Store handed Daniel a slip of paper and explained, "For your taxes. You can write off your donation. You fill in how much."

"Don't you worry that people will write in any amount?"

"You gots to trust someone, don't you?"

Daniel stood on the porch of the Highland home and watched the volunteers and the truck disappear from view. Then he went back into the house and wandered into Max's office, expecting to find it deserted. Instead, his wife was there, sitting in the worn rocker and staring out of the window at the barren garden.

"They just left," Daniel told her. "I can't believe we got it all done in such a short amount of time. We need to take Will and his friends out to dinner for helping us to pack everything. Maybe T.J. Ribs?"

"They'd love that."

"The St. Vincent people wouldn't take that rocker. There's a crack in the leg, and they don't have anyone to fix it."

"I don't want to get rid of this chair. Do you think it can be fixed? I want to put it on the front porch."

"We'll have to check around. We could get them to paint it while they're at it."

"Green would be nice."

"I didn't know you were attached to it."

"I am."

"I'll have to scout around and find me an old one to put next to yours. That way, when we're old, we can sit on the front porch and rock in the evenings."

"That sounds peaceful."

"Yeah, it does."

Sarah turned to look at him and asked suddenly, "Do you want to go through the box that Jamie and Carson brought back from

Samuels's place? I had Will put it on the kitchen table. That old suitcase is there, too."

"I've avoided it all morning, but I was always aware that it was there. I won't be able to rest until we've sorted it out."

"Are you certain you don't want to do it alone?"

"Very certain."

"Then let's go."

"What about Kris?" Daniel asked worriedly. "I don't think he should be around while I'm going through the box."

"He conked out on the floor of your old room while we were reading a book. It's so cute when he does that. I covered him with a blanket and put a pillow under his head."

"The way he naps, he'll be out for two or three hours."

"You look tired. Maybe you should take a nap, too."

"I told you, I can't rest until I've gone through that stuff. I can't put it off any longer."

Jamie and Carson had placed everything they thought worthy of Daniel's attention into a box that had once held copier paper. Daniel lifted the top and stared inside.

"Well?" Sarah asked impatiently. "Anything?"

"Not a whole helluva lot. I know all the business papers went to the lawyer's office. There are a few pictures." He briefly sorted through them before admitting, "I don't recognize anyone."

"What else?"

"An old paperback copy of *The Carpetbaggers*. It has Samuels's name in the front. And here's a hardback of *The Collected Works of Sir Arthur Conan Doyle*. Hm. This one has my mother's name inscribed on the title page. I'm surprised he kept it." He handed the book to his wife and said, "You like Conan Doyle. Do you want it?"

"I have a copy of Doyle's works. Keep it if you want."

Daniel lifted out a leather belt. Next to it, he placed a pack of Camels and a sharp knife.

"Jamie, Jamie, Jamie," he chuckled and shook his head. "He really missed his calling. Jamie Nesser, radical psychiatrist. I bet he would have given some of those yahoos a run for their money." Daniel held up the belt and asked, "Think we ought to keep it as a family heirloom?"

"Please, put it away before I throw up my lunch," Sarah said quietly.

"It's amazing how much power can be associated with an inanimate object," Daniel remarked, as he wrapped one end of the belt around his hand. "What do you think I should do with it?"

"Daniel, you're scaring me."

He stopped gazing at the belt and glanced at his wife. She did appear slightly afraid. He unwound the belt and laid it back on the kitchen table.

"You think I could use it like he did?"

"No. I…it gives me a queasy feeling to see you touching it like that. It's like you're…oh, *familiar* isn't the word I'm looking for…."

"Intimate?"

She paused to consider his choice then agreed, "Sick, but appropriate."

He tossed all of the items back into the box.

"I'll carry this one. It's light, so don't fuss at me for lifting it, okay? You get the old suitcase."

"Where are we going?"

"To the living room."

They knelt on the floor in front of the fireplace. Daniel opened the suitcase and removed his birth certificate and the bundle of letters. Then he pulled out his mother's old nightgown with obvious distaste and pitched it into the flames.

Sarah watched him burn the photos of the nameless people. She helped him to tear out the yellowing pages of Samuels's book and feed them into the fire. The cigarettes ignited with a burst of tobacco, and the leather of the belt gave off an acrid odor. The knife darkened with the heat and taunted them with its steel blade.

"What are you going to do with the letters?"

"Read them. After that, I don't know."

He untied the string and lifted the top letter from the pile. He opened it and read aloud,

January 4, 1958

Assumpta, it was good to see you at Christmas. Your husband seems to be a smart man of business. I'm proud of you. In one

year, you've graduated from college, married, and will have a child. Surely your mother smiles down on you from Heaven.

Da

"Why doesn't that surprise me?" Daniel muttered. "Maybe if he hadn't been so damned proud of what he thought she'd accomplished, she could have gone home."

The second letter read:

May 6, 1958

Assumpta, your son is a fine lad. I wish I could see you and him more often. Is everything all right between you and your husband?

Da

"Not one to mince words, was he?" Sarah quipped.

The third and last letter from Patrick Downey said simply:

January 28, 1966

Assumpta, I beg of you, come home.

Da

"That's it," Daniel said, as he replaced the 1966 letter back into its envelope.

"That can't be it. There are a bunch of other letters there."

"There are, but they're not from my grandfather."

"Who sent the other ones?"

"No one."

"What're you talking about? Somebody had to send them, didn't they?"

He flipped through the pile and said, "It's my mother's handwriting on the envelopes and Max's address. They even have stamps."

"It looks like they've been opened."

"I wonder who could have done that?" Daniel asked grimly.

May 18, 1958

Max,
I know you must hate me for running away like I did, but I've already gone over my reasoning in the note I left you. It would have killed me to see you disgraced.
You have a son. I've named him Daniel Warren. I wanted his middle name to be Warren because of your father. As for his first name, in Hebrew Daniel means "God is my judge." I thought that was a fitting name for the baby conceived in such illicit love and passion, a baby whose existence has forced that passion to come to an abrupt end. God has blessed me with his birth and damned you and me to be forever separated.
He is a beautiful baby. He looks like you and me.

My love always,
Tessa

Without pausing, Daniel laid that letter aside and opened the next one.

June 30, 1959

Max,
Our son is past one year old now. He is so advanced for his age. He can already say "MaMa," "dog," "milk," "car," and a host of other words. He took his first steps at nine-and-a-half months. He loves to play peekaboo and always gets excited when he hears Jerry Lee Lewis or Chuck Berry on the radio.

My love always,
Tessa

Sarah rubbed at the bridge of her nose and watched her husband reach for the next letter.

May 2, 1960

Max,
Daniel is such a bright and energetic two-year-old. He has been putting together complex sentences for several months and is no longer in diapers. He has a favorite toy bear that he calls "CoCo." It makes me think of CoCo next to you every time he says it. It makes me think of you.

My love always,
Tessa

Daniel hesitated as he began to read the next letter.

"What's wrong?" Sarah softly asked.

"The date. It's dated May 12, 1968. Did she stop writing for all those years? If not, what happened to those letters?"

"Maybe the letter will tell us."

May 12, 1968

Max,
Daniel is ten years old. He's so tall. A quiet boy, he's very single-minded when it comes to any task. He's also a voracious reader. I bought him a copy of Old Yeller *as a present. I know you would approve and understand.*

My love always,
Tessa

Daniel held out the last envelope to his wife and asked, "Would you read it to me?"

"If I can see it."

"The print's large and legible. You should be able to make it out fine."

"I need more direct lighting. Let's go back to the office."

Daniel sat in the rocker, while Sarah sat at the desk and turned on the lamp. She had to put on her magnifying glasses, lean close to the paper and squint slightly, but she was able to read with minimum strain.

She read:

November 27, 1968

Max,

I write to you now, even though I remain unconvinced as to whether or not you received my previous eleven letters. I don't know if my attempts to tell you about our son have failed; I suspect they have. Deep down, I guess I believe that if they arrived at your doorstep, you would have come for me. Even if you hated me that much, I figured you would have come for our son. I've prayed many times that you'd come for both of us.

If you've gotten my other letters and have chosen to stay away, then I am writing now to beg you not to punish our child because of my failings. He's suffered enough.

Eleven years ago I met and married a man I thought was kind and generous. He said he loved me, and I thought that I could grow to love him, too. He believed that the baby was his until the day the child was born. Once the doctor reassured him that Daniel wasn't premature, everything changed.

He never hurt our child. I told him I would leave if he did, and he loves me even now. And I, I do love him.

You would be appalled. You will be, if you get this note. My husband and I have become caught in a cycle of physical and emotional violence, an abyss of shame. I've known that the atmosphere isn't good for our son, but I could never leave Zachary. I can never leave him, not even to save my child or my own life.

I want you to come for Daniel and take him from me. I'm selfish. I love him too much to send him away, but it would be better for him. If I didn't love him so deeply, I would have put him up for adoption the day he was born. His life would have been much happier.

I tell myself that I will call you in case this letter isn't mailed, but the truth is that I'm so terrified that I can't do what's right. I'm afraid of seeing you again and of losing our son. I'm afraid of feeling unworthy of your love. Why, I don't know. I became unworthy of your love a long, long time ago.

I think often of those afternoons at the house and in your garden and that magnificent day at the lake. The time I spent with you was the most honest of my life. I rue the day it had to end. As much as I adore our child, his existence destroyed our future. I should have known it was too good to last.

Try to remember me as I was. That is how I will forever remember you.

My love always,
Tessa

Sarah laid the letter on the ink blotter and recoiled from it as if the paper was a poisonous snake.

"What do you want me to do with it? Burn it? Burn all of them?"

"No, I think I'll keep these, at least for now." Daniel began to rock slowly and pondered, "His existence destroyed our future. Man, she understood how sick her life was with Samuels, but she never did get it, did she? She could take responsibility for everything except her choice."

"I think she got it."

Sarah rose and came around to stand in front of the rocker. Daniel looked up at her and raised an eyebrow in an unspoken question.

Sarah bent to kiss his forehead and said, "*Daniel* is Hebrew for 'God is my judge.'"

"I believe she thought that the judgment was on her willingness to give herself to a man in an illicit relationship and not on her choice to leave her lover or lie to her husband. She certainly didn't perceive it as a judgment on her decision to stay with a man who yelled at her, beat her, and raped her continuously for over ten years. I wonder if she was mentally ill from the start. Maybe that's why she was attracted to a psychiatrist and why she and CoCo got along so well. I guess hearing it that way from her confirms what I've been suspecting all along – that she was an intelligent woman who had come to accept her role in a twisted and sadistic relationship."

"And that she loved you?"

Without answering, Daniel stood and went to retrieve the letter from the desk.

"I feel really dirty after going through those things. I'm going to go up and take a bath and then maybe lie down for a while. Mind joining me? I know you won't sleep, but –"

"I'll close the screen on the fireplace and pick up down here," Sarah said quickly. "What do you want me to do with the suitcase?"

"Pitch it in the trash. I'll wrap up the knife once it cools then put it in the garbage where it belongs."

"I'll see you upstairs then."

In the tub, Daniel soaped his skin and rinsed it; then he repeated the process. He coated his hair with a generous amount of shampoo and then stood under the spray until long after all traces of the white bubbles had disappeared.

Sarah was waiting for him in the bed.

Chapter Twenty-six: Tears in the Fabric of Our Lives

Daniel, Sarah, and Kris dined with Sarah's parents and siblings at Gino's Italian Restaurant that evening.

"Mom and Dad decided to put the farm on the market and move here," Vaughn informed the others as they waited for their dessert.

"Well, it's only taken them, like, twenty years to do that," Katie said wearily.

"Unlike you, most of us don't flit around like birds every two seconds," Will teased.

"Where will they live?" Kris asked. "With you?"

"They want to buy a home of their own," Tristan explained. "Nothing big, but not too small either. After living on a farm for most of their lives, I don't think they could handle a garden home or retirement community."

"Oh, I don't know. They might like it," suggested Vaughn. "What do you think, Daniel? You've been awfully quiet this evening."

"Hm?"

He seemed genuinely surprised that she'd spoken to him. Tristan, being more empathetic than his wife, had left him alone throughout the meal.

"Do you think Jim and Helen would ever adjust to living in a garden home or a retirement community?" Sarah offered helpfully.

He flashed her a quick smile that he hoped would convey his thanks.

"I think they'd hate it," he replied truthfully. He pushed back his chair and slowly got to his feet before stating, "I'm really getting tired. Tris, would you mind taking Sarah and Kris to the Highland house for me? Sarah, do you remember the code on the security system?"

"Of course."

"Are you sure you should go by yourself if you're tired?" Vaughn asked worriedly. "You're not going to pass out at the wheel, are you?"

"No," he said hastily and harshly. "Why do you do that, Vaughn? You're scaring Kris."

"Forgive me for being a little protective of my family," she said hotly. "I was only following my motherly instincts."

"I've already had two mothers. I don't need a third."

He shook hands with Tristan and Will; then he patted Katie on the back. Kris stood on his chair to give his father a hug, as his mother rose and stretched up on her tiptoes to kiss her husband.

"I'll be by Isabelle's for a while," he whispered in her ear before they broke apart. "Don't wait up."

By the time he reached the door of Isabelle's apartment, he wished that he had gone directly home. His abdomen was sore, and he was feeling lightheaded. He almost turned around and left.

An elderly man answered the door. Daniel stepped back and looked up and down the hallway to verify that he was at the right apartment.

"Ah, I…I was coming to see Dr. Elenstraub. Is she at home?"

"Yes, certainly," the man said kindly. He stepped back and beckoned for Daniel to enter. Extending his hand, he added, "I'm Noah Goldblum."

"Dan Nash. Nice to meet you."

"Daniel," Isabelle said behind him. "What a pleasant surprise!"

"I should be going," Goldblum said, gracefully excusing himself. "Perhaps I will see you again, Mr. Nash."

"Don't go on my account. I can come back another time."

Goldblum went over to Isabelle and kissed her on the cheek as he assured Daniel, "I have some things to attend to. Have a nice visit."

"Goodbye, Noah," Isabelle called out after him. "See you at 2:00."

"Hot date?" Daniel asked once the man had left.

"Not by a younger person's standards, I'm sure. We are going to the New Orleans Museum of Art and then to dinner in the French Market area before we return to Baton Rouge."

"I must be getting old, because that sounds like a hot date to me. Where did you meet him? Are you being careful? In today's age, one should always use protection."

"He is a fellow member of my synagogue." She came over to Daniel and laid one palm across his forehead. "Enough of that. I think you have a temperature. Sit."

"I don't have a fever. I'm just not feeling great."

"I can see that. You're pale, and you are obviously in pain. What did you do today?"

"Nothing," he said innocently.

"Nothing?"

"I drove for the first time tonight."

"You have a stick shift, correct? Did the doctor clear you to drive?"

"Yes."

"A standard?"

"I didn't actually tell him it was a standard. It slipped my mind."

"Conveniently, I'm sure. What else did you do today that was on your list of restrictions?" Let me guess. You and Sarah engaged in intercourse."

"Look, I had a rough morning and…and we took it easy."

"Haven't you had enough, Daniel? You should take better care of yourself."

"Okay, *Vaughn*," he said sarcastically. "I *have* been taking care of myself. I pushed a little too hard today is all."

"You had a disagreement with Vaughn?"

"A few angry words."

"She is concerned for your well-being."

As he lowered himself onto the couch, Daniel said, "I know that, but she's got this pie-in-the-sky image of how our lives should be, and she won't accept any other way. Remember when Sarah was diagnosed with macular degeneration, and Vaughn refused to believe it unless they went to Chicago for another opinion? Even then, it took Vaughn a long time to adjust."

"You came here to talk with me about Vaughn's ingrained personality traits? I doubt it."

"No. I wanted to sit here with you for a while. Is that all right?"

"Perfectly all right."

"Good."

He closed his eyes and leaned his head back against a cushion, as Isabelle went into the kitchen and poured him a glass of water. She placed it in his hands, and he drank deeply from the glass without opening his eyes. When the glass had been drained, she took it from him and set it on the coffee table. Then she sat next to him and once again laid her hand on his forehead.

"You do have a slight temperature. You need to rest," she said disapprovingly.

"All I've been doing is resting for the last month. My doctor says it might take me a year to fully recover. He won't release me to go back to work for at least four more weeks. Excuse me for wanting to get out of the house for a couple of hours."

"You are an adult. I will not scold anymore. We'll simply sit."

For five minutes, neither of them said anything. Finally, Isabelle took his hand in both of hers and squeezed it.

"What are you thinking about right at this moment?"

"This pregnant teenager I met a couple of months ago. I was wondering if she and her boyfriend will keep the baby and if they should. Something my mother said in one of her letters made me wonder."

"You read the letters, then?"

"There were a few from my grandfather. I read those, plus the ones from my mother. Well, Sarah read the last one to me. All of them were written for Max, but I guess Samuels intercepted them before they reached the mailman. And strangely enough, he kept them."

"And what did your mother write that struck you as important?"

"She knew what a warped life she was leading. She said something like she loved me too much to let me go, but she didn't love me enough to give me up. Does that make sense?"

"In its fashion."

"She said that my existence destroyed the future for her and Max."

"Do you believe that?"

"Technically, it was the cause of the end of the relationship."

"Technically, your mother was the cause of the end of the relationship. How did it make you feel to read those words?"

"Responsible, which is ridiculous. I know I wasn't responsible for being conceived. It wasn't my idea."

"How did it make you *feel*?"

"Hurt. Very hurt."

"You were an innocent child. It is quite natural for you to feel hurt by the words of a woman who is attempting to excuse her inexcusable actions by placing the blame on someone else."

"I wish I could forget."

"What? Your abuse?"

"My abuse and her abuse. What I know and what I think I know. Things have been coming back in bits and pieces."

"Such as?"

"The hitting and the rapes. What happened when Samuels beat me to a pulp that summer."

"Rapes?"

"Samuels used to hurt my mother in a variety of ways."

"And you witnessed this?"

"The beatings, always. The rapes, occasionally."

Daniel sat twisting a piece of the fringe that edged the beige afghan Isabelle kept draped over the arm of her couch.

"I – I had a visit from the doctor who delivered me. It was very informative but also confusing. My mother hinted in her last letter to Max that Samuels didn't start to hit her until after I was born. Yet, the doctor said that when he came to deliver me, my mother had bruises on her inner thighs. He treated her after that for various injuries and for six miscarriages in four years. During her last visit to him, she basically said that her attempts to get Samuels to cause another miscarriage had failed."

"And did the doctor perform an abortion?"

"He told her she was too far along, and that he wouldn't commit murder, so she left."

"And?"

"And I've been thinking back to that time period. I began to remember something that I must have blocked out of my pre-school mind."

"What do you recall?"

"Snatches of things. My mother was crying. There was blood and…and…." He covered his face with one hand and said hoarsely, "I can't even think about it. It makes me shake."

"You don't have to talk about it just now."

"I do. I have to tell someone."

"Tell me then."

"I swear to you, I…I saw a tiny foot in the tangle of sheets. When Kris was born, his feet weren't any bigger." Daniel rubbed his damp hands on the legs of his pants and said, "There was a great deal of blood, and I was afraid that she was going to die and leave me alone."

"Whom are we talking about?"

"What?"

"You said there was a great deal of blood, and you were afraid she was going to die and leave you alone. Do you mean your mother or your wife?"

"I never made the connection."

"How could you if you blocked out the early memories? But it does make perfect sense. As a young child, you witnessed things that are unthinkable, even to an adult. One of those things was a miscarriage –"

"Abortion."

"Abortion. You were too young to understand anything, save that there was a great deal of blood and that your mother was crying in fear and pain. You saw a tiny foot, and you know instinctively that something was wrong, but you did not know quite what. Nor did your mother explain this to you.

"As an adult, you married and your wife became pregnant. Months before the baby was due, she began to bleed profusely. You rushed her to the hospital and held her as she cried in fear and pain and delivered the premature infant. She almost bled to death because of the birth. All of those feelings you had as a small child were repeated.

"It's no wonder that the frequency and severity of your nightmares increased after that. Perhaps if you had remembered the earlier incident, you could have dealt with the trauma of Kris's birth from a more rational standpoint. Perhaps not."

"How could my mother do it? It wasn't unrecognizable tissue. It was a baby. How could she induce an abortion at that stage?"

"There are many ways that women chose to abort their unwanted babies when clinical abortion was not readily available.

Some continue these practices even today. Many die because of it."

"I didn't mean what technique did she use," Daniel snapped. "I meant, how *could* she? She would have felt it move by then. Kris was already giving little kicks. I can't fathom how she could do it."

"The abortion debate is a complex one, Daniel. I don't believe that we can solve it here. She obviously did not want to give birth to Samuels's child. It may have been because she did want to hurt him in some way as he had hurt her, or it may have been that she feared his offspring would inherit his sadistic tendencies, and she was striving to stop a new evil before it could begin. Both she and Samuels were obviously disturbed. It is a travesty that you were made to bear witness to such events."

"Will you help me, Isabelle? I need you."

"I could never turn away from such a heartfelt request."

He left her with a promise to return each Monday, Wednesday, and Friday afternoon to "sit" with her. He also swore to her that he would call his doctor and alert him about the fever.

Tristan was waiting on the front steps when Daniel pulled up next to the old Nash home. With the right side of his abdomen throbbing painfully, Daniel got out of the car and walked slowly around to the front. Sighing, he climbed up to where Tristan reclined and sat beside him. For a long while, neither of them spoke. There was no need.

Chapter Twenty-seven: Relapse

"Kris is asleep," Tristan eventually volunteered.

"And Sarah?"

"Baking something in the kitchen."

"What about Vaughn, Will, and Katie?"

"Will took Katie home. He'll come back for me and Vaughn when I call." Tristan leaned back, rested his elbows on one of the upper steps, and planted his feet on one of the lower ones before saying, "You hurt Vaughn's feelings."

"She's so unrealistic about things! How can you stand it?"

"Sometimes it's hard. The way Vaughn approaches life is one of the qualities that initially attracted me to her. She was so damned naïve. She still is, or at least she still pretends to be. Whatever the case, that Pollyanna attitude pulled me out of the fire more than once."

"I remember all that."

"I do, too. You know our marriage hasn't been that great for a while, but I still love Vaughn. Think about it. She agreed to marry a poor college student who had a recent history of depression and substance abuse. And the guy had a kid, too. That right there would have been enough to drive away most girls, but because she loved me – us – she saw things through. It's not that she thinks life is peaches and cream all the time. She wants to make it better for the people she loves in any way she can." He smiled in the faint glow of the porch light and confided, "As for how I can stand it, you could ask her the same thing. You think I've made it easy for her? How does Sarah put up with you? How do you put up with her? We can all be challenging in a variety of ways."

Daniel didn't answer. He gazed up at the stars that were visible in the patches of sky between the trees.

"Carson and Natalie left town for a while," Daniel said absently. "When they get back, Carson and I are going to go fishing. Maybe you'd wanna come."

"I'd love to. Where'd they go?"

"To find Carson's daughter. His ex-wife took off with her a couple of years ago, and he's never been able to track her down. He needs to find her."

"I'm sure he does."

"Maybe Frank Randall would come fishing with us, too. Do priests fish?"

Tristan laughed and asked, "You think there's a rule about priests not being able to fish?"

"No, I've just never seen one do it before."

"You've never interacted with a priest outside of Mass until recently."

"True."

"Some of Jesus's apostles were fishermen. I would think fishing would be a very priestly thing to do."

"I never thought of it that way."

"Jamie hasn't been fishing in about a year."

"Yeah, you're right. I'll have to talk with him about it."

Although he felt Tristan's arm go around his shoulders, Daniel kept studying the stars for several minutes. Finally, he allowed himself to be pulled against Tristan's chest. Neither man spoke. Neither man moved.

"I'm a poor substitute for Max," Tristan offered. "I wish there was more I could say or do for you."

"You do fine," Daniel insisted, as he shifted slightly and listened to the leather on his jacket move in tandem. "You do better than Max if you want to know the truth. You may not be a therapist, but you're more of a father than he ever was."

"He loved you, Dan."

"I know. He was an okay father, but he can't compare to you, Tris. It's not the same."

"I'm honored."

"Don't die on me any time soon, Tris. Mom and Lillian are gone. Max is gone. I don't want to lose any more parents for at least another five decades or so."

"I'll do my best," he vowed, wrapping a hand around the side of Daniel's head in a paternal gesture. "Are you running fever?"

"It's not high."

"Any fever is too high for you right now."

Releasing his son-in-law, Tristan helped the man up and walked with him into the house. They heard the women discussing a grocery list and headed in their direction. As they entered the room, both women turned and looked worriedly at Daniel.

"Vaughn, I'm sorry," he blurted out. "I apologize for what happened earlier."

"It's over now. Why don't you sit? You look exhausted."

Sarah had already come across the room and pulled Daniel's head down so that she could kiss his left temple.

"He's feverish. How long have you had a temperature?"

"Since I was at Isabelle's. Sarah, it's probably not even a hundred."

"Did you call the doctor?"

"No, but I promised Isabelle that I would when I got home."

The phone rang. Tristan reached out and lifted the receiver then said, "Yes, he's back. No, we haven't called, yet. I will. Thanks." He replaced the receiver but immediately lifted it again before declaring, "I'm calling him now."

"It's only a slight fever," insisted Daniel.

"Maybe so," Sarah said, as she began to unbutton his shirt. "Maybe not."

Daniel took her by the wrists.

"Daniel, I want to –"

"Not here."

"But –"

"Not here," he repeated more distinctly.

"Sure, I'll hold," Tristan was saying. He covered the phone with his hand and said in a loud whisper, "The answering service is paging your surgeon." Tristan returned his attention to the phone and said affably, "Hello, Dr. Beibee. Yes, it's good to talk with you, too. No he's not. He's got a low-grade fever. Uh-huh. No, I don't think so. Here he is."

Daniel accepted the phone from Tristan and said warily, "Hello?"

"John Beibee here. How are you?"

"I was doing better until tonight. Now, I'm running a little fever, and my family's freaking out."

"Can't say as I blame them after what happened before. Are you experiencing any vomiting or diarrhea?"

"No."

"Is the area around your injury any different than it has been?"

"I don't know. I haven't looked at it, yet."

"Would you check it for me?"

"Hang on."

He laid the phone down on the table and looking back and forth between Tristan and Vaughn asked, "Would you leave for a minute?"

"We can wait in the dining room," Tristan suggested.

Daniel fumbled with the buttons for several seconds before allowing Sarah to take over. She deftly undid each one and pushed back his shirt.

"It doesn't look any different to me," he told Beibee. "How about you, Sarah?"

"It hasn't changed since this afternoon."

"She says it hasn't changed since this afternoon. I'm just really sore."

"Hm. So, what did you do today?"

"Drove my standard; ate some salad at dinner; and had sex with my wife," he admitted sheepishly. "Nothing rough."

"Driving the car would have been rough enough," Beibee sighed. "I thought you didn't want to see me again anytime soon."

"No offense, but I don't."

"Too bad. I'm already over at the hospital. Meet me in the ER in twenty minutes. I want to check things out for myself."

"But if I lie down for a while here –"

"Be there."

Groaning, Daniel hung up the phone. He wanted to go to bed, not to the hospital. As Sarah buttoned his shirt, he called out, "Tris? I need a favor."

His father-in-law poked his head through the kitchen doorway.

"He wants to see me. Will you drive us? I hate to make you do this."

"Let me grab my coat."

"I'll get yours, Sarah," Vaughn offered. "Don't worry about Kris."

Not long afterward, John Beibee examined Daniel. Then he requested blood work and a scan of his abdomen. When he returned to his patient's curtained room, he stood next to the gurney and announced, "Good news. No ruptures or tears. The area is irritated, though. Your white cell count is elevated. I'm going to give you a round of some pretty strong antibiotics. I want you to see your internist on Monday if you still have fever. If it gets high, then I want you back here immediately. If not and all goes well, I want to see you in my office next Friday. And no driving, roughage or sex until I say so. Is that clear?"

"Crystal."

"Good. Before you go, I'm ordering an antibiotic injection as well as a dose of painkillers. Once that wears off, you can take Tylenol, Advil, Motrin, whichever you prefer. Now, go home and get some sleep."

Tristan, Vaughn, and Sarah had to help Daniel up the stairs. Tristan guided him to the master bedroom and supported him while Sarah removed his shoes, socks, and pants. Then, they laid him back on the pillow. He was already asleep.

"Daddy, will you help me get his shirt off?" Sarah asked, as she undid the buttons. "There's no way I can lift him to get it out from underneath there."

The instant she undid his shirt, Sarah realized her mistake. Vaughn had remained in the room and was now staring at her son-in-law with an anguished look on her face. She reached forward and brushed her fingertips along each scar, except for the recent incision.

"Don't tell him you saw this," Sarah said quietly. "He doesn't want people to see. Promise me you won't say anything."

"He'll know anyway," Tristan said. "She won't be able to hide it the next time she looks at him. God, it's been decades since I've seen that. It makes me scared and angry all over again."

"He remembered, you know," Sarah said, as Tristan raised the man so that she could slide the shirt away. "He remembered about the last beating."

"And?"

"And it was about what you'd expect. He may tell you about it someday."

She gently touched her husband's cheek. He moaned softly in his sleep.

"I should stay," Tristan told his daughter.

"No, Daddy. Don't you have some special site mapping in the morning? And besides, there's no place for you and Vaughn to sleep."

"But what if he needs to get up to go to the bathroom?" Vaughn asked. "You're too small to lift him."

"I've been taking care of him by myself ever since he came home from the hospital. We'll be fine."

Will arrived a half hour later, and Tristan and Vaughn reluctantly departed. Sarah slipped out of her jeans and sweater and hurriedly pulled on a warm nightgown. With Ralph following her, she went to check on her son. She kissed him and pulled up the covers. Ralph circled once then lay down at the foot of Kris's bed.

I hope nobody calls and wakes us up at the crack of dawn, Sarah thought, as she edged closer to her husband in the bed.

"Sarah?"

"Yes, Daniel?"

"How about if we get rid of the building downtown?" he mumbled, his words slurred by the narcotic. "I don't want anything of his."

"We could sell it and use the money to pay for the upkeep of this house."

"I'd feel dirty all the time. Every time I'd write a check for something, I'd know it was his money I was using. I can't use it for me or my family."

"We can talk it over in the morning."

"I want to give the money from the sale of the merchandise to…to…somebody," he went on. "Somebody who'll help kids whose parents whip, cut, beat, or scream at them or to help kids who have to watch it happen to somebody else. Maybe both."

"You could talk to Frank Randall about it. The church has to have programs to assist kids like that."

"Yeah, you're right. They could help."

"Which is worse? Watching abuse or receiving it?" she asked tentatively. It was a question she had been wanting to ask for years, but she'd found herself unable to say it aloud.

"When it's you…you…I don't know…but when it's somebody else, and you have to watch and…can't do anything…."

His breathing slowed as he gave in to the soft pull of sleep. Sarah never took her eyes off his face until she could no longer keep herself awake.

Chapter Twenty-eight: Calm in the Midst of the Storm

Daniel woke at 3:00 a.m. He realized his fever was high, but he wasn't confused or disoriented. He lay staring at the ceiling, not willing to move lest he wake his wife. Better to let her sleep for a little longer in case his fever didn't go down and a return trip to the hospital was necessary.

He eased out of bed, put on a t-shirt and sweatpants, then went quietly downstairs to his father's office to make a call.

"Sorry to get you up," he said apologetically, as he opened the door to Frank Randall forty minutes later.

"Priests are often on call. You get used to it," the man assured him, as he slipped off his jacket. "Is there something wrong?"

"Sorry. I've never seen a priest in jeans before."

"You need to get out more often," Randall chuckled. "Admittedly, it's not part of the uniform, but we don't have to wear the black suit twenty-four hours a day. It's difficult to unwind at home with the collar on." He peered at Daniel in the light of the hallway and exclaimed, "Good Lord, Dan! You're ill."

"That's an understatement."

"I'm serious," the priest said with concern. "Have you taken your temperature, lately?"

"Don't worry so much. I went to the hospital, and they gave me some shots and some pills. I'll watch it."

"Dan –"

"Frank, please. I know my fever's high. I'll call for Sarah if it gets any worse. I need to talk with you now. Why don't we sit in the office?"

The older man nodded then followed Daniel into the room without argument. He sat in the chair behind the desk. Daniel gritted his teeth and lowered himself into the rocker.

"I think my hip hurts worse than my stomach," he complained. "I wish they wouldn't give shots there." He sighed and rubbed at his eyes. "Oh, hell. Do you want something to drink? I got me a big glass of cold water after I called you. I should have gotten you something before we came in here."

"I'm fine. What do you want to talk with me about?"

"I want to donate the building and the profits from my stepfather's estate to help abused children."

"Have you discussed this with Sarah?"

"A little."

"Why approach me about it?"

"Because you're my friend, and I know you'll do the right thing."

Randall smiled and nodded.

"The money could go directly to the cause. In order to assure that the building would be used for that specific purpose it would take a miracle. The donation of property would be wonderful, but what if there were no funds to open or maintain such a place? If your request to use it only for that purpose is honored, then it might sit dormant for years if no money is allocated for its operation."

"Do you have a better idea?"

"You could sell the building and donate all the monies to an existing charity."

Daniel shook his head.

"Let me make a proposal then. But first, how much is your stepfather's estate worth? Not the building, just the money from the store and his savings or whatever investments he had."

"About a quarter of a million dollars."

"That's an awful lot of money. You aren't considering keeping any of it?"

"No."

"That's very admirable."

"What's your proposal?" Daniel persisted.

"Keep the building. Invest the money someplace where you can get a good return. Use it to maintain the structure and help to fund the project. You don't have to feel sullied by your ownership, because you'll be, in essence, cleansing the building of its dark past by allowing others to be helped there."

"Who would run the program?"

"You're the owner. You make the ultimate decisions as to who gets to use the space and what they do there."

"How can I make those decisions if I can't even make myself go in the building again?"

"You work downtown and so does your father-in-law."

"So?"

"So, Sarah is unemployed and has been battling frustration and depression, lately. Do you think she'd be interested in riding downtown with you each day and working at this place, or do you think she's had her fill of dealing with abused children?"

"Are you implying that I'm still a child?" Daniel asked mildly.

The man smiled and said, "Of course, she may not want to work there, but it wouldn't hurt to ask."

"I think it's definitely something to consider. It might be good for both of us to work it out like that. I'll talk to her about it."

"Good. We can discuss it when you're not so under the weather."

They listened as an owl hooted in the woods outside. Suddenly, Daniel asked, "Frank, is it a sin for me to hate the people who hurt me?"

"I thought you didn't accept the true existence of God."

"I don't, but I also don't want to lose your friendship if I tell you truthfully that I have no intention of forgiving anyone at this point in my life. If there is a God, then he can forgive all of them for me."

"If, during their lifetimes, your family members truly regretted what they did and were sincere about it, then, yes, God would forgive them. *Hate* is such a strong word, but I'd be hard pressed to find another if I was in your position. If you're a good person – and I sincerely believe that you are – God will forgive you for anything, even your hate and the stubborn refusal to consider His existence."

"I didn't say I wouldn't consider it."

"You didn't have to say it."

Randall left before dawn. Daniel climbed back into bed and immediately fell into a deep sleep. When he woke shortly before 9:00, his side of the bed was damp with perspiration, but the fever had broken.

"I want to go see Isabelle," he told his wife, as she brought him some hot tea and toast.

"Maybe she can come here. You're not going to leave this house today."

"But she and her boyfriend are going to New Orleans later."

"Isabelle has a boyfriend?"

"I met him last night. Noah Goldblum."

"I'll ask them over for lunch. Would that please Your Majesty?"

"Immensely. It would satisfy your curiosity, too."

It was all Daniel could do to shower and dress before Isabelle and Noah arrived. After the meal, the adults sat around the table, while Kris and Ralph played fetch in the backyard.

"He's a fine boy," Goldblum said genially. "He reminds me of my son."

"What does your son do?" Sarah asked politely, as she refilled his coffee cup.

"My son has been dead for fifty years, Mrs. Nash. Had he lived, I believe he would have been a carpenter like his father."

"Oh. I'm so sorry."

"Everyone else in my family was exterminated at Dachau. We Jews were herded like cattle by the Nazis into the Concentration Camps. I was the lone survivor in my family."

Noah Goldblum unbuttoned the cuff of his shirt and rolled up the sleeve until a row of black numbers was visible.

"Can't you have it removed?" Daniel asked.

"Removed?" the man echoed incredulously. "It is a part of me. Why should I want it removed?"

"Wouldn't it be easier to forget without that constant reminder? Your tormentors forced you to be tattooed. You didn't have a choice when they did it."

"If we survivors forget, then who will remember it? Who will stop it from happening again? That is why I was spared, so that I would not forget. I choose to be an instrument and prevent others from suffering as I did."

Daniel stared thoughtfully at the older gentleman for a few seconds before excusing himself and leaving the table.

"Wait!" Sarah called, as she sprinted down the steps. "Where are you going?"

"I need some air."

"I'll bet you do."

"You think the irony of this is lost on me? There's a Jewish carpenter in our dining room who was persecuted for his religious beliefs, and he's telling me with a few simple words how to let go without letting go."

"So, why aren't you happy?"

"Maybe I don't want to let go! If I let go of what was, what will be left?"

"What could be?"

"What do you want, Sarah?"

"To live here for now and not have to focus on anything except rebuilding our lives."

He went over to her and pulled her against him. Resting his chin on the top of her head, he said, "We can put our house on the market next week if you'd like."

"Mm."

They stood that way for a few minutes. Finally, Daniel said, "What did you think of Frank's idea about your working downtown? Have you thought about it, yet?"

"It's a good idea, but I can't commit to that. Not yet. Give it some time."

He kissed her forehead and confided, "I have another idea you might like."

"Daniel, the doctor just told you that you can't have sex again for a while."

"No," Daniel laughed. "No, that's not what I meant."

"Then what?"

"I think we should adopt Celeste's baby."

"Are you serious? What if they don't intend to give it up?"

"Then we can look into adopting someone else's baby."

"We've had this conversation before. What about the people with no children who are trying to adopt? They deserve a baby."

"Sarah, we deserve another baby and some happiness as much as anyone else in this world."

"What about an older child?"

"I still don't think I could handle that. I've had enough trouble dealing with my own abuse and neglect. I don't think I can tackle it with an adopted child. That may be selfish of me, but it's the truth."

"Self-protection and selfish are two different things. Honestly, I don't think I could handle it either. I need to get away from it sometimes. As much as I can get away from it with you."

"Thanks."

"You know how I meant that."

"Yeah. So, do you think it's a bad idea that I talk with Celeste?"

She shook her head and looked back anxiously at the house.

"We'd better go in. Isabelle and Mr. Goldblum have to leave soon."

As they climbed the steps to the porch, Sarah stopped and cried, "I have the perfect idea! You know how Grandma and Grandpa have been talking forever about moving to Baton Rouge. They've always said how cute our house is. Maybe they'd want to buy it."

"We can give Helen and Jim a call after Isabelle and company head out."

"Okay, then let's sit together with Kris and read a story. We need to get back to doing that."

"Fine. You call Helen and Jim, and I'll see what Max has in the bookcase that might be suitable for people under forty."

Clouds rolled into the area not long after. The sky outside became dark, and a heavy rain began to fall. The temperature dropped below freezing.

Inside the old Nash home, Sarah, Daniel, and Kris lay fully clothed under the covers in the master bedroom. Pillows were propped behind their heads. Kris, who sat between his parents, rested his small head against his mother as his father read to them both from *The Secret Garden*.

Daniel continued to read, even after Kris had fallen asleep. His own eyelids grew heavy, but he didn't stop. Finally, he closed the book and laid it on the nightstand. He looked over at his wife. Her eyes were closed, and her breathing was slow and even.

Daniel shut off the light and succumbed to the wonderful warmth of the house, the bed, and the proximity of his wife and child. Outside, the lightning flashed; the thunder clapped; and the rain pounded the roof.

With a deep sigh of contentment, Daniel let go of everything except the exquisite peace of the moment. He knew it wouldn't last, but that didn't matter. He wasn't going to waste this precious wormhole of tranquility by obsessing about how soon it might be over.

And life was good.

Other Books in The Real World Series

Over, Under, Across & Through
Mercy
Unfinished Business (Final Chapter)

ABOUT THE AUTHOR

Lauren Cutrera, who also writes under the name Barbara Cutrera, has published over 20 contemporary romance, romantic suspense, paranormal romance, mystery, and fiction novels. Diverse people and plots highlight her works, drawing readers into the characters' unique journeys as they navigate their way through their struggles and triumphs. Lauren and her husband, Budge, are the proud parents of a grown son. They live in southwest Florida and have a cute and naughty Yorkie, Hadrian, who sleeps next to Lauren as she writes each day.

Explore other published works by the author at amazon.com and goodreads.com

Check out all things Lauren (and Barbara) at www.laurencutrera.com

And connect with her there or on

Facebook: https://www.facebook.com/profile.php?id=100063631654302

Instagram: https://www.instagram.com/laurencutrera/

Pinterest: https://www.pinterest.com/laurencutrera/_saved/

OTHER BOOKS BY THE AUTHOR:

The Essential Elements Series

Kindred Spirits
Scorched Creek
Spirits Corner
Memory Lane
Homeward Bound

The Limitless Series

Sight Unseen
Better Left Unsaid
Unheard Of
Under Her Skin
Brain Storm
Out On A Limb

The Seneca & Michael Duet

A Lovely Dream
A Lovely Reality

The Gift Series

The Healer's Gift
Jordan's Way
Bound by Grace
The Nameless

The Real World Series

Over, Under, Across & Through
A Good Man's Life
Mercy
Unfinished Business (Final Chapter)

Standalone Novels/Short Stories

In A Manner of Speaking
Prim & Proper
Lucky
Compromising Positions
True: 3 Short Stories

www.ingramcontent.com/pod-product-compliance
Lightning Source LLC
Chambersburg PA
CBHW061312170626
46817CB00001B/149
9780985825584